RECEIVED
APR 23 2023
By
NO LONGER PROPERTY OF
SEATTLE PUBLIC LIBRARY

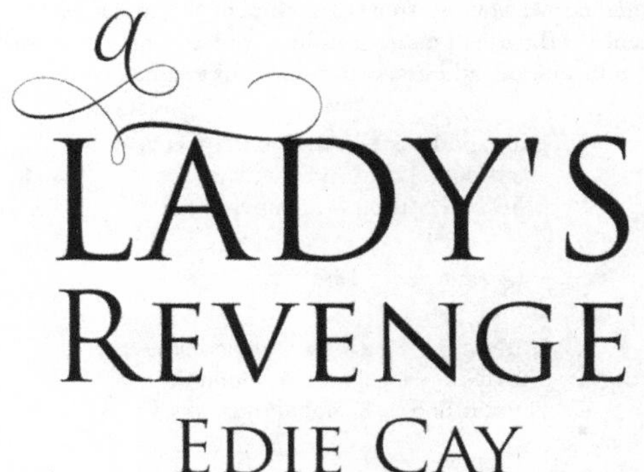

This is a work of fiction. Names, characters, places, and incidents either are the product of the author's imagination or are used fictitiously. Any resemblance to actual persons, living or dead, events, or locales is entirely coincidental.

Copyright © 2020 by Katie Stine
All rights reserved. No part of this book may be reproduced or used in any manner without written permission of the copyright owner except for the use of quotations in a book review. For more information, address: scarabskinbooks@gmail.com

First paperback edition February 2020
First digital edition February 2020
Second edition December 2020

*Cover design by Fiona Jayde Media*

ISBN 978-1-7344397-1-7 (paperback)
ISBN 978-1-7344397-0-0 (ebook)
Published by ScarabSkin Books

*www.scarabskinbooks.com*

*For every person who has ever felt not quite right*

# CAST OF CHARACTERS

**The Aristocrats:**

**Lord Lorian**, earl, father of William (deceased), Lady Lydia, and Lady Agnes
**Lady Lorian**, countess, mother of William (deceased), Lady Lydia, and Lady Agnes
**William** (deceased), eldest son and heir of the earl of Lorian.
**Lady Lydia Somerset**, eldest daughter of the earl of Lorian
**Lady Agnes Somerset**, youngest daughter of the earl of Lorian
**Vasily**, driver and friend to Lord Lorian from their war days.
**Charlotte**, lady's maid to Lydia and Agnes
**Robling**, the butler

**James Wallingford, Lord Andrepont**, viscount, nephew of Lady Lorian, cousin to Lydia and Agnes
**Lady Andrepont**, viscountess, mother of Lord Andrepont, sister to Lady Lorian
**Lord Andrepont** (deceased), father of the current viscount, husband to Lady Andrepont.
**Margaret Miller**, half-sister to James Wallingford,

daughter of the deceased Lord Andrepont and a maid. Taken in by Lady Andrepont.

**Lord Sebastian**, a close friend of William's before he died. Lydia treats him as a substitute for her brother.
**Lord Farley**, lover of Lord Sebastian

**Lord Elshire**, earl, an impoverished aristocrat until recently, guardian of his niece, Miss Rose Dorchester.
**Miss Rose Dorchester**, daughter of deceased Viscount and Viscountess, ward of the earl of Elshire.

**Lord Kinsley**, marquis, older aristocrat who has a great deal of money and political power. Father of Henry, Lord Leighton and Lady Jane Parks.
**Lady Kinsley**, marquess, mother of Henry, Lord Leighton and Lady Jane Parks
**Henry Parks, Lord Leighton**, heir to Lord Kinsley.
**Lady Jane Parks**, Lady Lydia's dear friend.

**Lady Agatha Beauclerk**, sister of Lord Seafield, and a friend of Lady Jane and Lady Lydia
**Lord Seafield**, heir to a dukedom, and a very eligible bachelor. Weak chin.

**Lady Marshall**, widow and possible lover of John Arthur

**Lord Hackett**, an old title that has lost a great deal of money, an old friend of Lord Denby and the deceased Lord Andrepont
**Lady Hackett**, wife of Lord Hackett, mother of Lady Isabella
**Lady Isabella Berchand**, daughter of Lord and Lady Hackett

**Peters**, butler at Hackett's country estate
**Chester**, a groom at Hackett's country estate

**Lord Denby**, a viscount widower with no children. Patron of Miss Bess Abbott.

**Count Denisov**, a Russian Count in London as part of the Cossack regiment being honored for their triumph over Napoleon

**Mr. Bernard Franklin**, a wealthy land developer and guest at Lord Hackett's country house, brother to Miss Franklin
**Miss Mary Franklin**, guest at Lord Hackett's country house, sister to Mr. Franklin
**Mr. Colby**, a banker and guest at Lord Hackett's country house, brother to Miss Colby
**Miss Colby**, a guest at Lord Hackett's country house, sister to Mr. Colby
**Mrs. Bartles**, a guest at lord Hackett's country house, Miss Colby's chaperone
**Mr. Snodfield**, a barrister and guest at Lord Hackett's country house

**The Commoners:**

**Mr. John Arthur/Corinthian John**, a prizefighter who has become a successful stockbroker. Continues to box for the joy of the sweet science.
**Miss Pearl Arthur**, younger sister of John Arthur, boards at Mrs. Tyler's Boardingschool for Ladies
**Miss Mathilda Perry**, friend of Pearl, boards at Mrs. Tyler's Boardingschool for Ladies
**Parsons**, butler at John Arthur's London townhouse
**Caulie/Marcus Breverton**, a prizefighter who became a jobber in the London Stock Exchange. No longer fights.

**Miss Bess Abbott**, a female prizefighter, acknowledged to be the best in London, John Arthur's best friend.
**Tony Farrow**, a pugilist manager and publican who helped John Arthur and Bess Abbott
**Basil**, boxing announcer
**Perry**, a young boy in the pugilists' world

# PROLOGUE

## LONDON, 1815

The hoofbeats couldn't pound fast enough to erase the feeling of dread that draped her like a cloak. Lydia hated being that close to the river, the creaking mastheads, the towering giants, the smell of sewage and rot. But perhaps that was the smell of her own soul, rotting her from the inside out. She'd know the difference as they retreated further into London—if the smell was her or if it was Wapping.

"We are never going there again," James said, leaning forward to peer out the carriage window for some unknown danger lurking about in the shadows. The carriage lurched as Vasily, the driver, climbed atop his perch. James pounded the carriage wall, and the vehicle eased into motion.

"I don't know," Lydia said, shivering in her pelisse. The area was still haunted by the gruesome Ratcliff Highway murders five years ago, giving them a false impetus to visit the area, as if they were voyeuristic aristocrats out to tour the misfortunes of others. "I thought I might ask Papa to buy some property in Wapping."

James rolled his eyes. "Fancy being a fishwife now?"

"That makes it sound like I would marry a piece of cod."

"Might make a good husband. Won't beat you and all that."

"Your standard for marital bliss is staggering." She could see her breath in front of her face. She had been glad to have both James and Vasily there for protection. "What will Margaret say about this?"

"You shouldn't have gone. I should have done this alone." James pulled a blanket out from underneath the seat. "Take this."

Their appearance an hour earlier in the Kings' Arms tavern was accepted as morbid tourism. No one had cared that two aristocrats and a foreign bodyguard sat down with a scruffy sailor. No one had noticed when James slipped that sailor a sack of coins worth more pounds than any of them would see in a year. James didn't trust the man, but Lydia didn't care; she didn't have a choice whether to trust or not. She needed the midshipman.

"Maybe we don't tell Margaret," James suggested.

"Margaret agreed to all the same sacrifices we did." Lydia arranged the blanket around her and pulled it up to her neck, but the shivering didn't stop because it wasn't just the cold. It was all of the darkness, pooled around her for so long. It was the odor of stale brandy from her childhood, it was the heavy weight pinning her down, it was the guilt for pulling James and Agnes and Margaret into it with her. If only she had kept her mouth shut. No one would have had to know, and while it would have killed her, at least the rest of them would have been free.

"We were just children. Agnes and Margaret more so. They didn't know what they agreed to," James reminded her.

"But they've made their sacrifices just the same."

Lydia's clothes felt wrong on her body. The chafing fabric, even the stockings on her legs, the hair on her head. "They have a right to know."

"It's a hanging offense. Do you realize that?" His face was nothing but harsh planes in this dim light. She did her best to ignore the resemblance to his father, the face of the monster in her dreams.

"I do," she whispered. "As did Midshipman Smith. As do you. This is the risk, and we are all taking it."

James fell back against the squabs, silent as the clack of the wheels turning on the road. It would be some time before they were home, back to Mayfair, back to clean rows of hedges and curated heirlooms and constructed histories.

"Do you think he can do it without hurting anyone?" Lydia asked. "You know Margaret will be concerned."

"And you aren't?" James scoffed. He shook his head. "He said he could do it."

"Needs must, and all that," she said. There was nothing right about this. Or her. Or the world. There was no blanket big enough to hide under, no embrace safe enough to hold her, no volume of tears big enough to calm her. Her body trembled, the panic threatening to take over.

"It's not just your revenge," James reminded her. "He hurt so many people."

"James." She said his name to bring him to his senses. "This isn't about your father. He's dead. Tonight was about Hackett."

James shifted in his seat, the muscle in his jaw flexing as he clenched his teeth.

Lydia flitted her hand out, trying for a gesture that meant they could drop the subject. Her temporary palsy didn't make it very clear, but James understood.

"As long as Midshipman Smith can manage his

commitment aboard the *Europe*," James said, "we will have only two of those bastards left."

"One," Lydia corrected. "Denby is on a trajectory that no one can help. Sebastian looked into his finances for me."

"Must you include Sebastian?" James's brows knotted together in a pout.

"Must you whine? You are impossible when you're petulant." Lydia pulled the blanket up around her neck again. The shakes were fading now that they were talking about actual plans.

"He isn't a part of us. He doesn't have any stakes."

"He was William's friend, and that's what matters," Lydia said. William's death had been the reason they were all together in that country house fifteen years ago. The family was shoring itself up, licking its wounds. It was unthinkable that the heir to her father's title would have perished with something as commonplace as catarrh, but he had. William was so much older that he'd already been out of the nursery by the time Lydia and James came along, but he was their hero. He took time to play with them whenever he was home. He taught Lydia how to ride and play cards. He carried baby Agnes around like he was her own nursemaid. Everyone commented on what a sweet boy the heir was to dote so on his sisters.

William got sick at school and was transported home white as a sheet, buried in blankets, his lips an unnatural color. Then he was gone. The girls had been kept from him to prevent any further illness.

So, they took to the country—Lydia, her father, mother, and sister. Her mother's sister's family, too: Lord Andrepont, Lady Andrepont—her mother's sister—their heir James, and, oddly, Margaret, the daughter of a housemaid, who everyone knew to be

Andrepont's bastard. But everything about James's family was strange. Sinister.

And Andrepont was a monster. Everyone knew it. Everyone whispered it. Even the nursemaids with children present. He was the shadow in the corner, the highwayman in the woods.

And they were right.

# I
## LONDON, 1816

The mill had been out of Town the night before. It had taken John hours to get back home, late, bloodied but victorious. His body didn't yet creak and ache, but he knew it would come the day after. Best to make money while there was money to be made.

Parsons entered the room with a tray.

"I'll eat at Garraway's, don't worry. Is Michael ready with the gig?" John tied his cravat in a hasty mailcoach knot.

"May I help you with your coat, sir?" The butler's tone of voice was imperious, commanding even. It wasn't a question so much as a nudge toward his desire for John to set up his house properly. Hire a valet, a cook, a kitchen maid, instead of leaving this lurching townhouse empty save Parsons, Michael, and the maid whose name he couldn't remember. He hadn't seen her but once, when he hired her. Lucy, maybe?

"Aye—I mean, yes. Please do," John said, trying to match his butler's unhurried formality. The crisp distance wasn't part of his nature.

Parsons held out the coat, and John shrugged into it as the butler pulled and pinched the fabric here and there, retrieving a brush to take off any stray bits of lint that may have stuck.

John said, "Am I fit to go gossip with all those rogues and cheats?"

Parsons inclined his head with a faint smile. "I will get Michael readied for you, sir."

John needed to work—it was as urgent a feeling as needing a chamber pot. He took a sip of the coffee Parsons had left for him. It was better than the swill he picked up at Garraway's, but he needed the company that the coffeehouse gave. He hated the days the Exchange was closed. The coffeehouse became the de facto Exchange, with runners from all industries reporting as brokers and jobbers congregated and poured over newspapers from all around. He thundered down the stairs, no doubt causing Parsons a fit.

But no, the unrufflable butler was by the door with hat and gloves waiting. Just once he'd like to catch the man out. "Michael will be out front shortly."

"Tell him I've started on. He can catch me up on Holborn," John instructed, pulling on the gloves. "Fine togs make me look a respectable sort, yeah?"

Parsons's face twisted. "If I may, sir, the clothes may do the service, but the state of your face after one of your events does not."

"It's a mill, Parsons. A prizefight. I see toffs there all the time. It ain't like it used to be."

"Some things, perhaps, are not. However, some conventions are not so easily brushed aside. You do look a bit of a..." The butler cleared his throat and looked away. "A bit of a highwayman."

There was the rancor! John laughed. He couldn't wait to tell Caulie about the discomfort of a man he paid to bring him his coffee in the morning and his liquor at night. It just seemed all backwards. Like living with money turned the whole world upside down. "Let me put you at ease, Parsons. It's just Garraway's, and all of those blokes have seen or had a bit of blackening of the peeper afore. Ladies ain't allowed."

"Very good, sir." Parsons returned to his full height and full distance.

John popped his hat on, giving it a thump for good measure. He could swear Parsons cringed. John supposed he should speak in his genteel accent with his butler, but it was so much more fun to needle that way. Besides, he still thought in those meaner tones. He couldn't be expected to get up in the morning with such long vowels.

Michael wasn't at the front gate with the gig yet, and John was not a man who did well waiting. But as he passed through the wrought iron fence, he spotted a different quarry.

Ladies Lydia and Agnes Somerset were leaving the townhouse next door. What a strange bit of luck. Lord Elshire rented the house, and his ward was just now having her debut. John had not met the girl yet, but Lord Elshire was an interesting cove who had never spent much time in London. This was the first time John had seen the Quality leaving the house. Society didn't always go as far afield as Marylebone. He checked his watch and there they were, upholding the rules of such ladies. They were on their round of calls. Three-fifteen. Formal call, then, not yet friends.

He itched to curl his hands into fists, just to shadowbox there in the street, blow off some nervous steam. But he didn't. He stretched his neck from side to side, feeling the comfortable crack on the right and on the left and on the right again. He hadn't planned this moment, but he'd dreamt of it.

Pearl needed a sponsor. He had enough money to line his pockets for all time, but his sister needed a protector, and a husband was better than a brother. But if she was going to marry well, she needed more than money. She needed friends in the right places, an entrance to the best parties, to the fashionable shops. Right now, she was mired in the lower middle class at Mrs. Tyler's Boarding School for Ladies. It was more than he could afford when she started, and it was less than he could wish for now that she was finishing.

To make Pearl's happiness come true, he had to find her some new acquaintances. He hadn't been able to figure out who, exactly, would be good mates for her. Henrietta had tried to be helpful during their dalliance, but she didn't know the unmarrieds.

But here on his doorstep was the fashionable set! Seemed like Fate. Nothing to it but to be bold. Best not think too hard; he was better on his feet.

"Excuse me, Lady Lydia, Lady Agnes," he called to the women as they walked to their phaeton. He cleared his throat, trying to remember to open his vowels, yawning to make those expensive sounds.

Lady Agnes, the tall one, kept talking. She was bigger all around than her older sister, and a bit plain. Lady Lydia was in front, her expression colder and even more distant than Parsons could be on a December day in Hell. She moved well, Lady Lydia did. A strange thing to notice, maybe, but she moved like someone who knew her business, not careless and flip with her limbs. Her dark hair was shiny, visible underneath her bonnet, decorated with lavender flowers. She wore a gray-and-violet dress tailored so well that despite it showing off her curves, it seemed just as impenetrable as a suit of armor.

"But I thought it was perfectly well done. Really, Lydia, sometimes you can be such a snob," Lady Agnes was saying. They approached the phaeton, but the step wasn't down and the driver hadn't noticed the ladies were ready.

"Pardon me—" John tried to cut in again, but Lady Agnes was back at her patter.

"I can see precisely what James sees in her, of course I can. What is shocking to me is that you cannot. It really is a selfish thing to not be able to see the very attractive traits in others," Lady Agnes continued.

He'd committed now, to anyone watching, to speak to these ladies. He would be a fool to give up, and especially a cur to abandon the acquaintance if Pearl needed it. He didn't think, he just acted. He put his hand out and landed it on Lady Lydia's arm.

Her head whipped around. Lady Agnes gasped. Wrong move.

"Pardon me," Lady Lydia bit out in a tone that should have poisoned every stray dog, cat, and rodent within a one-mile radius.

John gave the biggest, least threatening smile of his life. He willed his blue eyes to sparkle with charm. If there was ever a time a diamond could pop out of his peepers, now was the time. "Excuse me, Lady Lydia, I was hoping to have a word." Belatedly, he swept off his hat and gave a quick bow.

"We all face disappointment in life," she said, the poison receding just a bit. It was the first time they'd been face to face, but recognition flared. Her eyes were blue, but the dark and stormy type, the opposite of his own. They were offset by dark eyelashes and brows, and an almost star-shaped beauty mark near her right eye.

It was as if all the wind had been knocked out of him. He willed himself to breathe. He hadn't felt like this since he'd lost a mill to the Game Chicken three years ago. Those fists the size of pineapples and the brilliant midnight blue of this woman's eyes had the same effect.

The driver lumbered down off his perch. He was

the size of a small horse with hands like a porter's hooks. This man was the protection, not just the chauffeur.

"I don't care much for disappointment, my lady," John said, giving another great smile, this time including Lady Agnes, who he had momentarily forgotten was still standing there. He concentrated on breathing in and then breathing out.

"We haven't been introduced," Lady Lydia said, as if she were speaking to a child. It was like she knew all the tones that could put off a person and didn't mind using them.

"Walk with me for just a moment, here, in public, with chaperones." He gestured to her sister and the driver. "And that will surely remedy our acquaintance." He offered her his arm.

"That isn't how it works." She folded her arms across her chest. "Perhaps if you had better breeding, you would know."

If this had been a turn-up, all bets would be against him. "I've spent my life taking chances, my lady. I always weigh the risk to benefit. Making your acquaintance, however I can get it, is worth the risk. And knowing me is always a benefit." He meant to give another non-threatening grin, but he was in earnest. This was the grin that marked him as rubbish. The Quality didn't smile—they didn't need to. But it was the winning bits of his domino box that made folks relax and trust him.

She narrowed her eyes and watched him for a moment. It was only then that he remembered his black eye. He must be a wretched fright for a lady like her. No wonder she wouldn't talk to him.

"Agnes, get in the phaeton. We'll walk a single block, sir. Make your case. Vasily will follow us."

"But—" Lady Agnes protested.

"Done," John said, wanting to stick his hand out

to shake, as if this were a deal on the floor of the Exchange. It felt like the hardest bargain he'd driven that year. Maybe even that entire decade. Was he supposed to feel grateful? He wasn't sure.

The driver folded down the step and handed the taller woman into the phaeton. Lady Lydia spun on her heels to walk in the same direction the horses were pointed. Thankfully it was towards Holborn, and thus Garraway's. John hurried to take the street-side position next to her.

"Don't go far," Lady Agnes called from the open vehicle.

Lady Lydia turned to give her sister a sharp look. As she turned back, John caught a glimpse of a mischievous expression. Maybe she thought of him as a kind of adventure? Not the first time. The Quality was always entertained by a bit of mud.

"You may begin your inquisition," she prompted.

John cleared his throat. "I was hoping to obtain your help."

"Oh?"

He took a chance and glanced over at her face—still icy, still haughty, an eyebrow raised as a question. But was it in response to his question, or was it that he, himself was questionable?

"It's for my sister. I know that with our breeding, as you put it, she'd never get an invitation to Almack's, but an invitation anywhere would be a good start." His mouth started to run away from him. "She needs a chance. I've made my money, but it's different for ladies. As you know."

Michael drove up with his gig. John made a motion for him to circle around the block and try him again. They crossed a street, and he knew he should be thankful that she walked with him onto a second block of houses.

"A chance at what, precisely?" Lady Lydia asked.

He cut a sidelong look at her. She knew exactly what he meant. Why was she making him say it? Suddenly he felt very foolish, and he didn't like to feel foolish. She was mocking him, trying to make him say how very crass and crude he was. So he was born in St. Giles. So he grew up with a pig inside the house. So he could outpunch a cove twice his weight. So there weren't much more to recommend him than the massive jingle in his pocket. But he had a *massive jingle*, which was more than most of her lot could say.

"Don't play the air-headed *bon vivant*, my lady." Irritation seeped into his voice.

Her voice snapped back into ice. "I don't care for your tone."

John glanced back to see where their vehicles were. Michael was still circling the block, and the lady's phaeton was stuck at the previous intersection, which was blocked by an old, shabby carriage. The horse hitched to it was clearly in distress, its ears pinned back. John's attention returned to the woman next to him. She had twisted this conversation into something impossible. It weren't as if he were asking her to introduce his sister to the Prince of Wales. Just a silly garden party sometime. Or take her to buy a hat. Or ribbons, or hell, he'd buy them a whole haberdashery if it would get Pearl mixing with the right people. The right men.

A man that would treat her well. One that wouldn't go out cavorting and bring her back the pox. One that would listen to the fairytales she made up, the kind that he listened to for hours on cold nights when the wind whistled through the broken glass. A man that would love her. One that would see her through not just the ripening of her belly, but also the aftermath and all the bother a babe might bring. The kind of man they'd never met. The kind of man he'd hoped he could be, but knew that he wasn't.

Pearl's man needed to have money, but it didn't have to be much. John had the Midas touch enough for everybody. If this man were titled, that could be right fun. But the man needed to have respectability. That vaporous, elusive quality that even John wasn't sure what it meant. That was the man for Pearl. Respectable.

Which, according to Parsons, he was not.

"She needs a respectable man," John said.

The woman nodded her understanding but didn't say anything. So, John's mouth just kept running. "And since your lot is so obsessed with respectability, I thought—"

She barked out a laugh. Wasn't that rude? Or at least, a breach of a young lady's etiquette? He stared.

"Obsessed is the proper term, but you won't find true respectability amongst Peers, I'm afraid. I'd stick to your own."

"I beg your pardon, my lady?"

She halted their walk to turn and face him. "I know who you are, Mr. Arthur. Would you ever enter into a brawl with a man smaller than you who had no formal training?"

His pride flared. "Of course not."

"Even if he was saying mean things to you?" Lady Lydia questioned.

This was a trap. He didn't know where she was going with it, but he knew enough to want to sidestep it, to prove he was smarter. But since he didn't know what this had to do with respectability, he stuck to the truth. "Words are just words. They can hurt, but a person doesn't always recover from a beating."

Lady Lydia nodded her agreement again. Her hair caught the afternoon sun and it shined, showing deep, rich colors. He wanted to touch it with his bare hands to see if it was as silky as it looked. "Just so. Because your opponent is weaker, smaller, untrained. Ungentlemanly to attack, isn't it?"

"I agree with you, my lady. But what does this have to do with respectability?" He cracked his neck again, side to side, before he could catch himself. Rude behavior, he knew it, but old habits couldn't be erased so easily.

Her eye was caught by something up the street at the previous intersection. But she righted her attention back to him. "It is considered respectable to beat your wife. A man may bludgeon a woman, hopefully not to death, but certainly within a handspan of it, if need be, and still be considered respectable. Are those the type of men you would like your sister to meet?"

He was horrified. "Of course not!" How had this conversation gone so wrong?

"Respectability is in the eyes of the beholder, Mr. Arthur. It does not get transferred by patents of nobility. Excuse me." Lady Lydia made a move to cross in front of him, into the street. Before he could think, he gripped her elbow to stop her. No one should be so foolish as to walk into the middle of a crowded thoroughfare.

She gave him a look so lethal that were he not of hardier disposition, he would have fallen down dead. But he liked her elbow, and even through his gloves and her dress, he felt something—not electricity, more like the smooth stupor of good gin. Like he would get good and drunk just by being in her company.

"I don't know why you persist in the erroneous belief that you may touch me," she snapped.

He immediately removed his hands, holding them up and away from her. It was not for the likes of him to be touching the likes of her, right, right, understood. His head cleared instantly. Free of him, she moved into the street, deftly sidestepping the manure that dotted the terrain. She had her gaze fixed on the horse attached to the shabby carriage.

She was daft. That explained it. She was purely insane. Clicking her tongue, trying to get the wild-eyed horse's attention, she crept back towards the intersection. Michael appeared with his horse and gig on the opposite way, now blocked as well. Michael waved at John, but John ignored him, trying to ascertain what it was that Lady Lydia was after.

Against his better judgment, he stepped into the street as well. Michael whistled for him, causing the skittish horse to rear. Michael's horse whinnied in return. The reins slipped through the carriage driver's fingers. Michael whistled again. The skittish horse bolted, ears back, the carriage clattering out of control. The driver's eyes were wide, his mouth open as he scrambled to catch the loose reins.

John's legs were already in motion before he started thinking. He caught Lady Lydia in his arms, pushing her to the far side of the street. Their feet scrambled beneath them, and they fell just out of reach of the carriage wheels. They landed with Lady Lydia underneath him, a pile of horse dung not far from their heads.

For a moment, with her eyes closed, her face relaxed, she looked approachable. Fun, even. The kind of girl who could have a few rounds and kick up her heels. Make a body feel funny and charming, not worthless and crass. His palm cradled the back of her head, underneath her bonnet. He was right, her hair was silky, pinned up in swirls and twirls. He wished he wasn't wearing gloves. Still, it was a nice moment, it was. Soft and comfortable, without rules and order.

Her eyes opened, and he could swear they were violet. Whatever color that was, those sparklers were pretty. He wasn't supposed to talk so. No, he mustn't use such language. But they were open, and big, and she looked as if she would nuzzle into him like a baby kitten nuzzles into the crick of an elbow. He wanted her to do it, too—he wanted her to feel safe and warm. And he would nuzzle her back, drunk on her smell of oranges and vanilla.

But then he saw it: the wall came crashing down as she remembered herself. "I can't breathe with you lying on top of me."

He grinned because everything absurd made him smile. Even the resignation he felt as they returned to who they were, letting that smooth, heady feeling disappear. He rolled off to the side, giving her more room. "Apologies, my lady." He kept his hand in her hair. It was a pleasant thing, a woman's hair.

Then she began to tremble. Strange, sort of like the stray dogs that shake when certain people come near. Her jaw set so hard he wondered if she was going to break her teeth. Was it because of him?

There wasn't a moment he wanted her to waste being afeared of him, so he began massaging her scalp. It was a trick some of the other kids used to do when they were all holed up for the night, scared of the dark, too young to be imitating their elders with bedsport. Clever fingers run through hair melted away all manner of fears.

"Are you playing with my hair?" she asked. But her jaw muscle relaxed.

"No," he said. It wasn't playing with her hair. It was a real thing that helped people.

"I think you are," she teased. She really was mocking him now, trying to embarrass him. "I think you would like to kiss me."

That made him stop. He focused on her in the way he would focus on an opponent in the ring. The world melted away; all he could see was her. Her violet eyes became more vivid. Her scent of oranges and vanilla—dark and rich, not bright like oranges in the sun, but like a garden during a new moon—filled his head so completely it swam. Would he like to kiss her? Silliest question he'd ever heard. Her skin was smooth, her complexion pink with health. Only a body who was well-fed her whole life looked like that. She would have made his mouth water, but it was more than that: she was the personification of a hungering man's desire. His body desperately wanted to respond, but he kept control. He was very good at control. "Of course I would. You are a very beautiful woman. To say otherwise would perjure Nature."

Her expression froze over, even more walls, even greater distance. He was inches from her face, but he may as well have been in Manchester.

Two sets of boots came running up: one massive set, belonging to the chauffer Vasily, and the other still men's boots, but underneath the hem of an expensive frock. Strange.

"Lydia, are you hurt?" Lady Agnes yelled.

"I'm not deaf," Lady Lydia grumbled. John stood and tried to lend her a hand, only to be all but pushed aside by Lady Agnes and Vasily.

"What happened? Why were you in the street?" her sister asked.

Lady Lydia turned to John. "Please tell me you attempted to save my life rather than merely physically assaulting me," she said. "If it was the latter, then I'm afraid poor Vasily here will have to dirty his fists."

John barked out a laugh. "Vasily will have to get in line." He gestured to his black eye.

"Are you well, my lady?" Vasily asked, his voice thick with a Russian accent.

Her jaw muscle was back at full tension and John could see her hands shaking. She said, "Fine, Vasily, thank you."

"Please let me see you home," John offered.

"No, quite unnecessary, thank you," she said, her spine straightening, her shoulders pulling back so hard it was as if she were being tied to a post.

Stepping back to the sidewalk, he watched Lady Lydia limp over to the phaeton, using her sister and driver on either side as crutches. That had not gone well. He wanted to sweep her up in his arms, carry her to the carriage. Or to his house. To his bed. Those were not thoughts of a respectable man.

But while his thoughts were still reeling and drunken, her expression was perfectly clear: he was mud, and that was that. Michael pulled up in his gig, and John clambered on.

"That was a right mess," Michael said. "What happened?"

"No idea," John answered. "I was hoping to get my sister asked to tea."

"Funny way to do it," said Michael, urging the horse onward down to Holborn. "I've not tried pushing a lady down to get an invitation. Did it work?"

"No," John said. "I've made an ass of myself."

"I've made an ass of myself many a time afore." The boy shrugged. "Sometimes it works."

❧

VASILY'S MASSIVE HANDS WRAPPED A BANDAGE around Lydia's ankle while her father looked on, perplexed. Agnes sat in the corner with the best light, embroidering. Her mother stood at the window, looking out, a picture of serenity. Thanks only to Lydia's training was she able to discern the tenseness of her mother's shoulders, the strain in her forearms as she tried not to ball her hands into fists.

Sometimes it was hard to tell if her mother cared at all.

"Are you well?" her father asked again, anxious because a man held his daughter's ankle, even if it was just Vasily. The huge Russian had been a part of their household for years, familiar enough to have never induced a heart-pounding, abstract fear. Lydia's debut season had been difficult because every man in the ballroom seemed to cause her to break into a cold sweat. She'd sought refuge in the carriage with Vasily until her mother had come to drag her back into the party.

"Fine, Papa," Lydia said.

"Stay off it," Vasily instructed. "No walks or horses for one week. No meeting with Miss Abbott."

Her mother turned her head towards them with a flicker of interest at the mention of no meetings with Miss Abbott.

"But—" Lydia protested.

The big man held up his hand. "No." As a former mercenary, he knew injuries well. He treated Lydia's infrequent wounds, but also burns for the kitchen staff and other mishaps at the estate. The servants appreciated his talents, bartering what they could afford for his treatments.

"Most of your social obligations don't require much walking," Papa said. He was trying to be helpful. Did he not realize how much she loathed people? There were few exceptions, but removing her morning rides—charging through the underbrush and jumping fallen trees—made her days as dull and worthless as her acquaintances.

"Fine. One week, that is all I will agree to," she said. No horses for a week was inconvenient. To go a week without meeting with Bess Abbott might kill her. "The Beckersley ball isn't for nine days anyway."

Vasily narrowed his dark eyes at her, not pleased

with the idea that she might be dancing. Instead of fighting her on the subject of balls, her father nodded in acknowledgement. "Thank you, Vasily," he said.

The Russian grunted his assent as he left the room. "*Ne za chto*."

Lydia's papa came to sit next to her, gray fading his dark hair. "Vasily mentioned a gentleman who came to your aid."

She folded her arms and fell back against her pillows. "I'd rather not talk about it."

"He saved her life when the horse charged," Agnes said, letting the embroidery drift to her lap. "I watched the whole thing."

"Vasily said he didn't know him," her papa continued.

"No," Lydia said, although she believed Vasily was being purposefully obtuse to her papa to protect Lydia. Vasily likely recognized Mister John Arthur as a prizefighter, but perhaps not in the social context of paying a call in Marylebone. In that setting, Mr. Arthur was an upstart—a social climber who would do anything to break through the class barrier now that he had made his fortune. Why anyone would bother trying to get into this glass cage was beyond her. She'd be happy to do him a favor and block his entrance.

He wouldn't be the first prizefighter who tried to go respectable. She'd seen him fight, or *mill,* as it were. His popularity was deserved—he displayed theatrics while *peeling*—even she got a thrill in her stomach when his bare chest came into view. The muscle definition was an anatomic lesson. Who needed corpses to dissect musculature when they could just ask Mr. Arthur to disrobe?

"The name of this hero?" her papa prodded.

Agnes looked at her expectantly.

Lydia rolled her eyes to keep herself from

thinking about Mr. Arthur disrobing. "He's no hero. He's a stockbroker. A Mr. John Arthur."

Their papa started. "Really? How interesting."

"It really isn't," she brushed off. Should she out his pugilistic past? Would her papa care? He would care if he thought she knew him from that world. Her parents loathed her interest in boxing. She left her issues of *Boxiana* in her father's study and in the drawing room, particularly when Mr. Egan took to another rant of how pugilism was the most English of sports. Boxing was the height of nobility, and engaging in it displayed unparalleled moral character.

She wasn't sure if those musings were entirely accurate, and she wouldn't ascribe those qualities to Mr. Arthur after their brief encounter. But, if she could convince her parents it was true, then certainly such virtue was valuable in a woman as well, and they shouldn't be so disturbed by her study.

"He's another money-grubbing social climber. He accosted me on the street. I have no idea how he knew where I was."

"I was there, too," Agnes protested.

Her papa wasn't listening. Probably weighing the advantages of knowing this gentleman who was not a gentleman at all. "We should invite him to dinner. To thank him, as it were," he said, getting up from his chair.

"No, Papa. Papa?" Lydia leaned forward, trying to catch his attention. She wasn't entirely sure why she never wanted to come face to face with him again, but the clutching in her chest was insistent. "Business stays at business. If you want to work with him, you contact him at his office, or club, or under whatever rock men like him hide themselves."

"Quite right, a dinner is the best idea. After all, if he is the Arthur I've heard about from Sebastian, he is quite a talented young man. One hears the gossip."

Lydia flung herself back again. The gossip about his talent was from the widows, and they would know. Admittedly, she had stood with them, listening to the lurid details, curious but not willing to investigate. She knew she was not made for such things. Her entire adult life was subterfuge to cover that she was broken. She had to get Agnes married off and then find herself a hermit's lair. But first, revenge—then Agnes's marriage, then she and a few horses someplace where she didn't have to pretend to be whole anymore.

"Not until I'm better, please, Papa?" she asked, her voice getting small. "I don't want to limp in front of him."

Agnes gave her a look. Lydia returned it in kind.

Her papa finally turned toward her. "I'll send a note, unless you would like to do the honors yourself?"

She waved her hand. "No, by all means. But can you please let the dinner be after the Beckersley ball?" If she could get him to postpone, maybe he would forget all about it.

Truly, she didn't want to limp in front of Mr. Arthur. But it was more than just pride. When they first went tumbling and her head had fallen back, she'd expected to feel hard cobblestones. Instead, there was the soft cradle of his hand. She'd felt safe. Safer than she had felt since childhood. As long as she kept her eyes closed, she could let go of it all. Set down the heavy burdens. It was seductive, and she had indulged herself for just a moment. When she had opened her eyes and saw him hovering above her, his strawberry hair glinting in the sun, his light-blue eyes promising not rescue but care, gentleness even—she had wanted to fall into that oblivion. Like dropping into a pond without a bottom. Effortless.

But then she had remembered herself. Her broken

pieces, her vengeful heart, her promise to the world that she exerted more power upon it than the world exerted upon her. And her fury sparked again, dowsed only for a single, drowsy minute. She was not to be coddled, and she was not to be distracted. She itched to see Bess Abbott, to feel that stretch and power in her own shoulders.

She could respect Mr. Arthur from a distance. He carried power inside him somehow, constrained by sheer force of will. She liked that—it reminded her of herself.

"Dear girl," her papa said, "you don't need to walk during dinner." He kissed her on the top of the head. "I'll send a note."

# ☙ 2 ❧

Lydia, wearing a new midnight-blue gown, arranged herself on the sofa in the formal drawing room. She had opted for white gloves to contrast with the dark muslin of the sheathed overgown. A simple gold necklace highlighted her delicate neckline and slim shoulders. Gold ribbon hid the pins holding her hair in place.

Agnes sat opposite her, wearing a simple but well-made olive-green gown. The color did nothing for her hair or skin, and she hadn't bothered with any powder or jewelry. It was as if Agnes were trying to blend in with the furniture.

"You could at least get some practice," Lydia said.

"Practice what?" Agnes asked.

"Trying to charm a gentleman? Or at least letting them know you are sitting on the sofa before they try to sit down on top of you."

"We aren't all peacocks, Lydia." Agnes folded her hands in her lap, delivering the insult while looking as mild as milk.

Lydia suppressed the desire to fiddle with the ribbons or the necklace. Her lady's maid, Charlotte, had already chastised her once this evening. Lydia had been bred to never pace, never fiddle with her hair, and a whole host of other restrictions. Nervous habits were not ladylike. But why try to be a lady when she was already ruined? The damage had been done, so why make the Herculean effort to pretend otherwise?

Her mother surveyed her. "Stand up, dear. You will appear more advantageous."

"But she has a limp, Mama," Agnes protested.

Only a few days had passed since the incident with the horse, as the family had termed it. James had howled with laughter when Agnes told her version of events. Even Margaret had laughed. Lydia had sat there over the tea and treats, scowling until he was finished.

The ankle, in the meantime, had barely swelled. It was mildly tender, and only when flexed at certain angles. She wouldn't be able to run, but when was a lady ever allowed to run?

Lydia obeyed her mother, letting Agnes's protest go to waste. "Here, near the mantel?" she asked, wandering over to the fireplace. "Or perhaps we should try the quiet, modest approach? Agnes would approve of that." She retreated to the far doorway, which led to a private study, and posed with one hand on the doorframe, the other over her mouth.

Her mother rarely looked her age, but on the occasions when Lydia tried her patience, Lady Lorian appeared every one of her forty-nine years. Her dark hair was the same shade as Lydia's, but not as dark as her sister's, the dowager Lady Andrepont. James resembled the two ladies more, but the hard lines of his jaw and the stout muscle of his body were all inherited from his father.

When James moved too quickly, Lydia's heart caught with fear because the resemblance was uncanny. It was a primal part of her that she didn't think she would ever be able to turn off. Just as she would never tell James of it, his guilt already too great.

Her own father entered, glancing at the clock.

"He has a few more minutes before he'll be late," Lydia said.

"Be nice," her papa admonished.

Lydia picked at her opera-length gloves. Her breathing was shallower than normal, which grated her nerves. Perhaps her stays were tighter than normal. She was not, in any way possible, anticipating Mr. Arthur's arrival.

The thought of his chest pressed to hers, lying on the cobblestone street, caught in his arms, was not supposed to resurface. The feeling of safety, the ability to relax were no more than mirages in a desert. This dinner had been arranged by her father as a gracious thank you, with perhaps some business thrown in, nothing more.

Robling opened the drawing room door. "A Mister John Arthur," the butler announced.

The guest entered, well dressed as any gentleman. He wore black, the uniform of men going to dinner, though he and her father were matched in wearing old-fashioned breeches. She had expected him to be in trousers, but perhaps the conservative dress was intended to impress the nobility. His dark cravat was folded simply, held in place with a gold pin. His blue eyes were vivid as his gaze landed on each of them. He bowed low, a gesture she was accustomed to seeing, but his precise economy of movement fascinated her. Who moved like that, so purposeful in every muscle, as if he was trying to conserve energy as he used it?

"My lord, I thank you for the invitation," John Arthur said, eyes flicking toward the butler, a sure sign he was not of the aristocracy. Titled men rarely looked at servants unless it was with lechery.

"Mr. Arthur, I am so pleased you could join us," Lydia's papa said. "May I present my wife, Lady Lorian, and of course, you know my daughters, Ladies Lydia and Agnes Somerset."

The guest bowed again, his ginger-kissed head dipping in the air with the same precision of movement. Lydia took the opportunity to examine him again through lowered lashes. His breeches were not quite new, but finely tailored. The advantage of breeches, rather than trousers, was that they outlined powerful legs much more clearly. His waistcoat sported a dark brocade that matched the same dark hue of the background, an elegant variation to distinguish himself when men would all be dressed the same.

"I trust I meet with your approval, Lady Lydia," Mr. Arthur said.

The comment was meant to make her blush, to call attention to her study of him. He did not know she had steeled herself to unwanted emotional displays. "You'll do, for a dinner guest anyway."

He inclined his head, not showing any signs of offense.

"Lydia, be nice to the man," her father admonished. "He saved your life, after all."

Mr. Arthur's ruddy complexion flushed as he smiled. "I'm not certain Lady Lydia sees it that way."

All three of her family members glanced her way, looking for smooth compliments and a generous "thank you." All three would see right through the pretense she was tempted to put on. Instead, she curtsied deep, a show of respect she would otherwise only have given to the Prince Regent himself.

Mr. Arthur put out his hand to help her rise. It was an elegant move, and the touch of their hands—hers gloved, his bare—made heat pool in her belly. She lifted her eyes to meet his as she rose. This feeling was new, this heat, but it was not something to be felt while in the presence of one's father, surely. Her look betrayed nothing, but his shifted from smug success to uncertainty. Perhaps it wasn't so one-sided. That appealed to her.

"Thank you for the gallantry," Lydia said smoothly, still holding his gaze.

"I am glad to see your injury quite healed." His eyes bored into hers, as if the polite conversation could be a battle of wills.

"A sprained ankle is easily healed. Had you not acted, I fear how long I would have needed to convalesce," she said.

Then a bell rang, signaling dinner. She still had not looked away from Mr. Arthur, and he returned her attention without embarrassment.

"Have you used your whetstone?" she asked.

Curiously, the question sharpened his gaze, turning his expression into that of a hunter.

"To sharpen my wits?" he asked.

Her cheeks flushed. She quite liked his look, dangerous as it was. It matched her own. She hadn't expected him to understand her barb.

"Mr. Arthur, why don't you escort Lydia down to dinner?" her mother suggested, taking her papa's arm.

"Of course," he said, holding out his elbow.

Lydia glided forward, slipping her arm through his.

"You should not stand in front of horses," he said, just quietly enough not to be heard by her parents, who led them into the dining room.

Agnes followed behind them, and Lydia could almost hear her eyes rolling.

"Horses are prey animals, not predators," she said. "They are only unpredictable when they are nervous."

"Either way, it was a poor idea."

"If the whistle hadn't startled the animal, I

would've been fine," she insisted. "A loud noise would make any creature bolt."

"But a prey animal, as you put it, loses its mind."

"A prey animal bolts because it doesn't want to be eaten," she said.

The table in the dining room was formally set, as if they were entertaining an equal. The silver gleamed in the candlelit room, the chandelier throwing a pleasant light under which women looked enchanting. Her mother didn't leave any stone unturned when looking for beauty, and she certainly wouldn't allow a man to walk out of the estate not singing the praises of Lady Lorian and her daughters. Why Agnes wouldn't take advantage of this, Lydia would never know.

"So, would you say a man is a predator and a woman is prey?" Mr. Arthur asked as they separated, he to the seat of honor next to her mother, she on his other side.

"Good Lord," Agnes muttered, but Mr. Arthur's gaze never left Lydia.

The gossip amongst the married ladies mentioned him in some very flattering, if promiscuous, ways. Not surprising he fancied himself a predator, even if it was inaccurate. She knew some of the widows his name was connected with, and they were not the hunted type.

A footman held her chair out for her. She sat, gathering her skirts around her as the footman tucked her in at the table. "If you believe that women are prey," Lydia said, "you haven't near the experience the gossips say you have."

❧

THAT BARB WAS MEANT TO HURT. A BELLY-GO-firster, as Caulie would say. But Lydia brought up not only John's dalliance with Henrietta but also the rumors of his other trysts. Some of them were true, some not, but all were made with ladies whose husbands were no longer living.

"Darling, can you not wait until after the soup to inquire about the wine?" Lady Lorian asked her other daughter. The tall one, Lady Agnes, was almost impossible to see when the other women glittered so brightly.

Lady Lydia sat next to him, lit as perfectly as one would be for a portrait. He had thought her eyes were violet, but now they appeared dark blue, the color of her dress.

"Mr. Arthur," Lord Lorian boomed over the mild bickering.

"My lord?"

One footman brought soup to each of them, and another set glasses of Madeira at each place setting.

Lorian gripped his glass of wine. "A toast."

"Isn't it a bit early to be toasting, Papa?" Lydia asked, hand remaining on her glass. She had stripped off her gloves, and John could see more of her milky skin. The contrast of her dark hair and pale face was even more marked in the candlelight. He had thought her beautiful in the ballroom, or even on the street when they happened to meet, but now she was almost exactly as he had pictured princesses from the stories his sister had spun for him when he was tucked under a threadbare blanket.

He couldn't help but stare. His hand found its way to his glass on its own.

She caught him gazing and smirked. Fine with him. He wasn't ashamed of what was obvious: she was a sight to behold. It was damned difficult to turn towards her father.

"To quick thinking," Lorian said.

"Thank you, my lord," John said, raising his glass.

"At least to the quickness, if not the thinking bit," Lydia said over the rim of her wineglass.

Strange, that. So much bitterness for a pretty girl with no worry over bread or coin. Any woman with that much vitriol in her heart would end up a withered and pinched old hag, no matter how much natural beauty she possessed. Shame, that.

But then she looked up at him over that wineglass and his heart near melted. She gave him a small smile, her lips pressed together, forming a pretty red bow. There was something behind that wall. She had as soft an inside as anyone. Reminded him a bit of Tony, his trainer. Tough as the devil himself, but the man took in orphans and runaways, street urchins like himself, taught them the sweet science of pugilism, a way to look after themselves. Made money off the lot of them too, just look at them now. Famous London prizefighters—well, some of them anyway. Some of them should be more famous than they were. He was lucky there, too.

"I understand that in your line of work you must make a whole host of quick decisions," Lady Lorian said.

"Yes, my lady. I have to keep a great deal of information on hand to make the best deals for my clients," he said.

"And for yourself," Lorian chimed in.

John inclined his head. "Of course."

"I've heard you've done quite well for your circumstances," Lorian said.

The man was very focused. The earl clearly wanted something, probably an inside tip. That was what most landed gentry wanted from him. He was disposable until those lords remembered their failing crops and needed a good return on certain overseas investments. Too many aristocrats had lost their holdings in the South Sea bubble a few decades back and wouldn't let John or any other broker forget it.

"My lord, why don't we wait until after dinner to conduct business? I'd hate to bore the ladies."

Lady Lydia shot him a look of undisguised disgust. Lady Agnes just looked bored. Lady Lorian didn't bother to look up at him at all. Usually the lady of the house would be grateful for his manners.

"Your daughters are lucky to have such a competent chauffeur, my lord," John said, hoping to change the subject. "He seems quite devoted."

Lorian shifted in his seat.

"My father saved Vasily's life during the first coalition against Napoleon," Lady Lydia explained. "He doesn't like to bring up what a hero he was."

"Any man would have done the same," Lorian said.

"Vasily has been with us since I was a girl," Lydia said, her voice catching.

Interesting. She hadn't shown any emotion during any other conversation he'd ever observed. Weren't women supposed to be ruled by their hearts? This woman seemed like she held a venom-soaked sponge where a heart should be.

"He must be as one of the family." John tried to give her a soft, understanding look.

She shot back daggers.

"We are grateful for the influx of different cultures to our little island," Lady Lorian said.

"Quite," Lorian agreed.

The butler came in with a note on a silver platter. Surprisingly, the man went to Lady Lydia, not her father. It must be urgent to interrupt dinner.

She took the note, read it, and replaced it on the platter, nodding to dismiss the butler.

"James," she said as explanation to her parents. They nodded, making it clear it was a common occurrence for this man to interrupt dinner.

Who was this James that would have the bollocks to write to her at such an hour? John did his best to school his features into less of a scowl.

The footman came around with a platter and John helped himself, heaping food on his plate at Lady Lorian's insistence. Wine flowed freely. How could Lady Lydia manage not to be swaying? She seemed like a delicate thing. But she appeared unaffected by the alcohol, with the exception of a slight blush high on her cheeks that he liked. He tried to pace himself, too. There was more on his agenda tonight than just dinner with toffs.

"It's a pity that your profession is so lowly regarded when you do so much good for the economy," Lorian said to break up the silence.

John grinned at the clumsy compliment. "There will come a day when we will be a respectable lot, of that I have no doubt. We see too much money to be otherwise." He kicked himself. He shouldn't have talked about money. But his whole life was money. The only other thing he could talk about was pugilism, and that was even worse. Did Lorian even know his past?

"Of course," Lady Lorian said, giving a sympathetic smile.

With Lady Lydia sitting next to him radiating heat, John found it difficult to concentrate. He wanted to watch her mouth, and he was glad he had managed to put his name in for the fights tonight. He felt unfocused and out of his depth, but a mill would put him right back into sorts. Nothing like a man with his fist in your gob to make you pay attention.

Lady Lorian continued with her litany of upcoming events, asking which balls he would also attend. Did he go to the theatre? How to explain that he worked and fought, and then after he fought, he worked? It was how he made money, it was how he made Pearl comfortable. Most nights were filled with beef broth and long runs, training to keep himself in as good of shape as he had been when there had been nothing to do but fight. When the custard was finally served, John couldn't have been more grateful.

They adjourned, the men to Lorian's study and the ladies to the drawing room. It was as he suspected: Lorian wanted to discuss business, and worse, specifics. He stood next to the mantel, expounding on the type of investments he was seeking while John sat sipping a very good port: sweet but smoky.

The scene reminded him of his time at the boys' school, where he would sit in the common room in the evenings, listening to the lofty thoughts of the upperclassmen. He had managed the room and board through fights, gambling what little he had on himself, determined that he would never be poor again.

"What do you say, go to Brooks's to discuss this further?" Lorian asked.

"I couldn't possibly," John said, putting down his port, letting Lorian make his own assumptions.

"I would have thought you were more of a Whig man."

"Is there such a thing anymore?" John asked, a smile on his face. He hated talking politics. It interfered with money.

Lorian nodded. "I see your point. And I suppose the young money is all over at White's."

"Indeed," John said, standing.

"You seem nothing if not pragmatic," Lorian said.

"All of my friends say so," John said, affecting the broad stance and confidence of a man who had many supporters. "Thank you for your hospitality, but I do have another appointment this evening that I must get to."

"Of course," Lorian said, gracious enough to incline his head.

They stopped in the drawing room to say goodbye to the ladies. John gave another gallant bow, sweeping low, as if to supplicate himself to Lady Lydia. When he straightened, he saw a gratified twinkle in her eye. Perhaps that was the way to woo her then.

But that wasn't the thought he meant to have. He wasn't wooing anyone. Even if he could imagine being on his knees to worship at her altar. The thought was nothing if not appealing. But the likes of him don't touch the likes of her. The wine must have muddled him. A short walk before he hired a hack would be enough to clear his head.

The night was cool as he hurried away from the Lorian townhouse. He shook his arms out, craning his neck from side to side. That port had almost done him in. There was a match in an hour, and he was a long way from tonight's mill.

A carriage clambered by, and he could have sworn it was that giant Russian driving. Where could Lorian be going at this time of night? He was going the wrong way for Brooks's. The port was making John bold, but he grinned. An opportunity was an opportunity. He ran, picking up his feet so as to make less noise. As the carriage slowed to take the corner, he leapt onto the rear luggage bar.

Even if they were only going a few blocks in the same direction, the ride would help him arrive in time. Besides, it might do him good to know what Lord Lorian did with his evenings.

# 3

"I'm going out," Lydia declared after Mr. Arthur's exit left them all standing about in the drawing room. Her mother winced.

"Where?" her father asked.

"James only gave me an address. I don't know what that particular building is."

"When will this be done?" he asked, rubbing the bridge of his nose.

"When Hackett is ruined." How many times had they been over this? Since Lydia had revealed the pact, her parents had been laxer with her about the rules of Society, but her age of five and twenty was perilously close to being on the shelf, anyhow. Rules were of little use.

William, being William, had been worried for his younger sisters and persuaded their father to give the girls sizable inheritances that were not attached to a dowry. It meant that should either he or their father die without an heir, a cousin would inherit the title and the entailed lands, but Lydia and Agnes would still have a sizeable sum to live on. Lydia had known William was protecting them because he didn't believe he would have an heir. He was of certain peculiarities, as he'd liked to say, a grin on his face.

After everything that had happened, her father increased the sums. That and his leniency was his way of doing his best to protect Lydia now because he hadn't protected her then. Not that he'd even believed her—at least, not at first. Guilt afflicted him, but not her mother.

"I wish you would all stop," her mother said. "What's done is done."

That was her mother's chorus, the same words every time, and each time her mother made this comment, Lydia's whole body went cold. During that week in the country so many years ago, her mother had been so preoccupied by her father's absence—taking care of business in Town, settling things because William was gone—that she couldn't be bothered with her little girl's nightmares.

James was the one who'd comforted her those nights in the nursery, calming her as she sobbed at every shadow. Margaret and Agnes had been so young that they'd curled up next to Lydia and slept like a cat on her bed or snuggled down in her arms. In truth, their small, innocent presence had helped, even if it made no sense as to why.

When the truth came out, a truth she had discovered from James, she learned there had been a faro game, and the winning hand won not just money, but the chance at her. Those five men—how to even call them men—drunk and pox-ridden, wanted to heal themselves with the virginity of a young girl. But why any young girl when it could be a pretty one? One that would absolutely be a pristine virgin?

"You'll need to change," Agnes said.

It was the details that Agnes always noticed. She wasn't much for the adventuring or the risk-taking, but she kept Lydia safe with the small things.

The two women slipped upstairs, not bothering to ring for Charlotte. Agnes helped Lydia into the old gown, faded, even if well made. It was not much of a disguise, but far better than the magnificent midnight-blue beaded sheath she'd worn for dinner.

Adults had been the problem—their world had no room for Lydia's insistence. James was the oldest, and being a boy, he'd easily found out his father's actions. Lydia had never known if it was the look on her face when James told her or if it was because it pitted him against his father, but they were merely children when they formed their pact. Gambling was evil, practiced by evil men, and the four children vowed to take down all five members of that particular faro game.

Three of the players had been taken care of in the intervening years, including James's father, the former Viscount Andrepont. Baron Tottingham had been easy—his farms were already failing. The financial failure drove him to cheat at another game of cards, and he died in a duel with a Scottish stranger. They hadn't had to do a thing.

"Looks as right as it can," Agnes said, giving a sad smile. "Be careful."

"You know I'll be safe. Vasily, James, and Bess will be there," Lydia reminded her, taking the stairs as fast as she dared.

"And Mr. Arthur," Agnes added.

"Pardon?" Lydia slipped into her pelisse. Robling held her bonnet. White gloves were maybe not the best idea for going to the East End, but she was already late for her cousin's summons.

"He protected you from a horse, surely he would protect you in a...in a..."

"You can say it aloud, Agnes," Lydia scolded. "It's not like one could keep a secret from Robling anyhow."

The butler gave a mild nod.

"It's unsafe, what you do."

Lydia shrugged. "I'm already ruined. It's just that nobody knows it yet."

The other viscount at that faro game had been dispatched that very week, another victim of his own wickedness. A disgruntled husband had come round for words, and before anyone could stop them, the other man had accosted Viscount Beecher, giving him such a beating that later an infection set in. Months afterward, he died from an overdose of opium he had started taking to help with the agony of his shattered eye socket.

Vasily helped Lydia into the closed, unmarked carriage. Her reputation relied on her discretion, but also her native knowledge. She'd built trust with other members of the *ton* who didn't quite fit the particulars of a blueblood. She was a member of the Fancy, but they didn't discuss her presence at the mills, her interest in boxing, or her training. Her slender figure did not just come from avoiding desserts, but also from her work, the kind that most young ladies did not do.

Indeed, the biggest enemy of her reputation was her age: she was in danger of being on the shelf, having been out in Society for too many seasons. But because of her friendship with Sebastian, words spoken solely in the company of other men—utterances heard past midnight in a private club, blurred by brandy and a false sense of security—were scribbled down verbatim by his friends. They had an agreement, and a mutual love of William, and Sebastian helped her in any way he could, even if he despaired of her need to learn the sweet science of pugilism.

The ride to Covent Garden was long, and surprisingly bumpy. Looking out the windows could make a person motion sick, so she settled back against the squabs and tried not to think about Mr. Arthur.

He had addressed them all appropriately, but she could tell he had worked hard on his accent and manners. Why did he seek higher echelons when there was a perfectly comfortable middle class to exist in for merchants and bankers? He had the money.

Ah yes, the sister. He had the money for an excellent dowry, so why not find a title to make her nice and secure? Snug her in, tight and cozy, unaware that the *ton* didn't take to outsiders. Heiresses were always a sought-after commodity for the dissolute rakes, but would a man take a wife whose brother could (and had) beaten a man's face into resembling a pulped pineapple?

After word came back about the *Europe*, then she could help Miss Arthur. But she couldn't afford to get distracted while she still waited for Hackett's downfall. Her reputation depended on too many precarious dominoes. Not that it mattered much to her—but for Agnes to have a chance, Lydia needed to remain clean. Besides, if she was sullied, then she was of no help to Miss Arthur in any case. Later.

Finally, Vasily slowed the horses. The carriage rocked unexpectedly, but soon Vasily opened the door and extended the step. She hooked the large hood of her pelisse over her head to disguise her face, and they both hurried inside.

❧

THE LANDAU SLOWED AND JOHN ARTHUR JUMPED off the luggage bar. Of all the places he thought the carriage would go, this possibility had not occurred to him. John peered around the edge as the massive Russian opened the carriage door and folded out the step. Instead of the tall, trim form of Lord Lorian, he spied a slender white glove reaching out to take Vasily's hand.

John drew up short, gaping like a jolter-head.

A hooded lady emerged, and from the haughty air with which she walked, John was sure of the lady's identity. He grinned. So, he would have an advantage, at last. There was no way she had known he would be here, let alone fighting. After she crossed the threshold of the laundry, John slipped through the entrance at the back of the building.

While the boxing mills changed location, this was a common enough site when a mill was held in Town. The laundry's basement was large enough to accommodate a mob of a hundred spectators, maybe more if they didn't mind pickpockets. A proper prizefight would have been different, advertised, big names, a write-up by Mr. Egan, and then a discreetly agreed-upon site outside of London would be flooded with people looking for a bit of blood and money. The magistrates would have been bribed to keep quiet, and the local innkeepers would have been apprised to keep rooms at the ready.

A mill was already in progress when he slipped in, a couple of boys who looked like they couldn't even shave yet.

"Devil have me, the most illustrious Mr. Arthur!" Tony Farrow greeted, clapping him on the back with one hand as he shook John's hand with the other. Hard shell, soft middle, that one.

"Tony," John greeted him, feeling like he needed to stretch his jaw to drop the posh accent he'd spoken with all evening. "You didn't think I'd miss this, did you?"

"I was ready to send after you if you did," Tony said. "There's too much money in the room tonight."

"Good house, then?" John glanced around at the

spectators clutching sweaty wads of paper. Since Napoleon's fall, there had been more and more men crowded about. It had gotten rougher, all the ex-soldiers crammed into a tight space.

"Great house tonight!" the fat man roared. Tony had changed little in the twenty-odd years John had known him; not even a single hair on his head had turned gray. "You'll make some money."

"Winning or losing?" They walked into their corner of the room. John stripped off his greatcoat. "Having this kind of crowd is risky for an in-Town fight, Tony. Greed is making you reckless."

The big man waved him off. "Did you not see our patrons in the corner? We'll not have problems tonight. Paid off the dogberries proper this time."

Aristocrats huddled in one corner of the crowd, the members of Gentleman Jackson's Pugilist Club next to them, with the spread of tradesmen and the lower orders crammed into the rest of the space. "There's the Fancy."

The Fancy kept them safe and kept many of them afloat. They came to matches, lords and ladies alike, took lessons, and watched the boxers spill their claret —or, if the toff hadn't been in the Fancy long enough to understand the parlance—watched them bleed. But most importantly, they parted with the contents of their pockets.

"Perry's here, want me to send him over?"

"Aye," John said. "Who am I fighting?"

"A toff," Tony said, spitting into the corner.

John stretched his back, pulling one shoulder and then the other. He wouldn't mind showing an aristocrat the hardworking knuckles of the lower orders. After that dinner, he was glad to drop the affluent accent and slip into the familiar cadence of the old neighborhood.

Caulie elbowed his way through the crowd. He

was a friend from the old days, but he worked with John at the Exchange. He was a jobber—the lowest of the rungs on the financial ladder. Between his accent, his short stature, and his cauliflowered ears, there wasn't a way for him to climb up to real respectability, even though he had the blunt to do it.

"Them's thick out there," Caulie said, shaking his head. When he caught sight of John's togs, he pranced in mockery. "Oh, hellooooo sir, I thought you might be my friend John, not realizing we have a dandy about."

They laughed. "It's a bit far to keep your fighting name, but I weren't about to question it," Tony said.

John's fighting name, *Corinthian John*, was meant to evoke fineness and the Fancy who came down to slum. A true Corinthian would dress for dinner as John was dressed tonight, throw his coin about, drink too much, and maybe find a whore to keep company. But though John could dress the part, even give florid bows that John and Caulie had practiced for months, he could never bring himself to those habits. He remembered those whores as the girls they'd been when they'd all stayed in the abandoned buildings in St. Giles. He'd been terrified that would happen to Pearl, and he'd set her up as best he could, praying every day that he wouldn't get taken up to Newgate for stealing. They didn't mind hanging street urchins for taking anything worth more than five bob.

Instead, he found Tony, and he didn't steal, he fought.

Tony called Perry over to their huddle. "But here's the thing, see? Toff has wagered against himself. Secret-like. I think he aims to throw the match."

"Which toff? This one?" Caulie pointed to John. "Or that one over there?"

Thrown matches were never a good idea, and this crowd tonight wouldn't suffer a cheat. He looked across to where Caulie had pointed out the other toff but couldn't see him. John found the massive Russian in the sea of faces, but he couldn't find Lady Lydia next to him, though he was sure she would be there.

John's brow furrowed. Perry appeared, a lanky ginger boy who reminded John of himself, handing him a small, watered-down beer. The boy marked John's face from a container of grease. Without it, the other man's knuckles could tear the skin. With it, a blow had a better chance of glancing away. "You'll be my bottleman, then, Perry?"

The boy's eyes lit up.

"Are you even going to ask if I'll be your second?" Caulie said, arms folded.

"Do I need to?" John asked.

"Course not," Caulie said with a grin, revealing gaps from missing teeth.

"Who are the other mills?" John asked.

Tony only grinned that way for one fighter—Bess Abbott. She was terrifying, and Tony loved her. They all did.

"I'll go wish her luck," John said.

Tony pulled out a pocket watch. "Ye haven't much time. Better get to her now."

John walked into the crowd. The ring was marked out by lazy ropes on the floor, men crowding the lines. Typically, the ladies' fight was first, but some young amateurs must have taken the opening slot. Ladies' fights worked the crowd into a frenzy. Hopefully, Vasily could properly protect Lady Lydia when the time came.

Bess was nowhere to be seen. John pushed through the mob of people. The mill was still going and none of the men wanted to let him pass, so he elbowed the best he could. Before he knew it, he was face to face with Vasily, whose meaty, folded arms gave no unsure impression of his feelings.

"Hello, old friend," John said, restoring his aristocratic dialect.

Lady Lydia peered around the mountain of a man, surprise writ across her face. Her hood was still up, masking those who might try to recognize her, but anyone who knew Vasily would spot her instantly.

"What are you doing here?" she demanded. Her eyes trailed down to his undone cravat and partially unbuttoned shirt.

He'd fight bare-chested, but the first ceremony of any match was peeling off the garments. The room was already hot with anticipation of blood.

"I should ask you the same. This is no place for a lady," he said. "Are you part of the Fancy?" His eyes flicked to the big man. The crowd erupted. John didn't need to look at the ring to know that one of the fighters was knocked out. Money would be changing hands soon, the ring would be cleared, and the next match would be set.

Lady Lydia glanced to the ring and back to him. People elbowed past, everyone wanting the best vantage point. She was uncomfortable with him, that much was clear, but she didn't seem to be bothered by the jostling masses. She seemed the type to abhor the crush of this sweaty basement, but here she was, at ease with them and not with him.

"Should you need any further assistance," he said, glancing at the pony-sized driver, "I am at your disposal. However, I have a pressing matter in just a few more minutes."

"You took a fight on the same night as our invitation to dine?" She seemed insulted.

Should she be insulted? He fought every night he could, and the invitation was issued days before he knew the night of the fight. It was the only way they could keep ahead of the magistrates.

"A prizefighter must fight. That's in the name, is it

not? So what good would I be if I turned down such invitations, whether to dine or to bleed?"

"That's a pretty speech for a half-dressed man," she countered.

"You should hear my speeches when I am thoroughly undressed," he said, flashing a smile that he was almost certain would earn him a backhand from her driver.

"I'm not certain I could stand it," she said, not batting an eye.

He took a step forward, not thinking, just wanting to engage her further, smell her hair somehow? Oranges and vanilla would be a far sight better than the stink of unwashed men. But Vasily wedged his foot between John's and hers. He retreated, and Vasily gave a grunt of approval.

"I would be happy to help you push your limits," John said, bowing as best he could amongst the crowd.

"Fine manners, wot you got," he heard from beside him.

He straightened to see Bess Abbott standing there, hands on hips, towering over Lady Lydia and damn near looking the Russian bear in the eye.

"Bess!" He clapped his hand on her shoulder and shook her hand with the other.

"John," she said, grinning. "Like the old days, right? Me on first, then you bringing in the crowd for the crimson end."

"Nuffin' like old mates," he said, his accent shifting again.

He glanced past Vasily's meat barrier to Lady Lydia, who was looking at him with an expression he couldn't read. What better time to scandalize the highborn than when they went slumming?

"Lady Lydia, may I present my old friend, Bess Abbott," he said, returning to his proper accent.

Lady Lydia bowed her head. "Bess," she said, with no trace of hauteur or dismay.

Wasn't that a fine thing, then? What was she doing here, and why wasn't she appalled that he had called her name and introduced her to a lady fighter? In fact, why had she addressed Bess with her Christian name?

"M'lady," Bess said, giving an approximation of a curtsy. She was quick on her feet, Bess was, but she didn't possess the finest manners. Once, when they were both younger, she'd been clocked with a quarterstaff so hard at the end of a mill that she couldn't speak right for a week. The blow had ended the match, of course, and everyone agreed that she was lucky to keep most of her teeth. Since then, Bess didn't like to duck her head to anyone—she refused to limit her field of vision.

A warning bell rang.

"I'm to my corner," Bess said.

"Good luck, mate," John said, clapping her on the shoulder again.

"Don't need it," she said, grinning. "But maybe you do." Bess gave another approximation of a curtsy and then pushed her way through the crowd, shouting obscenities when someone took a drunken swing at her.

"If you are going to try to embarrass me, you'll have to try harder," Lady Lydia said, turning from him. "If you'll excuse me, the match is soon to start. I'd hate to miss it."

"I daresay it'll scandalize you, my lady. The fairer sex is not so gentle."

Her eyes flashed back at him, anger enhancing her beauty. The color in her cheeks he'd admired at dinner returned. "Finally. We agree on one thing, at least." Then she flicked her hand at him, dismissing him.

His temper, usually so controlled, flared at her gesture. He was no footman at her beck and call. He cracked his neck, first the left, then the right, then the left again. The bell rang and the match was starting, so he left, elbowing his way back through the crowd.

Tony's ample pockets were stuffed with notes. He was grinning like a jackal. "Bess is my girl," he crowed.

"You wish," John said, elbowing Tony in the ribs.

"Watch it," he said. "Those elbows are deadly weapons."

They stared out at the ring companionably for a moment, words unnecessary for men like the two of them who'd shared the rough life.

"That tart over there get you all worked up?" Tony asked, his eyes never wavering from the center of the room.

The women had their bottlemen undo their loose stays and take away their garments. The crowd whistled. Bess's opponent, an older woman he'd not seen before, shook her rump at the crowd, egging them on.

"Take i' off!" someone yelled.

Bess didn't respond, didn't waggle for the crowd. She was focused on her opponent, while the other woman was focused on the crowd. It would be her dominoes he'd step on in the ring, then.

Each woman wore nothing but a thin chemise, the straps loose on her shoulders, and damn near everything visible underneath the worn cotton. Bess banded her breasts, but not out of modesty. When she started the practice years ago, she claimed that not binding them knocked off her balance.

"Tits don't have controllable muscle, John," she had complained. "Don't get all lathered up on my account."

The opponent smoothed her chemise down against her body, showing off her tits to the crowd, which hooted and stamped in appreciation.

"You're supposed to be revealed!" someone yelled at Bess.

She didn't respond. Her stays were gone, which was all that was required. The bell sounded, and the two umpires got into the ring.

"I'll be your kneeman!" someone else yelled.

"Won't need one," John murmured to Tony, who laughed in response.

Any fighter—any—was instantly distinguishable from a performer. Bess wasn't famous because she was a showman. She was paid to fight, and fight she did. The muscles in her back, near to the twitch, were as wrought on her as on any man. She wasn't a beauty, never had been, and so she fought to feed herself, just as John had.

Still, the men who watched didn't appreciate her skill. They called her "Bes' Close Your Eyes First," mocking her homely looks—her ears cauliflowered, her nose having been broken a number of times. Her eyes were wide and brown, and her oversized stature made a man feel small.

But John would rather defend himself back to back with Bess than any other fighter he knew. His blood was up as they mocked her in the ring.

Between Lady Lydia's dismissal and the obscene jokes made at his friend's expense, it was all he could do to keep himself from tearing through the crowd. But he knew how to harness that, keep it at the ready for his opponent, when the time came.

The umpires conferred and released the fighters. They opted not to use weapons, which was probably better for the other woman. He'd seen Bess be lethal with a cudgel one night during a lurid match. She could've ended up in Newgate for that one, but luck was with her that night.

The other woman approached the line, her lip in a snarl. Bess toed the line, her face impassive. The umpires called the start, and the woman took the first swing. Bess shifted her weight and planted a facer.

The woman went down, the claret flowing from her nose and mouth. The match was over; the other woman was out cold.

"That's my Bess," Tony said. "She knows how to pop the claret!"

The crowd booed and hissed, screaming obscenities, angry at the lack of show. They wanted more Amazons, more bare-breasted women, teeth on display—like sex without sex, just a tease before the drunken, soft louts went to the brothel.

Bess pulled up her dress and conferred with the umpires, who checked on the other woman's health. Bess's bottleman, not much more than a lad, tossed her an orange. She caught it with ease, and they shared a smile. Easy money.

Across the room, Lady Lydia chatted with another man, her bearing comfortable and relaxed. Maybe it was only because John was about to fight, but he hated the idea of her talking so calmly with another man in this sort of place. Especially a man as pretty as this one, with dark hair and eyes the color of spring peas, clear enough to see at a distance.

He was in a state of undress, no waistcoat, and wore his shirt loose, so perhaps this was the toff Tony had spoken about. John had seen this other cove in the ring before but never fought him. If he were as good looking as that chap, he wouldn't step foot in the ring. But toffs took weird chances to prove themselves.

John's stomach soured as he watched this dark-haired man lean over and kiss Lady Lydia's cheek. She smiled back. So! He was a suitor. It dawned on him then that she had received a note during dinner, interrupting the flow of their overly polite, ultimately dull dinner conversation. This was the James that she had spoken of, whom her parents seemed unflustered about. If they knew where their daughter ran off to at night, they would certainly care more. Didn't she have a reputation to protect?

"You're up," Tony said, patting him on the shoulder.

"I can't lose this mill." Anxiety pricked at the back of his neck.

"I'd never ask you to, my boy," Tony said. "Go on, then."

Perry came running up behind him with a bottle filled with the cleanest water in the area and a few oranges, just in case the rounds went long.

After the disappointment of the women's match, Basil jumped into the ring. That little rat could talk Midas out of his golden touch, if need be. He had been a fixture of the underground rings since John was young, another urchin needing a way to feed himself. The years hadn't put any more weight on him, but his tongue only got faster. Basil started shouting about the upcoming match.

John stripped off his shirt, handing it to Caulie. He felt out of sorts. He was never out of sorts for a match.

"You all right? Need a minute?" Caulie asked. "An orange, more beer?"

Maybe it had been the rich dinner; turtle soup was decidedly not on the list of acceptable training foods. Not that he'd been seriously training. He hadn't had a proper prizefight in years, just these mills. Still, he wasn't used to the rich foods. That had to be the reason he couldn't focus. Not because of the lady in the hooded pelisse staring at him with midnight-blue eyes.

"Gents, gents!" Basil called to the crowd. "Next match, we have it for you! You know 'im well! Corinthian John!"

Caulie snorted, and John grimaced. His ring persona had come from years of sparring, where he wouldn't inflict more damage than he had to. If the man was down, he was down, and John respected it. Basil had started the name, and it stuck because of its allusion to Greek debauchery the dandies all participated in.

John shot daggers at the little rat as he walked into the middle of the ring and performed his courtly bow. He couldn't not think about Lady Lydia, her opinion, her safety—and he realized he wanted to see admiration in those dark-blue eyes. So, he made sure that he performed that courtly bow directly to her.

❦

THE ROOM FELT CLOSE AND HOT. SHE WANTED TO push her hood down, slip off her pelisse, and loosen her stays. Whalebone stays were a terrible idea all around. On the other side of the room, the Fancy gathered in a huddle. It was a rougher crowd tonight, veterans of Napoleon missing a hand or a leg, others just rough and sour looking. Lydia didn't feel like joining the Fancy, skulking about in the back as she usually did. She wanted to see James fight—he'd been particularly melancholy since he'd met Miss Dorchester, but things couldn't be helped.

She could find comfort with the aristocratic Fancy, but tonight, she wanted to just feel the sway of the crowd.

Bess had fought with surgical precision. The fighter had told Lydia during a private lesson once that her technique had come from being hungry all the time. The quicker a match was over, the quicker she could get food in her belly.

Lydia had starved herself on a number of occasions, wondering if she could feel that same drive, but in the end, the knowledge that food was abundant and nearby was too much of a comfort. Bess had also given her strict instructions for training, a diet of beef broth and thirty miles of running. Where on earth would a young lady run? Where would she be allowed to run for one mile, let alone thirty? Could an actual person run thirty miles in one day? She doubted it. Bess instructed her on how long to walk between the miles, and how long to rest, and when to eat. Thirty miles was to take the entire day. But still, to appear red-faced and disheveled for an entire day, as if one had nothing better to do with one's time? Even she couldn't flout convention that flagrantly.

The crowd jostled, riotous and grabbing. Vasily stood with his arms folded, scowling at any man or woman who came too near. The emcee, a skeletal man, jumped into the middle of the small cordoned-off ring. She could barely understand him through his gutter accent, shouting and crowing through his speech.

What she did understand, however, was that when the emcee called out "Corinthian John," Mr. Arthur stepped into the middle of the ring, peeled off his waistcoat, and pulled off his shirt. James did the same over in his corner, but she couldn't tear her eyes away from Mr. Arthur. He was lean, muscled like a stray dog. How was it that he took her breath away? Maybe he could run thirty miles in one day.

He executed a bow in the center of the ring that anyone would be proud to give a monarch. But there was no way she could tear her eyes away from his form. His long limbs looked perfectly sculpted, as if he was born to this.

Many men would argue that he was bred to it since he was born in St. Giles.

Corinthian John completed his bow, raising his head to look directly at Lydia. A warm flush travelled through her, settling lower than she thought it ought. Her pulse was racing again, though not from nerves. She wished she had a fan, like in a ballroom, where she could hide her expression, flutter away confusion.

Many in the crowd followed his gaze to her, a few whistling and hooting. "Corinfian John's got a proper lady!"

Lydia ignored them.

The little rat-man announced James, calling him "The Beastly Baron." She rolled her eyes. The crowd booed at James as he took his turn in the center of the ring, executing a bow so florid she thought he might fall over. As he stood, he caught Lydia's eye and grinned.

She grinned back, unable not to be pleased by her cousin, the most excellent brooding Viscount Andrepont, not a baron in the least. But what viscount would demote himself? Her breath caught in her chest. He meant to lose.

"No," she called out, hoping he might hear her out of the noisy crowd.

He looked back at her, his calm demeanor not helping her feel better in the least. He inclined his head, as if this penance was something she ought to understand. Oh, she understood it. He was in love and couldn't have what he wanted, so now he was going to alleviate his internal pain with a good dose of external pain.

"A bet, m'lady?" a man approached her.

Vasily growled and stood between her and the man, his hat off, his head bowed.

"The toff will get a taste of Corinfian John's fist right quick," crowed another man nearby.

Lydia didn't bother to look over. She shook her head, not wanting to betray herself again with her posh accent. Vasily's grumble was enough to get the bookie to move along to another target.

She balled her hands at her sides. There would be no wringing of her hands, there would be no tears, no more shouts, that much was for certain. These were two grown men who wanted to pummel each other; who was she to stand in the way?

The little rat-man rang the bell, and the two fighters met at the scratch line in the middle of the ring. They shook hands, a perfunctory nod as they focused in on each other.

Both were muscular, fit, with knees bent, showing good fighting forms. They both held their fists up, ready to either throw a punch or protect themselves from one. John Arthur was not as handsome as her cousin, but there was something she liked about his fine nose, a bit crooked as it was. If it were bent any more, she would be disappointed.

He moved smoothly, cool as he edged James against the rope, inch by inch. No punches were yet thrown. They danced instead as if this were another ballroom—dark, dusty, and sweaty.

James threw a jab. John Arthur caught it and pulled him in close, throwing swift body shots into James's side. John Arthur released him, and the crowd booed.

"Wipe that smirk off his gob, Corinthian John!" a man yelled.

Lydia met Bess's eyes from across the ring. Bess nodded in acknowledgement and moved her way through the crowd.

James threw a punch that connected, whipping John Arthur's head back. Even from her distance,

Lydia could see the flash of surprise in the stockbroker's eyes. Immediately his right lashed out, a lightning-fast hook striking James, then he followed through with a left jab that put James to the ground.

The umpires ran over, but James put his hand up to signal he was still conscious. The bell rang. The first round was over.

The crowd shifted, moving in all directions, more money exchanging hands, the boxers in their corners. The bigger lads were the kneemen; because of their small stature, they were on their hands and knees, their backs providing a bench for the athletes to sit on. Had they been older, the kneemen would have knelt with one leg down and the other up, their thighs giving the resting place the competitors needed. The boxers had thirty seconds to sit before they went to the line again.

Bess was near James's corner, moving amongst the crowd, sometimes getting a pat on the shoulder from someone who could actually reach that high. Lydia wondered what that would be like—to have a level of informality in so many venues.

The bell rang again and the men were up to the scratch line, still cautious towards each other, and the crowd hushed. There was still the rustle of paper, pound notes being folded and deposited in a pocket somewhere.

James let loose a fist, but John Arthur dodged it, swaying to the left so fast that he seemed a blur.

Lydia almost let out a gasp of surprise, as the rest of the spectators did, but caught herself. She was not the sort prone to hysterics.

Bess came to stand near her finally. They both continued to face the ring, ostensibly watching the match.

"I've got myself a new patron," Bess said in a low voice.

"Someone I know?" Lydia asked.

"A Lord Denby," Bess said. "Only one session so far, nothing untoward, but there is something I don't like about him."

"Then why did you take him on?"

"Money is money and food is food. Anyway, I thought it would interest you knowing which houses I'm in."

"Would it?" Lydia's hands became clammy under her gloves at the mention of Denby. She already counted him as ruined. He had to stay that way. "Or is it that you feel safer knowing I can find you, should you need assistance?"

Bess shrugged her shoulders, then lolled her head from side to side, as if she were merely stretching. "It seems like this is mutually beneficial."

Lydia acted like a predator, but deep down she knew she was a prey animal, skittish when threatened, unpredictable in the face of danger. "No, Bess. I apologize. Old habits and all that."

"Good," Bess said. Her head nodded towards the ring. "Your cousin is going to need some looking after once John is done with him. He's a talent."

Lydia couldn't help but agree. She'd seen James fight before, and a match never looked as graceful as it did tonight. "Will you come again for a lesson?"

"Of course, my lady. My patron is not at home this week."

"Then our usual hour will suffice. Good evening, Bess," Lydia whispered, but the lady boxer had already slipped through the crowd, light on her feet, pushing her way through the sea of red faces and screaming mouths.

John Arthur continued to punish James. They stepped apart only to come together again, John Arthur's swift, alternating punches finally causing

James's nose to erupt into red the color of claret. He fell, ending another round.

Lydia should have made her eyes follow James back to his corner, evaluating his gait, gauging his health. Maybe she should have even rushed to his side. But she did none of those things. Instead she stayed where she was, an impassive witness. The lithe John Arthur stalked back to his corner, unharmed. He remained as stone-faced as she was, not even bothering to check his knuckles for scrapes. He was in a ring, in a fight, hurting another human being and yet maintaining his neutrality. Was it different because it was for money? Or was it, like everything else, a matter of training and discipline? He glanced over at her, the smoky light making the sweat on his pale skin shine.

An undecipherable emotion flickered across his face, and if she were more naïve, she would think he was fighting for her, as if beating James was proving something. But she wasn't.

More crumpled paper changed hands amidst the crowd, and now there was so much yelling Lydia couldn't understand any of the words.

What he was planning, she couldn't say, and then she gaped like every other spectator as John Arthur took two wide steps and led with his fist. He clocked James square on the jaw, and James fell hard. The crowd erupted, the agitation instantly doubling in the low-ceilinged basement. James was down, fully unconscious. Corinthian John had won the match with a decisive blow.

Some men were yelling about breaking the rules, that they had not properly begun the round. The frenetic energy in the room crackled from spectator to spectator, the air growing closer and closer.

"My lady," grumbled Vasily as he watched the men surrounding them. "We should go soon."

"Should we not see to James?" The air was close and humid with the breath of so many people. She could smell not just the stink of the unwashed men near her, but the sweat of James and Mr. Arthur in the ring. She was jostled into Vasily by gamblers trying to make it to the moneyman. Money still had to be divided publicly in the ring. While everyone waited, it felt as if every corner was primed and ready to explode.

"For your safety, I think we should leave now. Lord Andrepont can take care of himself," Vasily said.

"Did you 'ear that?" screeched a man nearby. "That cove really is a lord!"

"No," other men said. "A man like that couldn't be from those inbred wankers."

The crowd shifted, a darker mood settling into the arena. "He expectin' us to bow jus' cos he's not woke yet?"

Lydia reached over to Vasily and took his arm. "An exit would do," she said.

"Coo, a lady in our midst!" a man shouted, pointing his dirty finger at her. He made a nasty bow. "Come slummin' for us? Got a taste for mud?"

Bess pushed through the crowd from across the room. Instead of waiting for a bodyguard, Lydia drew herself up as tall as she could. That prey animal was inside her, hooves tumbling and desperate for escape. The coolest expression she possessed overtook her face.

She let her eyes flick up and down the figure of the man who pointed at her. "I thought perhaps." Then she glanced over to John Arthur, who stood in the ring waiting for the referees' official pronouncement of his win. After that, the money would be divided and things would likely become chaos. Bess was almost to her side. Lydia's pulse galloped, and her whole body went cold. It wouldn't be long until her hands began to tremble. “But then.” She returned her gaze to the dirty man’s face. Her sneer was delicate and very well suited to the disdain required for this situation. “I thought not.”

John Arthur looked up, frowning at the crowd near Lydia as the referee pushed his arm up into the air to declare him the winner. She shouldn’t have wasted a backwards glance at the ring, but Lydia couldn’t help it. He met her eyes. If anyone could calm her, it was him.

But she didn’t need comforting, she needed escape from a dirty Covent Garden basement. Before the shakes could overtake her, she pushed her own way through the crowd, using her elbows to make her way when Vasily’s bulk couldn’t clear the path.

# 4

"Where's yer sister today?" Caulie asked, his dark pebble-like eyes glinting.

"Far away from the likes o' you," John said. The smell of unwashed moneymen grew worse as they bustled past. The expansive floor of the London Stock Exchange started to fill for the workday. The columns in the corners of the massive building were bigger around than a man's arms, and they hid the whispering transactions of before-the-bell dealings. The room felt sprawling and grandiose until the bell rang, and then it was nothing but elbow-to-bollocks as far as the eye could see. "Come with me to Garraway's."

"Now?" Caulie asked, looking around at the growing crowd. He leaned back to glance behind the far column, where the jobbers for the Dutch East India company usually began their day.

It was hard to say whose work ethic was more Protestant, his or Caulie's. Both had the same upbringing—scrapping, thieving, and fighting before being elevated: Caulie lifted by catching the attentions of a wealthy patron and John by the guilt of an older cousin who'd fled England for a better life in America. They went to the same boys' school to learn to read and write and found they needed to stick together. At first glance, John was the talker and Caulie the muscle, even though their skills were the reverse. John was all fists, and Caulie loved a good negotiation. Still, as a jobber, the ears helped Caulie ward off the pranks of the other men, earning him a little more respect than the others.

"We've got twenty minutes before the bell," John said.

"But my holdings are good today, John. Today is a money day for me," Caulie protested. "And with your face looking all a fright, you'll probably trade well."

The swelling had gone down, and all he was left with was the cut across his nose and some yellowing around his eyes. He was lucky the Beastly Baron, or whoever the toff was, had not broken his nose. Not that it hadn't been done before, but John hated that crunchy feeling in his face as it healed back up. And while his nose wasn't perfect, it was adequately attractive to find companionship. Lady Lydia probably didn't find crooked noses appealing.

"I'm healing well enough," John protested.

Caulie shrugged. "Aw rite, mate."

A man cut through the men on the floor. The ceilings were high, letting the clamor of noise lift above the heads of the men making it. "Mr. Arthur!"

Squinting, John made out Lord Elshire pushing his way through the men already mingling about before trades opened.

"Lord Elshire, what a pleasure to see you," he said, sticking his hand out for a handshake.

"My good neighbor!" Lord Elshire said, ignoring the outstretched hand. "I was surprised you'd left your home so early this morning. I thought surely I would catch you before you came to the Exchange."

"I had a great deal of business to conduct today," John said, catching the strange face Caulie gave him.

Truthfully, he had left early because he couldn't concentrate in his own quiet house. He took some of his papers and set up shop at Garraway's, drinking coffee and letting his eyes run over the newsprint. He let everyone think he was keeping up with the markets, but his head was replaying those moments from a few nights ago: Lady Lydia with her gloved hand on his while they went down to dinner. Lady Lydia's shocked expression at the laundry when he bowed to her from the middle of the ring. Her glance back at him, as if asking for his help, as she fled the mill.

He wanted to go after her, clear the path as Vasily had done for her. Protect her. He was good at protection. But if there was anything he had learned from dinner with her family, it was that he was beneath them, and a lady did not belong at a basement boxing match. With only two exits and all those disgruntled, unpredictable soldiers, even with a bodyguard, she had been in danger. All the more reason to give such a punishing blow to that ridiculous toff. He lured her there. It was that toff's fault, and John was glad he'd knocked him out.

"I need to rearrange my holdings," Elshire said. "Critical, really. I need to exchange my three-percent securities for something more lucrative in the short term."

John frowned. "Are you certain, my lord? Three percent is standard."

Elshire nodded, his deep furrowed brow showed his age. "The investment returns from my previous expedition were quite helpful, and thank you for having the foresight to see to it. However, my ward, Miss Dorchester—perhaps you've met her?"

John shook his head. Shouldn't the man know who has made his ward's acquaintance? Poor girl must need the attentions of the Ladies Somerset for guidance if she was left on her own in this shark-infested water. That was why he sought a guide for Pearl. He knew the rules after a fashion, but not all the details.

"Ah, well, she's a lovely girl, and I want to make certain her dowry is as attractive as she is, but I haven't much time."

"My lord, are you not already well into the Season?" If the girl was already getting serious offers, there wasn't much time to grow the investment. There were a few risky securities he knew about, but not one he would gamble a young girl's dowry on.

"I honestly hadn't thought she would catch the eye of someone so grand." Elshire sighed. "Please don't mistake me, but the odd little thing was raised in the country by her uncle."

John nodded in sympathy to the lord's self-reference. "We're all a bit odd, my lord. Some of us just hide it better than others."

Caulie grinned, showing a gap deep in his mouth where he'd had teeth knocked out. Elshire glanced over and caught sight of it, chuckling.

"I need to start a longer-term investment portfolio at the same time," Elshire explained.

"Both a short term and a long term? You are confusing me today."

"A three percent for the next, I'd say..." The man broke off to calculate. "Forty years ought to do it."

"Forty?" John asked. "What happens in forty years?"

A sparkle seemed to flicker in Elshire's eye. "I may actually have children. I need a dowry, or perhaps a small income for a second son."

"I would not think of correcting you, my lord, but might I suggest a slightly shorter term, and of course, compound the interest to grow the capital?" John asked, bowing slightly as he did so. He'd found in working with aristocrats, one had to show deference at every turn, regardless of how much more he knew about the markets.

Elshire frowned, thinking. "I suppose you're right. A young lady doesn't typically marry at thirty-five, does she?"

"No, my lord. As for the short-term, is a five percent return enough?"

"She might have an offer in as little as a few weeks. Can you get more than five?"

"The five percent Consols are government backed and carry little risk. This isn't the same market as we had during the war. We no longer have gains of twenty percent in an hour."

Elshire nodded, hanging his head. "Invest in higher risk if you can get a better return. I need to give her the chance. Surely you understand?"

"I'll see what I can do," John said.

"Wonderful! You know, I do recommend you at the club when I am in Town. You've performed miracles." Elshire clapped John on the shoulder and then moved out of the stream of men pouring in through the colonnade. John watched the lord work his way through the crowd and exit the building. It was dizzying for civilians to be in the Exchange after the bell rang. It was loud and busy, and no one was above throwing elbows to get what he wanted.

"I've got stocks to sell," someone shouted.

"Bell's not rung, ya bounder," another man yelled.

There were sects amongst the members of the Stock Exchange, and they migrated to separate corners. There were the aristocrats, the Huguenots, the Hebrews, the ministers, the bankers, the Foreigners of various stripes. But John prided himself on being able to glad-hand them all, making good trades regardless of the man involved. Money was money, and it didn't care whose pocket it was in.

The bell clanged, and the noise level increased. Only a man trained to trade could pick apart the voices as a broker mounted the rostrum to announce his needs.

"Borrow money? Borrow money," a jobber yelled, turning in a circle and hoping to find a broker.

Caulie clapped John on the back. "Time to go to work, my friend."

Would it be too crass for him to leave a card at Lady Lydia's house? One for her father, really, since he knew enough that men didn't leave cards for unmarried ladies. He could find a way to talk to Vasily, make sure Lady Lydia was unhurt. He couldn't just sit around and wait for Fate to push them together again. After the Exchange, then. There would be ample time to get to Mayfair and leave a card for Lord Lorian.

"WHAT ELSE?" JAMES ASKED, HIS LEGS CROSSED, balancing his small notebook on his knee. His face sported two black eyes, and his lip was cut in two places. The swelling had gone down, but he was still quite a sight.

Bess handed Lydia a small sparring club, despite her protestations that her arms were already near shaking with fatigue. Every time the wooden sticks connected with force, the impact rattled up to her shoulders.

Both women were stripped to their waists, their breasts bound as Bess had invented for herself. Lydia was positively drenched from the encounter. Her mother would say she glowed, but no woman could glow this excessively. She still wore her chemise up over her shoulders, while Bess had her straps down and tucked in about her waist.

"Denby prefers grappling," Bess called over her shoulder.

*Of course he does,* Lydia thought, but she was too out of breath to say it aloud. They sparred in the Lorian ballroom, a space big enough for Lydia to show off her footwork to her mentor. It was funny to think of the *ton* dancing and gossiping in the same room where she was punching and hitting, being all ways indecent.

"Of course he does," James said from his perch on the bench at the far wall, his inflection different from the way those same words had sounded in Lydia's head. James jotted down the information anyway.

"How many sessions?" he asked.

"We had a first meet." Bess grunted as Lydia finally connected her club to Bess's ribs. "And one session."

"Anything untoward?" James asked.

This time, Bess's club connected with Lydia's shoulder as she spun to avoid the weapon. Lydia stifled a cry of pain.

"Nothing that wasn't pre-contracted." Bess spun to make their way back down the ballroom, advancing quicker now that they had warmed up.

"And what, exactly, is pre-contracted?" James asked.

"Why do you need to know?" Bess asked, her blows becoming stronger.

Lydia moved faster, the rhythmic clack of the weapons making conversation difficult. Bess wouldn't keep her strength to herself. If Lydia were going to appear without injury at the Beckersley ball, she would have to work to defend herself more heartily.

The door creaked open as James left the room. She heard it close, and she focused on Bess. This woman was the best female boxer in all of England, and Lydia was determined to fight her off.

Bess and Lydia had been training off and on for a few years, once James returned to London permanently. He'd found Bess, and he'd been correct: training made Lydia feel more in control, more prepared, less scared. She'd blossomed, as her mother would say. But it wasn't true. Training had helped her harden.

Every time Lydia had stopped training and later restarted, the restart became harder. In past years, she had taken the Season off to ensure she had no visible injuries, but this last year she hadn't been able to bring herself to put the sport aside.

They were so close with Lord Hackett floundering financially, and if their plot succeeded, he would be ruined permanently. Ruin seemed the best they could do for a man like that, though she hated to inflict it on his wife and daughter. Still, sparring kept her hungry and focused. She couldn't think about the wife and the daughter, even though Lady Isabelle had debuted just a year behind her. They were both in danger of being on the shelf, and while it didn't matter to Lydia one whit, it surely mattered to Lady Isabelle.

While Lady Isabelle wanted to marry well, Lydia's one goal was the pact, which bound her to her sister and cousins, and them to her. When the last man from that horrible faro game was ruined or dead and the pact was fulfilled, then the four could be free to live their lives as they saw fit.

Well, the other three could. Lydia would always be weighted down by Andrepont's specter. Because those men had all feared they had contracted the pox, Lydia was subjected to inspections by physicians for years. The anniversary of the country retreat was marked by a glass of warm apple brandy, her mother standing stoically by her bed as a physician delicately folded up a sheet around her knees. Did she or didn't she have the pox, too?

If she did, who would marry a pox-ridden debutante? She wouldn't be able to bear children. When to disclose that piece of information? When signing a marriage contract? When courting? As if the *ton* would keep its mouth shut over that piece of gossip.

Even if she didn't disclose, she still wasn't a virgin. And how to prove that it wasn't due to her poor decisions, but rather an act of brutality? Who would believe that, and when could she disclose that?

Her mother decided that after so many pox-free examinations, held annually up to the date of her debut Season, they would assume she hadn't contracted whatever the former Andrepont had tried to cure, and they would proceed as if she were the snow-white virgin she ought to be.

But that wasn't something to be powdered over, as if it were a blemish on her face. It was a blemish inside of her, something that made her change irrevocably, and it awakened a need inside of her to destroy anyone who might think the same as James's father. Anyone who might take from another girl what that monster had taken from her.

Lydia's focus ripped back to the present as Bess came at her with a flurry of parries, wielding the cudgel more like a sword than a stick. Lydia narrowed her focus to respond in kind, blocking each attack and anticipating the next blow.

Finally, Bess lost concentration for a second as her eyes flicked towards the door. Lydia used the moment to deliver her own crushing hit to the shoulder and then followed it with a light right cross, a finishing move that she didn't dare deliver with force.

Bess stumbled back, surprised. Blood trickled

from her nose. Touching the injury, she smiled. "Very good, my lady."

Behind Lydia, there was applause, and the sound of two sets of hands pricked her ears. She turned, seeing not just James watching, but Mr. Arthur as well.

His presence did not help Lydia's heart return to a slower beat. She had an impulse to pull up her dress, but a lady did not scramble. She'd never been this exposed to anyone but Bess, Agnes, and James. Propriety dictated that she not ever be this naked in front of anyone, including a mythical future mythical husband.

But she refused to be ashamed, not of her body, not of anything. So she stood proud, glowing profusely, trying to catch her breath. She'd rather be ruined for what she did than for what had been done to her. Mr. Arthur gaped at her in confusion.

Recovering her best ballroom manners, Lydia glided over to where he stood, despite the urge to limp. Bess had thwacked her in the leg earlier, and a knot had formed under the bruise. She twirled her stick out as if it were an extension of her arm.

Mr. Arthur took the opportunity to bow low. As he rose, she nodded her head in acknowledgement.

"Such courtesy," James commented. "I wonder that the older generation grouses about our manners."

Lydia tore her eyes from Mr. Arthur's figure—and he cut a handsome one. He was understated, his clothes unadorned but well fitting. Surprising even herself, her eyes flicked down to his buckskin breeches, which were tight across powerful thighs. Well, if she hadn't been out of breath before, it was certainly reasonable to be so now.

"John," Bess said, walking up with a smile of genuine pleasure at seeing her friend.

Unreasonable jealousy stabbed. Lydia pushed all of her interest and emotion away. Now was not the time, and he was not the man for her. There could be no man for her. She was broken; she was marked and undesirable.

"Bess," he said with an incline of his head, his smile easy.

"Oh, now that makes more sense," James said, standing finally. "You and Bess know each other."

"My lord," Mr. Arthur inclined his head in respect.

"Please, I don't bother with the formality. I haven't the need for it, unlike some people," James said, pointedly looking at Lydia.

"If we hadn't manners, how would we distinguish ourselves from animals?" Lydia asked, keeping her voice breezy, as if she weren't standing around with two champion fighters and her dress stripped to her waist.

"We don't," James said, frowning. The expression had to have pained him, given the extent of his injuries. He pushed his notebook into the breast pocket of his coat, a secure place for his espionage.

"'Savages we call them, because their manners differ from ours,'" Mr. Arthur quoted.

"Quite pretty. Who said it?" Lydia asked before she could check her interest. It wouldn't do to prolong this interview, given the state of her dishabille.

"Benjamin Franklin," he said.

James groaned. "Well versed in the enemy, I see."

"Creating a new country demands a great deal of wisdom," Mr. Arthur said, pulling at his sleeves. "But I suppose we could settle this in the ring."

"John, enough," Bess said. "Let the man's wounds heal first."

"I would, if he would give me his name," Mr. Arthur said.

"You do not know him?" Lydia asked, turning to her cousin. "Is he not here for you?"

"It's your house," James said. "Why would he look for me here?"

"Then why did you admit him?" Horror dawned upon her. "You are here to call on me?"

James quirked his eyebrow at her, goading her to crack her façade.

"I was only leaving a card for your father," Mr. Arthur protested.

James laughed. "Of course you were."

"I was concerned for you, of course, after the mill the other night. I had no idea you were so closely connected to this gentleman."

His words were clumsy, but he didn't lose his poise. Was he embarrassed to be caught out like this? He was taller than James, and on this morning, less purpled than James.

"I don't understand," Mr. Arthur said, looking between the players. "Shouldn't you be ruined for this state of undress in the presence of a gentleman? Mustn't you marry?"

"What do you say, James?" Lydia asked.

"Marry you?" James repeated, stifling a laugh. "Why, I'm flattered. This is so unexpected. I think I shall faint."

Bess snorted.

Lydia turned her gaze back to Mr. Arthur, whose skin was flushed in embarrassment. The sight of it made her feel mean and small. "If word got out that this is how I spent my afternoons, then yes, I would be ruined. And if it was found out that James was here, then yes, I would have to marry him. Or someone anyway."

"Someone?" Mr. Arthur asked, clearly with someone else in mind.

"For no one would believe that I wasn't *enceinte* after being in this state."

Mr. Arthur glanced over at Bess, bewildered.

"Proper lady talk fer having one in the basket," Bess said, gesturing a round belly.

"Oh," Mr. Arthur said, looking slightly less bewildered and more cross. "Well, how do they expect you to do anything while wearing restrictive clothing? That makes no sense."

"Precisely, Mr. Arthur," Lydia said with a tight smile. "I'm not allowed to do much of anything at all. Restrictive clothing is immaterial for a well-bred lady."

"My lady, if you would excuse me. Our session for today is over, and I have other engagements to attend to," Bess said, untucking her sleeves to pull up her dress.

Bess smiled at Mr. Arthur as she pulled up her chemise and dress, walking to the door of the ballroom and glancing back with a clever grin. Lydia watched her go, holding the feeling of jealousy below her still waters as if she could drown it.

"I should go, too. I have someone else's appointment to ruin," James said, unfurling his long legs and standing.

"My lord, before you go, I beg you, tell me who you are," Mr. Arthur said. "Surely we have made our acquaintance."

Lydia expected her cousin to be confrontational again, but James flicked his eyes over at her while deciding his course of action. She was tired of the posturing. "This is James Wallingford, the fifth Viscount Andrepont. James, this is Mr. John Arthur. As you know."

Lydia watched Mr. Arthur's face, doing her best to read him, but he betrayed very little. His eyes were on her, lingering more than they should before returning to James. He gave a bow, the inferior in the introduction.

"Cousins, then," John Arthur said.

Lydia raised a brow. "What did you think we were?"

He gave a polite smile. "Then, my Lord Andrepont, I hate to hold you up on your ruinous appointment."

"It's nothing, really. I just need to save my dear friend from wooing a young lady," James said.

"You should let him be," Lydia said. Despite her wish for James's happiness, he had fallen in love with the wrong woman: the wide-eyed Miss Dorchester, Lord Elshire's ward. An engagement between his ladylove and his best friend, Lord Leighton, needed to be manufactured to save Leighton from his scandal last year. However, if Hackett's daughter, Lady Isabelle, married Leighton, Leighton could save Hackett from financial straits, regardless of what happened to the *Europe*, ruining all of Lydia's schemes. Therefore, the innocent Miss Dorchester had to marry Leighton, regardless of James's amorous feelings. They would pass.

James turned his purpled face to her, his expression as pitiable as she'd ever seen it. "I can't. Another ring, another time?" he added to Mr. Arthur.

"It would be my pleasure," Mr. Arthur said, bowing again as courtesy dictated. James exited, closing the door behind him, knowing the soft click of the door latch might as well have been a church bell signaling inappropriate behavior.

Lydia needed a chaperone. She knew she should send for Agnes, and she should get dressed. All of this was nothing but ruinous. But there was something so delicious in it, so freeing. *Just a few minutes.*

She turned and walked away from Mr. Arthur under the guise of putting away her weapon. She was no match for him, but still, she wanted to know what it would be like to square up against him.

"And why have you really come, Mr. Arthur?" Lydia asked, feeling every inch of exposed skin prickle.

"I came to make sure you returned home safely last night. It was a dangerous crowd," he said, following her at a distance.

"I am quite safe," she assured. Though this moment felt very unsafe in a very different way. Shouldn't her hands be clammy and shaking by now? By rights, she should be a panicked mess, clamoring for escape. Instead she was trying to prolong this encounter—this entirely inappropriate, disastrous encounter.

"I see that," he said, picking up Bess's weapon, feeling the weight of it. He was a man who was able to judge how well he could use it.

Trying to remain casual, she turned to watch him, remembering what Bess had said about not showing her back to a potential enemy. She'd held the axiom to be as true in a well-gossiped ballroom as in the more bruising lessons Bess had taught her.

He watched her as well. "I was only returning it to you," Mr. Arthur said, holding the weapon outstretched.

❧

A BETTING MAN WOULD HAVE LOST. ANY SANE MAN would have thought she'd scurry away or direct him to place the weapon back in its storage. But he was learning that nothing that happened near Lady Lydia made any sense.

He gripped the short cudgel well enough that

when she darted forward to knock it away, he brought it up to meet hers. The impact took some of the force of her parry away from her and compelled her to take a step backwards. It was habit, it was training.

"I'm sorry," he said, lowering the cudgel. "I didn't mean to—"

But there she was again, lightning-fast, darting forward, pushing him back with a flurry of attacks that left him doing nothing but blocking her attempts at his face. He was doing his best to be mannerly, but she was making it impossible. Wasn't it some kind of felony to attack the upper class like this? And a lady, of all things. His career would be ruined if he put a hand on her. He'd be in Newgate by nightfall.

He pushed back, returning a block with enough force to spin her off her mark to his left. The time that it took her to stabilize her footing was enough for him to counterattack, but not so long that she didn't have a chance to defend herself.

Again, they waltzed the length of the ballroom, him pressing forward, careful not to deliver blows with full force, but with enough to jar her delicate arms. After her session with Bess, she should have been too tired to put up this much of a fight. He grinned. This kind of endurance was fun to push and hard to find.

Color rose high in her cheeks, dark hair loosed from its pins, and her beauty became his greatest distraction. Still, she hacked at him, blocking his blows, turning them into counterstrikes. But he couldn't retreat from her, even as she struck at him. His blood was up, and it was hard to not want to be closer to her, to be drawn in, moth to flame.

He closed the distance between them, a way to slow her attacks and to get closer to her. His heart pounded in his chest, but not because of the fight.

No, there was no aggression here. This was something else, something he knew from St. Giles. This was flirting.

She took her eyes from the weapons for a second, and her smile nearly felled him. His heart lifted. Perhaps she understood; perhaps she saw that pugilism wasn't violence, it was fun.

When he had been ushered toward the ballroom, he had thought that perhaps she was engaged in some kind of dance practice, flower arranging, or some other enhancement young women of the aristocracy were required to perform. He had recognized the sound of the practice sticks clacking as he'd followed Lord Andrepont down the hallway. He'd assumed it was a demonstration, her bodyguard perhaps. But no, there she was, stripped down in all her glory, Bess working her hard.

Closing the gap between them, watching her chest heave, he would have gladly died in that instant for this opportunity. Surely some fop would enter, challenge him to a duel for insulting a lady—no, *assaulting* a lady, no doubt overlooking that she assaulted him first. But it was worth it. She was panting with her effort, her lips parted.

He reached out and caught hold of her weapon. She held fast despite their disparity in strength and size. He wrested it from her, but she did not back away. The smile on her face dissolved, concern replacing it.

"Now what?" she asked, her chest still moving fast, but more controlled. "You wrestle me to the ground? Knock me out?"

"If this were a match, yes." He was too warm, and he wished to God he was at least in his shirtsleeves. He'd always fought without a shirt on, and the restriction on his movements was unfamiliar. Being fully dressed and sparring was a challenge.

"Why isn't it a match? A match is fair, is it not?" Her eyes were blue today, still dark, and he again noted the small, star-like beauty mark near her right eye.

"It can't be a match," he said. "I'm not dressed for it."

"I am," she said, surprising him with her boldness. "Or perhaps you didn't notice."

"I've noticed," he said, hoping he sounded nonchalant, not like the lecher he was. Could he help trying to peer underneath the gauzy chemise? "And I've noticed you cosseting your left leg, though you seem to be right-handed. Did Bess get you there earlier? She likes to go for the back of the thighs."

Lady Lydia's eyes narrowed. He had said the wrong thing, but he didn't know what it was that had angered her. She rabbit-punched him in the ribs. "Prepare yourself, then, and let's finish this."

Her jab had deflected off of him. It wasn't the first time an opponent had tried to talk him to distraction only to surprise punch him. It was a favorite strategy of Caulie's, though it was the first time a proper lady had done so.

"As you wish, my lady." He backed away from her, both weapons in hand.

"Are you not going to perform another of your ridiculous bows for me?" she taunted.

"I'll not take my eyes from you." The cudgels clattered as he threw them far away. He meant it. He couldn't if he wanted to. She was the most glorious thing he'd ever seen, better than any angel in any church.

She put her hands on her hips, a move in a man he would have seen as a show of dominance, or even just trying to cool off. Her hands merely accented her small waist, the flat expanse of her stomach, the smooth ridging of her ribcage. John had to will himself to think about this encounter as a fight and not a preamble to the bedroom.

He removed his coat and laid it out on the floor. The knot in his cravat was deucedly unimportant now as he tugged at it. Was that interest he saw in her eyes? That arched eyebrow could mean anything. He peeled, just as he would for any mill. The collar and the waistcoat followed the cravat. He unbuttoned the first few buttons of his starched shirt and then pulled it over his head, bare-chested as he faced her. He still had a few bruises, but Lord Andrepont hadn't landed very many body blows.

"You needn't have undressed on my account," she said.

"You didn't protest." Prey animals, she'd spoken of at dinner. Prey animals were those whose instincts told them to run, to not be eaten. They were the hunted. Lady Lydia did not look hunted in the least.

"I am merely here to test my skills," she said.

He took small, measured steps towards her. This arena was much bigger than the eight-foot squares he typically fought in, but it somehow felt much smaller. "And how long have you been training?" he asked.

She shrugged a delicate white shoulder. He had a strange urge to bite it. Her flesh would be salty by now, covered in sweat. The most advantageous thing she could do right now would be to seduce him. There was no way he could resist her at this point. The great Corinthian John, felled by the fancy-nancy blue-blooded girl.

"A few years," she said, her head angled just enough to the side to show off her high cheekbones and elegant lines. Did she do that on purpose? Did she know how he fought with himself to keep decent? The buckskin breeches showed every change to his state of mind. He was trying to be polite, damn it.

She was playing him, and the worst part was that

he knew it. But he continued forward, small steps, buying himself time.

"And you think a few years is long enough to fight me? I've been training my whole life." He balled his fists for effect, flexing his muscles as if he needed to stretch them out. He would never hit her, but just as she showed off her best angles, he could do the same.

She blinked, and he heard her slipper skid backwards. To her credit, she did not appear to move, though it was clear her balance had shifted. "Surely, you had years where your parents put you through schooling. You must not have had all that time to train."

"Oh, aye, but I did," he said, letting his accent take on its Irish-colored St. Giles roots. "I scrapped for me and me sister. My father ran off early on, or so I was told, and me ma died of one of those diseases so common no one remembers what it was. So, I scrapped and I stole."

"You're saying this to shock me," Lady Lydia said, a steely look coming over her. "You cannot be the broker you are without an education. A middle-class sort, anyway."

"I did get an education. I scrapped until some family came looking for me, felt guilty, left some money for me schooling. Weren't much. I put my sister wiv family wot moved to Paddington until I had enough money to put her into a school for young ladies." He closed the distance between them. He looked down at Lady Lydia, unsure if he was scaring her. He elongated his tones to the posh accent she was familiar with. "So, you see, my lady, I am the authentic article."

The smell of her wafted up to him in the still ballroom, the work of her afternoon, pungent in a way he was glad to know a lady could smell. He had never smelled a perfume its equal—still faintly oranges, still a touch of vanilla, but also something more animal. The front of his breeches seemed smaller.

But he couldn't think that way. No, she showed no fear, no pity. He had to remember that she was a willing opponent. He bent his head, his eyes locked on hers. She was like the best gin; just the scent of her made him lose inhibitions. As if drunk, he nuzzled her cheek, and to his surprise, she gave way. He slid his lips to hers, pressing soft and hopeful. Here he was no warrior. Here he was a pagan priest.

For a moment, one shining, kingly moment, she kissed him back. It wasn't just that she let him press against her, she invited him. Her hands touched his chest, and he felt her threading through him, as if he were caught in a loom made of nothing but her. There was no choice, no other option but to take a step forward, deepen the kiss. It was instinct. It was need. He would die without it. His arms came around to envelop her.

Suddenly, she pulled away. "Is that a threat?"

Her words were like a bucket of cold water. "A threat?" he repeated. Confusion was becoming his constant companion.

"If you win, you have your way with me?" There was an unnatural tinge of bitterness to her voice.

"No," he said, backing away. This turn confused him. What was she talking about? It was just a kiss. An incredible, heart-stopping, need-inducing kiss. "I would not hurt you."

"Really? Even though I am outright asking for a fight?" She folded her arms in front of her. "Could you not help yourself if you won? Would that be your excuse?" she moved forward, closing the gap between them.

"I never have, and I never would." He shook his head, not knowing where a right answer lay.

"It weren't just at the end that you favored your left leg. You're tired, and that makes you sloppy. I had more than one opening to take your weapon, or at least knock it from your hands. If I were a rascal or a scoundrel, I would have."

"You are a broker and a brawler. Why would I not think you a scoundrel, or worse?" Instead of tilting her head to look up at him, she only looked up with her eyes, those unreadable pools ringed with thick, dark lashes.

He put his hands up. Formality was the screen to hide behind. ""Deuces, Lady Lydia. *You* kissed me."

"Yes, well, be that as it may," she said, her hands on her hips, and still she swayed closer.

Words were never his medium. But actions were. He dropped to his knees in front of her. He could be her priest. "I forfeit."

"You can't forfeit," she cried. Her hands were warm, scrabbling at his shoulders, trying to make him rise. "Get up!"

He shook his head. "Not until you understand that I will not hurt you, cannot hurt you."

"I demand that you rise," she said, putting her hands back on her hips, where her dress sleeves gathered.

He looked down, a supplicant posture, because if he looked up, he would not be able to see her, all he would gaze at was the gauzy chemise, the rough bindings about her breasts. If he could just put his tongue there, where the sternum ended, an inverted heart on her abdomen. But he knew about discipline. He emptied his mind of the chaos she caused in him, trying to focus as if he were facing an opponent. Slowly, he moved his gaze to her eyes, rising to meet her. "And now?"

"Now, what?" She was off-balance, for once. Perhaps for the first time since he'd met her.

"Now what do you demand of me?" Had he moved closer to her? If he had, it wasn't on purpose. It was as natural as breathing.

Her breath caught. Her eyebrow quirked, and there it was—she was back in control, recovered from herself, and her persona appeared. Just as his Corinthian John strutted, hers flirted. "What services do you offer?" she purred.

"Don't do that," he said. There was no need for Corinthian John here, between the two of them, and thus there was no need for her *haute ton* persona either. She could just be her. He liked her better that way. She was a boxer, like him.

The eyebrow went back down. "Do what?"

"Hide behind whatever character you've dreamt up. Do you wish me to leave?"

"No," she said, rushing through the word as if it came out of her mouth before she could think better of it.

"I am an excellent sparring partner, though not much of a teacher," he said.

"That's not what the widows say," Lydia said.

He barked out a laugh.

"According to Countess von Verschler, you were life-changing. She was happy to let the world know you came with the highest recommendations."

He couldn't help but smile. "She spent too much time in Prussia with her geriatric husband."

"Did you ever meet him?" she asked.

"Of course not," he said.

"He was practically dead already when he wooed her father with his cod of money."

The very young, very widowed countess's enthusiasm made more sense now. They'd only broken off the affair because he felt she was becoming indiscreet. But still, a good review was nice.

"It isn't as if you don't have suitors falling at your

feet. I've heard your name linked with Lord Sebastian, not to mention your cousin," John challenged.

Her spine stiffened. "Leave Lord Sebastian out of this."

"Is your cousin not charming enough for you?"

"No one ever is," she quipped.

"What is it that you require, Lady Lydia?" He didn't want her to be thinking of another man while he stood in front of her.

"I require many things, but you mean in a man?" The eyebrow arched again. Knowing she would push him away, he stepped forward, their faces so close he could smell the sweetness of her breath. Her nose was even with his mouth. Just a little bend of his head and he could kiss her again.

"Yes, in a man. Let's say for argument's sake that I was wooing you. How could I be successful?" He cocked his head to the side, deliberately changing the angles at which they held their bodies. He wasn't sure how long he could not kiss her standing so close.

Sure enough, she backed away a step. "You couldn't."

"I'm wealthy, well heeled." He paused. "Well-reviewed."

She smiled—a real one, not her cold expression of amusement, but a real sign that she could maintain a genuine conversation.

"But sadly, you are not well-mannered," she said.

"I beg to differ, my lady."

"Truly? You accosted me in the street though we had not been introduced, and now you've called on me. Have you any idea the damage you are doing?" She pulled her shoulders back even further, and had she been fully dressed, it would have been an intimidating move. Wearing nothing but bindings, however, it pushed her small breasts out in a display she obviously hadn't thought through.

His mouth fairly watered. "This is the first you've protested."

Her eyes narrowed. Was she angry, or was she scheming? It was hard to tell. "Is it? I protested on the street when we met. I protested your presence when I realized you were here to call on me."

"But you didn't ask me to leave." His brain was swirling. Realization dawned. He didn't even have the sense to know when he was being a boor. Because the consequences of his boorish actions weren't up to her. It wasn't her opinion that decided her fate—it was the rest of her world's opinion. By asking for an introduction on the street, he had already compromised her. Walking with him was her way of making him leave quicker. His card being left in the wrong dish, where it could be seen by anyone following him on their calls, would put her in scandal. She hadn't a choice. Her staff might lie about his presence here, but the card was irrefutable evidence. He wouldn't want a man to impose that on his sister, so why did he do it to her? Because he was a scoundrel. He hadn't known—or he hadn't paid attention. "Oh."

The look of anger on her face melted into one of pity. He scrambled for his clothes. He pulled on his shirt and waistcoat, hastily tying his mailcoach knot.

Fully clothed, it felt different to be near her. Far less of a possibility to be together than it had seemed when they were sparring. These layers of fabric reminded him of who he was, and who she was, and why it truly was impossible for him to woo her. How he was so backwards he had no idea how deeply inappropriate he had been. How much his interest had cost her.

She had likewise made her clothing decent. It

made her look smaller, tamer. More like a lady. "Mr. Arthur," she said, her tone tinged with pity.

He bowed, unable to do anything else. "Lady Lydia, my sincerest apologies."

She inclined her head, gracious in his mistakes. Coming here had been yet another grave miscalculation on his part. He had to escape before he made another one.

# 5

Gold fixtures dripping with beeswax candles adorned the Beckersley ballroom, and hothouse flowers were tucked into every available corner. Most importantly, the champagne was cold—essential to a successful evening. If this were a more proper sort of ball, there would only be ratafia for her to drink, which was just short of intolerable. Private balls were so much more preferable to public ones.

The dowagers and wallflowers sat in the corner watching the young people, passing judgment and making predictions. Agnes made her way over to join their ranks. No doubt they discussed who would be next invited to Almack's and whose family ought to be slighted. Most of the *beau monde* was in attendance, notable exceptions being Miss Rose Dorchester and her uncle, Lord Elshire. They probably hadn't even noticed they'd been snubbed.

Lydia left the company of her parents to join Lady Jane and Lady Agatha Beauclerk, both working their fans in flirtation with gentlemen across the room. As tiresome as the crush of Society could be, at least Jane was amusing to behold. She appeared gilded and light as air, assuming the grace of an innocent—not the calculating, cold-blooded manipulator that Lydia knew her to be.

Lady Isabelle was off in another corner, chatting with the older matrons. No sign of Hackett. The grotesque little man was probably off in some gentleman's smoking area, hawking his daughter's virginity. The crush was still milling about. Her family had not arrived early, but neither had anyone else.

Lady Beckersley swept over to the doorway, greeting new guests, escorting them to a group of acquaintances, reveling in her position of power. Lydia froze when she saw Lady Beckersley's next couple, the young widow Marshall and her escort, the now-familiar Mr. Arthur. He stood tall, his broad shoulders filling out his evening coat in a way that other gentlemen's didn't. Fabric should be loose about the arms, as if the coat were as effortlessly genteel as its wearer. Instead, his coat strained on his upper arms, tightening around him as he drew breath. The cut on his nose had healed. All the purpling of his bruises had disappeared; not even a hint of yellow was left.

The room warmed, and she suddenly felt the need for air. Lydia whispered her excuses to her group and made for the terrace. The estate wasn't much for gardens, which made it a safer and more respectable ballroom for in-the-market young ladies. With no possibility of a clandestine tryst in the shrubbery, no one cared if she took some air alone. She glanced back to see where Mr. Arthur navigated Lady Marshall. He cut a dashing figure, each stride marked by physical self-discipline.

The days since their encounter in her ballroom had left her unsettled. She had behaved indecently, stripped to the waist as she was, only her chemise to cover her. And then she had kissed him. Had they been caught, either a duel or a wedding would be in short order. Or would it? She was already broken. If he knew, then—cold washed over her. He didn't know, did he? Was that why he kissed her? Sought her out? Because he knew she was already ruined, and therefore could be dallied with?

She viewed him as he and Lady Marshall moved about between couples. He looked around, surveying the crush. No, he couldn't know. He was just ignorant of the rules, that was all.

Perhaps it was the epitome of irony for her to point out his social missteps. She clearly didn't abide by every rule, but she did when she was in view of other people. Anyone who called after him might find his card in the salver by the door. Anyone could have seen them on the street when he first accosted her. True, fewer society gossips in Marylebone than in Mayfair, but it didn't matter. There were rules.

Her transgressions were calculated and necessary. His were blunders. When that realization dawned on him, she had seen for the first time how hard he was trying. He really had come from nothing, and he wanted to not only better himself but also aid his sister, which was an admirable goal. It made her feel bad—something no one seemed to think was possible.

Of course, if it turned out that he knew about her past, she wouldn't feel bad for him at all, and she would repay him with the nastiness she reserved for Hackett and Denby.

Mr. Arthur matched his pace to his companion's, keeping step with her but not hurrying her along, as any well-bred man would. There was something in that movement that made it difficult to turn away from him. Like watching a superiorly bred racehorse canter. It wasn't the act of moving itself, it was being able to marvel at the way the body itself fit together.

Her heavy muslin overgown shuffed and clicked, bead against bead, as she carved her path toward Jane and Agatha. It was an extravagant design, a piece Lydia had commissioned from Madame Vergary last year and had not yet worn. The pearl beadwork along the bodice made the silver dress shimmer as if she were the moon herself.

"Lydia, darling," her mother called, not so loud as would have been unseemly. Lady Lorian was still a beauty of the *ton* even though she was married and mother to a grown daughter, and it was no surprise to see her escorted by a gentleman Lydia had never encountered before.

Her mother wore the Grecian style, as so many other women did, but in a more flamboyant fashion, with an extra ruffled layer at the hemline of her dress and a brooch accenting her décolletage at the neckline. Not only was her hair done up in pinned curls, but she also sported a large white feather, pinned at an offset angle.

The man at her side wore a foreign military uniform, crisp dark-blue with a high collar and gold epaulets. The coat came down lower than the military red coats of the British Army, brushing at his calves, and it was also tighter at the waist, giving him even more of an exotic air as he glided across the floor with Lady Lorian. His dark hair was unruly, even more so than was the style amongst English gentlemen.

"Count Denisov, I would like to introduce you to my daughter, Lady Lydia Somerset." Lady Lorian dropped the count's arm. "My dear, this is Count Denisov, a lieutenant in the Don Cossack army and a witness to Napoleon's defeat at Waterloo."

The count bowed at the waist, lower than Lydia expected. In return, she curtsied deeply, showing off the extent of her intricate gown as the candlelight caught the gleam of silver thread and pearl beading.

"Lady Lydia, it is an honor," the count said, his voice a rich baritone with scarcely an accent. "Word of your beauty precedes you."

Introductions were made to Jane and Agatha. Again the count bowed, and the ladies curtsied as Lydia's mother named them. Lydia's eyes narrowed on the unusual flush in Jane's cheeks. An easy tell, betraying that Jane was taken with the dashing count. Peculiar, since she was vocally devoted to the weak-chinned Lord Seafield, Agatha's brother, who had also accepted the invitation to tonight's event, as Lady Beckersley told all who entered.

The minuet that had opened the dancing finally completed, and the couples promenaded. The next dance would start soon.

Denisov offered his elbow to Lydia, but at that moment, Sebastian came swooping to her side.

"I do hope I'm not late," Sebastian announced, giving appropriate courtesy to the matrons of the group. "We have a standing appointment."

She couldn't help but smile. "My apologies, Count Denisov."

Her dress clicked and shifted with her movement. She placed her arm on Sebastian's, feeling the familiar warmth of him, and they promenaded to the dance floor.

"Did I save you, or did I make a hash of things?" Sebastian asked.

"Aid was most appreciated," Lydia replied.

"What's the dance? I just arrived." Sebastian pulled on his sleeves. He seemed out of sorts, which was unusual for him.

"So, you haven't seen Lord Farley yet?"

"Is he here?" Sebastian feigned indifference.

Lydia smiled. Being with him was so easy. "Since you both are wearing white roses in your buttonholes, I can only assume whatever your quarrel was, you've since made up."

Sebastian returned her smile. "If only you didn't know so much."

More couples gravitated toward the middle of the ballroom, and the small orchestra began to play the lilting rhythms of a waltz.

"Oh my, how scandalous," Sebastian said.

"My reputation can take the gossip if yours can," she said.

"Can it? You're practically on the shelf," he reminded her. "Have a care."

"Which is why waltzing with a man will make me appear like I'm trying to land a husband."

The steps guided them, bodies close together, one of his legs between hers, which was why many of the mamas fretted over this part of the evening. She followed the steps, suddenly not enjoying herself very much.

"I don't make this offer lightly," Sebastian began, the color suddenly gone from his face.

"Please don't," Lydia stopped him. They kept dancing, now more distant despite their physical closeness.

"You're William's sister. I have to," he protested.

She looked everywhere but at him. Weren't marriage proposals supposedly to be full of giggling and delights? Or at the very least, some parody of joy? Not stodgy obligation. She hated it for him and for herself. It was then that she saw Mr. Arthur watching them. She blushed.

"If at the end of the Season—oh." Sebastian

followed her gaze to see Mr. Arthur. "He's a handsome devil. What about him as a prospect?"

"He's a pugilist," Lydia said, shaking her head.

"Sounds delicious," Sebastian replied, moving her to get a better view. "He could do the job, don't you think?"

"You hate boxing," she reminded him.

"But not box*ers*."

"It would be scandalous. A former prizefighter?" Lydia protested. "What about Agnes?"

Understanding dawned, and Sebastian danced them away from that side of the floor. "Does she want an advantageous match?"

"What do you mean, does she want one?" Lydia asked.

"Well, you have no intention of marriage, that much is clear. What about her? Does she?"

The question tripped her, causing awkward footwork to return to the dance. Of course Agnes wanted an advantageous marriage. One just had to look at her, with the embroidery and the piano, the demure manner. Why else would anyone conform to such standards?

"Why don't you ask her before you start sacrificing your future?" Sebastian said.

They finished the dance and Sebastian escorted Lydia back to her mother. Lord Seafield had joined the growing ensemble. Lydia spotted Agnes in the chairs up against the wall, along with the older matrons and the other wallflowers. She was tall and not terribly graceful. But what did one expect if she spent all her time sitting at a piano or with the mending on her lap?

Lydia's father arrived with Mr. Arthur in tow. The trader stood tall amongst his betters, admittedly elegant in bearing. He wore the conservative style of the older gentlemen, tight black breeches and black stockings, a simple white waistcoat, and a black tailcoat, still straining against his broad chest. Lord Seafield, in contrast, wore the latest fashion, the baggier trousers, affecting the lazy slump of a dandy. Had Lord Seafield not been an heir to a dukedom, she doubted Lady Beckersley would have allowed him inside.

Lydia didn't want to talk to Mr. Arthur, not when she felt so confused. Sebastian was suggesting that Agnes didn't want a marriage, even with her pristine reputation. Which, then what would be wrong with —? No. She had one thing left to do, and that was ruining Hackett. To do so was to free them all to marry whomever they wished. Therefore, she needed to pay attention to the task at hand and not waste time thinking about blue eyes and corded muscle.

"Mr. Arthur saved our dear daughter," Lord Lorian said, after making introductions.

Words were one thing, but no one could believe that the timing of such a display was coincidence. By singling out this particular stockbroker in front of a foreign count, and an heir to a duchy, her father was rewarding him handsomely for his boldness.

"Lady Lydia, you look beautiful this evening," Mr. Arthur said quietly, as if he didn't want the rest of the group to hear his compliment.

"Thank you, Mr. Arthur. You also look well," she said, her eyes darting around the circle of people to see if anyone noticed. Sebastian was watching the exchange with amusement. Jane fluttered her fan, trying to pay attention to Lord Seafield, though she couldn't manage to tear her eyes away from Count Denisov.

"I'm glad to see you are in good health," Mr. Arthur said, stretching his neck from side to side—a motion she'd seen him use in the ring when he was tired.

"Thank you. And I should thank you for your quick action." She meant in saving her—not that moment when they were sparring. "I meant with the horse."

He finally glanced down at her, flushed. "I know what you meant. I would be happy to assist you in such a manner anytime."

Lydia whipped out her fan and began fluttering, a mirror of Jane. It was so warm in here. She raised her eyes from behind her fan. "Should you not attend your lady?"

"My lady is attending to other matters. I do not wish to intrude."

Out of the corner of her eye, she watched as Mr. Arthur took stock of the Russian lieutenant and then Sebastian.

"I confess that some social rituals are beyond me, but I believe it would be rude to not dance with every young lady," Denisov said, his eyes fixed on Jane.

Jane curtsied, her fan trembling. Denisov extended his arm and she placed hers atop, her big doll-like eyes fastened onto his dark ones. They retreated back to the dance floor, Jane looking even more porcelain in his arms.

Lord Seafield coughed, his hand covering both his mouth and the weak chin so proudly displayed by his family as if it were evidence of the royal European Hapsburg line. Fortunately, his sister, Agatha, didn't suffer from that particular family trait. "I find dancing disagrees with my constitution," he announced to the group.

"If it is not too bold to ask, I would be honored to dance the next set with you, Lady Lydia," Mr. Arthur said.

"Surely—" Lydia protested, wanting to shove Agatha into his arms.

Lady Lorian clapped her hands together. "How

very elegant. Lydia darling, that is such a beautiful way to thank your protector."

Trapped, Lydia curtsied, a way to accept without provoking a verbal retort. When it was clear the next piece would begin soon, Mr. Arthur held out his arm to escort her. He was tall and trim, quiet and economical in his motion, his power muted here.

The second waltz began. Mr. Arthur put his hand on her back, clasping her hand with the other. She stood in the same position as she had with Sebastian, but it felt so different. Everything felt so muddied.

His steps were precisely the same distance apart, unless he wished to move their pairing, in which case it was exactly the same length every time. The space between their bodies was appropriate, perhaps even further apart than when she'd danced with Sebastian, but she felt every inch between them.

"You dance well, sir," she said, not knowing how else to start a conversation.

"Dancing is not difficult," he said.

"It is for some. Lord Seafield, for instance." She glanced back to the group they'd left, still chatting amiably.

"A future duke has no need of physical activity," Mr. Arthur said. "He is a Peer. That is enough."

"Many Peers still enjoy dancing and hunting, both admirable sorts of exercise." Lydia almost gasped as he spun her before cossetting her again in his arms, a gesture of which her father would definitely disapprove.

"Admirable exercise, yes, but not terribly exerting," he said, his voice too close to her ear.

"This suggests that you get your exercise in some deplorable way," she said.

He chuckled. "More fun, anyway."

She willed herself not to blush at such a remark.

"That is not what I meant," she said, trying to regain control of the conversation.

"I only meant a good mill," he protested, but he seemed to relax.

"Yes, who doesn't adore a good pop in the nose?"

"Invigorating," Mr. Arthur agreed.

A silence settled between them, neither companionable nor awkward. It felt full of promises that could never be made, hopes that could never be shared. The understanding that their paths had crossed as they ought, and now they were to move on.

The music ended and disappointment swept through her. When she rose from her curtsy, his face mirrored her own.

"That's it for waltzes, then," he said.

"Indeed," she said, wanting to say more but having no other reply. She took his hand to return back to her family. "Thank you for the dance, Mr. Arthur," Lydia said as they rejoined the group, loud enough for everyone to hear her. "I do hope Lady Marshall isn't bemoaning your absence."

"MY LADY, IT WAS A PLEASURE." HE MADE ALL THE appropriate bows, paid all the correct respects. He'd consulted several books before tonight, suddenly unsure of the rules once Lady Lydia had pointed out how uncouth he really was.

How long before he could go home? When Viscountess Marshall had invited him, he'd been enthusiastic. He'd been her husband's broker, and he had dined at the Marshall house a number of times as a guest. They weren't close, and they certainly did not have the association that Lady Lydia had suggested.

To prepare for the evening, he brushed up on his etiquette and dancing, knowing Lady Lydia would be in attendance. But then to see her face when she danced with the tall, skinny fellow, Lord Sebastian. She smiled, he smiled, he'd never seen her so in her element. How could he not have noticed the way the man held Lady Lydia too close while they waltzed? How could he not notice the exchange between them that for all the world looked as if he were proposing to her?

He wandered out of the ballroom and into a card room. At least there he could drink uninterrupted, without the obligation of dancing with every eligible woman on the property.

There was a smattering of women in the game room, only one table of ladies playing. The rest stood behind the chairs of the men they supported, regardless of whether they were the men's spouses. They looked elegant in their Grecian white gowns, ostrich feathers dipping and waving as they laughed and batted eyelashes.

A woman fluttered her fan at John, but he ignored the invitation and kept walking toward the back of the gaming room, hiding, in effect, from the Quality. In the back there would be high stakes games, men who gambled away their livelihoods, men who might be in need of a skilled broker come tomorrow morning.

Lords Denby and Hackett sat at a table. An acquaintance, Mr. Severnson, sat at their table and waved him over. He knew the lords by reputation. They were always in need of financial advice, clients to be wary of taking on. Waning fortunes always needed shoring up. Severnson was a second son of a second son, and his clientele was the aristocracy.

Against his better judgment, John went over. They were introduced, and to his relief, Denby brought up his talents in the ring.

"An Exhibition, just as the sort they're doing at Drury Lane," Denby said.

"Exactly so!" Hackett said.

"And Miss Abbott has already agreed to it?" John asked.

"Of course she has," Denby grumbled. "Why wouldn't she? She spoke highly of you."

"My country estate, of course, has ample room. We'll make a time of it, no need to always be working," Hackett said.

A clumsy way of telling him he wouldn't be expected to dine in the servants' hall. "If Miss Abbott said she needs me for this Exhibition," John replied, "then I'll be happy to do it."

"Wonderful," Hackett said. "My wife will send out invitations."

John bowed and made his excuses, not wanting to sit at the table with those men. He knew Bess took on private clients—most boxers did—but he didn't like the proprietary way Lord Denby had grumbled after being asked if she had agreed to an Exhibition.

Being partners with Bess in an Exhibition would be like the old days, a bit of fun, showing off, scandalizing ladies as he peeled before the mill. He weaved between guests. He looked the part tonight—from the breeches to the gloves—but his insides were still clogged gutters and hungry nights, stealing handkerchiefs in the yellowed London fog. This lot had no idea.

But he walked among them. Did he want to join them or did he hate them? Yesterday, he would have entertained the idea of joining them, striving, pushing to win Lady Lydia. It wasn't impossible, just improbable. Her shoulders bare, that impish smile as she beat him back with the practice stick—but no.

After having seen her face with Lord Sebastian, wearing a smile that was true and easy, the kind he could give to Bess or his sister, he knew his efforts would come to naught. The likes of him didn't touch the likes of her.

He found a spectator's seat near a high-stakes table, hoping to be invisible and bide his time until Lady Marshall was done teasing her latest married paramour. Everyone was their own sort of monster.

# 6

Lydia stifled a yawn. The muscles along her ribs ached with the sudden inhalation. Her spencer tightened around her chest, causing her breath to catch. Training with Bess took much of her constitution, and the balls and the dinner parties that stretched late into the night also took their toll.

"Honestly, Lydia, is my company such a bore that you must repeatedly sigh?" Jane rolled her eyes.

The carriage jostled along the streets. A pothole sent both of the ladies off their seats for a moment.

"Perhaps if you made conversation," Lydia said. She wasn't in the mood for Jane this morning.

"Did you receive an invitation to the Hackett's country estate?" Jane asked.

"I did," Lydia said. "And you?"

Jane laughed. "Of course I did."

They sat in silence as they jostled along. Lydia looked out the window at the ladies on the street, walking in pairs. They looked so pleasant, as if they were enjoying one another's company.

"Will you go?" Jane asked.

"I am still undecided," Lydia said. News of the *Europe* would be arriving soon, and she wanted to see Hackett's face when he realized his ruin. If that meant spending a week in the country with him, then she would do it.

"Your mother won't want to go."

True. But if she knew they could watch Hackett shatter, she would be willing to make the excursion. "And you?"

"No," Jane said. "Lord Seafield will not attend."

"Tragedy," Lydia said.

Jane turned her eyes to the window as well. They were getting closer to Bond Street. At least they wouldn't have to talk to one another when they were browsing for the latest fashions. She wished Agnes were here. With her talent for chatter, she and Jane would be able to keep an animated discussion going and leave Lydia to rest.

"Count Denisov is going," Lydia added.

Jane's blue eyes snapped to Lydia. "Pardon?"

"You were introduced at the Beckersley ball, if you remember," Lydia said.

Color rose in Jane's cheeks. "I vaguely recall."

Lydia didn't know if it was a kindness to let that piece of information slip. Count Denisov had been invited, but Lydia was unsure as to whether or not he had actually accepted. Lady Isabelle had intimated that she had invited him as a match for Lydia.

"I hear the Hacketts are expanding their social circle," Jane said, recovering herself.

"Not surprising, since Lady Isabelle is not seeming to make much progress with your brother."

"Nor will she," Jane said.

"Miss Dorchester has caught your brother's eye?" Here was a careful ground, as she didn't want to reveal how much she knew about Miss Dorchester from James.

"Miss Dorchester or not, Henry would never ally our family with the Hacketts, no matter what Mother insists upon."

"I didn't realize your mother was so appreciative of the Hacketts," Lydia said.

Jane waved her hand. "It is as if she is frozen in time, set at the moment of her own debut. She has not realized that the world has changed."

"I beg your pardon?" Lydia asked.

Jane sighed. "She doesn't realize that men can be judged for the type of business they engage in, and if one still supports the slave trade, regardless of whether or not it is legal in the British Territories, one may risk being a social pariah."

"Just so," Lydia said. "I had no idea you were so politically minded."

"Perhaps I have a hidden talent for it," Jane said, staring out the window.

Lydia strongly suspected that Jane's bored expression was nothing more than affect. "Perhaps you needn't hide a talent like that."

Jane tittered. "Please, Lydia."

"Would it be so terrible to be known as a thinking woman?" she asked.

"A bluestocking? No, thank you. Look at your poor cousin, Margaret. Absolutely not."

❧

"Please let's go," Pearl begged. "I am dying to see something new." She and John sat in the receiving room of the Mrs. Tyler's Boarding School for Ladies. The room was well appointed but not extravagant. The carpet was thicker than those John remembered from his boys' school.

Pearl had picked this particular establishment based solely on its proximity to the rooms he had rented so long ago, and he was flattered. He had been unprepared for setting her up in his own household when he first started out—a young lady's requirements seemed so daunting and exacting. Better to send her to a boarding school where she would learn all that was proper so that she could inform him, too.

Funny how extravagant and expensive it had seemed when they first enrolled her there, and now, just a few years later, flush with blunt, it seemed shabby and a bit worn. Too much time spent in grand houses. He'd ask Pearl how she felt about it, but not here, where the titular Mrs. Tyler might hear her.

Now that he had rented a townhouse, he was trying to get things set up so that she could move in as well. But he wasn't sure what all was needed. Instead of researching it, he worked at making more money, sure that with enough money, all of his problems would be solved.

John scratched at his chin as if he were thinking. "What is this business? Art, you say?"

He had offered her every luxury, even suggesting that he pay extra so she might have her own room in the warmer confines of Mrs. Tyler's own house. But she demurred, wanting the camaraderie of her peers. They slept in a dormitory, in tidy rows of beds near a stove. It all seemed unnecessarily cold to him, but Pearl never complained, no matter how hard he pressed.

Pearl grinned, her light-blue eyes lighting up. It was lucky that she hadn't inherited all of the ginger-hued freckles that he had. "An Art Exhibition is quite an event."

From the doorway, he felt eyes on him. He wouldn't be so foolish as to look over and make eye contact with any one of Pearl's classmates, but he could hear the light dashes of slippered feet on the floor, the suppressed giggles in the hallway. He should be glad to be found attractive. Somehow, because of these entanglements with Lady Lydia, the lighthearted gaiety of flirtation no longer seemed simple.

He furrowed his brow, shaking his head. "Sounds expensive," he said.

"Oh no," she cried. "You know it is free to the public."

A smile cracked his face, and another round of giggling erupted in the hallway. "I will be happy to escort you."

Pearl nearly clapped her hands, but the finishing school had beaten any show of enthusiasm out of her. Instead, he had to content himself with the sparkle in her eyes and the straightening of her shoulders.

That was the very sentiment Lady Lydia lacked as well. No enthusiasm without a shield of sarcasm. She was surrounded by nearly visible barriers that seemed as treacherous as any dragon-infested moat. Why should he not then glory in the attentions of these simpler girls? Young ladies who found him dashing cared not a whit for his lack of title or humble beginnings.

"If any of the other young ladies of your acquaintance need an escort, have them come with us. I can play big brother to any number." He stood, straightening his waistcoat and throwing back the side of his coat, displaying not only his buckskin-clad leg but also his expensive pocket watch, much to the excitement of the ladies on the other side of the doorway. "When does it open?"

"Not for another few weeks, but I wanted to get on your social calendar. I know it's quite busy." Pearl looked down at her lap.

Was that the demure motion that ladies did to hide disappointment? "Pearl, I'm trying."

She gave him a wistful smile. "What I have now is more than I could have imagined. It's just that while you look the part, you don't seem happy."

"I'm happy enough. I'm making more money than before, and I can keep you in better luxury. Do you need more dresses?"

More tittering from the doorway.

"No, John, I've plenty of dresses. You remember what Mrs. McEnroe always said: 'A happy person is more attractive than one who shows misery on her breast.'"

"Mrs. McEnroe ran a brothel," John reminded her.

"She knew what she was about," Pearl pressed. "And you are wearing your misery on your breast."

John sighed. His sister wasn't wrong, but she wasn't entirely right. "I've committed to going to the country for a few days. I came by to tell you that I will be out of Town."

"Sounds exciting," Pearl said.

"I've been asked to partner with Bess for a demonstration," he explained, suddenly not wanting to seem as if he were a proper guest.

"Ah." Pearl hated the pugilism. She'd nursed him too many times after bouts with blokes too big for him.

"It's just an Exhibition fight, not a real mill. Bess won't hurt me."

Pearl harrumphed. Finally, a gesture that wasn't from the caged young lady handbook. She was proper now, and he should be proud, but he also felt like he had held her down and put a collar around her neck.

Crossing the room, he got down on his knees in front of her, clasping her hands. "Pearl, you all right here? You 'appy?"

She smiled at the slip in his accent. "Wotchu fink?"

John cleared his throat and willed himself back to his learned speech. "I think a gilded cage can still be a cage."

"I'm safe; my belly is always full. It is a holding ground, that much is true. But it is meant to be a purgatory before marriage." Pearl shrugged. "It is perfectly adequate. As long as you take me to the Art Exhibition. Open to the Public. Two weeks from today."

"Fine," he said. "We'll go look at Art."

"The Arthurs will go look at Art." She flashed a smile like in the old days—big, bright, where her lips thinned into almost nothing, showing her pretty teeth. She always had pretty teeth. Lucky that way, too.

"Hilarious," he said.

"And you'll take all my friends as well." She looked down her straight nose at him.

"Yes," he agreed.

"So, you'll have to rent a very large carriage."

"Oh, I will?" he said.

"Yes, especially to take us to Gunther's afterwards for ices," Pearl said.

"My negotiating tactics are getting rusty." He stood, his knees creaking as he did.

"No, mine have always been better," Pearl said. "Let me walk you out. I'd hate for Mathilda to accost you on the way out."

"Mathilda is the guard dog?"

"No, Mathilda wants a husband and thinks you'll do nicely." Pearl stood and took his arm. "This way, sir."

They took the stairs down to the front door, where John collected his hat and gloves. "I'll call the moment I return. It should only be a few days."

"You seem unhappy," Pearl said again. "I can see it around your eyes."

John shook his head. "Haven't a care in the world."

Lady Isabelle greeted Lydia, Agnes, and their mama personally. The girl's thin, upturned nose, a replica of Lady Hackett's feature, could make her appear either haughty or pinched, but with the extra glow of country air, it was the first time Lydia had found her passably pretty. Fewer flounces than when she was at a ball.

Lydia's maid, Charlotte, stood behind them. She would be the only maid attending Lydia, Agnes, and their mother, but she could manage. She'd been with them for years. Agnes could help Lydia while Charlotte tended their mother, and Agnes—well, Agnes required little from a lady's maid.

A valet unloaded the last of their trunks, ogling Charlotte before giving his instruction. She had a dark complexion, one which was not uncommon in London, but less so in the country. "Come on then," the valet said, not bothering to acknowledge the woman's nervousness. Apparently, Charlotte would get to meet the staff inside the house. There must be quite a stir if both the butler and the housekeeper were busy elsewhere when guests were arriving.

The country house was larger than Lydia's family's country seat, but then, the Hackett name was a generation older than her own. The boxy-looking manor appeared in decent repair, despite the problems of the Hackett fortune.

Lady Isabelle herself was dressed in a fashionable country tweed riding habit, looking pleased. At least that meant there were horses.

"I am so glad you have arrived, Lady Lydia, as we have some lovely steeds on the property this week. Lord Denby has arranged for several of his best to be available to only the most experienced riders, and I'm certain he would count you among those." Lady

Isabelle did not stop prattling, but at least Agnes was there to keep up the banter.

"I'm not much for riding, I'm afraid," Agnes told Isabelle. "But I do love country air. A lovely walk in the morning does so much for one's complexion."

"I couldn't agree more," Isabelle returned, leading them up the staircase.

The house was decorated in dark greens and deep reds, giving the impression of sumptuousness. Gilded portraits of Hackett ancestors, squat and plain, lined the hallway.

"I am so pleased that we will be able to provide entertainment for our guests as well. Everyone says the country is boring, but we will have our Exhibition, the horses, and of course, we'll have a ball at the end of the week," Lady Isabelle continued.

The spiral ringlets in Lady Isabelle's hair bounced as she walked. It was a pity that female intelligence was given so little weight, but the bouncing curls did little to change that view.

She brought them to the corner rooms, a wide suite with views of the open meadow. The adjoining suite held two beds and a smaller adjoining room for Charlotte so she wouldn't have to sleep in the servant's hall.

"What lovely rooms, Lady Isabelle," her mother said. "Please let your mother know that I have arrived."

"Of course, Lady Lorian. I'll send up some tea so you may rest at your leisure." Isabelle gave a short curtsy and excused herself.

Lydia followed the young woman out into the hallway.

"I hadn't a chance to ask who all is coming," Lydia said.

Isabelle giggled, the ringlets bouncing. It made Lydia want to slap her.

"Quite the crowd," she said. "You know Papa; he loves to entertain. But I slipped in some new friends on Mama's guest list. I mean, if we are dining with Lord Denby's mistress, then Papa can have no objection to my friends."

"Oh?" Lydia felt her stomach twist at the idea of Denby's mistress—which was what people thought of Bess.

"I know you won't be shocked, but I put the *Franklins* on Mama's guest list." Lady Isabelle's ringlets bounced with her enthusiasm.

"I don't think I know the Franklins," Lydia said, unclenching with no mention of Bess.

Lady Isabelle frowned. "Mama is now digging up untitled money for me to marry, just in case I can't land Lord—oh, never mind. But I like the Franklins, I do. They're nice. Mr. and Miss Franklin, and their mother was from the West Indies. Mr. Franklin took over his father's real estate firm. They're simply *flooded* with money."

"I didn't think Lord Hackett would—"

"Oh, I have heard quite enough out of Papa." She put her hands on her hips to imitate her corpulent sire. "'Young ladies mustn't talk to men like that, they'll think you no better than a harlot.'" Lady Isabelle put her hand on Lydia's arm. "I shall be so vulgar with you, Lydia, since we are the same, but money can be a great equalizer when it comes to my future husband."

"If we are being vulgar, who is Lord Denby's mistress?"

"I spied her on the way in, and she's not terribly attractive. Taller than a man by a good piece, and even though she wore a long-sleeved dress, I could tell her arms were like tree trunks. Can you imagine? A woman like that? An *athlete*?"

Lydia's stomach tightened. The girl could only be

describing Bess. Denby wanted to show off his latest toy, a lady boxer. At least Mr. Arthur wouldn't be here to witness his friend's humiliation. Lydia hoped Bess would be well-paid. To be put on display for this empty-headed bunch was like the lion that lived in the Tower of London. Caged and ogled, it was no life for such a powerful animal.

Isabelle recovered herself. "Anyhow, dinner is at nine."

"And the Exhibition?" Lydia asked.

"End of the week, day before the ball." Lady Isabelle turned to leave but looked back over her shoulder. "I'm glad you came, Lady Lydia."

Lady Isabelle left Lydia alone in the hallway. Lydia's mother and Agnes were already settling into the rooms, and Lydia went to where they stood in their mother's room, surveying the wide pastures and forested enclaves from the corner window. These would be good riding lands, and she would be happy to exercise any of Denby's new horses. They had discussed their own recent acquisitions at a Hackett dinner earlier in the Season.

That dinner had been most awkward, as Lady Isabelle had thrown herself at Leighton. Lydia had passed the time discussing horses and keeping the necessity of being pleasant to Denby from completely repulsing her by drinking large quantities of wine.

Lydia didn't like that Bess would be perceived as Denby's woman. There ought to be an opportunity for her to talk to Bess alone before dinner, or before the Exhibition at least. Maybe they could sneak in some early morning sessions. Too bad Mr. Arthur wouldn't be coming. A week spent in close proximity to him, the chance to learn something new, to find herself in—

"Do you mind which bed?" Agnes asked.

Lydia shook herself out of her thoughts. "Pardon?"

"In our room. Do you care which bed? I'd prefer closest to the window. Better morning light." Agnes liked to wake up reading if she could. She and Charlotte swapped books constantly, as Charlotte could obtain titles that no one would sell to a young miss like Agnes.

"Fine. I'm going to lie down on the bed furthest from the window. Wake me when the tea comes." Lydia said.

"Do you not want to go for a walk?" Mother asked.

"Perhaps after tea," Agnes answered for her.

Lydia retreated to the other room, which still had a chill. She lay back on the plush four-poster bed. The carriage ride had been long, and closing her eyes without feeling the road bumping beneath her was some small comfort. She let herself misbehave with thoughts of Mr. Arthur, the things she would never do. Of what would have happened if she'd let that kiss go on longer.

❧

IT WAS DARK WHEN HE ARRIVED AT THE ESTATE. The public carriage had broken a wheel in the afternoon, causing a significant enough delay that John missed dinner entirely. The carriage had been hot and crowded; the only decent time of it was helping the driver make repairs. He was grateful that travel was over.

"Did you bring a valet, sir?" the aged butler, a pale man named Peters, asked. The man's face reflected the same disdain John had seen on his own butler's. Low birth was apparently tattooed on one's face.

Without thinking, John pulled at his waistcoat, as

if he could smooth out the wrinkles from the daylong carriage ride with a simple tug. "No valet," he said. "If you could spare a footman in the evenings, I'd be grateful."

A look of irritation creased Peters's expression. "Of course, sir. I can show you the room."

The butler led John up the stairs, giving him a chance to take in the opulence of the front entryway. The stairs were carpeted with green fabric, but the steps themselves were marble, like the rest of the foyer. They reached the landing, and from either side, hallways extended down, lit by flickering gilded sconces. Peters took him up a second set of stairs.

The carpet on the second set was a bit more frayed, despite the fact it must not have received quite so much use. Peters took him down the hallway to a cramped room in the corner. Just that morning, taking his coffee at Garraway's, a runner from the docks had come to give reports. The boy said a ship belonging to Hackett's shipping company had foundered in the Atlantic. A fire aboard the ship, all cargo lost. It had left Antigua, part of the triangle trade, and was full of molasses, sugar, and wood. No one yet knew about it—likely Hackett would get the news today or tomorrow. But it made him wonder how the week would play out. Would Hackett still host everyone, knowing he'd lost his fortune? He had a little time before the news would make its way onto Lloyd's Marine List and the whole world would know. But it certainly wasn't up to him to inform his lordship that his fortune was in peril. He hoped he'd gotten good insurance. Not all ships were covered for fire.

"A footman will be up shortly with your luggage and a tray," Peters said, leaving before John had a chance to ask any more of him.

The room itself was tidy, with a double bed, a

washstand, and a reading chair in the corner. There was a small fireplace in the room, and he could smell smoke from a fire lit in the room below him.

He peered out the double bank of windows into the night. Despite the butler's snobbery, he knew he should count himself lucky for having a corner view. For a brief moment, John's ego prickled. Didn't they know how much money he had? Didn't Hackett realize he could buy this estate three times over without having to take out even half his investments? Especially now that Hackett was effectively broke? He didn't know the rest of the man's finances, but to lose a ship like that, laden so heavily with slave products, it would break most men.

But men who dabbled in the exploitation of people were asking for comeuppance. How could a person hold with suffering? The Empire was built on it, the wealth wrung from the blood of others. The money he touched wasn't clean, but he felt like he could make the world better if he could funnel it the right way.

Yet he couldn't count himself clean if he enjoyed the hospitality of his host. If it weren't for Bess, he wouldn't have been invited, and there was a part of him that had wanted to be here. But he was beginning to think such a move was folly. These people would never accept him, and even if they would accept Pearl, with her better refinement, they would never let her forget where she came from.

And they weren't better people. It's just that their wealth was older. Wasn't that Lady Lydia's point when they spoke on the street? That respectability wasn't necessarily enough? The whole thing confused him, and he didn't like being confused.

John slid off his coat and untied his cravat. He was here now, so he might as well make the effort to fit in. He and Bess would put on a good show for everyone, and at dinner he would still be able to make connections, if only for business.

He lay on the bed, which was surprisingly soft, even if the comforter was a bit threadbare. He should be grateful, street urchin that he had been. This was a fancy manor, run by fancy people, and he was going to enjoy being waited upon, no matter the look of condescension on everyone's face. Well, everyone except Bess. They were together again, fighting back to back, as they had when they were children. Who said time changed things? Life so far had been one big circle: the further he got from pugilism, the more pugilism seemed to follow him.

He was asleep before the footman arrived.

# 7

Lydia rose early the next morning, immediately donning her riding habit. Agnes didn't stir. Charlotte looked bleary-eyed as she opened the adjoining door to assist Lydia in dressing.

"Don't worry about me," Lydia said, dismissing her with a wave.

Charlotte went to check for fresh water for Lydia's toilette, returning with a small ewer. "Will you be riding all morning, my lady?" she asked.

"God willing," Lydia answered, pulling on her boots. "I am not too keen on our little company." Lydia regretted saying the words as soon as they were out. She glanced over to the fireplace, where a weak fire burned, but the open chimney must stack onto another room above her. Who knew who was staying up there? Perhaps no one, but there was no need to make enemies at the beginning of a week. "Please don't repeat that, Charlotte."

Charlotte nodded. "Of course not, my lady."

Lydia had gotten a chance to lay eyes on Bess at dinner. She hadn't been sure the lady boxer would have been allowed to dine in the hall with all of the

Quality, but to her relief, she saw her seated at the end of the table.

Bess cleaned up tolerably well, wearing a dress that could not very well be considered a gown but would suffice for a country evening at least. From Lydia's vantage, Bess seemed to have decent conversations, as the company seemed engaged.

After dinner, however, Bess disappeared. Perhaps she had gone to train, or perhaps she was advised against mingling with the ladies in the drawing room. Lydia didn't blame her. The conversation revolved around the exact hue of pink that would be most becoming for Lady Isabelle. The chorus of two unmarried young misses, whose names Lydia did not remember, decided that salmon pink was in fact the best and most proper shade, and Lydia thought she might feign whooping cough just to excuse herself from the torture. Agnes had whispered to her to be nice, and Lydia did her best to school her expression back to neutrality.

"Should I wake Lady Lorian to accompany you?" Charlotte asked.

Lydia sighed. She didn't want any company. "I'll find a groom."

The hallway sconces weren't lit, and the gray morning light creeping through the windows didn't illuminate much. The portraits lining the walls now appeared as pale oval faces floating in fields of darkness. An old feeling of cold nausea crept up on her and she quickened her step. Light flooded the landing, allowing her to slow her speed as she descended the front stairway.

The breakfast room was empty, with food still being set out as she entered. She asked for morning coffee and helped herself to a small meal of eggs and toast.

The butler, Peters, appeared as a footman

delivered her a small cup of coffee. “Do you need any assistance this morning, my lady?” Peters asked, giving the courtly sort of bow Lydia would expect from a man of his advanced age.

“Thank you, Peters, but no. All I need is to be pointed in the direction of the stables.”

“Very good, my lady. I can have a groomsman escort you there.” Peters turned to go, but Lydia stopped him.

“Are any of the other guests up yet?” she asked.

“One gentleman is already out of doors, but he has not yet breakfasted,” Peters said. “And one of the...” The butler paused, searching for the right word. “One of the female guests, also.”

The female guest could be no other than Bess. The butler wouldn’t have stumbled in describing the other women as ladies. But Bess was her own category. As for the gentleman, Denby typically rode early in the morning, as she remembered from his dinner conversation. The idea of meeting him alone out in the stables didn’t sit well with her, but she wasn’t about to let him get the better of her. They were likely together, and she wouldn’t mind seeing if Bess would give her a training session if she could scare Denby away.

“Thank you, Peters.” Once finished with her breakfast, she met with a groom who asked her to follow him to the stables.

They were bigger than she anticipated. Hackett clearly had an ancestor who’d appreciated horses, even if he himself did not. She asked the groom about the different horses, which was whose, and the temperament of each animal.

The young man seemed not at all impressed by Lydia’s question. He stood in one spot, directing his hand towards each horse. “This’un is Majesty, or maybe Majestic. Belongs to Lord Denby, and seems fairly calm," he said, describing nearly every horse the same way.

She stopped the groom midway through his recital. "Saddle Majesty for me, please," Lydia said, glancing down the row of stalls.

The groom nodded and went to work. While he retrieved a saddle, Lydia walked down the aisle, trying to get a better view of all the horses. "Quite a full stable," Lydia commented.

The groom grinned, hoisting the saddle onto Majesty, or perhaps Majestic. She was a sleek-looking animal with a powerful front and sloping withers.

"This is the fullest I've ever seen it, my lady. I don't mind the extra work for these kinds," he said, finally warming to her.

"Am I the first to ride today?" Lydia asked, approaching Majesty's stall. The horse's dark eye rolled to focus in on her.

"Yes, ma'am. I was surprised at so early. Thought all you types slept 'til noon," he said, cinching the saddle.

Lydia laughed. He was right in his assessment of most of the Quality, despite the insult.

The groom's face colored. "Oh, I apologize, my lady."

She waved off the apology. "You aren't wrong. What was your name?"

"Chester—but please, I don't normally speak with people of rank, and the words just came out." Chester finished the saddle and stood hat in hand.

"Not to worry. Your secret is safe with me," she said. He was a strong lad, probably not quite twenty. "Is Majesty an Arabian? She looks it, but something isn't quite right," Lydia said, approaching the horse even closer, extending her hand to pet her.

Chester's head snapped up, now that he realized

he wouldn't get a tongue-lashing. "Quite right, my lady. Only Majesty ain't an Arabian. She's a Barb."

Lydia nodded, reaching up to pet Majesty's blonde-brown nose. The horse sighed with pleasure. A man like Denby would love to own a rarer breed that had belonged to the Royal Stables before Cromwell's revolution had sold them all off.

"She's beautiful, in any case," Lydia said.

"Not as beautiful as the Arabian in stall four," Chester said. "But Majesty's much sweeter of a girl."

"Will she run?" Lydia asked.

"She'll do whatever you ask. Best of the lot, I think," the groom said, leading both horses out of the stalls.

The poor boy must be uncomfortable with people of rank. He probably didn't get many visitors out here. Indeed, with every stall full, the guest Peters had mentioned must have foregone his early morning ride.

Chester pulled at the saddle blanket to make sure it was smooth, and then he helped Lydia mount. "Do I need a groomsman with me in these woods? They don't look particularly forbidding."

Chester shrugged. "I'd let my little sister roam in there."

"Excellent. Thank you, Chester." Lydia clicked her tongue and Majesty started a slow amble towards the woods that she had seen from her window. The trees looked pleasant, not so dense that a horse wouldn't be able to maneuver well.

Glancing back at the manor house, symmetrical and boxy, she wondered if anyone else was up yet. The world felt so still and empty, the way she felt most at ease. Not even the birds were fully awake yet.

She reached the woods and ambled down the dirt path, blocking the great house from her line of sight. There was no one about, so she'd take a bit of a meander to get her bearings, and then, when she got to an open space, she could urge Majesty to speed.

The path was wide and well maintained, though blades of green poked through, indicating its level of use. The sun dappled in amongst the leaf cover. Lydia leaned back in the saddle and tilted her face up, letting her eyes close. Majesty was a steady girl, continuing to stroll on as Lydia relaxed.

After a while, the horse's gait shifted—not a startle, just a change. Lydia opened her eyes to see why. The trail had become grassy, cushioning each step. Ahead there was a small clearing with a pond, and a man's coat hung on a tree branch. Lydia searched the clearing for the man who owned the coat but saw no one.

She considered calling out, but then hesitated, as she couldn't be sure whom she would meet. As she came closer, she saw the man's shirt hung beneath the coat. So, there was a half-naked man running around in the woods? She halted Majesty and turned in the saddle, looking into the trees that surrounded her.

"Are you in need of assistance, sir?" she called out. Nausea returned as her heart tripped faster. She'd much rather meet an attacker than be ambushed by a robber.

Majesty's massive head swung around at a noise. Lydia followed her gaze.

A muscled form broke through the trees. Light freckles were sprinkled across his chest, and it took a moment for Lydia to register his identity.

"Hello, Lady Lydia," he said, as if they were meeting by chance in Hyde Park and not in some isolated glade in the countryside.

"Mr. Arthur," she said, doing her best to cover her shock at seeing him here of all places. The early morning light caressed his well-formed body, highlighting his pectoral definition, perfect squares, as if he were a geometry puzzle more than man. His broad shoulders tapered into a slimmer waist—the golden triangle is what the Classicists called it—but she had never thought of it in this context.

"I was expecting Bess, but she seems to be lost." Sweat rolled down his temple, and a fine sheen coated his chest.

Tempting as it was to gawk, she collected herself. In spite of herself, she felt her shoulders relax. The panic that threatened to grip her ebbed. "Is that why you are here? The Exhibition?" she asked.

"When an old friend asks you to do something, you do it." He grinned. "Even if you don't enjoy the company."

She didn't let her expression betray anything even though she agreed with him.

"I didn't know you would be here," he said, clearing his throat.

His chest had a fine sprinkling of red-gold hair. From this distance, she could see freckles dotting down his chest, following the line of hair to...well. Other places. It was her turn to speak, but she couldn't think of a thing to say.

Suddenly, Mr. Arthur shook his head. "My apologies, Lady Lydia. I forgot your position. Please forgive me for holding you up, and you must be awaiting a chaperone or finding a chaperone, or—" He looked around. "Where *is* your chaperone?"

"I opted to ride alone this morning. No would-be attacker could keep up with Majesty." She patted the horse's neck.

He ambled over to where his shirt and coat hung on a low branch.

"I meant to give Majesty her head when we found a clearing." Some part of her desperately wanted him to keep his shirt off. She noticed some wrapping around his knuckles. "What do you have on your hands? Are you hurt?"

"These?" He held up his hands, stepping toward her. "Just hand wraps. Don't you use them?"

She shook her head, looking down at him. "What are they for?"

"Practice, mostly. Gentlemen use them to keep their hands tight-fisted during sparring sessions."

The strips of cloth didn't look particularly strong. She didn't understand what use it would be to wind them about, but she was curious. Bess had never mentioned them.

"My lady, you should really go," he said gently. He reached up and patted the horse's neck.

"But I have so many questions," she said.

"If Bess were here, that would be one thing, but it's just you and me, and I'm in a state of undress. You accused me of being unaware, so let me remind you of it here and now. You should go."

But she didn't want to go. She wanted to stay and learn about hand wraps. Standing before her was one of the best fighters in London, and she was just going to leave?

"I could stay for just a moment. Bess should turn up any minute." Lydia dismounted.

"This is exactly the sort of thing you shouldn't do," he reminded her, holding Majesty's bridle.

"I suppose that's true. But we're in the middle of the woods. Who's going to come upon us here?" Lydia led Majesty to a tree across the clearing and tied her. Was it silly to be glad she was wearing her favorite riding habit? The kind that fitted well across her hips, with trim that made her eyes turn the color of sapphires?

"But—" he protested.

"I won't compromise you, I promise."

Mr. Arthur's mouth was open in mid-protest, but he closed it. "I am not worried about that."

"Well then." She took off her riding gloves. They both ignored the unspoken truth that hung between them: if they were discovered, she would be compromised and a marriage would have to take place. "Would you be so kind as to wrap my hands? I'd like to see what it feels like."

The water in the stream babbled. Majesty huffed, snuffling out what else was around in the grass and roots. Mr. Arthur stretched his neck from side to side, the vulgar crack audible.

He stared at his hands. She stared at his bare forearms, snaked with muscle, trying very hard not to think about what it would feel like to be enveloped by those arms. How she'd felt before with him wrapped around her: safe, warm, calm.

"The way I grew up, early on anyway, there was no line of girl and boy. There was only cold and hungry, or watching someone else be cold and hungry."

"And I suppose no impropriety occurred?" Lydia held out her hands as if he were going to tell her fortune.

He snorted. "Constantly. Lads had mistresses as soon as they knew how to steal. One lad I knew kept a girl since he was nine years old." Mr. Arthur unwound the bit of cloth.

"Does a boy of nine know what to do when keeping a girl?" The question came out before she could stop herself.

His ginger head snapped up. "You do shock me now, my lady."

She fidgeted. It was a terrible comment. But hadn't he been trying to shock her first?

"A fair question, which I will ignore for both of our sakes." He stepped next to her, one hand wrapped, the other not. "You see how on my unwrapped hand; my knuckles can be moved." He squished his knuckles with his other hand. "You do it."

"Pardon?" Had he just invited her to touch him?

"Push my knuckles around a bit, so you can see how moveable they are."

She squeezed his knuckles together with thumb and forefinger, as if she were testing a pear for ripeness.

"Not like that," he said.

"Well, you didn't give terribly clear instruction, now did you?" She protested.

"Think of how a fist lands on an object."

His hand was freckled a bit. Just lightly so, without hair on the knuckles. She was glad of that. It was a small thing, but she didn't care for a man with hairy knuckles. It seemed dreadfully unnecessary. "Straight on, I should think." She pushed her finger between his second and third knuckles.

"Get in there. How hard do you think I hit?"

At his goading, she pushed her finger harder, willing a knuckle to slide over.

"There! See how it moved? Now, what if that was somebody's nose? Or worse, their jaw?"

"It would hurt," she said.

"Yes, and in a proper mill, that's fine. But what if you just need some practice before a proper mill? Why get your hand bloodied? You need it for the real thing. So, you wrap it. Do the same on my other hand." He held up his wrapped fist for her inspection.

Once again, she pushed her fingers between his knuckles, this time covered with that bit of rag. Bound tightly, the knuckles wouldn't move.

"I see!" She wanted to try it but didn't dare ask again. It would seem too much like begging, and that would not do. Instead, she waited for the next set of instructions.

"It keeps the hands from getting scraped up and bloody, which is helpful," he continued. "But the best part is what it does up here." He tapped his temple.

Now it was him looking at her expectantly. "I don't follow."

"Not yet. Hold out your hand."

She fairly danced as he wrapped her hand. He started at her wrist and wound around her knuckles and then back down again, tucking the tail of the rag into the binding at her wrist. His touch felt no more intimate than a maid's as he wrapped, but then, tucking in the tail, it seemed to warm. He held her bandaged hand. She looked up at him.

Promises seemed to form in the air around them. Hope and permission and dreams all transformed from wisps into viable thoughts, able to be spoken aloud. The clearing felt even smaller, and the closeness seemed to draw him to her.

They had kissed once already. Was it such a trespass to see what it felt like a second time? His eyes flickered down to her lips. She closed her wrapped hand, drawing his hands in with hers, pulling him to her. This. This was real. He stared at her mouth, and soon all she could think of was the taste of his.

Suddenly he shook his head and cleared his throat. He backed away, freeing his hands from hers.

"Where is your chaperone?" he asked plaintively, facing away from her.

Lydia was once again without words. "Where's Bess?"

He put his hands on his hips and hung his head, as if he were exhausted from a long fight. "I haven't the foggiest."

"Well." She looked down at her wrapped hand. It felt stiff, but she curled it into a fist. The motion felt so natural, as if the rag wanted her hand to be fisted. She threw a couple of jabs, just to see how it felt. Instead of her normal form, the wrap helped her feel even more pointed, truer. As if she couldn't help but hit her target.

Mr. Arthur turned around to watch her. "You have good form."

"I see what you mean about the mental aspect of the wrap," she said.

His eyes sparkled, and he took a few steps toward her, then stopped abruptly. He cracked his neck from side to side once again. "Exactly. Most of pugilism is mental. Stamina, endurance, pain control, it's all in a body's head. If you think you are tired, you fail. If you think you cannot endure one more round, you might as well forfeit."

That was something she knew well enough. Just when she wanted to crawl into bed after yet another round of slights, or failed schemes to ruin Hackett, after another fight with her mother over yet more liberties she wanted to take, she straightened her shoulders and kept on. She refused to lose this fight.

"I'd love to spar with hand wraps on. Bess tries not to make actual contact with me."

"I understand her point," he said, taking another small step before stopping once again and cracking his neck from side to side. "It's dangerous for the likes of us to lay hands on the likes of you."

"That's not quite a fair thing to say." She itched to have the other hand wrapped. It felt like a talisman. Or just a token of authenticity.

"You could hurt us and you would suffer no consequences. A story, any story, of how we wronged you, and we would hang," Mr. Arthur said. "But for us? No amount of defense could ever justify my hands on you."

Her mouth went dry. Heat pooled in very

inappropriate places. "But I could put my hands on you, and I would suffer no consequences?"

Closing the distance between them, she was once again aware of how very bare he was. "No consequences whatsoever."

She was tempted. What harm, here, in the glade? She reached up with her wrapped hand and traced his square jaw. His eyes fluttered. She traced her fingers down his neck, across his collarbone, down his chest. She followed the trail of lightly sprinkled hair down to his stomach. His muscles flexed and twitched in response. His hands stayed at his sides. There was power here.

Watching his face, she stood on her tiptoes and brushed her lips against his. His skin prickled against her feather-light touch. "No touching?" Lydia whispered.

His breath hitched in response.

She sank down to her heels and ran the palm of her unwrapped hand across his chest and down his stomach. "Not even now?" She taunted.

"Not even now," he repeated through gritted teeth.

This time she reached up and put her hand through his hair, just to feel the texture. He closed his eyes, his features softening. She liked the way he looked, so she took her time before dropping her trace down behind his ear, running it along his jaw.

His eyes opened, chips of blue resting on her in a way that should have made her nervous. She was the center of his tightly focused attention, and it felt unlike anything she'd ever experienced.

"Hallo there," called a voice that was thrashing through the underbrush.

"Oh!" Lydia dropped her hands and took a step away from Mr. Arthur.

Mr. Arthur cursed.

❦

BESS MATERIALIZED FROM THE MIDDLE OF THE trees, trudging through the brush. Twigs were stuck in her hair and her dress was covered in mud. "Had a bit of a go back there."

*Not the only one*, he thought. The torture Lady Lydia had exacted on his body was almost more than he could take. The feather-light kiss, her hands in his hair. His whole body was ringing with desire, a church bell clanging its need. He was surprised no one could actually hear his bollocks crying out.

"Why did you not use the trail?" Lady Lydia asked.

"There's a trail?" Bess asked as she stepped onto it. "Well."

John laughed, or tried to. He sounded strangled. Because he was. Even though Lady Lydia had moved away from him, she was still in sight. He could still smell her. "You've been too long in the city, Bess."

"Too long? My whole life." She brushed herself off and ran her fingers through her hair. "Surprised to see you here, Lady Lydia."

"I was as well," John said, trying to cover for her presence.

Bess grunted. "You manage to get Lady Agnes up this early?"

Lady Lydia hid her wrapped hand behind her back. Damn. He'd forgotten about that.

"Lady Agnes is still abed. The stableboy assured me that I was safe on horseback."

Bess glanced at the tethered horse. Black riding gloves were tucked into the saddle. She spotted John's one wrapped hand, then glanced over to Lady Lydia. "I ain't soft in the head."

"No one's saying that," he said.

"Let me see your hand," Bess instructed Lady Lydia.

She brought it out, the hand wrap tight across her knuckles. "I still very much appreciate your instruction."

"I'm not worried about that," Bess said.

"She saw that I was wearing them and was curious," he said. Bess flicked her gaze to him, assessing, weighing, making decisions. He could read her face like a gazette.

Lady Lydia unwrapped her hand, letting the long rag spool in the air. "I should be going, if you'll excuse me."

"It was hard enough to convince Denby I needed to spar with John this morning. He doesn't want me training anyone else." Bess said, looking pointedly after Lady Lydia. "We'll train today, John, but we don't get any more practice before the Exhibition."

"That's fine," John said, trying not to watch the lady tug on her black riding gloves and untether her horse. She took the horse to a downed log and used it as a mounting block.

The horse stepped and swayed as Lydia adjusted her skirts out of view. "Good day, Mr. Arthur. Bess."

He bowed—he couldn't help it—and Bess inclined her head. Off Lady Lydia went, back toward the estate. Her world.

Bess shook her head and tutted. "Not the best idea."

"I got no ideas," he protested, retrieving the hand wrap from the ground where Lady Lydia had left it.

His friend stretched her neck and windmilled her arms before pulling her arms out of the sleeves of her dress.

He rewrapped his hand, the bandage warm and smelling of oranges and vanilla. Kind of like he was holding her hand. In a way.

"Don't start with that," Bess said. "You're smiling like a fool."

"I'm not," he said.

"Yer looking at her wrap like it's her actual hand, a grin like I ain't never seen on yer face."

"Yer blind," he said.

"That's it? That's all you got? It must be bad." Bess shook her head. "Well, I'm telling you true right now that I can't train her while I got this business with Denby. But if you want, you could train her. She pays well."

It was like ice in his gut. "Wot?"

"This place has got her nerves all frayed, just look at her. She's going to need to train. Ladies are supposed to be still and quiet-like, but that one don't work like that. I can't train her, but maybe you could."

John made an indistinct noise, like a snort and a considering hum all at once. More time with her. More torture.

"She needs it. But I don't want to see you getting hurt. She's pretty, but she's got complicated bits to her. So, no foolin' with her, got it?"

"I wouldn't," he protested.

"I mean that for yer sake jus' as much hers."

John wasn't sure he could train Lady Lydia, not because of the fisticuffs bit but because he didn't think he could be in this glade with her again and not lay hands on her. But why was she on edge? He'd thought it was because of him, but Bess seemed to believe otherwise. He wanted to help the lady. And he would keep his grubby hands off her.

But that didn't mean she couldn't lay her hands on him.

# 8

At dinner, their differences could not have been more pronounced. Lydia was escorted in third during the procession, Lady Isabelle fourth. Agnes followed Lady Isabelle, and the rest of the young misses and matrons behind them, all on the arms of the young bankers and barristers who made up the male half.

Count Denisov, the Russian lieutenant, escorted Lady Lydia while Lord Denby escorted Lady Hackett, and Lord Hackett was paired with Lydia's mother. At least the succession spared Lydia the squalid man's company. Her mother could handle him. Had always handled him in the polite, massaging way a lady must.

"So lovely to see you again, my lord," Lydia said to the Count.

His thick black mustache wriggled as he smiled. He was handsome, even with the facial hair. Despite not donning his military costume, he was still very clearly a military man in bearing. The straight back, the puffed chest—he was not a standard English gentleman. She could see why Jane liked him.

"Likewise, Lady Lydia," he said.

They processed to their seats, he on her left, Denby on her right. It was the second dinner party that Season where she was seated next to him. At least they could speak of horses—or Bess, if Lady Lydia could find a way to discuss her without showing her knowledge. The rest of the guests filed in and, at the end, the very end, Mr. Arthur escorted Bess.

Mr. Arthur looked very fine in his dinner attire. The white shirt clung to him, starched and precise. Every man in the room wore the same, but he wore it better. With his head held high, he looked as if he belonged, or, rather, dared them all to call him out and accuse him of not. Bess, on the other hand, looked nervous. Her eyes darted all around the room, perhaps not sure of what to look at, but also perhaps assessing potential targets. It was hard to say.

Bess and Mr. Arthur sat last, at the far end of the table, nearer to Hackett and Lydia's mother than to Lydia. Discussion hummed all around as she slipped her gloves off and laid them in her lap.

Denby turned toward her and greeted her with an incline of his head. "Here we are again."

"So it appears," she said, giving him a thin-lipped smile. Dinner would be interminable now that she'd lost her appetite.

❧

ETIQUETTE BOOKS WERE HELPFUL. HE'D HAD A library of those. And small dinner parties were excellent practice, but large parties such as these still made him nervous. He'd been told by other ladies that he ate too fast for polite company.

He'd whispered the tip to Bess as they'd entered. Neither too fast nor too slow.

"Wot's that mean?" Bess demanded, as if he couldn't make her even more nervous than she already was.

The dining room held more silver than he'd seen

in his life. This was a way for the Hacketts to show off their wealth, probably to dangle Lady Isabelle's prospects to the unmarried barristers and bankers of their party. But he was too lowly to be considered even a base match for someone of the Hackett lineage. No, Lady Hackett threw her attentions on Mr. Snodfield, who was a barrister, and, when conversation shifted, to Mr. Colby, who worked at the Bank. As for the lady who needed a fortune-filled match, Lady Isabelle divided her attentions between the Russian count and Mr. Franklin, a real estate developer. It was his firm that had built up the new area around Regent's Park. Paddington was never the same after they'd gotten ahold of it.

He knew conversation was to go one way at the table, and then the next, but he wasn't quite sure which was first. Glancing about, he saw that it went opposite to his escorted lady. Made sense. This would be easy if he could just relax. Miss Franklin, the sister of the developer, was next to him.

"Speak to the bloke on tha 'tother side of ye," he whispered to Bess.

Bess startled, drawing off evening gloves like she was flaying her own skin. "A'rite."

He turned toward Miss Franklin. She was pretty, with a sprinkle of dark freckles across her nose, and skin a darker tone than his own. Her dark brown eyes were round and set a bit far apart, and she had an upbeat sort of spirit. She was easy to like.

"We are having quite lovely weather, are we not?" Miss Franklin asked.

The weather? Surely two people who didn't know each other had plenty of other things to talk about than the weather.

"Unusually sunny," he said. "Have you been able to enjoy it?"

"We've taken a turn around the grounds, which was very refreshing."

Soup appeared in front of him. Turtle soup. Again. What was it with toffs and turtles? It wasn't really that good of a flavor. But it was expensive, so they must eat it. As if everything with a price tag was worth consuming. And anything they wanted to consume that didn't have a price, they'd put one on it.

"John," Bess whispered. "Wot is this?"

"Turtle soup," he whispered back, giving Miss Franklin a charming smile.

"But why?" Bess asked.

"Just eat it. Rude not to eat soup."

"Wot if I don't like soup?" she whispered.

"Just. Eat. The soup."

"Miss Franklin," he said, clearing his throat. "Do you ride?"

"Oh," she said, coloring.

Why did she blush? Did he do something? Was he being vulgar? Probably. Shite.

❧

When the ladies adjourned to the drawing room after dinner, Lydia made a point of maneuvering away from Agnes and sitting next to Bess.

"Who am I supposed to talk to?" Agnes whispered after Lydia. Their mother gave Agnes a withering look.

"Did you enjoy your first dinner?" Lydia asked, taking a cup of tea.

"I'd prefer a tray in my room," Bess said. "Much more enjoyable up there. Wouldn't be worried about mucking up every little thing."

"It'll get easier," Lydia assured.

Bess grumbled into her teacup, adding more sugar.

"Would it be possible to arrange some training sessions here? Discreetly, though. I'd prefer it if this party doesn't know."

"It ain't shameful," Bess said.

"No, but—" Lydia glanced around the room. The middle-class misses and their mamas or chaperones, Lady Isabelle, Lady Hackett—they didn't know about her. Not anything. Not the pugilism, not her ruination, not the pact, none of it. She'd like to keep it that way.

"I can't. Denby has asked for exclusivity in my attentions and paid me accordingly."

"He hasn't the backing to pay you accordingly," Lydia huffed.

"I got the banknotes." Bess blew on the cup of hot tea.

Lydia recoiled. "Don't do that."

"'S hot," the boxer complained.

"Then wait before drinking it." Across the room, two misses glanced over at Bess, then shifted to Lydia.

Bess let the cup and saucer drop into her lap with a tinkling of the china. Lydia winced.

"You can get in a session, but not with me." Bess glared back at the young misses. "John said he'd instruct you."

Heat poured through Lydia as if she'd dumped her own tea in her lap. "Really."

"He says he ain't much of a trainer, but I've seen him work. He'll do well. And I made him promise he won't touch you."

Bess looked at her, flicking her eyes around Lydia's face, assessing, calculating. It was all Lydia could do not to fidget.

"Thank you for your concern," she said.

"But you'll need a chaperone still. Maybe Lady Agnes wouldn't mind 'cos yer maid is shite at it."

"Language," Lydia said, pasting on a smile for the room. Hopefully no one else had heard the obscenity. "Agnes is not an appropriate chaperone."

"Well, you need someone there to keep both yer paws where they oughtta be."

The men entered the drawing room, causing many of the young misses to sit up even straighter, as if they were just coming to life. Indeed, what was a performance without an audience?

The men parted, Mr. Arthur coming in last. He was in deep conversation with Mr. Franklin, another man amassing a fortune. But Mr. Arthur looked up and locked eyes with her.

"Well, I suppose I ought to go check with Agnes then," Lydia said, rising.

As she crossed the room, she found herself falling into step with Mr. Arthur. She hadn't planned it, but it evolved naturally, and, she hoped, not in a way that would be gossiped about.

"Good evening, Mr. Arthur." Her evening gown was not as magnificent as the midnight-blue sheath she'd worn when he came to dinner, but it was still flattering. The pale-yellow dress was from last season, but still in fashion. It made her appear a soft young miss, perhaps even biddable. Did he prefer biddable women? Hopefully not.

"Good evening, my lady."

"Bess has informed me that you would be willing to instruct me." They were almost to her mother and sister. Their conversation would have to change once they made those final steps. To something her mother could approve of. She'd speak with Agnes tonight. Charlotte would be relieved.

"Has she?" Mr. Arthur cleared his throat and looked around. "I can, if you need."

"Bess also made clear that she has extracted promises from you."

He chuckled. "Yes, promises have been made. But you still need a proper chaperone."

"Will tomorrow do? I will come prepared this time."

"Of course. I'll bring an extra set of hand wraps for you."

Closing the distance now to her family, she caught the attention of her mother. Mild conversation covered the anticipation that bolted through her. It was hard to follow everyone's comments on the weather and the walking and the food. But it was just as well. In the morning, she would be boxing.

❧

MR. FRANKLIN APPROACHED HIM AGAIN AS THE ladies were beginning their departure. Teacups were abandoned and skirts rustled as they left the drawing room with single candles to light their way.

"My sister tells me you've shown an interest."

Lady Lydia and her mother and sister had abandoned their teacups as well. As Lady Lydia's pale-yellow skirts swished out the door, John turned his attention to the man in front of him. "Pardon?"

"You asked if you might take a ride with her. That's an aggressive show of interest." Franklin gestured toward the window to gain privacy. "But I know your history. I can see that you are a man who won't waste time."

"Pardon?" he repeated, following the man. When had he asked to take a ride with Miss Franklin? The conversation at dinner had been all sorts of convoluted, and he hadn't followed half of what was being said. Somehow, he'd blundered from polite conversation to asking for more time with the young miss. "I—" John tried to defend himself, but considering he wasn't sure what he had to defend, he stopped.

"You're not from much, but neither are we. I know you're in financials and that you do well. Well enough that you have the support of the aristocrats in our midst." The man grinned, a boyish look.

"It's true," John said. He did have the support of some of the titled in Town. Still, what was he getting at?

"We can talk more about it after you and my sister take your ride. Though, just to let you know, she is more of a keen driver. If you've access to any kind of vehicle, she'd prefer that to actually being on the horse itself."

Fair points. He'd prefer a pleasant experience over a terrified woman any day of the week. "Ah. Did Miss Franklin say when she would prefer to have an outing?" What was he supposed to do? Did this mean he was supposed to dig up a vehicle from Hackett? Who would chaperone? Her brother? Was he supposed to find a chaperone, or was she? Was it something that was better in the morning or the afternoon, or did it matter?

After the port was finished and all the ladies had departed, John made his way up to his chamber. Such a mess. He undressed and slid into bed. Sleep was elusive, the picture of Lady Lydia looking up at him sidelong as she asked for instruction embedded in his dreams.

---

AGNES TRUDGED AFTER HER TO THE STABLES. SHE was not happy. It was all Lydia could do to keep a scowl from her own face.

"Majesty again, my lady?" asked Chester,

recognizing her.

"Please. And Bluebell for my sister."

Chester brought out the two horses and helped them mount. They were well into the woods when Agnes began her bargaining, just as Lydia knew she would.

"When I have a favor to ask, I expect you to repay it without protest," her sister whined.

"When that day comes, I will." Lydia's teeth were set, and it was all she could do to keep from grinding them. There had been endless complaints last night as she tried to sleep. In the dark, whine after whine had wafted from Agnes until she'd finally exhausted herself.

It had taken Lydia longer than the whining lasted to find sleep for herself. She kept thinking on how Mr. Arthur had fallen into lockstep with her in the drawing room. How easy it had been to have their discreet conversation. How well he'd done in conversation with her mother and sister. He was clearly trying very hard, and it was touching.

He'd no idea how much he was helping her by agreeing to train her. Staying in Hackett's manor house was a trial in and of itself. But news of the fate of the *Europe* should come soon. They should have left Antigua within the last few weeks, laden with trade goods. Shipping was an expensive venture, lucrative only if the goods were sold once back in England. She'd checked his insurance as well—he'd insurance against weather and pirates, but had skimped in an effort to save money and had left off a policy against fire. If Midshipman Smith had honored his commitment, Hackett's ruin was imminent. Finally. She wanted to see the look on that man's miserable face.

She spurred Majesty, who was happy to give her rider more speed.

"Lydia!" Agnes called.

"Oh, keep up," Lydia threw over her shoulder.

When she arrived in the glade, Mr. Arthur was already there, his coat and waistcoat off but his shirt still on. There was a bundle by the tree that held his clothing. "Good morning," he said.

"Good morning." She returned the greeting as she dismounted and tethered Majesty to the same tree as she had the day before.

"I thought you were bringing a chaperone," Mr. Arthur said, looking back through the trees.

"I am. My sister is slow on horses. She doesn't care for riding. Or being out of doors in general."

"There's a place for all of us," he quipped. As she approached him, he surveyed her. "I doubt you could spar in a riding habit," he said, fingering the corner of her jacket.

The tightly tailored spencer left little room for maneuvering, but at least it didn't have to stay buttoned down the front. It was designed to be worn open, which helped with movement. "I'll train with you the way I train with Bess," she said. "It really doesn't matter."

He ran his finger along the stiff collar of the jacket. "What is the difference between your riding habit and your normal dress, anyway?"

"You mean aside from the military decoration?" she asked, pointing to the jaunty gold epaulets on her shoulders.

His forehead creased, as if he were trying not to frown.

"I have a neckcloth," she said.

"Excellent knot, by the way," he said, examining it. "Though a bit on the sloppy side, don't you think? You'll have to fire your valet."

She laughed. "I don't have a valet; I have a lady's maid."

"No wonder. A lady's maid could not possibly handle a neckcloth," he said. "Is it supposed to be a mailcoach knot?"

She gasped. "No, it's supposed to be a horsecollar."

He tsked, stepping closer and untying the careful tie. "It's gone all wrong."

"And I tied it myself," she protested.

"As I well know, it is impossible to do a fine job on anything but a mailcoach knot if you are tying your own neckcloth. You need a proper valet," he said, rewrapping the thin white cloth about her neck.

"And you think you can do the job?" she asked, her eyebrow raising.

"Consider this my job application," he said, glancing up to meet her eyes.

She lifted her chin to give him access to the cloth, and she wondered if he would kiss her. Instead, his fingers brushed her neck as he folded the cloth over. Finally, he pulled it through into the knot. Agnes would be here any moment to make her behave. By the time they got to any sort of undress, Lydia would be properly chaperoned.

"How does it look?" she asked.

"Quiet. I'm concentrating," he said, gently tugging this way and that on the knot. He stopped and stepped back.

"And?" she asked.

"Quite tidy," he announced. "Have a look for yourself in the pond."

"Oh no," she said, taking a step backwards. "I know how that game goes. You forget that I was raised with James. I get close to those banks, and you push me in."

Mr. Arthur put his hand over his heart. "My lady. I would never."

"You're a big brother. It was your job to push girls

into ponds," Lydia said.

"If I wanted you in the pond, I would pick you up and throw you in," he said.

Lydia raised her arms into a defensive posture. "I beg to differ."

"I won't come for you."

Her arms drooped. "That's kind of disappointing," she said.

"I just want to hear your praise at my excellent knot-tying skills," he said. "Besides, I did promise not to touch you."

She couldn't help but smile. His eyes darted to her lips. "Even though you just tied my neckcloth."

It took but a few large steps for him to close the distance between them. The clutching feeling she'd had all morning evaporated as he angled his mouth toward hers. "But I didn't touch you. Just the cloth."

"Details," she said.

"This doesn't bode well for your training."

"No," she agreed. "You're supposed to be a substitute for Bess."

His face drew closer. "Where is your chaperone?"

It felt as if she had no more air left in her body, as if her heart might stop. She had no choice but to meet him, to finish the distance. Raising herself onto her toes, she pressed her lips to his, and it felt as if he was saving her. From what, she wasn't certain. His gentleness was not enough, and she wrapped her fingers in his hair, pulling him tighter to her.

A small grunt came from him, as if he were an animal. He responded in kind to her aggression, pulling her tighter, pressing against her more. His leg went between hers, closing any gap between their bodies.

She felt unable to think, like she'd had too many glasses of champagne before dinner.

"It's too hard not to kiss you," he gasped.

"Then kiss me," she said.

He broke from her lips, trailing his down to her jaw, to her ear. It was a new sensation, and she couldn't help but gasp at the thrill of it. No nerves, no panic, just the hot thrum of her blood pooling in new parts of her. This was pleasant, better than nice. She was beginning to understand what the widows were talking about. Her body felt good, and it was because of him.

"I'm coming through the forest," Agnes called. "On my big horse. Here I am, on this horse. Look out for any persons in my path!"

Lydia shoved away from him. She took big, steadying breaths, and watched him do the same. He raced over to the bundle he had by the tree, trying to appear as if he'd been across the glade the whole time.

Agnes and Bluebell sauntered into the grove. "Well, hullo," she said, in a much too loud voice. "There you are. Not near each other at all. So very appropriate. I'm certain that's been the way the whole time."

"Be quiet, Agnes." Lydia shot her a withering look, untying her bonnet.

"Come help me off this beast," Agnes said.

Lydia crossed the grove, giving Mr. Arthur wide berth. She held the bridle as Agnes dismounted, handing her the bonnet. She tethered the horse near Majesty. Agnes pulled a book out of her pocket and settled on a log.

"I'm here now, so you can commence your fisticuffs," Agnes announced.

❧

THIS WASN'T GOING TO WORK. HE COULDN'T TRAIN Lady Lydia. Not when he was drawn to her like a fly to honey.

Peeling off his shirt suddenly felt like an embarrassment, but he certainly couldn't ask her to go into a state of undress if he didn't. He had so many plans for today, but they all evaporated. He felt like a fool. He hated it.

She undid the buttons on her spencer jacket.

"I think we can just go half undress for today, my lady," he said.

Even Lady Agnes looked up from her book.

"Given that today I've brought weapons," he said, nudging open the bundle at his feet.

"I've done some weapons work with Bess," Lady Lydia said.

"I remember," he said. The day of their first kiss, where he'd nuzzled his silk cheek and she turned and —that was not helpful thinking. Back to weaponry. "I brought some cudgels and quarterstaffs this morning. They are the most commonly used weapons in women's mills, so I thought we could start there."

She finished peeling off her spencer, handing it to Lady Agnes for safekeeping.

"Pick up a quarterstaff," he instructed, taking one for himself. He should feel bad for what he was about to do, but he had to focus. He was the instructor. This was his job.

She strode forward and was bending to pick it up when he brought up his quarterstaff in one swift motion, connecting with her shoulder and pushing her backwards. She fell onto her rump.

"Never keep your footwork off balance," he said. "Stand up."

"I wasn't prepared," she said, standing, dusting off her skirts. She went for the quarterstaff again, quick as she could manage, but he was ready for her, thwacking her in the ribs hard enough to push her off to the side.

"Will this be the extent of your training? Beating me while I am unarmed?" she asked, standing once again, holding her side. "Thank goodness there are a few days before the ball. How would I dance?"

"This is just to warm your muscles. We will begin training when you can retrieve the quarterstaff."

She ran for it, and again he connected his quarterstaff to her body, but not well enough to push her over into the dirt. Time and again she tried to dodge past him. Lady Agnes had stopped reading her book and watched as her sister was thwacked with a stick. He hated it for her, but Lady Lydia was tougher than she looked. Finally, she stood bent over, her hands on her knees, panting to catch her breath.

"You will hit me no matter what," she said. "This isn't about dodging you at all."

He inclined his head. She'd finally figured it out, not for lack of trying. Her expectations for his lessons seemed low. "I instructed you to pick up the quarterstaff."

"You're trying to make certain I can take the pain and still accomplish the task."

"Pugilism isn't about throwing a punch, it's about being able to take a punch and still being able to think," he said.

"So, you're here to teach me about pain?" she asked, lifting her eyebrow, closing the distance between them. The look caused his member to twitch.

He stepped forward until they were toe to toe. "I will give you pain until you cannot take any more." Their eyes were locked, and he felt like he should receive an award for his restraint. He wanted to throw her on the ground, use his mouth to guide his hands in removing every stitch she wore. The committee in his pants agreed with the plan.

Lydia licked her lips as she kept his gaze. Moving

her mouth as if she were about to speak, she instead ducked and darted around him, making for the quarterstaff.

This time he wasn't prepared, and his weapon caught her on her backside as she retreated. Agnes burst with laughter.

He shouldn't have been fooled by her seduction efforts, but he smiled anyway. Praise the student when she does well. "Excellent tactic, my lady. Now we may begin."

They went over the basics that she had learned from Bess. Her grip was sloppy, and her stance was a right mess. It wasn't Bess's fault; it was just what happened when a student's confidence outweighed her experience. He corrected almost everything, from head to toe.

"But I know how to do this," she protested, cutting the air with the quarterstaff.

"Now you'll be better." Technique wasn't something learned once, it was something to be refined through perpetual practice. Tony liked to say that. Thought it made him sound smart.

As he put her through the paces of basic moves, they both grew warm. He had even managed to not think about his body lingering too closely to hers. Still, every time he touched her, adjusting her grip or correcting a motion, his hands tingled with desire.

Lady Agnes stood. "It's time."

"Of course, my lady," he said, gathering the weaponry into a bundle. He at least had an excuse to be sweating out in the woods with a bunch of sticks. "Cool yourself with water from the stream."

She nodded, her cheeks red and her hair mussed. While she tended to herself at the stream, they both had a moment to return to themselves. Once they had gotten to actually working, training went well. She was a fast learner, and Bess had instilled decent basics. He buttoned his shirt back up all the way and slid on his waistcoat.

"If you are able, try to take a hot bath tonight," he said, trying not to picture her in a porcelain bathtub, a foot extended out, him grasping it—nope. Not helpful. He pictured Caulie in the bath. That pulled his lust back to heel.

"Why would I not be able?" she asked.

"A hot bath is quite a lot of water to haul," he said, frowning. The staff must already be groaning under the weight of so many guests.

A hard line set in her expression. "That isn't the sort of thing I worry about."

"Your muscles will be quite sore," he said, trying to cover that difference in their upbringing. He worried about the difficulties for the staff, she worried about her toilet.

"Of course," she said, crossing the grove to her sister. Lady Agnes handed off the spencer jacket, waiting as Lady Lydia buttoned it before handing her the bonnet. Once attired, Lady Lydia readied Bluebell for her sister and then mounted Majesty. "May we meet again tomorrow morning?"

Lady Agnes grumbled.

"I look forward to it."

❧

"I've spoken to Miss Franklin," Agnes said. They trudged through the field toward the stables in the early light. The morning dew wetted their boots. Or rather, the dew wetted Lydia's boots. Agnes's boots were some sort of atrocious men's work boots that she'd made Vasily obtain for her. They were impervious to all manner of things, the least of which was water. "And I now formally request my due for rousting myself out of bed these past two mornings."

Contrary to her scowl, Lydia was in a good mood. Dinner had gone well last night, and she had again been paired with Count Denisov. They spoke about Jane, which endeared her to the man. This time they had sat in a different arrangement, however, and she'd spent the evening chatting with Mr. Colby. He had a birthmark in his hair, a white spot amidst the dark brown that was quite singular, but aside from that, he was a mild soul. His preferred horse was the gentle kind, and his preferred pastime was having someone read to him near the fire. Lydia thought she might try to introduce Agnes. A banker might be a bit below rank, but if they suited, why not?

"And what's that?" Lydia asked.

"We are to be chaperones this afternoon for Miss Franklin."

"Even if it is the country, I think we are underqualified for the task."

"It's only for a walk. Besides, Miss Franklin is also speaking with Mrs. Bartles, Miss Colby's chaperone."

Lydia rolled her eyes. A stroll in full view of every window in the manor was perfectly safe, but certainly, a young lady required chaperones. Lest she be pulled into the bushes. She shuddered. There were some men that would pull a young lady into the bushes. But shouldn't they find those men and oust them, lock them up in Newgate, rather than constructing cages of air around their young ladies?

"Fine. Who is the gentleman?"

"I don't know."

Lydia stopped and turned around, and her sister plowed right into her, almost knocking her down. They were nothing but arms and giant boots everywhere. Agnes ended up on the dew-covered ground. "Excuse you, what are you doing? Pay attention to where you're walking."

"I'm sorry," Agnes whined. "I was thinking about

something else."

"While you were talking?" Lydia's fists came to her hips. "Honestly, Agnes."

"Just because you can't think of two separate things at the same time doesn't mean I can't." Agnes stood, her skirts wet.

"Let's go."

"I can't ride when I'm all wet," she protested.

"You aren't all wet. Your dress is barely damp. I bet your feet are dry as a bone. Come on."

Chester was waiting for them at the stable with Majesty and Bluebell. "Thought you might be riding again, my lady. Er, my ladies." Chester scrunched up his face in confusion. Agnes giggled, which heartened Lydia. At least the entire morning hadn't gone sour. They mounted and were on the trail quickly. They reached the clearing to find Mr. Arthur still wearing his overcoat.

"Good morning," Lydia called to him as they approached. Dismounting as she spoke, she walked Majesty over to the tethering tree.

"Good morning," he said in return. His red-gold hair shined in the early morning light.

The overcoat seemed to accent the broadness of his shoulders, and the way he moved was efficient and smooth. Perhaps not a preferred quality one would list in a man, but one she appreciated nonetheless. Agnes greeted him as well, dismounting and handing the reins over to Lydia so she could tether Bluebell next to Majesty.

"Lydia," Agnes complained. "I'm cold."

"Sit in the sun," Lydia advised, undoing her bonnet.

"Here," Mr. Arthur said, shucking off the overcoat Lydia had admired. "I've got to take this off anyhow."

He draped the overcoat over Agnes's hunched shoulders. She shivered, just to top off her theatrics.

"Really, Agnes," Lydia said. "You ought to tread the boards at Drury Lane."

"That should keep you warm," Mr. Arthur insisted, ignoring Lydia's jibe. "How did you get so cold?"

"Took a tumble in the grass," Lydia said.

Agnes shot Lydia a mean look. "I wasn't paying attention to where I was going, that's all. I tripped over something ridiculous."

"Oh?" Mr. Arthur asked.

"You needn't be polite to her," Lydia said.

"And what did you trip over?" Mr. Arthur prodded.

"Her," Agnes said, pointing to Lydia.

He laughed, his head thrown back.

"It isn't funny," Lydia said, folding her arms in front of her chest. The glade was cold still, and the grass was thick with dew. "I'm not ridiculous."

"I'm glad to see you're both human." He shook his head and chuckled, stripping off his jacket to hang on the tree. "May I offer you this coat as well, Lady Agnes?"

Lydia pulled off her riding gloves. She disliked being laughed at as a general rule. But his laughter was soft, inviting her to join in, not ridiculing her from afar.

"One article of clothing per gentleman is what I always say," Agnes said. "Thank you, sir."

"Since we worked with weaponry yesterday, I thought we could wrap your hands and work on some basic combination punches." Mr. Arthur fished four small bundles of rags from the pockets of his coat, which hung on the branch.

Lydia bit her lip to not give away how much she'd hoped for exactly that. She discarded her bonnet and her spencer. "That sounds lovely."

"'Lovely' is perhaps not the most accurate word,"

Agnes said from her perch, huddled in the overcoat.

"To each her own," Mr. Arthur said, slipping off his waistcoat.

Lydia didn't hide her smile that time. Finally, someone who could understand what gave her a thrill. It wasn't the next ball, another dress, or a new novel. It was movement, action, the heavy thud in her chest as she worked hard to better herself. And it was precisely what a lady like her wasn't supposed to do. Here was a man who would help her be exactly who and what she was. She held out her hands. "Please."

Tucking two of the wraps under his arm, Mr. Arthur began wrapping Lydia's hands.

"And thank you for saying 'her,'" Lydia whispered to him.

"Of course." He looped the strip off cloth around her knuckles. "I was talking about you."

"Yes, but." She sighed. Was it even worth explaining it? Yes. To him, it was. "But when you are a person like me, 'her' means all manner of things that I am not, expectations that I cannot rise to, no matter how much façade I hide behind. I find I enjoy things that typically have a 'him' attached. So, thank you for noticing."

His rough, wide hands held hers. They stood for a moment, quiet in the glade, the stream babbling. It was Mr. Arthur that fell out of the reverie first. "I ought to rewrap that hand so you can learn the process."

"Please." Anything that kept her hand in his a little longer. She tried to pay attention, she really did. He unwound the bandage and started again, explaining the science behind it. He showed her how, and then had her demonstrate on her own hand. They unwrapped and tried again. Soon they were shadowboxing. Mr. Arthur corrected her stance, pulled back her shoulders.

"Refinement is something altogether different here," he said, placing a single fingertip on her ribcage, a reminder that lifted her bearing. "It isn't elegance, it's practice."

This time, she didn't object. She followed, trying to embed the feeling of proper form in her body. She felt warm enough now to try to work without her dress sleeves. She'd bound her breasts that morning, just as Bess always had. Then they might spar.

It was the chatter of Agnes's teeth that drew them out of their lesson. Lydia turned to see Agnes huddled under Mr. Arthur's overcoat. Her lips were tinged with blue.

"Oh Agnes!" Lydia was horrified to see that she'd ignored her sister for so long that an illness might actually occur. Her mother had always accused her of selfishness—it seemed she was right. "Get dressed," she told Mr. Arthur.

"I'm cold," Agnes repeated.

Lydia threw on her spencer and bonnet and untethered the horses. She mounted Majesty. "Help Agnes up to sit in front of me."

"You'll have to ride astride to fit both of you," Mr. Arthur said.

The suggestion wasn't amiss. Gritting her teeth, she stood up in the stirrups, rucked up her skirts, and swung her leg over. "Come on now, Agnes."

Mr. Arthur helped Agnes to the log that served as a mounting block. Between the three of them, Agnes hauled herself onto the saddle.

"I've got you," Lydia whispered to her sister. "Mr. Arthur, would you be so kind as to take Bluebell back to the stables?"

He swept into a bow. Lydia curled her arms around her sister and spurred Majesty back to the manor.

# 9

"You have to go to Miss Franklin," Agnes urged from her sickbed.

"Another swallow of broth and I will consider it," Lydia said.

Agnes was swathed in blankets, warm bricks laid in every crevice of the bed. The tray near her elbow and the patch where Lydia sat were the only parcels of land not heated by some device.

Their mother sat on the other side of the bed, near the window, stitching. She'd been so angry with Lydia for taking Agnes out into the cold morning that she could barely speak. The stabbing of the needle was the only current sign of her emotional state.

"Hand it to me," Agnes insisted. When Lydia did so, Agnes took it and drained the bowl. "There. Go. Use your influence with the young man, whoever he is."

"I have no influence," Lydia protested.

"Isn't it you that says there's always an angle? You're clever. You'll think of something. If only James were here. You're cleverer together."

"Now I'm convinced you have a fever." She slid off the bed, smoothing her skirts. "But, if I must go do a good deed, I will." Lydia glanced over at her mother, who was still pointedly ignoring her. "Cheer up, at least you won't have to go down to dinner tonight."

"I don't know," Agnes said, leaning back into the pillows and frowning. "I've quite liked the discussion amongst the young ladies in the drawing room."

"Then perhaps they might come visit you this afternoon while you convalesce. If Mama's scowl won't frighten them."

Lydia's mother gave a sharp look, but at least she acknowledged her daughter. Lydia gave her a hopeful smile in return. "I'll be off, then."

Lydia wound her way down to the drawing room, where she found Miss Franklin and Mrs. Bartles. They stood and curtsied to her.

"Is Lady Agnes occupied this afternoon?" Miss Franklin asked.

"Sadly, yes. I'm afraid I drug her out this morning for a ride and she caught a chill."

Mrs. Bartles tutted. She was young, perhaps Lydia's age, but her status as married gave her so much more freedom. That alone made marriage palatable. To not constantly fret and look over one's shoulder for proper supervision. To just do something, without constant arranging and planning and scheduling.

"Lady Agnes asked me to come in her stead," Lydia said.

Niceties were exchanged and more sympathy laid out for Agnes's welfare. They sat quietly for a moment. "When will your young man show up?" Lydia asked.

The clock on the mantle chimed the hour in response. The fire was dying down.

The door flung open. Mr. Arthur appeared, his hair a bit disheveled and his eyes wide.

"Quite the dramatic entrance," Mrs. Bartles murmured.

Mr. Arthur entered and bowed. His chest was heaving as if he'd just been running. When he rose and saw Lydia, something akin to panic flashed through his eyes. So, this was Miss Franklin's young man. She pushed away the sting to her pride, the sourness in her throat.

"I apologize for my tardiness," he said.

All three women looked to the clock that had just chimed, announcing his arrival.

"Only just," Miss Franklin said.

"I learned that you were keen on driving, Miss Franklin, so I took the liberty of arranging a phaeton for this afternoon, instead of a walk." Mr. Arthur ran his hands through his hair, calming both himself and the strands of red-gold.

"How thoughtful," Miss Franklin said, standing.

Lydia brought herself to her feet, as did Mrs. Bartles. There was a decidedly sour pit in her stomach. "Indeed. Thoughtful."

"Shall we?" Miss Franklin swept out of the drawing room. Mrs. Bartles and Lydia followed, but as she passed Mr. Arthur, she couldn't help but stare him down. The nerve to kiss her the day before and then to ask Miss Franklin for an outing the next.

His sky-colored eyes seemed full to the brim—perhaps with explanations and excuses, but she wasn't interested. Actions were what counted.

Properly bonneted and gloved, the party arranged itself in the phaeton, Mr. Arthur and Miss Franklin in front, Mrs. Bartles and Lydia in the back. The horses shifted as they waited, their hooves scraping across the gravel drive. Miss Franklin chattered on at length about driving, the horses, different vehicles, thoughts on cornering at speed. Lydia couldn't listen. All her concentration centered on keeping her face as pleasant-appearing as possible. The phaeton lurched into gentle motion.

The day was still overcast, and there was hope that rain might force them to return early.

"And where is Mr. Bartles?" Lydia asked in hopes of making conversation that would prevent her from hearing Mr. Arthur discuss his gig with some enthusiasm.

"At sea," Mrs. Bartles said with a pleasant smile.

"You seem contented with that," Lydia said.

"Oh, I am. Pleasant man, Mr. Bartles is, but we're both spirited souls. We do better posting letters and reuniting after some months apart than we do in a regular domestic life." A curly wisp of brown hair escaped the woman's bonnet.

Mrs. Bartles wasn't a meticulous sort. The ribbon of her bonnet was not tied particularly well or securely, and while she was tidy, she wasn't precise. Not the way Lydia was. Lydia glanced to the front. Nor the way Mr. Arthur was. But there seemed some happiness to be found in that, without expectations of perfection—the constant striving that underpinned all of Lydia's endeavors.

Miss Franklin laughed. A little too freely, her mouth open and wide, as if she were catching flies. Lydia looked away. The small shrubs that lined the drive were well-manicured. A bitter thought rose: Her goal would be accomplished when Hackett could no longer afford such well-trimmed hedges. Mrs. Bartles spoke, but between the clopping of the horses, the wind, and Lydia's dour temperament, she didn't hear. Fisting the fabric of her skirts, Lydia willed herself to turn toward the chaperone.

"Pardon?" Lydia asked.

"I asked if you were looking forward to the Exhibition," she said, her gaze sliding to the front, where Mr. Arthur's coat strained against his shoulders. "It's a refreshing idea, to end the week with an Exhibition and then a ball, isn't it?"

"I suppose it is." Lydia knew what those shoulders looked like bare, in action, covered in the sheen of sweat.

Mr. Arthur threw a worried glance over his shoulder. Good. She didn't want him to enjoy his afternoon with Miss Franklin. A deep sulking feeling overtook Lydia. Mr. Arthur was *hers*. It was childish to want him to only pay attention to her, but it was still there. Lydia focused on keeping herself still. Calm. Imperturbable, implacable. Impervious.

In the end, the rain did threaten, and then followed through. Miss Franklin was forced to drive the phaeton—at great speed—back to the house. The party alighted, and the grooms took care of the vehicle and the horses while Mr. Arthur and the ladies scurried inside. Wet bonnets and shawls were shaken and handed off.

Peters escorted them to the drawing room where they were given hot tea to warm themselves. The fire was stoked, and Miss Franklin and Mrs. Bartles were bright and flush in the excitement. A dusting of raindrops was not enough to stoke Lydia's passions.

"Quite the outing, wouldn't you say, Mr. Arthur?" Mrs. Bartles asked.

"Rejuvenating," he said. Was his smile genuine? Or was he acting? He inclined his head as he spoke. Was it in acknowledgement or in respect?

Lydia drained her teacup. "If you'll excuse me, I would like to go check on my sister."

"Of course. Give her my best," Miss Franklin said, her arm outstretched, as if she might actually touch Lydia.

She eyed the hand. "I will, Miss Franklin. I'm certain she'll appreciate your concern."

The ladies dipped a short curtsy and Mr. Arthur gave a brief bow as she left, the reminder of her rank. The hallmark that she didn't belong in their circle.

Trudging up the stairs in her damp shawl, she wondered if her mother would fuss over her as well.

Agnes was sitting up in bed, embroidering yet another pillowcase while Charlotte read to her. Their mother was nowhere in sight.

"How was it?" Agnes asked when Charlotte paused.

"Miss Franklin gives her regards," Lydia said. If she hadn't been so out of sorts, she would have asked why that comment elicited a blush from Agnes. At the moment, she couldn't care.

"So, who was the suitor?" Agnes asked.

"Mr. Arthur," Lydia said, her tone sharper than she wanted.

Agnes sighed in disappointment. Charlotte put down the book and tutted at Lydia. At least someone would fuss over her. Charlotte helped her out of the shawl and then, without a word, started to undo the dress.

Agnes flipped over the blankets on the bed to make room. "Get in."

Stripped to her chemise, Lydia slid in next to her sister. Charlotte continued her ministrations, pulling out the towel-wrapped brick and replacing it with another from the fire.

"Should I continue reading, my lady?" Charlotte asked.

Lydia nodded, putting her head on Agnes's shoulder. Charlotte began again, a novel of some kind that Lydia didn't know. The maid's accent changed as she read, gaining a lilt of her original accent.

Here was where she belonged. This was comfort and belonging. If she were another sort, she might have cried, but instead, she fell asleep.

❧

THE COUNTRY WAS NICE. THE AIR WAS GOOD, better for taking gulping lungfuls when a cove needed. But all in all, the country could hang, for all John cared. He liked meeting Lady Lydia in the woods for a morning spar. He had been nervous about it at first; he wasn't much of an instructor, even if Bess encouraged him. And he liked sparring with Bess before dinner in the Orangery.

But the rest? Dinner was the worst. Even worse than the ones he attended in Town. Interminable, and he was always saying something wrong. Like the whole mess with Miss Franklin. He'd somehow asked her to go riding with him, which he hadn't meant to do; he was only making conversation. But that was wrong, too.

When her brother told him she preferred driving, he'd spent all afternoon arranging the phaeton, only to find he was going to be late if he didn't sprint back from the stables. He was embarrassed enough for that, and then to walk in to find Lady Lydia there, ready to amble along with them. Damn it all. She had given him those icy glares the whole ride.

And now it was dinner time again. Always dinner. Like a perpetual Hell every night. He wanted to feign sickness just to get out of it. Couldn't he just get a toasting stick and have some toast and cheese in his rooms? A cup of wine to wash it down, and, if they had it—and rich folk always did—a bit of hot cocoa for the pudding course.

His collar starched and his cravat tied, he went down to dinner. Once the last guest arrived, the procession formed, as it had every night since he arrived. He and Bess stood, arm-in-arm, dead last, stiff and silent. Unnatural was all that was.

The ladies looked beautiful in all their pale skirts, flounced and ruffled and whatnot. The men all dressed alike, some tall, some short, some lean, some fat, but all in black. At least he knew the expectations of the dress code. Bess floundered around with it, but the group seemed generous to bend its rules for her. She looked like a different sort, standing half a head taller than most of the men in attendance.

They marched into the dining room, the other guests seating themselves, just as always, but tonight there was a seat next to Lady Lydia. As the last couple to enter, they never had a choice of where they were seated, though Lady Hackett had insisted that they change seating selections every night to vary conversation.

"Good evening, my lady," he said when Lady Lydia looked his direction. He'd learned in the last few days that they would have the chance to chat for the first part of the meal. After some amount of time, he wasn't sure how much—he hadn't caught on that far yet—the direction would change, and he would talk to Bess again.

Lady Lydia looked beautiful as her hair gleamed in the candlelight. He leaned in just a little. She smelled wonderful, still oranges and vanilla, but warm, like the best towel stepping out of a bath. But it was there that the softness stopped. There was nothing but icy politeness all over her face.

"You seem to be well-recovered from our afternoon rain shower." The tablecloth was so white and so starched. Was there a person whose whole job it was to starch the tablecloths? It must be. There was a person to do everything around here.

"Quite," she said.

"Did you enjoy the ride? Miss Franklin seemed to be an experienced driver."

The footmen—so tall, all these footmen—delivered the soup course. Lady Lydia picked up her spoon and pushed it around.

"No one was injured," she said.

"The air was pleasant."

"Until the rain," she countered.

John turned his attention to his own soup. It appeared to be some kind of broth. He took up his spoon since Lady Lydia didn't seem to want to talk. They sat in silence, elbow to elbow, for quite some time. John thought about how he'd worked so hard over the years to make friends with men above his rank. How he was able to be on friendly terms with every group of brokers and jobbers at the Exchange. He excelled at getting people who hated him to like him. So, he started running his mouth.

"This is my first country visit, you know. Haven't done one of these yet. It's been a different sort of experience, having to meet so many new people all at once. I know how to speak to all the blokes, of course, but having so many young ladies to converse with is a bit o' a challenge for a cove like me. I mean, I talk with my sister all the time, but it's different when in an elegant house with elegant females, and I certainly don't want to offend anyone. Like the other night, I was seated next to Miss Franklin. I was just making conversation, asking if she liked horses, and the next thing I know, her brover is comin' to me in the drawing room, giving me advice on courting. I was just asking after the horses, and the next thing I know, I'm going on a phaeton ride!" His accent had eroded. He took another slurp of soup to recover himself, lodging expensive vowels in his mouth. "Well, you know, you were there."

Lady Lydia thawed. She turned to him, her walled-off expression dissolving into merely a guarded one. "You didn't mean to ask Miss Franklin for an afternoon excursion?"

"'Course not." He slurped the soup and looked around the room at the other guests. "I wouldn't presume."

A smile played at her lips. They were very plump, and pretty. He wanted to kiss them again. "No," she said. "I shouldn't imagine you would presume."

Heat crept up his collar. Was she referring to their kiss? He had presumed there, in the glade with her. He glanced around again, this time to see if anyone was listening. A footman came around and poured the wine. "I know my place," he whispered when the footman had withdrawn.

"That's a pity." She gave him a sidelong glance—the kind you might expect from an actress or a flower girl, not a lady. Because a woman who looked at you like that had plans. Wants. He hoped he was a part of her plan. "That's a pity."

Hope flared in his chest, and lust flared somewhat lower. Suddenly, or so it seemed to him, conversation turned the other direction and the soup dishes were cleared.

"Yer as red as Mrs. Nagy's stew," Bess said, turning toward him.

"What? No, I'm not," he sputtered. Though he would rather eat Mrs. Nagy's stew than the fish that was laid out on the table. Chunks of meat, probably beef, but it didn't matter when she cooked it for so long in the onions and whatever that spice was. His stomach growled. He just wanted some normal food, not this prancy shite with another white sauce. Brown bread, red stew. That's food.

"Lady Lydia givin' you the what-fer?" Bess asked, waiting for him to serve her fish. It really was the stupidest rule. Why couldn't everybody just get what they wanted on their own terms? How was he supposed to guess how much she wanted?

"No," he said, attacking the fish.

"Oh, the opposite then? Heard you went fer a drive with Miss Franklin over there."

"Didn't mean to, but it happened."

"Didn't think she was the marrying type, if you know what I mean." Bess watched him as he cut into the fish.

"Yeah, don't think she is. But who am I to tell people what to do?" John portioned out some fish for Bess and for himself and served them without too much trouble. A drip or two of white sauce on a white tablecloth wasn't that bad.

"Right?" Bess said as she dug into the fish. "Between you and Denby, I never get a moment's rest. I'm right famished."

The rest of dinner proceeded along interminably. He and Lady Lydia spoke, but never about anything real. Her interest in pugilism was something she didn't want public, and he respected that. So, they searched for other topics, waylaid by flirtatious comments and innuendo. It was a pleasant way to pass the evening, mostly, except that he kept wanting to reach out and touch her hand. Or feel her hair. Some connection.

The ladies withdrew to the drawing room, and the men took turns at the chamber pots in the corner, lighting up cigars and swirling glasses of port. Mr. Franklin settled in beside him.

"My sister was delighted that you found her a vehicle this afternoon," he said. "High marks for that, sir."

John inclined his head. "No sense in spending an unpleasant afternoon."

"She was touched by your thoughtful gesture," the man said. Now that John had spent time with Miss Franklin, he could see the resemblance between the two. Both with brown eyes and hair, a dusting of freckles to each. Mr. Franklin, though, appeared to be not quite twenty.

"Tell me, is it you or your sister who is older?" John asked.

Mr. Franklin chuckled. "If you want to ask my sister's age, let me tell you, she is young enough."

"I meant no disrespect, sir." The smoke from Mr. Franklin's cigar wafted closer, and John suppressed a cough. He didn't care for the things.

"When we discuss terms of a dowry, we can discuss her age." A generous smile appeared on the young man's face.

John squirmed in his seat. How had he gone from sitting next to a young lady to discussing her dowry with her brother? Sometimes, when negotiating at the Exchange, he wanted something so badly that he would take whatever terms were offered, and that's what it felt like was happening. He needed to escape, and he would endure any conversation necessary to facilitate that.

"Of course, sir," he said. When were they going to the drawing room? He downed his port. "Excuse me." He went to find the chamber pot in the corner.

When the last cigar had been extinguished, the men joined the ladies in the drawing room. Lady Lydia was nearest to the door, entertaining Lady Isabelle, Miss Franklin, Miss Colby, and Mrs. Bartles.

"I should think my mother and I will exchange rooms so that she may dote over my sister even in her sleep," Lady Lydia said in jest.

The ladies tittered with amusement, muted because of the men's entrance. John was aware of what an interruption he and the others were on a world that must seem far easier without them.

Bess sat on the sofa with Lady Hackett, her jaw clamped shut and her shoulders slumped. She looked both uncomfortable and bored. As much as he wanted to go save her, he needed to talk to Lady Lydia. The need to see her tomorrow morning clawed at him.

"Lady Lydia, Lady Isabelle, Mrs. Bartles, Miss

Colby, Miss Franklin," he greeted all of them. Mrs. Bartles alone was the woman who blushed. It hadn't been long ago that married women—though with dead husbands, not seafaring ones—were his specialty. "*Tomorrow* will be quite a day," he said.

Lady Lydia's expression sharpened; she looked almost hawkish.

"Yes, the Exhibition!" Mrs. Bartles said. "I hope we shan't be too shocked."

"I, for one, hope it is shocking," Lady Isabelle said. "It is supposed to be pugilism, after all. If it weren't shocking, we'd all be doing it before tea."

"Excellent point," Lady Lydia commented. "But I agree, *tomorrow* will be quite the day."

John did his best not to look too interested.

"Perhaps, but aren't you looking forward to the ball more?" Mrs. Bartles asked. "What with the music and the dancing?"

"But I've been to a ball," Miss Franklin said. "I've not ever been to a boxing match."

"And a woman, too!" Lady Isabelle said. "Have you ever heard of something more unnatural? I mean, just look at her."

John's temper flared. There wasn't anything unnatural about Bess. Nor about Lydia. The pampered, coddled girl in front of him didn't know the first thing about survival, about the world.

Still, they all turned to watch Bess and Lady Hackett.

"I think she's attractive in her own way," Miss Franklin said. "Not every woman has the same kind of beauty."

"Well said, Miss Franklin," John said through gritted teeth.

"Just so," Lady Lydia added.

"Oh, come now, Mr. Arthur," Lady Isabelle prodded. "You must have an eye for women's beauty, do you not? You stand amongst five women, have you not already ranked us?"

"I beg your pardon?" John felt like the walls were closing in.

"If number one is the most beautiful, and number four is the least, which of us is first?" Lady Isabelle asked in a coy tone.

"Oh, I don't like this game," whispered Miss Colby.

"Well," he cleared his throat. Lady Lydia's gaze was like the weight of a stone on him. "I find that beauty changes as a person gets acquainted. And thus, I would say that the most beautiful woman..." He paused for dramatic effect. Lady Isabelle was about ready to fall over herself in hopes of being named number one, while he could feel Lady Lydia withdrawing in disgust. "Would be a woman I know well and respect. And in that, I cannot say a more beautiful woman exists than my sister, Pearl."

Miss Franklin chuckled, and even Lady Lydia gave a satisfied laugh. Lady Isabelle huffed. "But your sister isn't a part of our group."

"Then it would have to be Bess, since we've known each other since childhood."

"You have?" Miss Franklin asked, wide-eyed.

Conversation turned towards how long he and Bess had known each other, and fighting in general. Lady Isabelle lost interest in her quest for compliments. Eventually, a footman appeared with a tray full of candles so that the ladies could retire.

*Tomorrow*, she'd said. They had at least tomorrow.

"I APOLOGIZE, CHARLOTTE," LYDIA SAID AS THEY crept down the hallway. The overcast morning made it seem as if they were sneaking out of their rooms at midnight and not merely going down to breakfast.

"Not to worry, my lady," Charlotte said, stifling a yawn. "I've worn my thickest stockings and I have a book."

"Good. I'll meet up with you after I've breakfasted. I won't be long." She'd bound her breasts beneath her stays, just in case they would actually spar. The idea of him undoing her laces was one she liked. The idea that his fingers might brush her skin, a soft touch on her shoulder blade, or tucking up a wisp of her hair on the nape of her neck, she couldn't think of anything else.

"The weather doesn't look promising," Charlotte said.

Lydia rushed through a piece of toast and nibbled on a bit of ham. Bess had always counseled her to eat a little before meeting, just not too much.

"Will you go riding, my lady?" Peters asked, jolting Lydia out of her speedy reverie.

"Of course, yes," Lydia answered, willing herself to slow down.

"May I recommend that you either forego your exercise this morning or postpone until the afternoon? The weather may not cooperate." The butler bowed.

"Thank you for your advice, but I think I will still try to get out before the rain." Lydia threw down the last swallow of tea and hurried back to the foyer, meeting back up with Charlotte. They bustled their way to the stables, but even before arriving, fat raindrops fell all around.

The irrefutable evidence of a spoiled morning slowed Lydia. She huffed in frustration. "No!" she insisted at the sky.

Charlotte watched with her hands clasped in front of her. When Lydia was done with her stomping, Charlotte spoke. "I'm sorry my lady. We should go back to the house. We can't have both you and Lady Agnes ill. Your mother wouldn't survive it."

"My mother would welcome any effort to dampen my spirits." Lydia trudged back towards the house, the raindrops falling faster and faster.

"That's not true," Charlotte protested.

Lydia threw a backward glance at the trees. For a moment, she thought she saw Mr. Arthur standing in the copse, watching her retreat.

❧

THE MORNING HAD BEEN DREARY. RAIN CLATTERED on the windows. Lydia excused herself to go down to the drawing room, in search of other entertainment besides Charlotte reading aloud and Agnes's embroidery. The room was stuffy with heat and stillness while outside the rain continued, heedless.

And Lydia meant to go to the drawing room. She meant to find the other young ladies and a card game or charades or something to do that was suitable. But on her way there, she realized it might be interesting to see how the Orangery was set up. Since the Exhibition was to be held that night after dinner, would there be a ring marked out? Or would it be more like the stage shows they held at Drury Lane, where James had taken her to see Molineaux before he retired?

When she entered, she found chairs lined up in one half of the room and an undressed Mr. Arthur in the other. There were only a few candles lit, and while an Orangery ought to be bright with all the windows, the rain kept the light muted. He shadowboxed, and the candles traced his hard lines. Each hard jab threw sweat into the air, which made it look as if he radiated light. It fairly stopped her heart.

Maybe it wouldn't matter to him that she was broken. Perhaps a man like him, a man of hardship and gain, he could see past such ruin. The attention he gave to his sister was admirable. And his friendship with Bess—a lifelong friendship with a woman! He was a different sort of man: respectful, even if he wasn't truly respectable in the social sense. But she preferred the former over the latter anyhow. She moved through the chairs, unable to keep her eyes off of him.

Her dress caught a chair and the legs dragged against the wood floor, causing Mr. Arthur to look up from his exercise. When he saw her, he broke into a grin. A real grin, full of teeth and effervescence. The look people give when they are truly excited to see someone. It made her tingle to think he wanted to see her.

Maybe, after everything was over with Hackett, maybe there was space for Mr. Arthur in her hermitage out in the country. She wouldn't have to wait to marry off Agnes, although a match might be more difficult given Lydia's marriage—no, she needed to stop. Her plans were tripping ahead of her. She chided herself to enjoy the moment. They were in the country, where rules were relaxed. He was a charming man, and she could just be herself. That would be enough.

"Lady Lydia," he said, sweeping into a bow. An arc of sweat followed his gesture. She should think him dirty or somehow disgusting, but she didn't. The evidence of his hard work drew her across the room, her feet propelling her with a will of their own.

"I didn't think I would find you here," she said. "But I'm glad I did."

"I saw you this morning," he said, closing the distance between them.

"I tried," she said. He was close enough to touch.

Heat radiated off of him. It should be overwhelming, but it wasn't. She reveled in it. There were so many *shoulds* in her life.

"Me too," he said.

"I thought I saw you," she said. "I didn't want to go back to the house."

"Just because of the lessons?" He searched her face, his gaze lingering on her mouth, and while she knew she shouldn't invite him in any way, she couldn't help but moisten her lips.

"No," she said, being honest. Because she was done with *should*.

"Good," he said, and his hands surrounded her face, pulling her towards him, kissing her lips.

Her hands landed on his chest, and she knew she shouldn't get too close—his smell would be on her for the rest of the day, marked. But she kissed him in return. Her thoughts were lost and she pushed forward, reached her arms up around his neck, his body slick. He turned and walked her backwards, his lips fluttering now to her nose, her cheek, her jaw. Being with him felt like drinking too much wine.

"The only good thing about this place," he said as he nipped at her with kisses, "is you. I couldn't stand being here without you."

"I couldn't agree more," she said, gasping when she collided with the wall. His hands were all over her, slipping under her derriere, pulling and kneading. "Would you have done this in the wood?"

"'Course not," he said. "We had a lesson to complete."

Before she could laugh, he covered her mouth with his. He pulled her leg up, and her dress tore. The sound was the bucket of cold water they both needed.

He pulled back, releasing her leg gently to the ground. His expression was full of shock.

Her heart thudded in her chest. She could retreat

up the stairs quickly and Charlotte could have it mended. She had plenty of others to wear.

"I beg your forgiveness," he said, backing away. "I don't know what came over me."

Lydia pushed herself off the wall, trying to sort through the behavior such an occasion might need. Mr. Arthur was all formality again.

"No need," she said, unable to muster her usual false confidence.

"I promised not to touch you." He hung his head. "My blood was up, and it isn't an excuse, it's a reason. Shite. I promised."

"And last time I saw you, I gave you permission," Lydia reminded him gently. She moved towards him again, all those *shoulds* falling away in favor of what she actually wanted. What she wanted was to feel good. To feel wanted. And though she was not clear on a great deal of other things, she knew John Arthur wanted her.

"But still. It's important." He searched her face. "Lydia, I would never hurt you. Never."

Her hands landed on his chest, and he wrapped his arms around her shoulders. "I believe you."

"I would marry you if we were discovered."

She grimaced. Could she have one proposal that wasn't conditional? One proposal that didn't have an *if* in it. Sebastian would marry her *if* she were going to end up on the shelf. James had once said he would marry her *if* she were shamed by their revenge. And now Mr. Arthur would marry her *if* they were discovered. "That's not quite the worst proposal I've ever had, but it's close."

At least he had the decency to look abashed. "I want you to know that I would do the gentlemanly thing even though I'm not an actual gentleman."

Because it all came back to that. She just wanted it to be about her, no titles or responsibilities, and just him, no pasts, no rankings. She bent her head and rested it on his chin. He kissed the top of her head. It was maybe the nicest kiss she'd ever received.

"I should go and have my maid fix my dress."

They stood for a moment, she tucked into him. It felt safe and right. Lust was still zinging through her—she'd heard enough from the widows to know that's what it was—this comfort she felt with him was the reason why she could feel the lust as well. She needed both. It made her want to cry, and she wasn't a woman who did.

Finally, she extracted herself from him. His face was etched with concern, but he let her step out of his arms. He nodded and she turned, making her way towards the chairs and the door. But nothing felt right now. She wanted all of those things they had been doing earlier—the holding, but also the desperate hands roaming all over. But that silly rip was a reminder of what lines they shouldn't cross. *Should*. What a terrible idea.

"I meant what I said," he called after her. "About this place. You are the only good thing here."

She turned. "I meant it too. And just so you know, I like breaking rules with you."

"You like it?"

"I hate doing what I'm supposed to." She fisted some of the fabric of her dress, waiting for him to respond.

"In that case," he said, charging after her, tossing a chair out of the way. She laughed, she couldn't help it, and again he swept her up. This time, it was her hands about his face. He sank down in one of the chairs, pulling her onto his lap. She could feel the hardness of him against her thigh.

"This—this is all I want to do with the rest of my life," he breathed as she took her turn with exploratory kisses. Such a perfect space between his ear and his square jaw to fit her lips. He tasted like salt.

"Your clients will be most disappointed," she murmured.

"If they knew you, they would understand completely." His arms snaked around her, pulling her closer. "I feel like an opium-eater, and you are the opium."

"Is that a compliment?"

He licked the underside of her jaw. "If you knew the indecent thoughts rioting in my mind, my lady, you would understand the compliment that it is."

This time it was she who took his mouth, and without understanding how or why, she opened her lips and let her tongue explore his. He returned the gesture, his hands flat against the outside of her thigh.

"I want to pull your dress up, but I won't," he panted.

"Because you shouldn't?" she teased.

"I really shouldn't."

She began pulling her dress up, showing her stockinged ankles, and then her calves. He gripped her ankle, circling his hand around it. He kissed her again, his hand inching slowly upwards, stopping when he reached her knee.

She scrabbled at her hem, pulling high, exposing more flesh. All rational thought had left her brain. When she thought she wanted to feel good, she'd never dreamed she could feel this good. That her body could make her feel so perfect, and not broken in the least.

"You have to stop," he said, gasping. "I'll spend myself in my trousers otherwise."

"So soon?" she asked, mocking.

His face darkened. "Don't test me, my lady. I

know all sorts of ways to make you scream even after I spend myself."

She had no experience in this arena, but she knew he didn't say things unless they were true. The idea of his attempts made her mind go blank. As she sat dumbfounded, he kissed her neck and the hollow between her collarbones. And then he trailed down lower, grunting in frustration when he got to the neckline of her dress. But he was unwilling to move his hand from her knee.

"We can't be doing this," he said.

"Why not?" she asked. This was the only thing she wanted to do. The dinner, the Exhibition, the ball—all of it could be wiped off the schedule so far as she was concerned.

"I have to perform tonight. I need to keep my edge."

"You don't need an edge with Bess," she protested.

"No, not for Bess. For Denby. I don't like him, and I don't know what he wants." He punctuated his sentence with kisses along her clavicle.

But as soon as he mentioned Denby, the heat in her body cooled.

"So, you have to go. For the sake of pugilism." He raised his red-gold head.

She slid off his lap, and he groaned softly as she did so. "For the sake of your art."

"You look a proper wanton, you know."

Posing as if in a tableau, she gave him an innocent smile. "So, I ought to sneak back upstairs with my torn dress and disheveled coif?"

He stood, his chest flushed and a decided strain in his trousers. He caught her looking and gave a mischievous grin. "But then again. Why should I limit you? Have a seat, my lady."

"Oh?" She complied, sitting in the chair they had

just occupied, smoothing her skirts over her lap. The expression he wore made her curious.

He went to his knees in front of her. "Stop me if you're uncomfortable."

Taking the hem of her silk dress in both hands, he began to roll it, catching the cotton petticoat as well. Slowly, her ankles were revealed, then her calves, then her knees. He took a moment to run his hand along what he had found. He glanced up, looking for her approval. Her lips were parted, and she could barely manage to nod her head. She'd never felt desire like this before. The clear, imminent opportunity for pleasure.

He grinned, continuing his task, now catching up the hem of her chemise as he exposed more and more of her. Letting go of the fabric, he ran the flat of his palms along either side of her legs. "I wish to make you happy."

Her mouth opened, but no words came out. The air of the Orangery was cool on her skin. He pressed a kiss on the inside of her knee and she opened her legs for him. He scooted forward, lifting one of her legs to hook it over his shoulder. He pressed another hot kiss to the inside of her thigh. It was shameless. It was reckless. It was the most beautiful moment of her life.

"Would you like me to continue?" he asked.

All she could manage was a nod. Another kiss on her thigh, trailing up and up. Until she could feel his breath between her legs. It was a sensation unlike any other. One she was wholly unprepared for.

"Would you like me to continue?" he repeated.

She swore.

He pressed a firm kiss against her apex, a place she didn't have words for. "Language, my lady," he chastened her.

She felt every word he spoke. Every breath was a

new, overpowering pleasure. And then she felt something stronger. Still soft, still dreamy and beautiful, but coalescing into a pattern, a pace.

Her hands gripped the edge of the chair. Her muscles ached with tension. "How—"

He broke off and lifted his head.

She panicked. "Bloody hell, keep going."

He laughed and buried himself amidst her skirts once again. This time the pressure intensified. Her pulse raced faster. Every muscle in her body was tensed. She did her best to keep her legs open, trying not to crush John, wanting him to continue forever if she could withstand it. Her hand went to his head, pushing him harder and faster. He complied, and it was like there was humming inside her head, a noise that was like a vibrating piece of glass just before it shattered.

And then it did.

She pitched forward, out of breath, her muscles clenched as pleasure coursed through her. John's ministrations ebbed, her self-control returning. The light shifted in the Orangery, brightening the corners of the room, and catching John's reddish gold hair.

"Have you a handkerchief, my lady?" he asked.

She nodded, fumbling in her pocket to extract one. John wiped his face and then turned back to her nether parts, cleaning her.

"You still look as though you've been thoroughly kissed," he said, rolling her skirts back down to her ankles.

"Because it's the truth." She should hide herself, of course, be ashamed, slink away, but she didn't feel ashamed. In fact, part of her wanted to parade around in the evidence of her wantonness. This was how to be properly ruined. They could take their Almack's waivers and hang. She'd rather spend a lifetime in the Orangery with John Arthur.

"You really ought to go before someone sees you." He stood and offered her his hand.

"You expect me to stand after that?" Her legs had all the structural integrity of *blancmange*.

"Don't worry. I'm good for a follow-up match." He leaned in and kissed her cheek. "In the woods tomorrow. It's the best part of my day."

# 10

The Orangery looked different in the twilight. The last fingers of purple sky lingered on the horizon, soon to fade into black. Beeswax candles lit the room, casting dark shadows behind them. John had taken dinner in his room, a relief to not stare at Lady Lydia from across the table. Even he had been shocked at his boldness that afternoon. But something about her seeking him out, and the timing of him being at the height of his exercise, he couldn't see straight when she was around.

"Well?" Bess asked as she strolled in. She held out her arms, displaying the new dress Denby had gotten her. It was a strange dark-blue affair, recalling the samurai robes he'd seen in a few of his trade magazines. These sleeves were slimmer, conforming to the shape of her arm, but roomy in the shoulders, which would give her space to throw punches and block effectively.

The skirt was, well—not a skirt. It was this aspect that reminded John of the images of the samurai from Japan. The skirt was made up of two extremely wide legs. When Bess stood straight, she appeared to be wearing a dress. When she dropped into her fighting stance, it was clear that she wore loose trousers.

"How's it feel?" John asked.

Bess approached, swinging her arms across her chest, loosening up her muscles. "So far, so good."

"Have you fought in it yet?" he asked.

Bess shook her head. "It only just arrived," she said.

John feinted towards her, reaching out to catch her belly with a body shot. Bess blocked it with ease, the wide legs billowing as she danced backwards.

"Seems to work," he said.

"Of course it works," Denby said, entering the Orangery. He closed the doors behind him.

"My lord," John acknowledged him with a short bow.

"I researched many fighting cultures around the world," Denby continued. "Though most seemed to keep combatants naked."

John noted that Bess didn't meet Denby's eyes for that remark.

"Doff the togs and grease up," John said. "You make a hell of a target."

Denby countered his remark. "Greco-Roman. I know."

Something protective in John roared to life. He wanted to get into the smug little man's face and see how much he knew about fighting. But no, it was clear that wasn't how the lord operated. He didn't use the brute force that John and Bess understood. This man used different methods of manipulation to make people dance for his pleasure. And sure enough, what were they about to do? Dance for their betters.

But he was proud of his prizefighting past. So, let them look. Let those young ladies ogle and scandalize their chaperones. Let Lydia ogle. He wanted her to think of him with pride, to think of him as her man as he fought. If he thought about their afternoon together, he couldn't be in public.

She had no idea the amount of control he'd exerted to keep his hands where they were. The sound of the dress tearing had scared her, but it had awoken a fierceness in him. He wanted to keep tearing, keep pawing at her, rip her clothes off and claim her all at once. But he'd made a promise, and even though she'd given permissions, he knew better.

There was something in her, warring, for her attention. He'd known others like that, brooding and without peace. Granted, they'd been men, but it seemed like the philosophy ought to be the same. The best strategy he'd found was to knock on the door to whatever the scary bit was, and then wait. If they opened the door, stand aside. If they didn't, wait some more, and then knock again.

He'd knocked.

Dear God, he wanted to knock some more. And more. And more. He'd meant it when he said that's how he wanted to spend the rest of his life. Yes, his face buried in her hair, his hands up her skirts. Worse things than that.

His body was starting to react again, so he glanced over at Denby. He hated him. The man was barking instructions at Bess. And he hated how Bess just averted her eyes and obeyed, like a mastiff on a lead. It was humiliating. So much power, so much strength inside her, and yet she agreed to a collar.

The doors opened and Peters announced the crowd. The ladies filed in, a few still tittering behind gloved hands. The men joined them, many still with glasses of port in their hands. Lydia sat front and center, Count Denisov to her right, and Lady Isabelle after him. Lord Hackett sat on Lydia's left, and Lady Hackett next to him. Miss Franklin sat in the second row, next to her brother and Mrs. Bartles and Miss Colby and her brother.

John backed himself into the far corner, where a small stool was set. He still wore his coat and waistcoat. He'd taken off his pocket watch and cufflinks to make the transition from gentleman to boxer easier.

Denby positioned himself center stage. The chairs were set in a semicircle, as there weren't enough to be on all sides of them. Bess sat on a stool in the opposite corner, her face neutral. Her new garment was draped in such a way that it appeared as a dress. This would no doubt be part of Denby's program, as the entire thing seemed designed to show his prowess, despite his complete lack of it.

The lord greeted them, holding up his arms to garner their attention. "Ladies and gentlemen, every person should witness a pugilistic display at least once. It is the most English of all sports, where a fighter is honest and true, his courage displayed with nobility."

John couldn't listen anymore as Denby droned on with his ridiculous sentiments, so he watched Lydia's face instead. She was beautiful in red. Her dark hair seemed to pick up the richer tones, and her eyes became blue. The tiny mark next to her eye, the star-shaped one, became nothing but a dot at this distance.

She met John's gaze, and it fueled him. He was her man, no different than if they lived in a little garret in Paddington. Except much less gin. And fewer pigs.

John grinned back. If anyone could turn a sobered-down boxing show into an actual event, he could. It would have been better if Caulie and Basil were here, but he and Bess could make do.

Denby introduced Bess. She stood, making her way to the center, her skirt parting into two legs as she walked. The ladies gasped at such a garment. Denby was pleased by the reaction, standing taller, though still comically small next to Bess.

Pointing out innovations in the garment, Denby had Bess move and pose in different manners. He gave no thought to her modesty when he touched her inseam or ran his finger along the low neckline. If he'd seen a man do that on the streets, John would have no qualm challenging him to a fight, though Bess wouldn't have allowed it in the first place. She took care of planting all her own facers.

Fans began to flutter amongst the ladies, perhaps a reaction to the indelicate touching. John didn't like that the lord treated Bess like a doll. He risked a glance at Lydia, whose expression was distant and stony.

After Denby detailed these innovations, in which he didn't bother to downplay his own genius, he set up opposite Bess. The two of them demonstrated some basic moves where Bess was at the disadvantage. Not a situation that would occur naturally. John hoped everyone in the audience knew that.

As he demonstrated, Denby reasoned out Bess's apparent disadvantages to the crowd: "As a woman, she is weaker than any man."

A statement that was patently false. Bess was weaker than some men out there, but not many. Certainly not a spalpeen like Denby.

Denby wore his shirt bloused loosely, still in a state of undress without a waistcoat and bare sleeves, but nothing to upset the crowd. If this were an actual fight, and Denby didn't have the decency to disrobe, John would pull the back of the shirt up over his head, blinding him with it and punching him until he passed out or choked on his own blood. The thought alone cheered him.

Bess didn't even look warmed up. She still had no color in her cheeks and continued to breathe through her nose, exerting about as much strain as she would while standing in line at a market. Finally, Denby beckoned John.

"For your delight, we have Mister John Arthur, an accomplished pugilist. Anyone reading Mr. Egan's accounts will be familiar with his successes. He and Miss Bess Abbott will demonstrate as I narrate." Denby motioned to John again. "The first of the act is always what is termed by the Fancy as 'peeling.'"

John got off his stool slowly, stretching like a cat. He had always been Corinthian John, understated and polite during fights, but a peacock of a man nonetheless. But this wasn't a fight, this was a show. He had typically played the straight man, letting his opponent ham it up for the crowd as he had stared frowning at the antics.

Stealing a look at Bess to see if she knew what he was up to, John licked his lips and yawned with an exaggerated stretch. A twitch of a smile crossed Bess's face. She knew. Of course she knew.

"Get on with it," Denby hissed at him.

John flung his arms back, peeling off his coat. He flexed his arms as he did so, knowing his biceps would show through the soft cambric shirt. The coat shed, draped over the stool, John started forward, then stopped as if he remembered something quite important. He unbuttoned his waistcoat, peeling that off as well.

Denby gave an exasperated sigh. "Theatrics have long been a part of boxing phenomena," Denby explained to the crowd, taking back control of the show. "But due to the tender company, we have taken the animalistic components out of tonight's Exhibition."

So, the man wanted to own this show?

John strode forward, his swagger exaggerated. "Boxing can be a sport of fools or a sport of gentleman," John said. It wasn't until right then that he realized he was also an entire head taller than Denby. He hammed it up for the crowd. Denby's hands curled into fists, not that John cared.

"Boxing is a sport where a man can display his masculinity by not shifting about too much, taking what he is owed with aplomb," Denby protested, his voice pitching higher.

"The most important aspect of boxing is to prevent oneself from getting hurt," John said, sliding his gaze over to Denby. "Everyone has a plan until they get hit in the face."

He stepped over to Bess, who was waiting for her role to be revealed. "Bess, er, Miss Abbott," he asked, addressing her before the crowd. "What would you do if you faced an opponent dressed as I am?"

Bess grinned, stifling a laugh. "I'd pull his shirt up over his nob and punch until my hand hurt."

John turned back to the audience, smiling. "Exactly." So, John untucked his cambric shirt from his breeches and pulled it off over his head. The crowd murmured and tittered in response. John looked at Lydia, who looked about to laugh, though perhaps those eyes were darkened with lust?

John tossed the shirt to Denby. He dropped his high-class accent. "'Ere you go, mate."

---

SHE'D TEASE HIM ABOUT THAT LATER. CONSIDERING the appreciative murmurs around her, apparently the young ladies were not so much shocked as intrigued by the man's undress.

Bess looked more relaxed now that John had started talking. Her shoulders weren't as stiff, and she was engaging John in conversation, her expression lively. When Denby had shown off Bess's garment to the audience, Lydia had barely enough control to sit still as he traced areas of her body that were totally unsuitable for a man to touch in public.

Though John had touched Lydia in exactly those places, in this exact room, earlier in the day. But they had been alone, and she'd very much appreciated his exploration.

"Boxing in its purest form is punching," John said. He threw a one-two combination at Bess, slower than his normal rate, and Bess blocked appropriately. "But in the sweet science of pugilism, a number of other things are within a fighter's arsenal, such as hair pulling."

Bess reached over and ran her fingers through John's short hair, shining like copper in the candlelight. She did her best to grab a handful, but John was able to duck out of the way.

"It might not be fashionable, but it saves me a bit of pain," John said, dancing away from Bess as she advanced. He used the length of the room, far larger than a standard ring.

"You might say that's a bit too much freedom," Bess said.

Lydia was surprised that Bess decided to talk, but John did somehow manage to put everyone at ease. They were childhood friends, Bess and John, so they had a connection unlike anyone else's. A pang of jealousy flooded Lydia, but she tamped it down.

"But in an actual match, we are confined to an eight-foot square," Bess continued.

"'Ow big is that?" John asked in a gutter accent.

Bess went to Lady Hackett first. "My lady, would you mind helping me for a moment?"

"Of course," Lady Hackett said, rising from her

seat, taking Bess's hand as if the fighter were a man escorting her onto the dance floor.

Bess also pulled Lady Isabelle, Count Denisov, and Mr. Leeds up, using the four of them to mark out an eight-foot square.

"That's not very much room," John protested as Bess pushed him inside the square.

The audience and four posts laughed, even Count Denisov. Now that the fighters had taken over the show, Lydia looked around to find Denby sitting on one of the corner stools, sulking.

"Now you can't just run away from me," Bess said, chastising John as if he were a small child.

Everyone laughed. The whole audience leaned forward. Lydia felt something on her thigh, and at first, she had the odd idea that perhaps it was a bug. They were in the Orangery, after all, and it seemed reasonable. She brushed her hand across the offending pressure, only to find it was a hand.

Not knowing what to do, what with people everywhere, Lydia froze. Lord Hackett was to her left. A quick glance down confirmed it to be his hand. How was it that when John did this, it was all she could do to keep herself from dragging him to the bedroom, but now she felt as if she might vomit? Her breath caught and she suddenly felt cold all over.

The show continued on, Bess acting stern and John preening and dancing away from any of the lazy jabs Bess threw at him.

"Don't pout, Lord Denby," John called. "Footwork has long been called a foreigners' game, underhanded and tricky. But it ain't tricky not to get levelled by a facer."

No one else noticed Lord Hackett's hand roaming her leg. Her breath came up short as if Bess had landed a fist.

There was nothing anyone else would do. She brushed the hand away again.

The hand returned, halfway up her thigh. This time, instead of freezing her up into inaction, she became angry. She glanced down, found the fat wrist, and plucked it off, tossing it back into Lord Hackett's lap.

Lydia was quite content to continue sitting where she was, as long as she remained unmolested. But it wasn't long until the hand returned, this time squeezing her leg hard. Without thinking, she shot her arm out, thumping Lord Hackett square in the chest. Finally, her body was responding, as if she had been blocked up in ice. But no longer.

The thump to Lord Hackett was enough to knock the wind out of him, and he coughed. She stood, willing the rising panic to dissipate. The dark waters pulled at her legs, sucked at her chest, threatening to swallow her. She pushed the feeling aside, as she always had, but it would not be so easily vanquished. The moments with John had made her feel light, as if that panic might not overtake her ever again, but now she knew the freedom she'd felt was just temporary. This was her life. Her past. What a fool to think otherwise.

She was marked. And it hadn't been by John. It had been long ago, and Hackett knew it.

As she made her way towards the double doors, she glanced back at the fight. John watched her, glancing between Lydia and Lord Hackett, a bewildered look flashing briefly across his face.

She hurried to her room, checking behind her every few steps to guarantee that Lord Hackett wasn't following. Panic was still inside of her, still frantic, still sucking at her bones, squeezing from all sides. The sconces were lit in the hallway, keeping her sane until she got to her room.

Memories that she would give anything to forget flooded her now: the sour smell of wine mixed with cigar smoke on a man's hot breath, his pores sweating stale alcohol. The fragmented shadows that fell across the nursery floor as he lay on top of her. The numb scrambling of cold fingers pulling up her nightdress, her skin warm from sleep.

She shouldn't have come to the country. With so many intervening years, why would her body betray her like this? Cold sweat persisted under her arms and the small of her back. Her chest felt compressed, as if she couldn't get enough air.

As she approached her door, she could hear Charlotte humming.

"My lady," Charlotte said, hopping up to give a small curtsy. She held in her lap Lydia's dress and a thin needle, making repairs. Agnes was still in bed, reading. Their mother sat by the fire, working on embroidering a chemise.

"You're back so early. Is the Exhibition over?" Agnes asked, closing her book. Charlotte stopped humming.

"Not yet. I just had to leave." Everything was fine. She was a grown woman with privilege and position; none dared touch her. She was inviolable, and she repeated that to herself again and again. Inviolable.

"Did something happen? Did that man—" Her mother's voice began to take a sharper edge.

"No, everything is fine. I'm just starting to get a megrim. Perhaps too much wine."

Agnes threw open the blankets to her bed. "We're quite cozy here."

❦

THE APPLAUSE SURPRISED HIM AND BESS. THEY both had worked up a light sweat, and while they had each taken some swings, none of the blows hit with any force. It was play-acting, like they had as children. They fought on a street corner, and depending on the audience, sometimes John won, putting Bess "in her place." Other times, Bess won, triumphing over a boy who would presume to inflict violence on a girl. Not that Bess was always recognized as a girl.

"The most English of sports," Lord Denby announced as his final statement to the crowd.

"Forgetting Molineaux," Bess whispered to John.

"And whoever else isn't English enough for that bastard," John whispered back, gathering up his shirt.

Lady Isabelle approached them, her eyes darting in all directions but returning again and again to his naked torso. She had made her interest plain in her eyes, taking him in as he pulled his shirt back on over his head. Strange how he had seen that look on Lydia's face and welcomed it, but on Lady Isabelle, it seemed, well, crass.

The forwardness made him look away from her ringlet-framed face. Count Denisov congratulated Lord Denby in another corner of the room. Miss Franklin, Miss Colby, and Mrs. Bartles all spoke with Bess. The other gentlemen stood chatting amongst themselves in the chairs.

Of course, the moment he turned his attention to donning his waistcoat, Lady Isabelle's eager face was pressed to his shoulder. Normally he thanked the stars when a woman's desire crossed his path. But Lady Isabelle was taken by his pugilist self, the stage persona—to her, he was a prize to be obtained. He didn't like how that felt.

Was that how it felt to be the wealthy daughter of a privileged man? To be seen as a treasure chest full of gold coins and pieces of paper with the word *Lord* writ large across them? But it wasn't her money that made John want Lydia, and it wasn't her status. It was all of the contradictions she embodied. It was her haughty demeanor coupled with her eagerness and perfectionism during their sessions. It was her unabashed physicality, her need to gather up everything around her and squeeze it through her fingers.

And he knew Lydia appreciated him. But was it just as Lady Isabelle did, for his celebrity? Yes, his physicality was part of it, which seemed to likewise captivate Lady Isabelle, but Lydia also seemed to be interested in his intelligence, his accomplishments, his ambition. He was more than just the prize. Or so he hoped.

---

A YELP WOKE HER.

"Agnes?" Lydia called in the dark. She was answered by soft snores. She listened in the dark.

There was movement next door, and the soft thud of someone bumping into furniture. Through the connecting door, she could hear her mother speaking softly but couldn't understand the words. Who would she be talking to? She lit a candle and opened the adjoining door.

Hackett held onto her mother's bed. He had the audacity to look surprised to be found in a woman's bedroom wearing his nightshirt.

"Lord Hackett," Lydia greeted, as if this was a perfectly acceptable scene. No more tendrils of sleep lingered. She was wide awake.

"Lady Lydia," Hackett whispered, tiptoeing towards both her and the bed. "I thought this was your room."

"Get out," hissed her mother. Lydia wasn't certain who she meant, but there was no way she would leave her mother alone in a room with that man.

The panic from earlier in the evening started to rise. Lydia's body went cold. "That's even less of a reason to be here in the middle of the night." Her body went cold. The panic from earlier in the evening started to rise.

Lord Hackett crept closer to her, leaving the anchor of her mother's bed. Her mother lit the candle by her bedside.

"I do hope you realize that with one scream, I can alert the entire household to your presence," Lydia said.

"And I hope you know that should you scream, I will tell everyone you invited me here," he said with a smile.

"I invited you to my mother's room? Or to the room I share with my sister, who has taken ill? Either way, not terribly convincing."

"I heard you say it in the drawing room after dinner the other night! You and your mother had switched rooms!" He looked like an overgrown child, throwing a temper tantrum. The low candlelight caught every poxy crag in his face.

"And you are the low sort who eavesdrops on the conversation of young ladies?" Lydia's voice was thin and pinched, verging on shrill.

Her mother rose out of bed and pulled her wrapper around her. Squaring her shoulders, she thundered out a command as befit a countess. "Remove yourself from this chamber."

"She invited this," he insisted to her mother.

"You putrid little man," Lydia said. She didn't mean to say so, but the idea of his hands on her was more revolting than anything else she could imagine.

Hackett shook his head. "I know what young debutantes like you are up to. Nothing but balls and dresses, and, and..." His voice was hoarse. "And young men."

So here was his fetish: youth and the ideas of frippery. He liked the empty-headed, the pleasure-seekers, and he thought her one of them. She had cultivated the reputation for several years, so she couldn't blame his perception.

"I saw you leave the Orangery today with your reddened lips. Only loose favors make a young woman look like that!"

Her mother gave her a sharp look.

"Even if that were true," Lydia said, "it doesn't mean I would bestow favors on a poverty-stricken, pox-marked pedophile like you."

"Do you not see the beeswax candles?" he sputtered. "The servants in livery? The fine meals?"

"Bait for a husband for Lady Isabelle," Lydia said. "Clever, I suppose, in a very ordinary sort of way. Seems silly for a man like you to pin his hopes on his daughter."

"You don't know what you are saying, you stupid chit." His expression lost all traces of lechery. "I'd thought to do you a favor by warming up the ice between your legs, but now I see it's an impossible task." He grabbed the candle from the dressing table and waddled out, a great swaying ghost in his nightshirt.

Her mother hurried over and turned the key in the lock.

Lydia began to shake. "Are you well?" Lydia asked her mother. If she could focus on something else, anything other than herself and the quickening panic that was sucking all around her, she could stave it off.

Her mother staggered back to the bed. By the light of only two small candles, Lydia saw tears streaming down her mother's cheeks.

"Nothing happened," Lydia soothed her, barely

quelling the shaking of her own hands. "See? All is well."

She sniffed now that she was caught in her tears. "But he was going to—"

"He thought he could, but he didn't. I'm safe, you're safe." Lydia forced herself to keep the softer tone. She wanted out of here, out of this house. The darkness threatened to overtake her, press in on her chest, and pull her down into hell.

"Is Agnes still asleep?" her mother asked.

Lydia turned to see Agnes approach the adjoining door. "I'm here," she said.

Her mother nodded and exhaled a shaky breath. "We must leave."

"Tonight?" Agnes asked.

Lydia was relieved. Her skin prickled and crawled. She wanted to be home, and in the bath. Her teeth chattered, but she clamped her jaw shut.

"I'll wake Charlotte," Agnes volunteered.

"I'll start packing," Lydia said.

Not that Lydia had ever packed anything in her life, but if there was ever a moment to try, this was it.

There was a soft knocking on the door. Her mother stared at her, eyes wide with terror.

"He can't hurt us," Lydia said, creeping towards the door. Her heart beat wildly. She turned the key in the lock and opened the door.

❧

"I HOPE I'M NOT THAT TERRIFYING," JOHN SAID. He held a candle aloft in the dark hallway.

"What are you doing here?" Lydia asked.

He hadn't thought about how his presence might compromise her. Indeed, he'd only wanted to make sure she was uninjured. He'd been awakened by harsh words wafting up through his fireplace, and in his sleepy fog had not quite comprehended what was happening. After he heard the door slam beneath him, he figured she was at least not in acute danger, so he took time to dress and light a candle before coming down to check on her.

She was more frantic than he'd ever see her. Her hair was in a loose braid, frayed with sleep. Lady Lorian stood behind her, clutching her wrapper like a shield and holding a candle that flickered as she shook.

"May I come in?" he asked, still standing at the threshold.

Lydia didn't bother to look up. The long line of her neck was lit by the meager flame. He couldn't help but appreciate her in this moment, too, beautiful like a painting, all contrasts of light and dark.

"Yes. Please shut the door," Lady Lorian said, motioning him inward.

He raised his eyebrows. When he didn't immediately comply, Lydia sighed in frustration.

"Honestly. With my mother here, our reputations are quite safe," she said.

"I'm prepared to do the honorable thing," he said, entering the room and quietly latching the door behind him.

"The trunk is under the bed. Would you please fetch it, Mr. Arthur?" Lady Lorian asked.

Why would they need trunks at this hour?

"I heard a commotion. My room is just above yours." He got down on his hands and knees and searched for the trunk.

"Thank you for your chivalrous thoughts," Lady Lorian said. "We are fine now."

The heavy trunk was under the bed. He pulled it out and flipped it on its side so it would be ready to receive dresses.

"Here." Lady Lorian shoved an armful of dresses

at him. "Pack these and I'll take care of the dressing table."

"Shouldn't a maid do this? I would hate to ruin any of them," he said, holding the pile of fabric as if it were an armload of week-old fish.

"We're leaving. Be quick about it. Please." Lady Lorian tacked on the courtesy at the end. He noticed her gritted teeth, and her nervous flutter was impossible to miss. Lydia had disappeared back into the other room.

He arranged the dresses as best he could into the trunk. "I can offer my assistance to you in whatever capacity."

"Not to worry," Lady Lorian snapped as she poured her jewelry into small bags.

Lydia appeared in the doorway, holding a candle. She was dressed now, her hair bundled up in a knot. Dark circles sagged under her eyes. "Mama, please let him help."

"What could he do?"

"Protection would be nice," she said. And then her shoulders began to shake. "I can't do it alone."

"I happen to be one of the best bare-knuckled boxers in London," he chirped.

The frantic pace of scooping her jewelry into a small cloth bag slowed.

"See, Mama?"

"And I can cover any costs along the way. If we need to stop at an inn before we reach Town, I would be happy to pay. I can take care of it all."

"That's very kind of you, sir, but I would never impose that upon you." Lady Lorian finished with her small bags.

"It isn't an imposition at all." John wished in that moment that he could ease their pain. Whether it was to allay her fears about money or highwaymen or anything. "I'm happy to do it."

"Please excuse me so that I may dress." Lady Lorian pulled her wrapper even tighter.

"I'll send in Charlotte," Lydia said, ushering John into the adjoining room.

Deuces, she was beautiful. Her dark hair melted into the darkened corners of the room. Her pale face and cherry-colored lips stood out, mesmerizing him. He ached to help put them all at ease.

The maid passed by and the door closed. Lady Agnes packed her trunk on the other side of the room.

"Good evening, Lady Agnes."

"Good evening Mr. Arthur," she returned. "Will you be accompanying us on our journey home? It never hurts to have a prizefighter in the carriage."

"I believe your Lady Mother has accepted my offer."

"Thank you," Lydia said in a low voice.

He grabbed her hand. "You know, *now* if someone came in, your reputation would be ruined."

"Fine," she said. "If we are compromised, I'll marry you. But it's still a terrible proposal."

His heart gave a hard thump in his chest, as if he were in the ring with a nine-foot giant. Had she really said yes to marrying him? Did he actually want to marry anyone? What would Pearl say?

"Don't go planning the wedding just yet," she said.

He laughed. The sound was thin and pitched too high. Was he really thinking about marriage? But if his motivations were so obvious, why wasn't she clear? He didn't want to prod too hard—they were all clearly frantic. Too much questioning and one of them might break down entirely, which would definitely make the situation worse.

"Trunks are packed," Lady Agnes said. "We need to call a carriage."

"When Charlotte is finished dressing Mama, she can go down. We'll get the trunks," Lydia said.

"Why are you fleeing in the middle of the night, Lydia?" he asked softly.

Her eyes flicked up to meet his, and he could tell she was thinking about lying. "Lord Hackett," she said.

When no other explanation came, he assumed the worst. Manners dictated that he not pry, but he also didn't want to think ill of his host. "What about Lord Hackett?" he pressed.

"An unwanted advance, and then an unwanted visit," Lydia said, drifting away from him. She stopped in front of the mirror, made a tsking sound, and began to fuss with her hair.

"He came here?" Those were the voices that had woken him.

"Yes," she said. "Are you surprised?"

The tone in her voice sounded unfavorable. Perhaps he was supposed to be surprised, or perhaps he wasn't. But he felt a familiar surge of heat, that same one he'd felt whenever Pearl had been threatened when they were kids. The feeling when crowds jeered at Bess. The feeling when he'd seen Lydia pushing her way out of the basement last week, trying to escape the angry spectators of the mill.

"Well, yes, I am," he said. There was no perceptible change in her demeanor. "If you had a room alone, that would be unforgivable, but you share the room with your sister, do you not? That seems to be the height of stupidity."

"If the shoe fits," Lady Agnes said.

The maid opened the adjoining door.

"If you're ready, perhaps we should go downstairs," Lady Lorian said from the darkness. "Can you manage the trunk?" Her face was shadowed, her figure a silhouette in the candlelight.

The maid went ahead to rouse a carriage. John made several trips to carry down the trunks, Lydia carrying a candle so that he could see the steps in front of him.

The maid paced in the foyer, wringing her hands. "I'm sorry, my lady," she whispered. "It's taking so long. No one is awake."

"I'd like to go put a note under Miss Franklin's door," Lady Agnes said.

"You can write to her when we get to Town," Lady Lorian said.

"I'll return shortly. Do not leave without me," John said. He took the stairs two at a time. He was not about to let Lydia travel alone at night. While it was unlikely for their carriage to be set upon at this hour, he didn't want to let her out of his sight.

He threw his things together and thundered back down the stairs as quickly as he could. The carriage was ready when he arrived, horses shaking their heads in the cool hours. The driver was tying the trunks down and the maid's valise sat in the dirt, next to be added in the pile. John added his own valise as the driver flicked his eyes up with a question.

Lady Lorian, Lady Agnes, and the maid were already inside the carriage, but Lydia was soothing one of the horses. She murmured apologies to the animal, stroking the horse's nose as he burrowed his head towards her hand.

"If the horse were a cat, his purr would be deafening," John said.

Lydia glanced over her shoulder at him with a smile. "This is a good team. I want them to know how much I appreciate them."

The driver came around, finished with the luggage. John went to the carriage door to help Lydia up.

"This isn't the best move, leaving in the middle of

the night," he said.

"I won't stay another night," she said. "None of us will."

She seemed so matter-of-fact, as if this was a run-of-the-mill assault, nothing more than a nuisance. Her equanimity staggered him.

He hoisted himself into the carriage, pulling up the step. After he tapped on the wall, the horses began the long amble back to London. Lydia sat with her spine straight, adjusting her gloves.

"I will never return," Lady Lorian vowed.

"Even if it isn't Hackett's any longer?" The words fell out of his mouth before he could stop himself. Lydia stiffened beside him. He wasn't normally so loose-lipped. He blamed the early hour.

"What do you mean?" she asked. There was something in her tone that was more than curiosity.

"I mean Hackett has taken a financial hit. But I shouldn't speak of it. I apologize, my lady." If he could have bowed and scraped in the carriage, he would have.

"Speak of it," Lady Agnes commanded.

"The *Europe*?" Lydia breathed.

"You've heard?" He was surprised. Some ladies followed the markets, but most didn't, in his experience. But then again, Lydia surprised him constantly.

"No," she said. "News has come?"

"The morning I left London. A boy came to Garraway's—we have runners from all over, and he told us that news came from Antigua. The *Europe* sank just after leaving port, laden with goods. It won't be in Lloyd's for another week, maybe more. They'll want more confirmation."

"How?" Lady Lorian asked, looking at her daughter with an expression he couldn't read.

"Fire. All the goods were lost."

"Fire," Lydia whispered, sounding almost giddy.

Lady Agnes leaned forward. "And the people?"

"All accounted for."

Lydia squeezed his arm. Lady Agnes slumped back in her seat, breathing a sigh of relief. He searched all three faces, receiving no answers. Why did this ship signify attention?

"Is it over?" Lady Lorian searched her eldest daughter's face.

Lady Lydia nodded and her eyes glassed over. Lady Agnes began to cry softly. Lady Lorian leaned back against the squabs and dabbed at isolated tears before they could roll down her cheeks.

"We have to tell James and Margaret," Lady Agnes said, sniffing.

John offered his handkerchief, hoping he might get at least a wayward glance and an explanation. "Is what over?" he asked.

"When we get back," Lady Lorian said, ignoring him completely. "We'll have them all over for tea."

"And Sebastian," Lydia added.

"I beg your pardon, but—"

"And Mr. Arthur," Lady Agnes added. "So he can know how grateful we are for the messenger."

He glanced around, hating to be left out of the conversation. At least Lady Agnes could remember him, but then he saw Lydia shake her head in dissent.

"I'd be honored to be there," he said. If he could get answers, he'd go anywhere. "I—"

"Don't," she said, cutting him off. "I don't want you to be there."

His pride took a bit of thrashing, but she slipped her arm through his, and slowly, as the miles crept on, and as her mother and sister drifted off, Lydia's head lowered to his shoulder. He'd knock on the door again, a little later, and see what happened. Her breath evened out. He'd never enjoyed silence more.

## 11

Safely ensconced back at her father's London house, Lydia changed out of her travel dress. They had spent most of the hours in the carriage not speaking. After news of the *Europe*, what was there to say? A weight lifted from her chest. Something she'd not realized was so very heavy.

Somewhere before sunrise, with the other ladies steadfastly asleep despite the jostling of the carriage, Lydia found herself leaning on John Arthur's shoulder. Unable to recall the exact way it unfolded, whether she had fallen asleep and woken up there or had been so fatigued by the evening's events that she had needed his physical support, she allowed him to envelop her in his arms.

Strange that such an easy gesture felt so intimate. His arm around her as she dozed, cozied against his chest, felt closer than even their interlude in the Orangery. He protected her when she was too tired to protect herself. Worry and weight evaporated under his care.

But now they were back into London—prematurely, at that—and while she had no social obligations for a few nights, she might have to do some preemptive rumor-mongering. Who knows what Hackett would say in the morning, once it was discovered their party had left?

She dashed off a note to James, Margaret, and Sebastian. She sent for James because he could help keep the gossip in the men's clubs to a minimum, and for Margaret because her practical nature made her an excellent strategist. She should wait for her mother's formal invitation for tea, but she didn't know when that would happen. They should know about their success.

As soon as she sanded the note to Margaret, she took another slip of paper and began writing to John. She hadn't thought it through; she had just followed her impulse. She put down her stylus. Of all the things that John Arthur made her feel, quite against her will, it was safe.

She leaned back in her desk chair, acknowledging that she wanted a moment of quiet indulgence that she would never, ever confess to. He had proposed to her, technically. True, the circumstance was only if they were discovered.

But what if they had been discovered in the Orangery, and she really did have to marry him? Would they be like her parents, proper and formal, never a touch between them in public? Answering to each other not by first names but by titles when others were present? Lydia had caught her parents together before, a giggling sort of love between them, full of teasing and swift caresses, meant to be kept private, even from their daughters.

She tried to picture their domesticity and failed. What she could imagine was waking up in a bed next to him, the maids giggling as they opened the window curtains, seeing both master and mistress in the same room. They would have a sparring room where they would train together, pushing each other's physical limitations. She would staunch the blood on a cut above his eye, he would apply poultices to the bruises along the backs of her thighs, where Bess liked to hit with cudgels. Perhaps they would even open their home to children who didn't have the benefits that Lydia had experienced. Children who had lived like John had lived, exploiting themselves for food and shelter.

Odd that she couldn't imagine children of their own. Surely, John would want a son to carry on his name. Isn't that what all men wanted?

He would need to know that she was broken. And she wasn't ready to tell him that. She frowned as she finished writing. She debated about sending the letter and sanded the ink slowly, giving her time to think. The pact was over. They were freed from their obligation. They could marry. All of them. Even her.

But would he still want her when he knew?

John's back was stiff from the carriage ride. The nap he'd indulged in had not helped his muscles, though his mind felt a little less foggy. In the carriage, those magical dark hours where Lydia had rested against his chest, he'd believed in all sorts of fantasies that could not be true.

There was something about that hour where light touched the darkness, heralding a sunrise yet to come, making all manner of things seem believable. He had believed that the iron-willed woman who slept in his arms could love him. She had sagged against him, her exhaustion clear, and he'd pulled her closer.

The carriage had been chilly, and she'd sought the heat of his body. When she stirred, he had stroked her hair until she stilled again, breathing slow and even. The sun had risen, peeking in through the small carriage windows. Lady Agnes had woken, looking across with alarm at the tableau he made with her sister.

Tensed, John had silently begged her for her silence. He couldn't comprehend why, but the girl merely smiled and closed her eyes again. He thanked the stars.

After changing, John rang the bell for Parsons. Seeing how well Lydia got on with her maid, John began to consider the idea of hiring on a valet. He could use a man in his corner, even if he was paid to be there.

Parsons came to the room with a tray and the mail, anticipating John's needs. He was good, Parsons was, but he seemed to disapprove of John's meager bachelor household. John had taken the townhouse to give Pearl a respectable place to live, but he hadn't quite gotten it up to snuff yet.

As the butler turned to leave, John couldn't help himself. "What would make this household more agreeable, Parsons?"

The butler turned on his heel, a neat gesture that John appreciated for its economy of movement. "Propriety," he said.

John couldn't help but laugh. "And what prescription would you have for propriety?"

"A valet, a footman, a groomsman, a carriage, and a family," Parsons said without hesitation.

"In that order?" John asked.

"Yes sir," he said. "And if there is to be a family, there will be more to hire."

John stared at his tray, a single cup, a small carafe of coffee. The walls of his bedroom were bare and in need of a fresh wallpaper.

"Are you suggesting I start my own family then, Parsons? It seems a bit impudent," John said.

"Impudent or not, you asked my opinion, sir,"

Parsons said.

John laughed. "Let's start with a valet then."

"I will put an advertisement in the paper," Parsons said.

John turned to look him in the eye. "Ask around in your circles, Parsons. I'll pay top rates for a loyal man who doesn't mind getting blood stains out of a shirt."

Parsons actually seemed pleased at the mention of the onerous task. "Consider it done, sir."

The butler departed, allowing John to turn his attention to the letters that had accumulated. He poured his coffee. There was a bill from his tailor and a personal note, the feminine handwriting more familiar. His heart ticked faster as he fumbled with the paper.

*Dear Mr. Arthur,*

*Thank you for your assistance in departing the Hackett residence. I should like to continue our training. Please advise when we may continue.*

*Cordially,*

*L.*

Of course. Training was what she wanted. She'd been accosted by Hackett, and training would help ease her anxiety and fear. She had slept against his chest for hours. Gratified warmth spread through him, though he wouldn't mind an explanation of the conversation that had taken place around him in the carriage. He'd delivered news of the *Europe* but was then promptly ignored. Her closeness was a balm for his ego, but balms didn't last forever.

Could the mention of training just be an excuse to see him? An opportunity for them to be together in a manner that was purely their own? A way for her to tell him whatever this secret was that haunted her entire family?

He tossed away the letter. This was not like him at all. How many affairs had he engaged where letter-writing had been the lifeblood, full of romance and explicit desires? How is it that those took graphic descriptions to bring a smile and the stirrings of desire, but with this one very short directive from Lydia, he was goggle-eyed?

By not dictating a time for training, she invited his response. She wanted him to write to her, which should feel like a triumph. But somehow, it only muddied the waters in his mind. No, he needed to be realistic. He had meant it when he'd said he would marry her if they were discovered. And if he was a more devious man, he could have arranged a discovery in order to force her hand. But that wasn't the type of marriage he wanted; he wasn't so underhanded and disgusting of a man. He needed her to choose him. Not require his services.

His rational mind told him there was no room for romance between a stockbroker—worse, a boxer—and the daughter of an earl. He stood, pulling on his coat. There was still time to go to the Exchange. Perhaps love was better shown than stated. A lady like Lydia was probably unimpressed with flowery speeches and sentiment. Besides, he could do something for her that no other man could. He could make sure that any insurance claim from the *Europe* would be denied.

❧

THE LATE SUN STREAMED INTO THE DRAWING ROOM. The tea service had been amply used, and Lydia was so full of tea she didn't think she'd eat for another few days at least. Margaret had insisted she needed the practice of pouring tea, and so everyone had drunk cup after cup, allowing Margaret to refine her skills. There had been some spills. The only thing Lydia could think of was John's words about refinement and practice, even if it was tea in front of her and not throwing jabs in a wooded glade.

"I hate it and I don't want to do this," Margaret said after spilling Agnes's tea for the umpteenth time.

"Oh, come now," Agnes tutted as she returned to the chair between her mother and Sebastian.

"I told you that Margaret hosting a ladies luncheon was a terrible idea," James said to Lydia as he lounged on the loveseat, kicking one foot onto the arm of the furniture.

Sebastian frowned at James's feet on the furniture. He sat in a high-backed chair turned away from the fireplace, balancing a saucer on his lap as he sipped his tea. Lydia sat in a chair next to him, opposite her mother. Margaret and James shared the loveseat, though James took the lion's share of it.

"You pour very well, Margaret. It'll be fine," Lady Lorian said, trying to soothe Margaret, who was uncharacteristically emotional. Lady Lorian then turned her eyes to her nephew. "Feet off the furniture."

"Why must you always invert your person?" Agnes asked.

"Old injury," he said.

Sebastian narrowed his eyes. "Liar."

"All right, fine. I prefer to sit this way," he said, kicking his leg even higher.

"I would prefer you to sit like a gentleman," Lydia said.

"Oh, sit how you please, James. Who cares? Who cares about any of it?" Margaret said, standing.

Sebastian sprang to his feet as well, out of

politeness. James remained reclined.

Margaret wrung her hands, her long dark hair streaming down her back. She'd arrived perfectly coifed, but in the anxiety of tea-pouring lessons, she'd claimed the pins made her head hurt.

Lydia's mother tutted at the impropriety of having hair unpinned in the presence of two eligible bachelors, but given that Sebastian would not be tempted by Margaret's dark tresses and James was her half-brother, she didn't make any overt protests.

"I don't want to have my staff cleaning whatever is on the bottoms of your boots off the back of my love seat," Lydia said.

"I beg your pardon," her mother said. "It is my staff and my love seat. When you marry, you'll get your own."

Sebastian stifled his chuckle in his teacup. Lydia thought about strangling him with it.

"Margaret, sit back down and try to have a fine time. It's just us," Lydia said. "A tea party isn't nearly as difficult as repairing all of those bizarre artifacts in the basement of that museum, and you do that all day long. Besides, I would like to give you all some good news."

"Finally," James said. "How much tea must a man drink before he can get some information?"

Margaret bent at the waist, resting her hands on her knees. "I can't do this," she panted.

"Are you hyperventilating?" James asked, finally sitting up and putting his feet on the floor.

Lydia leapt up and returned Margaret back to the sofa. James helped guide her in.

"Why does he want me to do this? I don't understand. Elshire and I have never been in public together," Margaret wailed as she collapsed onto the cushions.

"Elshire wants to give you everything he can, and

he mistakenly believes you want a position in Society," Lydia said. Who wanted a position in Society? But then, it had been so much of her life until now. Would she truly give it up? It was one thing for Margaret, who had never known it, to not want to engage in the strict etiquette, but for her? She glanced over at Sebastian, who looked precisely as concerned as a gentleman ought. Enough to fetch a doctor, but not enough to pull slippers off. Or give a head massage. Or envelop her in strong arms and ask for nothing in return.

"Society is just a damned nuisance," James added, dropping to his knees in front of Margaret to fan her with his kerchief. "Feeling better?"

"You aren't helping, James," Lydia said.

James gave her a look of annoyance and stood. "It's just some stupid tea, isn't it? If you don't want to go, don't go."

"Miss Dorchester is quite worked up about hosting these ladies on Margaret's behalf. Showing friendship with Margaret shows family solidarity. Margaret is going to have a difficult time as it is becoming Elshire's wife." Lydia said, glaring at James. "You certainly haven't been helping her position."

James folded his arms across his wide chest but declined to comment.

"I don't want to let him down," Margaret said.

"No, of course not, kitten," Lydia said. "Lord Elshire is a fine man, and he loves you for the time you've spent together in that awful basement. He loves you because you love the bugs and the dirt, and..." she looked to James for help.

"Yes, the experiments you've conducted together," James added. "And you keep all of the glassware spotlessly clean. Who wouldn't love a woman like that?"

Lydia rolled her eyes at her cousin.

"What? Cleanliness is next to godliness. Just ask the Quakers," James said.

Margaret nodded. "We talked about living in the country, where we could have our own little laboratory out there in an old greenhouse. Doesn't that sound lovely?"

"Deathly boring," James said.

"I mean, once I can actually marry, of course," Margaret said, looking down at her hands. "Thank you all for understanding and letting us announce an engagement."

"It won't be long," James promised.

"Tell them," Agnes prodded Lydia.

Lydia threw a pillow at James. "I have news."

"I'm listening," Sebastian said. James rolled his eyes.

But then they all looked at her, waiting. "I have reliable word that the *Europe* caught fire off the coast of Antigua and sank, laden with goods to bring back to England."

"The whole shipment?" James sagged back on the loveseat.

"What about the people?" Margaret asked.

Agnes smiled at Margaret's echo of her sentiment. Lydia noticed that her teacup was still full. "All safe," Lydia said.

"So, I can marry Elshire?" Margaret said. Her voice was tremulous, as if she didn't believe it.

"Whenever you wish," Agnes said. "Tomorrow, if you could get a special license."

Margaret giggled at the idea.

"No need to rush," Lydia's mother added. "Do things properly so that everyone knows he is marrying you for love, not obligation."

"Because that happens," James muttered.

Lydia agreed with him. All of her proposals had been obligations. Even John. It was always an *if.* Or perhaps a *should*. She was tired of conditionals. She wanted a man to choose her for what she was and what she did, not to feel obligated or tied to her in some way.

"Well," Sebastian said, slowly rising. He replaced his teacup on the tray in front of the loveseat. "I'm happy to hear that the machinations have been completed."

James ran fingers through his dark hair. "But it isn't over, don't you see?"

The members of the group stared at each other. The only sounds were the scraping of porcelain as they fiddled with their cups. Lydia worried that he was right.

"There will be an insurance claim. Hackett will be out some money, yes, but it might not break him. Shipping companies always have insurance. Too much can happen at sea. This isn't over."

"He skimped and didn't have a fire policy. I checked with Lloyd's," Lydia protested.

"But what about cargo insurance? Was there inclement weather that could be the cause of the fire?"

"Lloyd's would never pay a claim like that," Sebastian said. No one agreed with him. "Would they?"

"The important thing is that it's over enough that Margaret can get married," Agnes announced, setting her jaw firmly, as if waiting for an argument.

"Agreed," Lydia said.

"And what about Denby?" James asked, his voice rising. "He's still up, walking around."

"Denby is on financial crutches. He hasn't enough to convince anyone to marry him, and he barely keeps up his estates. Why push him over when he's already toppling?" Lydia smoothed her skirts. It had seemed like such a success just five minutes ago.

"Because then it would truly be over," James said.

"I disagree," Agnes said.

"If you topple a failing man, then you become the monster you sought to destroy," Margaret all but whispered.

Sebastian looked at Lydia. There was a plea in his eyes. Her mother stared at the teacup in her lap. The fatigue that cloaked her was palpable. And poor Margaret. Anxious as she was over a tea party, she just wanted to get married and live in the country with the love of her life.

If the pact had formed because of Lydia, shouldn't she be the one to dissolve it? So many other lives were intertwined. And they had done it out of selflessness, out of loyalty. What she wouldn't do for these people. What they hadn't already done for her.

"I declare the pact dissolved," Lydia announced.

Her mother exhaled a quiet sigh.

"You can't do that," James said. "There's still work to be done."

"And I will do it. Alone," Lydia said. She would find out about the cargo insurance and what was eligible for reimbursements.

"And what about Lady Isabelle? Her marriage could save the Hacketts," James said.

"I can't control it all," Lydia said. "But Hackett has taken a hit, and I will work to make it permanent."

"Don't hurt Lady Isabelle, please," Agnes said. "Why inflict that on an innocent? You of all people know how awful it is to be helpless in a world that refuses to let you control your own life."

"If Lady Isabelle marries a wealthy man for love, I won't lift a finger to stop it," Lydia promised.

James growled with displeasure. The vein in his forehead grew prominent, as it did when he was about to lose his temper.

"I think that's a wise position," Sebastian said.

"You are not a part of this," James roared at him. "Why is he even here?"

"Because he's helped us so many times. And because he was William's dear friend," Lydia protested. Having Sebastian around was like having William back, in some small way. A guiding hand.

"I, for one, am glad that the pact is dissolved," Agnes said.

"It isn't," James muttered.

"Don't do anything stupid, Andrepont," Sebastian said.

James glared at him. Lydia held her hands out, as if she needed to separate the two physically. Not that it would be a fair match. James had seemed to grow broader as he sunk more and more into the world of the Fancy. And Sebastian's tall but waifish figure, accented by his well-tailored waistcoats and breeches, would break under the pressure of a handshake from James, let alone a more aggressive gesture.

"And we look forward to celebrating Margaret's nuptials," her mother said.

"Let's get your hair pinned back up," Agnes said, joining the crowd on the loveseat.

"Thank you so much for the tea." Sebastian bowed to Lydia's mother. "And for the excellent service thereof." Another bow, this time to Margaret, who blushed.

"Lady Lydia," Sebastian said, "I would like to formally invite you and your chaperones to the public Art Exhibition next week." Another bow.

"Thank you, Sebastian. I would love to go," she said, glancing about the room, hoping not all of them would accompany them.

The rest of the party rose from their seats, including Margaret, whose hair was pinned back into place. As they made their goodbyes and filed out of the room, James told her in a low voice, "I'm not done."

"We'll work on it," Lydia whispered. "But let's dissolve the pact for everyone else. They need it."

James swung his heavy-lidded gaze at the rest of them. "Fine. They can marry, have babies, leave London, live their lives. But you and I have to finish. We will make this right."

The familiar knot settled back in her stomach. The weight of the burden rested on her once again, all the more oppressive now.

JOHN WAS READY FOR THE OPENING BELL AT THE Exchange. He had given Caulie fistfuls of paper to authorize the short sale of nearly one hundred stocks.

It was John's money to spend, and he knew he would make it back. In a short while, he and Caulie had managed to find out the holdings of both Hackett's and Denby's stock portfolios. John had some of the same stocks, and after some deliberation, they figured out a way to sell all of his shares in those companies, drive down the stock prices, and create financial havoc.

If they could whip up a panic, that would cause the entire stock to tank. After Hackett's man pulled his money out of the stock, then John could buy the stock back and preserve the company whose sad misfortune was only to have caught the interest of a particular lord.

"You sure about this?" Caulie asked, shifting his weight from foot to foot.

"Absolutely," John answered. "Don't be nervous."

"Feels dishonest," Caulie said.

"It isn't," John said. "It's business."

Caulie flashed a grin at him. "I'll remember to never cross you."

"It wasn't me," he said.

"Right, right," Caulie said. "Don't cross your paramours."

"She's not my paramour. I'm courting her," John said.

"Ooh," Caulie said, raising his pinkie finger as if he were drinking a cup of tea. "Does she know that?"

"It's understood." John looked around the Exchange, trying to clear his mind for the task ahead.

"How is it understood? What, you put on a funny hat, jump up and down, and before you know it, the toffs say you can court one of theirs?"

"No," John said. "There's no funny hat."

"Oooh, pardon me, my ninth lord of Bloody Knuckles."

"Shut yer face hole, Caulie. We got work."

The bell rang, clanging high and loud, interrupting them. Caulie set out to spread rumors and short money availability to anyone buying the marked stocks while John went out to ruin two lords. The effort would take a few weeks of concentrated effort, but John did not doubt the results.

He'd stopped by Lloyd's to ask after the insurance policy for the *Europe*. It had been busy in there, and the clerk looked exasperated with him. John had been able to buy the debt of the cargo, but he hadn't gotten the details of the extent of the insurance policy on the ship. Not all ships were insured against fire. It was a hope.

Hackett's ruination was for Lady Lydia, but while he was at it, he had disliked how Denby had made Bess dance. Besides, he would make sure both women profited from the short sale of these stocks. As Bess's broker, he had permission to trade her shares for an ultimate advantage. He could make her rich in the process. Since he wasn't connected to Lady Lydia on a professional level, he created a new account to cover the costs of the cargo debt.

While he would be happy to absorb the expense of the cargo—massive as it was—he knew she would hate to be indebted to him. And he didn't want her to feel like she owed him anything, either.

Maybe it was unethical, what he was doing, but the entire Exchange engaged in far more serpentine plots. During the wars, men would create elaborate plans and shows, ride into London breathless, announcing the capture of Napoleon just to drive market prices. If that wasn't illegal, short-selling and insider trading certainly weren't.

He pushed through the crush of men shouting and trading money. There was an order to which groups he would approach and when, hoping to spread the panic and cause the most damage. The French Huguenots were first to spread the word for the short sales. When dealing with the merchant brokers, he added hints of sordid personal details about Hackett without naming names. They didn't hold with aristocrats using their position with impunity. To the Catholics, he fanned the flames of anti-Catholic discrimination at the hands of the Anglican government. To the abolitionists, he spoke of the Triangle Trade route, of which the sunken ship from Antigua had been on, and how sugar was the only alchemy to make gold from the sweat of an enslaved man.

At least with the constant demand, he wouldn't think about Lydia with her blue-violet eyes, accented by her star-shaped birthmark. If he cupped her jaw, the pad of his thumb would cover that mark, not that he would want to hide it. He shook his head. Now was not the time. He had to focus. They trained in two days, and that was soon enough.

# 12

John was already warming up in the field when Lydia's carriage arrived. He walked over to his pile of clothing to check his pocket watch. She was early, too.

The two days away from her had given him plenty of time to examine all the options before him. Try for her or let her go; weigh the risk and the benefit—she may find him lacking in respectability, but not in other areas, and the benefit was clear. She would be in his corner, and in his bed, forever. Thus, here in the cold foggy morning on the outskirts of London, the only scenario acceptable was the one where Lydia belonged to him and only him.

How that would happen, he wasn't quite sure. But he was working on it. He had already proven how useful he could be while escaping from the country. When she discovered the short sales and the cargo debt, she would see how generous he was. What else did a respectable husband need to prove? He had no idea. Manners, probably. Well, uphill battles were his specialty.

Lydia opened the carriage door herself, letting down the step. Her driver sat on his perch, clearly not inclined to descend. John waved to the man, and to his surprise, the man returned the gesture. The maid from the country, Charlotte, poked her head out of the enclosed carriage. She was wrapped in a shawl, but she shivered.

"You can chaperone from the window," Lydia told her maid. The woman closed the door, her face framed like a headless portrait. She looked miserable.

John met Lydia halfway into the field. "You're early," he said as she approached. He wanted to pull her into his arms, to show her how amorous he was. Husbands should be amorous, shouldn't they? And he was. Well, desirous anyway.

In contrast to the two people still at the carriage, Lydia's eyes were bright, no trace of sleep at this early hour. The sun had barely risen.

"You are too," she said.

Before he could stop himself, he reached out to take her hand. He brushed his thumb across her knuckles. She didn't pull away. All his thoughts of respectability and usefulness fled. The desirous ones remained.

"I think training might get more difficult," he said. How was he to concentrate on her technique when all he could see was how at once she had strong shoulders, toned and firm, but also smooth curves and supple hips? Since the Orangery, how often had he fantasized about the rip of her dress and continuing to tear at her clothes until he could see every bit of her?

"I like difficult," she said.

"I've noticed," John said, refusing to release her hand. He shook himself out of it. Usefulness. He was her trainer, and trainers trained. "You need to get warmed up."

She nodded, pulling her hand from his grip but not bothering to turn away as she unbuttoned her garment. This dress wasn't made like others, for it had buttons in the front. No need for assistance.

He glanced at the carriage, where the driver was pawing through a hamper, and the maid stared at him from the window. This audience was the kind that made him nervous. One wrong word and Lydia would be whisked away from him. Points tallied against him.

Did she understand his intentions? Could there be any misinterpretation of what he desired? If he were a dishonorable man, plenty could be misunderstood. However, a respectable man—because he was trying hard to become one—a man like that would have only one thing on his mind.

Each button Lydia opened revealed another section of soft skin, and in his dreams, he had sanctified every inch with his tongue.

Marriage.

Yes, that was what a respectable man would be thinking about right now.

Without thinking, he pulled at his own shirt, untucking it from his breeches. Shouldn't they be having a conversation? He exhaled, and a puff of breath appeared in front of him. By the time he got his shirt off, she was already undressed, tucking the long sleeves about her waist.

"What would you like to learn today, my lady?" he asked, approaching her as casually as he could. His heart thumped as if he were going to enter the ring with a man over seven feet tall.

There was a band covering her breasts underneath her chemise. He stared at it, suddenly knowing they were mad. What were they doing here? It was one thing to meet in a secluded glade in the country, but here, in Town? Nothing was private in Town, even at an ungodly early hour.

"Grappling?" she suggested.

Proof that she was, in fact, trying to kill him. Or get him killed. He swallowed hard.

"Ah," he said, as if there was anything he could say. How could he veto her plan unless he told her of the nightly visits she had most unwillingly paid him? That seeing her like this nearly brought him to his knees? He turned away, hoping that removing her from his sight would give him time to think.

To be discovered might be a blessing.

"I am ready to learn such a skill," she insisted.

"Yes, of course," he stuttered, coming to his senses again. Where was the confident demeanor he'd had when she surprised him in the wooded glade? His back still to her, he stretched and rolled his bare shoulders.

Grappling was a mistake. It was one thing with the weapons, even the physical corrections, but quite another to physically lay his hands on her. If the wrong man spied them, he could end up in Newgate for his troubles. Would Lorian believe his daughter's pleas and not press charges against him?

Or would they obtain a special license and be married by tomorrow morning? He turned back to her, trying so very hard not to imagine a quick wedding feast for none but close family, followed by locking the bedroom door for at least three weeks straight. He'd have to hire a cook, but Parsons could bring them trays to keep up their strength. Because he would want some very strenuous days.

Marriage, usefulness, generosity, control. That was what a husband had to have. Self-control. He turned back to her, banishing all thoughts of wedding nights, locked doors, and large beds.

Color was already high in her cheeks, hair pinned back securely, the swell of her breasts pushing against the bindings. If there was a Hell, he was already in it. How strange that it looked surprisingly similar to

Heaven. He just had to get through this morning controlling himself. And then he would call on her properly, like a suitor. With flowers. At the proper time. With his sister. Be good and proper. If he could just not think about his hands against her skin. "Grappling it is, then."

"Good," she said, stepping back.

Even in the short time since he'd first seen her boxing with Bess, her shoulders had changed, now showing striations of muscle, her arms carving out the hollows between the biceps and the triceps. Her across-the-ballroom glide maintained its civilized perfection while she improved vicious forward attacks. Their work together had already changed her.

The sun had risen, and the air warmed. He couldn't help himself; he took a deep breath in, eyes closed and arms out, inhaling the sweet smell of grass, clean and wholly different from the aromas that assaulted him in other parts of London. It almost felt like the country again. The good parts of it, anyway.

He opened one eye and saw that Lydia had taken the opportunity to mimic him. Letting go of his misgivings, he felt good down to his bones. Being in the field with her felt right, despite what Caulie had said and what his own rational mind thought. There was precedence for a stockbroker to become wealthy enough to marry into Quality. Uncommon, but not unheard of.

"Ready?" he asked.

She dropped her arms to her sides and focused her storm-colored eyes on him. "Basics, then," he said, moving towards her, willing himself to think of her as any other student. A male student who didn't smell faintly of oranges and vanilla.

He explained the first maneuver, a standing take-down. He showed her in slow motion, then in real time, as if she were a real opponent. It happened in a flash, one moment standing, the next minute not. He could see the surprise in her stunned expression.

They were in the grass, his body covering hers, the heat of their skin mingling with the dew. There was a definite smell of vanilla, but John fought against his baser nature, willing himself to be stronger than his needs. He had control of his body, not the other way around.

"This feels familiar," she said, the dryness of her tone unmistakable.

All he could think of was the last time he had lain with a woman. Images tumbled through his mind, Lydia's head thrown back in ecstasy, some faceless lothario the cause of her joy. Jealousy flooded him, causing his heartbeat to thump far faster than this level of exercise warranted. He hoped she didn't notice the pulse in his neck. "Does it?" he asked, not moving.

She exhaled, her breath heavy. "Yes, this was how we met," she said. "And I still can't breathe."

He scrambled off of her, the tension dissipated. Vasily seemed more interested in the pasty he'd discovered in his hamper than what they were about. The maid still sat her vigil in the carriage window, unmoving but with eyes wide.

"The runaway horse?" she prompted.

"I remember," he said, extending his hand to help her up. She took his hand, her expression searching. They had distance. He should use the opportunity to instruct. "Now your turn to practice."

"Fine," she said, resuming their face-to-face stance.

She learned quickly, only needing to try a few times until she was able to put him on the ground as quickly as an amateur could. He moved on to the next standing maneuvers, and they practiced until even he became accustomed to feeling her plush skin slide across his.

After she became adept at the standing maneuvers, he taught her a few holds that might be of use in the real world, even though the positions originated in Greco-Roman wrestling.

"You're improving the weight distribution between your feet. Very good," he said.

She smiled at the compliment, and he knew that expression. He, himself, had looked like that as a child when Tony praised his work. He'd been a scrap of a boy, and Tony was already the rotund gambler, no longer able to demonstrate.

Being able to share the knowledge that had kept John alive, gotten him and his sister through school, felt worthwhile. Fighting had not just been a way to survive; it was how his life had meaning.

To reinforce the lessons, John had Lydia take him from a standing tackle to an on-the-ground hold. They were in the grass, her arm around his chin, her hands clasped on the side of his neck, about to cut off circulation to his head if she squeezed her hands together, flexing her forearms. He tapped her arm and she relaxed the hold, her hand brushing across his bare chest. His head was near on her lap, and they locked eyes. He had never been more aware of how much flesh he exposed, and how much of it was touching her.

"Lydia—" he began. How could he say all of the complicated things that whirled inside of him? There were things he felt and thoughts that he didn't have words to describe. But he knew what he wanted, and that was her. She deserved to know his intentions were real, that he was doing what he could to honor her at the Exchange, and that whatever she needed him to do in order to be worthy of her, he would do it. "I want you to know—"

"Oho! What do we have here?" a voice shouted.

John sat up, his hackles rising. The underbrush amongst the trees shook as two figures emerged.

❧

LYDIA WAS MORE IRRITATED BY THE INTERRUPTION of John's sentence than by the element of discovery. He wanted her to know something. *Tell me what you want*, she was tempted to shout. But then her attention focused on the interlopers, who kept approaching.

They were well-soused, by the way they walked. But it didn't matter if they were drunk; anyone finding them was disastrous. At best, they would wheedle a bribe out of her. At worst, well, she couldn't think about what that even might be.

The thin man was taller, wearing a top hat to appear of greater height. The other man was rotund. A glint of gold caught the pale light. She went cold as she recognized the pair.

"A tryst, of course. It looks like we've blundered in too soon. We should've taken advantage and hidden in the trees," Hackett said, a wooden case swinging in his hand.

"Lady Lydia!" Denby exclaimed, before bursting into laughter. "I had no idea you were part of the Fancy. Perhaps I should have included you in my Exhibition."

"No thank you, my lord," she said through gritted teeth. More than anything, she wanted to pull her dress back up, bundle herself away in the carriage, go home, and hide under her blankets. She wanted John to run in front of her, take care of them while she curled up somewhere safe.

But these were her demons. They walked the Earth, free to torment, and she and James had sworn to finish this. In order to feel any sort of peace, she had to take care of them herself. And here, in the field, exposed, she would have to take an aggressive stance.

"How well do you take a fist?" Denby growled.

Her stomach twisted. "How well do you?"

"Lady Lydia, you should have said there was another gentleman in line for your affections," Lord Hackett called. "I wouldn't dream of jumping the queue."

John stepped close to her, trying to shield her from their view. "Go," he whispered. Then he called across the field to the men. "What brings you gentlemen here?"

"A duel, of course," Lord Hackett replied. "I hate to interrupt yours. Pray, continue, don't stop on our account."

"Perhaps we can all have a turn," Lord Denby said, as if he were suggesting another round of port after dinner.

Her hands began to shake, her flesh puckered with goosebumps. The binding about her breasts seemed to constrict even further. Air couldn't come fast enough.

"Don't speak that way about a lady," John warned.

"I beg your pardon, sir, but your state of undress says otherwise," Lord Hackett said. "There was always suspicion that Lady Lydia was a whore, but now I know for certain. A girl can't be so popular with so many Seasons under her belt and not have some kind of secret."

But enough. She'd not let John fight her battles. James, Margaret, Agnes, and Sebastian had stood shoulder-to-shoulder with her. It wasn't right to pull in another person, not when she was so close to finishing it herself. What was it that John had said about the hand wraps, back in the glade? That if one believes the fight is over, one might as well forfeit? She stepped around John. "I'll not have the likes of you call me names."

"We cannot help the accuracy," Lord Denby said.

"I have some accurate names I should have called you at every dinner party I've ever attended," she spat, advancing on the two men across the field.

Rage radiated off of her in waves, and it was almost surprising that she couldn't see it. John trailed a few steps behind her, taking soft steps in the wet grass. If there was ever a time she believed she could commit murder, it was now.

"This is a surprise," called a familiar voice from yet another direction. James sauntered up through the field, his dark coat flowing behind him, the rest of him in a state of complete dishevelment.

"James," she acknowledged, not looking at him. "What are you doing here?"

"I could ask the same as you, especially in your boxing costume," he said.

She glanced over to him as he came into her peripheral view, noticing that he wore a pistol pushed down the front of his trousers. Dueling pistols were supposed to be transported in a case, not waved about for all to see. She glanced at the other men and realized that Hackett carried a case, battered and well-worn around the edges.

"Fine English walnut," John quietly commented behind her, remarking on James's pistol. James turned and smirked, as this was a reference to the hilt of every new weapon of James Purdey's make on Oxford Street. It was a common refrain to overhear at balls, or any place men gathered and discussed weaponry, not that she knew much about it.

The pistols in Hackett's case were likely of an older issue, not as accurate as the new weapons to be found on the London streets.

"Boxing costume?" Hackett sneered. "You know what the ladies do after the match is over, don't you? Will you be masquerading there as well?"

"That's not true," John said.

"I'm sorry, I don't believe you should be dissenting against your betters," Denby snapped. "Besides, I know exactly what Bess does after our matches."

"You are such an ass," James said to Denby. "This is why we are here for a duel."

"You are despicable," Lydia spat at both Denby and Hackett. Perhaps it had been a mistake to say that Denby was ruined enough. And maybe it had been a mistake to leave Hackett's ruination as purely financial. James was right; they should burn it all down.

"Why, of all the people here, am I despicable? Because I speak my mind?" Denby challenged.

"Because you prey on little girls," she said through gritted teeth. Now her hands were shaking, not with cold or panic or fear, but with incandescent rage. Heat poured through her, and it was all she could do to contain it as she stalked up to him. The man didn't have the sense to cower or step back. Before she could think, her fist was flying.

Denby fell back on his ass, his hand over his eye. "How dare you!" he screeched.

"Excellent form," James murmured to John.

"Thank you—she's an excellent student. Doing quite well," John said.

If Lydia were in a better state of mind, she could have responded to them, but as it was, all she could do was turn her attention to Hackett, who dropped his gun case to attend to his friend.

"You're supposed to put your hands up, my lord," James called to Denby.

"Your defenses are quite lacking," Lydia taunted,

watching with her hands on her hips, her expression carefully schooled into neutrality.

John came up behind her, and she could feel his hands hover about her shoulders, as if he would touch her, and then thought better of it. "Come on now, that's enough."

"Don't touch me," Lydia snarled. If Hackett would only stand up, she would go after him as well. She felt like a gas lamp that had been turned up too high.

"What the devil is wrong with you?" Lord Hackett cried. "This is obscene!"

James joined John, his slow walk masking his careful attention to the scene at hand.

Denby stared up at her, holding one hand over his eye. "Whoever heard of such unnatural behavior?"

Lydia stalked back and forth, as if she were a cat waiting for a mouse to emerge from a hole in the wall. "Yes, what unnatural tendencies should we discuss? The word is that your first wife was bought and paid for before she had enough birthdays to debut properly."

"Her father agreed. What of it?" Denby spat, still holding his eye, swearing as it swelled.

"Quite terrifying when she's worked up, isn't she?" James murmured to John behind her.

"I forgot that women are merely breeding animals to you," Lydia said. "We don't deserve air if we aren't carrying a child."

"What is happening?" John asked James.

Hackett struggled to his feet, his arms outstretched to Denby, dragging him up as well. "Andrepont, I demand that you take your cousin home!" Hackett yelled.

"No," James replied.

Lydia stopped her pacing, now able to take in all the players at once. James stood with his arms crossed, amused. John looked confused, glancing from face to face. But she had scared the two older men. And it felt good.

"Make her stop," Denby said.

James nodded, as if he were deep in thought. "This is your own doing, I'm afraid. You are the one who must make amends."

"Lady Lydia, you are behaving like a spoiled child," Hackett said. "You shan't like it if I force you to leave."

Lydia laughed, an awful sound tinged with darkness. He dared to threaten her now? "Your hands aren't any cleaner. Pedophiles, deviants, slavers," she spat. Her pride surged. She wanted Hackett to know it was her who took his fortune. "You were so worried about the *Europe*, weren't you? All of that money from selling off yet another country estate went into your last hope. It was a big risk, but a calculated one."

"What do you know about the *Europe*?" Hackett's pallor faded to the color of chalk.

"I know that if you can't profit from misbegotten wares, then you have to pimp your daughter to maintain your wealth. Can you stand to be so beholden to a young woman?"

"How do you know that?" Hackett demanded.

She liked his panic, how squeaky his voice became. Behind her, the carriage creaked as Vasily lumbered down from the driver's perch.

"I paid for that arson on your boat. It is me that crippled you," Lydia said, trying to regain her composure, not wanting to show her glee. "So, you see, a girl-child is worth something to you, isn't she? Her marrying well is the only path you have left, and she doesn't seem to be too cooperative."

Finally, Hackett reached the edge of his own anger. "Whore!" Hackett roared and rushed her.

Everything happened so fast. In the space of just a

few moments, James pulled the walnut-handled pistol, cocking it as he strode two steps forward.

She readied herself for Hackett's hit, wanting to sidestep him rather than let him take her down. But Hackett never reached her.

A loud bang reverberated through the field, causing the birds to take flight. Trees shook with the sudden vacancies. The report was much louder than she expected. It was as if the whole of London could have heard it. Hackett crumpled to the ground, and they all staggered back.

"There. Now." James looked among all of them standing in the clearing. He peered over the rotund body of his victim, seeming pleased with his firearm. "We have had a duel, you and I."

Hackett groaned in response. The older man didn't even try to cover the hurt with his hands. Lydia stared at the blood seeping through Lord Hackett's dark trousers, wetting the fabric stretched across his thigh.

"Denby, you're an ass, so it is me that beat your face in. I wouldn't mention the truth of who was here," James continued.

"He needs a tourniquet," John said.

There was more and more blood. She'd never seen a gunshot wound before. She'd never seen anyone fire a gun before. Having spent most of her life in London, she'd never gone on a hunt or seen anyone else do it either.

"Not until he gives his word," James said, holding John back with his arm.

"Fine. A duel," Hackett gasped, and James dropped the arm that had been blocking John.

"My lady?" Vasily rumbled, just a step out of reach.

Lydia nodded her permission, though she wondered if he would tend Hackett anyway, out of a sense of duty to the wounded. Vasily knelt next to the injured man and tore the cravat from the man's fat neck and bandaged it about the thigh wound.

John came up next to her. "Get dressed," he told her.

Defiance flaring up. She was still exuding heat and power.

"You're going to get cold soon," he explained. "Once that feeling of triumph passes, you'll crash."

He was telling her that she couldn't ride this crest forever, and she wanted him to be wrong. She glanced over at James, disheveled just like herself. He nodded in agreement with John. Lydia pulled the long sleeves out of the banding at her waist and slid into them. She did the buttons up the front, a disorienting motion.

"Do you have a carriage?" Vasily grunted.

"It's on the other side of the park," Denby answered.

Vasily nodded and then said to Hackett, "You'll have to stand."

John left her side to help pick up Hackett. She didn't like him helping, but if he did, the odious men would leave faster.

James came to her and put his arm around her. "How did you know I would be here?" she asked.

"Didn't," he said, fishing in his interior coat pocket. "If you weren't here, I would've killed them both."

"I told you not to do anything stupid."

He produced a flask. "You were here. Did it seem stupid?"

Between Denby with the swollen eye, Vasily, and John, they brought Hackett upright. Hackett looped his hand over Denby's shoulder, but Vasily was much too large to assist in the same way. Instead, Vasily offered his arm as aid. The three of them slowly made their way through the trees. John watched them depart, Hackett's moans echoing through the park.

"Stiff upper lip," John called.

"Come on," James said, steering her back to the carriage. As they walked, he dropped his arm from her shoulders in order to unscrew the cap of his flask.

"You already smell like that pub in Wapping," she said. "Haven't you had enough?"

"It's not for me," he said, handing it to her.

"I'm made of sterner stuff than you," she said.

James snorted. "Probably true. But you'll want it in a minute."

"You couldn't possibly know that." Behind them, she heard John swishing through the grass as well, following them back to the carriage. Charlotte stood guard outside, her shawl wrapped tightly around her shoulders. Poor thing was likely cold. She shouldn't have been out here. None of them should have been. This was all a ghastly, stupid idea. And Lydia had wanted it more than anything.

"It's your first real fight," James said. A proud smile crept onto his face. "A brawl."

"My lady?" Charlotte asked, a dozen questions hidden inside the one.

"I'm fine, Charlotte, thank you."

James ushered Lydia into the carriage, and as she sat, all of her spirit drained out of her. Exhaustion took its place. James hauled himself up across from her, as did John, now wearing his shirt and coat. Charlotte slid in next to her.

"Here," James offered the flask again.

She took it, noticing that her hands were beginning to shake. Cold crept in. The urge to cry welled up, but she pushed it down. She was not the sort of woman to make a display of herself. Or at least, not in that way.

"Would someone please tell me what's happening?" John asked.

"I've had a duel, and Hackett was shot in the course of it." James answered with a smile. He looked pointedly at Charlotte. "None of you were ever here."

"Yes, my lord," Charlotte answered. She reached over and squeezed Lydia's hand. It made Lydia feel better to have that small comfort.

"Yes, but why did you insist on a duel? What was the business at his house in the country? What is the manner of whatever it is that is supposedly over, because clearly it isn't, if you took to a dueling ground to shoot the man?" John huffed in frustration.

James looked to her. "May I tell him?"

Her heart went to John. He was trying to support her, trying to help. But she wanted him to keep looking at her like he had in the Orangery. He thought her valuable, desirable, precious. If he knew the source of all this darkness, he would know she was broken. And she wasn't ready to lose that yet.

"No," she said, and she squeezed Charlotte's hand harder.

John threw himself back on the squabs. "I'm trying Lydia, I really am trying."

She knew he expected an answer from her. And that he wanted explanations as well. "I know," she whispered.

Vasily opened the door to the carriage, returned from his onerous task. "Shall I take you home, my lady?"

"Thank you," she said.

John shook his head. "You can trust me."

Trust him not to think she was broken? Not possible, when everyone believed it to be true. Even herself. "I'm afraid I can't."

The look on his face was not one she'd ever

wanted to see. He was disappointed in her. He was hurt, and worse, he looked like she had betrayed him.

"Sorry, mate," James said, hopping out of the carriage, holding the door open to encourage him to follow suit.

John opened his mouth to speak. He had wanted her to know something before they'd been so rudely interrupted.

She knew what he wanted. He wanted to know why. Why was the *Europe* important, why had they cried with relief when they'd heard it was destroyed? Why did she hate Denby and Hackett so? Why did James shoot him? But it all returned to the same origin: her and her shame.

And shame was not something one shared.

"Goodbye, Mr. Arthur. Please return home safely."

He clamped his jaw shut and exited the carriage, following James out into the grass.

"Get some rest," James said before the door clicked shut. He pounded the outside of the carriage with his hand, and it lurched into motion. Lydia watched through the window as John walked away, the wet grass dampening his trouser legs.

# 13

If she couldn't trust him, he wouldn't beg. He'd knocked on the door, and she'd refused to answer. It was clear that she didn't think him worthy, and so instead of gathering up Pearl to properly enter the Lorian drawing room, he trained. He couldn't call on Lydia, so he called on Tony. In between, he worked. And in between that, he visited Pearl, who reminded him of his promise to take her and her friends to the Summer Exhibition.

"Your coat is too loose," Pearl complained, sitting next to him in the rented carriage. It was open-air, and the young women all complained as they held their bonnets and checked one another's coifs. "You're losing weight."

"I'm fine, Pearl," he said. At least the sun was shining. There was a touch of warmth on his shoulders. There were four of them and one of him. And Miss Mathilda Perry wouldn't stop trying to catch his attention. He looked out at the street going by instead.

They arrived at the Exhibition Hall to witness the full flux of the crowd. He sighed. More crowds. They would be more faceless nobodies gawking, just like everyone else. Elbow to bollocks, day in and day out.

"It's the first day," Pearl explained.

He handed them all down out of the carriage and, once the ladies were collected with skirts smoothed and bonnets adjusted, they bustled their way into the Exhibition Hall, where people brimmed out of rooms and hallways. Even the building's normally cool marble seemed too warm with so many bodies pressed together.

Pearl navigated them through the crowd of aristocrats and commoners alike, into the main room. Its walls were stuffed with framed paintings. Most of them depicted some kind of war memorial. Many pieces marked the Battle of Waterloo, which caused Miss Perry to sidle up to him and espouse romantic ideals of a war neither of them had seen.

The crowd whispered and surged behind them, pushing their little party to the front of the room. They kept pace, taking the opportunity to stop and look at the wide landscapes in front of them.

"Do you care for landscapes?" Miss Perry asked him.

He had absolutely no position on landscapes whatsoever, and he was tired of her repeated ploys to draw him into conversation. Turning away in an attempt to shake his foul mood, he ran into his saviors.

"Miss Franklin, Mr. Franklin, what a pleasure to see you here," John said.

Miss Franklin made no attempt to hide her surprise. As they exchanged pleasantries, Pearl came over and John introduced her to his new, very respectable friends. They were exactly the type of people he'd hoped she would meet. Finally, something was going well. They chatted amiably, and the other young ladies were introduced.

The crowd surged and crushed their party together.

"Perhaps we can visit the sculptures," Miss Franklin recommended. Pearl took a step to fall in with Miss Franklin, but Mr. Franklin suggested they switch siblings, and thus Pearl walked with Mr. Franklin and John with Miss Franklin, while the rest of the young ladies trailed behind them.

They walked down the hall to the sculptures room, but before they arrived, they saw Lydia arm-in-arm with Lord Sebastian, Lady Lorian and Lady Agnes behind them.

He felt like Caulie had landed a blow in his breadbasket. She looked well. Healthy, in far better shape than when he'd left her on that field the day Andrepont shot Hackett. Somehow, they managed to lock gazes. He quickly swept the hat off of his head as he bowed low to her.

The young women surrounding him also curtsied low, sinking into the cotton dresses, their straw bonnets bowed as one, making each indistinguishable.

"Lady Lydia," John said. "What a pleasure to see you."

❧

John Arthur was handsome in his red striped waistcoat and buckskin breeches. His green velvet coat caught the light in a pleasing way, making Lydia want to remove her gloves and touch it. He looked the part of a dandy, a Corinthian, as it were.

It made her ache, as if the interior lining all along her body shriveled to her bones. For a week, they'd spent every morning together. Despite Hackett's profound misbehavior, his hospitality had given them a chance to have that time. But that had led to questions, and then there was the shooting, which only raised more questions.

And she couldn't bear to see the pity on his face when he knew the answers.

But then again, when one has the company of a gaggle of women, and the favorite Miss Franklin, why did he need any answers at all? He clearly had no problem making friends.

John turned to Sebastian, making another low bow, the ladies following suit. Sebastian acknowledged the courtesy with a nod. Lydia was aware that each man sized the other up, just as clear as if they were in the ring, circling one another.

"Lord Sebastian, a pleasure," John Arthur said, rising. "We met at the Beckersley ball."

"Mr. Arthur," Lydia said, meaning only to acknowledge him, but as he turned to her, the crisp blue of his eyes made her want to stay where he could see her, talk to her. "You have quite a company with you. Miss Franklin, Mr. Franklin, lovely to see you again. And how wonderful you have found the same company once again in Town."

While the Franklins gave their courtesies, Agnes pushed her way forward. "What luck to see you here, Miss Franklin!"

"May I present my sister. Lady Lydia, this is Miss Pearl Arthur." John handed the girl forward. She was young and slight, with the same arresting blue eyes as her brother. She executed a curtsy well, and looking at her clothes, which were well-made but not overly fashionable, she would easily make a decent middle-class match. She was pretty, but with her small, pointed chin and broad face, she looked almost fey. When Lydia looked closer at her face, the indirect light bouncing off the wide planes of her cheekbones, she was almost relieved to see the girl didn't possess the same reddish-gold eyelashes as her brother. Her complexion was pale and clear of any hint of the ginger freckling that haunted John.

Miss Arthur curtsied, and Lydia began to wonder just what it was that John had thought she could do for the girl. He'd made acquaintance with the Franklins, and surely more were to follow.

"Miss Arthur, I am pleased to make your acquaintance," Lydia said, surprised at how sincere she sounded.

"Oh, John, will you not introduce us?" One of the young ladies asked. She too was pretty in a shrill sort of way, pinched face, with crowded features. Her clothes were well-made, and like Miss Pearl's, not at the height of fashion. Surely, she was well-acquainted with the family if she used Mr. Arthur's first name in public.

Very well acquainted, Lydia judged, by the way the young lady leaned herself over his shoulder, practically laying herself along his arm. She had thought he was above cradle-robbing, but then why she should think he would be interested in a grown woman as opposed to a malleable, empty-headed trollop was beyond her comprehension.

A flush crept into Mr. Arthur's face. "Yes, of course," he said, and the introductions continued—all the young ladies, Sebastian, Lydia's mother and sister. So many new acquaintances needed to be made.

But this interminable display made her time with him seem all the more distant and dream-like. Had they seen him fight? Seen how his muscles coiled in his back before he unleashed?

Lydia found that she couldn't even hear each lady's name as they curtsied. Once all introductions were conducted, her disappointment had flowered. These were young women who were as they ought to be: polite, not too eager—except for the one—out to look at fine art, unbroken. She should have been like them. With so many seasons out, she should have been married by now. *Should*.

"If you will excuse us," Lydia said, unable to bear their youthful faces, looking exclusively at John Arthur. She hated that the broad angles of his face were so well contoured, that he seemed so at ease in the company of a gaggle of women. "We have not yet seen the main gallery," she added.

Another round of bows and curtsies, and Lydia escaped with Sebastian. Her corset felt too tight.

"I'd like to stay with Miss Franklin," Agnes said.

Their mother glanced between her daughters. "Go on," she said to Lydia.

Her near-to-the-shelf status finally gained advantage. Lydia pulled at Sebastian's arm before any more could be said. She couldn't bear John looking at her with his questioning gaze.

"Lovely people," Sebastian said.

"You are kind to withstand all of it," Lydia said, letting him lead her through the hallway.

If anything, the proximity of other people and the encounter with John—no, he was back to Mr. Arthur—made her itch to go home and work through more of Bess's training regime. She resisted the urge to shift her weight between her feet.

---

LADY LYDIA AND LORD SEBASTIAN MADE QUITE A pair, and Pearl's friends sighed over his understated politeness. The couple strolled to the main gallery mobbed by the rest of London, and only once did Sebastian catch sight of the lady's face, smiling as if he had already proposed.

Perhaps he had. The idea of it was like a jab to the kidney. John had never kidded himself that Lydia was a possibility for him, but how could he forget about the heat they generated between them?

"Mr. Arthur, do you not think sculptures are better than the paintings?"

John could barely pay attention. He swung around to the origin of the voice, pivoting his sister on his arm too fast. Pearl had to grab onto him with her other hand to keep her balance. Thank goodness it was her and not Miss Franklin on his arm.

"Pardon?" he asked, he wasn't even sure which young lady had commented.

Miss Perry fluttered her eyelashes at him as she repeated her question. She looked down, lifting only her gaze to his, a show of modesty, but also a way for a young lady to make her eyes appear bigger, more innocent. Pearl had told him of Miss Perry's trick.

"Sure," he said. Lady Lorian walked with Lady Agnes and Miss Franklin, but she kept her eyes on John. Watching. Observing. Miss Perry needed to not talk to him anymore. He wasn't doing anything wrong by having a discussion with the young lady, but he certainly didn't want Lydia's mama watching him do it. Did she know what he had done with Lydia in Orangery? She wouldn't have told her mother, would she? Another glance back to the Countess showed nothing but bland attention on her face. She must know. But if she knew...? He felt the flush as it worked its way up his face. "I do beg your pardon, Miss Perry, I need to discuss some business with Mr. Franklin."

He unhooked Pearl's arm and shamelessly abandoned his sister. Her laughter followed him. But he didn't care. He'd find something to talk about to Mr. Franklin. At least that conversation could be held without judgment from the Countess. Did she know? She couldn't know. She knew.

And worse, she didn't care enough to force him into marriage. That's how lowly he was.

# 14

There were comforting smells in life. Sometimes they made sense, and sometimes they didn't. For instance, John was comforted by the smell of junipers so strong it made his eyes water. Gin smelled like home. He was supposed to be above that. Blunt in the pockets, fancy home rented in a fancy neighborhood. French wine was supposed to be his drink of choice.

But he preferred gin that could peel wallpaper.

Parsons knocked. Or he probably did. John was too drunk to notice. This was his office in the house, which he had never used because he was always at Garraway's. The room was a nice enough place. There was a desk, which was a useful place to keep one's glass of gin. Or what-have-yous.

"You have a messenger, sir," Parsons announced. He seemed annoyed. But he always seemed annoyed.

John sat up and put his feet on the floor. Might as well try to look respectable, even if one was soundly, very clearly in fact, not respectable.

A boy of about ten entered. He didn't wear any formal livery, but his clothes were clean and his hair was tidy.

"Yesh?" John prompted.

"The lady told me to come get you," the boy said.

His heart jumped. Or maybe it was just the booze. But if Lydia needed him for something, he would go in an instant, drunk or not. "The lady?" he asked.

"Er, yeah. The lady boxer. She's been staying wif Lord Denby. Says you need to come straight away."

John got to his feet, swaying as he fished in his pockets for a coin to give the boy. If Bess needed him, he would go, undoubtedly. His drunkenness was not ideal, but it was the situation. "Tell Michael to ready the gig and meet me out front," he told Parsons. "Show the boy to the gig, too. I'll be down after I find a chamber pot."

He met them downstairs, feeling slightly soberer. The night air should help on the ride over to Mayfair, and he could see what Bess needed of him.

They rocked as they piled onto the gig, and the trip to Mayfair was quiet. When they arrived, the kid disappeared around to the back of the house before John knocked, while Michael sat in front with the gig and the horse, waiting for instructions.

The butler at Lord Denby's home was a thin, sour man who reminded John of Denby himself. The house was dark, with few candles lit in the public spaces, just enough for the butler to see where he was going. The halls were cold, as if no one had lit a fire in weeks. John was shown into the drawing room and instructed to wait.

The drawing room was formal and impersonal. Paintings with generic hunting scenes and dogs adorned the walls. The room was chilly and stale; it was clear that it did not receive much use. A maid entered to light a few more candles, as it was barely light enough to see one's own hand.

John waited as the clock ticked the minutes past. The paintings were at least entertaining enough to examine as he waited, but after a while, he exhausted even those. The butler returned and offered brandy. John refused and was left alone again.

Finally, the door opened, and John turned away from his third inspection of a Scottish hunting scene done in oils. Bess stood in the doorway, her face drawn, her figure diminished.

John rushed towards her. "Bess, you all right?" He took her by the shoulders, running through the same checklist of wellbeing he surveyed his sister with.

There were dark rings under her eyes. Her face was puffy from lack of sleep, and while he couldn't be sure, she seemed to have lost weight since he had last seen her.

"I'm fine, John," she said. "Thanks for coming."

"Anytime you need," he said. "Is there something I can do?"

Bess flopped down onto one of the chairs. "I'm just tired. More tired than I've ever been. I've gone from trainer to nursemaid."

"Nursemaid?" John asked, standing back to give Bess room to enter and sit. He waited for her to find a chair before he sat as well.

"Denby's sick," she said, looking down at her hands.

John noticed how red and chapped her hands were for the first time. It was true that they didn't look like the hands of a fighter; they were the hands of a caretaker or a laundress. She must have been bathing him regularly or washing his clothes in hot water to get hands like that. "When did this happen? He was fine a few weeks ago."

"It was after the country," Bess said. "First he was just really tired. He doesn't keep many servants on, so he asked me to stay so that I could help him up the stairs."

"Surely he has some hearty footman that could do the job," John said.

Bess shook her head. "He doesn't hire anyone new. Mr. Ferguson, the butler?" Bess gave him a wry smile. "Then after the exhaustion came the puking."

John held his hand up. "You needn't give me the blow-by-blow accounting."

Bess shrugged. "I've stayed on because he's got no one else. Even the servants are leaving, afeared that it's the plague."

"You don't think it's a plague?" John asked, returning her smile to let her know that he thought it unlikely, too. He walked over to the cold fireplace. Denby had seemed hale enough when they met on the dueling field a few weeks ago.

Bess glanced over her shoulder. "I think it's poison."

John's heart skipped a beat. "You think someone is killing him?"

"Killed," she said. "I think what's done is done."

"Good God," John said. Doubt crowded his mind. He was terrified of his first instinct, terrified that his sinking feeling confirmed his fears.

Bess shook her head. "He ain't well-liked. And more than one angry creditor has banged on that door."

He didn't want to volunteer that Denby had profound enemies in Andrepont and Lydia. Either of them could be responsible. His gut twisted. Lydia wouldn't do this, but would Andrepont? He didn't want to know. Not that he'd ever be allowed close enough to know what that family would be capable of. "What about you, Bess? If you stay here much longer, you'll be blamed."

Bess shrugged. "I couldn't forgive myself if I abandoned any creature as sick as Denby. That should be proof enough."

"But people don't care the good you've done. They'll want to put the blame on you because of what you do." John wished he'd accepted the butler's offer of brandy. If Bess were blamed for this, he didn't know what he would do. And if Lydia was behind it, he would lose his mind.

"I'll not waylay my good judgment out of fear, John." She stood. "I don't like to leave him alone for too long, even when he's sleeping."

"What could happen while he's sleeping?" John asked, rising to his feet.

"He," Bess stuttered and licked her lips. Exhaustion was taking its toll. "He cannot control himself. He could choke on his own spit-up."

"Jesus," John breathed.

"I doubt it will be long," Bess said. She pulled a wad of paper out of her pocket.

He was impressed she had that kind of blunt. But she'd mentioned more than once that taking the job with Denby was worth it.

"If you could get this to Mrs. Martin, and tell her not to let my room to another, I'd be grateful," Bess said.

"Yeah, 'course," he said, taking the money. "But you could have had your boy do that errand."

"Yeah, but I needed to see a friendly face," Bess said, slugging him in the arm. "It's easier if I know you're here."

His mouth was dry and his mind swam with possibilities—none of them good. He'd go tomorrow to Mrs. Martin in Paddington. That would be easy enough.

"And, I was hoping you'd let Lydia know," Bess said.

His heart sank. "You don't think—"

Bess shook her head. "I don't think anything about anybody, and neither should you."

"What should I tell her? That he's been poisoned? That he's dying?" John shoved his hands in his pockets. He felt helpless again. That feeling he'd had before he'd gotten good at boxing. Useless, helpless, with no footing whatsoever.

"It could be tonight, it could be a fortnight before he goes. I don't know. I've sent for a surgeon, but he doesn't know either."

"Dying it is," John said.

"They don't live far from here," she said. "You could tell her tonight."

He scrubbed his hands through his hair. Sobering did not mean sober. "Must I?"

"Well, if he's dead in the morning, she'll find out a different way. I'd prefer it if she knew before he went."

"Why? What is this all about?" John said, his voice raised. "Sorry. Sorry Bess. It's infuriating."

Bess shrugged and leaned against the wall. "I don't rightly know. After we trained fer awhile, she told me two names, and if I ever came across them, to tell her everything. So, I did. I do. Denby is one of those names."

"It makes me want to punch the wall," John said.

Bess considered him. "Dumb idea, but go ahead. You'll hurt yer hand."

"I hate being jerked this way and that. I hate feeling a fool."

"Miss, miss—" the old butler's voice rang throughout the house.

"I've got to go, John," Bess said, heaving a sigh. "Tell Lydia. I'll find you when this is over. And give Mrs. Martin my apologies for not helping around the house. Just been busy."

Bess walked him to the foyer, and she went up the steps while he let himself out of the dark house, feeling much more deflated than when he entered.

John dropped out into the dark evening streets, his hands shoved into his pockets, his shoulders pulled up high as he trudged. He didn't want to think about it. He didn't want to know anymore.

In the streets, if you wanted to kill a bloke, you hit him with a hammer until he stopped moving. Inelegant and messy, but effective all the same.

❧

THE CARRIAGE SLOWED AND SHOOK AS THEY crossed over the threshold of the property. Lydia felt it shift as Vasily got down off of the perch to close the gate behind him. Again, the vehicle shifted as Vasily climbed back up to finish their journey up the drive. Agnes was still holding Lydia's hand.

Robling met them at the door, taking their hats and shawls. "Should you need any refreshments, my lord?" the butler asked her father, who sighed and looked to her.

Dinner had been long. She couldn't even remember the menu. Food had been placed in front of her, and then it had been whisked away.

"A tray would be lovely," Agnes said, looking around both of them.

"Very good," Robling said. "Also, Lady Lydia has a caller in the drawing room."

Her father's light eyebrows raised, despite his tiredness. "Oh?"

"At this hour?" her mother asked.

"A Mr. Arthur," Robling said.

Her heart tripped over itself. She hadn't seen him since Miss Franklin was on his arm at the Art Exhibition and that other miss was draped over his shoulder.

Lydia's father looked at her, the creases that appeared only when vexed now apparent. "What time did he arrive?"

"Not long ago," Robling said. "Perhaps a quarter of an hour."

"There must be something wrong," Agnes said, her eyes going wide.

"Did you not tell him we had gone out for the evening?" Lydia asked, stripping off her gloves. She shot Agnes a look, trying not to think the same thing.

"Indeed, but he insisted," Robling said. "He is in the drawing room now."

Something terrible must have happened. As she made her way up the stairs, she tried to think of reasons that he would be here, fear clutching at her. All ended in disaster.

She opened the door to find John on the sofa, arms crossed and entirely asleep. A small fire glowed in the hearth and the candles were lit, highlighting the palm-width expanse of his cheek, the shadows causing his jaw to look even more severe. He looked as if he were sculpted raw with a chisel in the side of a mountain, an old god waiting for sacrifices so he could wake and protect his people.

Perhaps she should have told him everything in the carriage, when he asked it of her. But every other person had reacted in the same way, and thus why wouldn't he? When he discovered she was broken, he would look at her with loathing and pity.

Agnes was on her heels. "He's so peaceful," she whispered over her shoulder. Her voice was enough to startle him.

"I apologize," John said immediately, his voice not even thick with sleep. He was on his feet with lightning speed.

His ability to come round so quickly from unconsciousness was a feat nothing short of miraculous. "For what are you apologizing?" Lydia asked.

"I oughtn't have come at such a late hour, but I

must deliver dire news." He cleared his throat and cracked his neck to the left, the right, and then the left again.

Lydia's parents filed into the room. An earl and a countess were enough to make anyone nervous. Her mother gestured for them all to sit, as if this was a proper call at a proper hour.

"Bess?" Panic gripped at Lydia.

"In a way," John said, glancing over at her mother and then her father.

"What it is? Is she ill?"

"No," John said, keeping his voice low. "But Lord Denby is. Mortally so."

Agnes gasped.

"Poor fellow," her father said.

But there was something in his hesitation that made Lydia brace herself. "He was perfectly healthy not two weeks ago. How could this happen?"

"I had hoped you could tell me," he said, turning to face her.

"How would I know?" She went cold all over. His expression said it all. He thought she was somehow responsible.

"Bess says he is quite ill, and the doctor thinks he could expire at any time. Bess said you would want to know before it happened," he said. Looking around the room, he gave a tight, polite smile, barely different from a grimace. "And now that I have delivered the message, I will be on my way. If you'll excuse me." John stood, bowing to Lydia's parents before he hied himself out of her house.

Her stomach clenched. He couldn't just leave after implying murder. She followed him out of the drawing room and into the hallway.

"Are you accusing me of something?" she hissed after him.

He turned to face her. "You know a great deal of

secrets," he said. "I don't think it's unreasonable to think you would know about this kind of thing, too."

"Is this your way of insulting me?" she asked.

"Not at all," he said.

"It's my fault when a man catches a cold? It isn't as if I carry that around in jars with me," she said.

"Bess believes he's been poisoned."

That resonated around the hallway, stunning her.

"You think I would poison Denby?" She couldn't look up at him. All she could see was the thick red carpet that lined the hallway.

"I wouldn't know."

She recoiled as if he had slapped her. But she didn't shy away from hurt. Pain was something she knew, and so she lifted her head to take it straight on. "If you have something to say to me, say it."

He stared at her, his blue eyes glowing in the low light, burning with betrayal. "You can't possibly understand what it feels like to be shut out of something based on the conditions of your birth. And to shut me out just because—"

"The conditions of your birth? Sir, are you not aware of my womanhood? It is the quintessential closed door."

"Don't talk over me. Your opinion doesn't mean more than mine."

"I interrupt only to show you how blind you are to your own importance!" Lydia huffed.

"If I held myself half as high as you, I'd be laughed off the street before I got home!"

"Is that your way of saying I'm—"

"You're arrogant, self-centered, and lack awareness of the world around you!" His face was red as he spit the last words at her. "How can you traipse around half-naked and expect the world to still fall at your feet?"

And that was when she knew for sure. He might

as well have hit her with his fist; it would have hurt less. As unconventional as he seemed, John still wanted the modest virgin. He didn't approve of her boxing, didn't think she ought to engage in the only thing that made her feel at home in her own body.

His words echoed in the hallway and in her ears. She pulled herself up to her full height, as regal and arrogant and self-centered as she could manage. "Your character is on full display now, Mr. Arthur. Thank you for illuminating your opinions so clearly. It is quite late. I'll bid you goodnight."

He bowed, maintaining their fixed gaze. "My lady." He turned on his heel, making for the door.

❧

THE PINTS DID LITTLE DAMAGE. CAULIE LIFTED HIS finger, ordering another. John lifted his finger to do the same.

"This rum doxy's doing a number on you," Caulie said.

"I don't want to talk about it," John said.

"And Bess can't help? She deals with those toffs," he said. "The lords 'n ladies 'n such. His Royalty SuchitySo." Caulie bowed his head, making fanciful circular gestures as if he even knew how to present himself properly. "At yer service."

"Bess is busy," John said as he and Caulie both caught their fresh drinks with open palms. He didn't want to think about Bess—if he thought about Bess, he thought about Denby. If he thought about Denby, he thought about the Orangery, and if he thought about the Orangery, he thought of his own hand sliding up Lydia's leg, his mouth nibbling on her neckline. And that, that was all the things he should not be thinking about.

"She's all right, though, idn't she?" Caulie took a mouthful of foam off the top of his pint.

"Who, Bess? Better than me," John said. "And she's always better than you."

"Never a truer word spoken," Caulie said, raising his glass as if to toast her. "Never a day gone by that I wisht I weren't taller so I could woo her proper."

"Yer in yer cups," John said.

"Don't disparage old Bess," Caulie said. "Ain't her fault she's a Long Meg."

"I'm not. I'm disparaging you." John used his finger to swirl the foam on the top of his beer, flinging the extra wetness off onto the floor.

"Don't get mean," Caulie said. "If you get mean after this many pints, they might not let us in th' pub no more."

They sat in silence, drinking down to yet more empty glasses. The place held a few other regulars such as themselves, more Exchange men there at the end of a long day. They were other non-faction brokers and jobbers like themselves. The other sects seemed to have their own pubs, dividing up the streets into territories and gangs—like the old days, just with more money.

"Clique-ish sort, aren't we?" John asked.

"Who? Jobbers?" Caulie asked, raising another finger to signal the barman.

"Nah, the English," John asked.

Caulie frowned as he considered the topic. "Don't know about that," he said. "I mean, what about th' other ones, the French?"

"They lopped the heads off those that were clique-ish," John pointed out. The Reign of Terror hadn't bothered him that much, as that sort of unrest didn't seem possible in England. It would mean that the lower orders cared more about the nobility than they actually did.

"I don't think it would be very easy to put my head on a pike," Caulie said.

"Say you lopped off me head. What do you grab to put it squarely on a pike?" He mimed picking up an object. "You ain't gonna pick it up from the bottom, it's all bloody down there. No, you use the ears." Caulie wiggled his ill-shapen cauliflower ears. "Mine's too smooth to get a good grip."

"P'haps you'll be spared the trouble then," John said.

"A man can only hope," Caulie said, exhaling loudly. "I'm tired now, I think I'll go."

"You just ordered another round," John protested, pointing to the almost full beer sitting in front of his friend. He downed the rest of his own.

"You take it," Caulie said, getting off the barstool. "I can't think about cutting off heads without getting tired."

John slid the beer over.

"See you tomorrow, Corinthian John," Caulie said, waving goodbye without turning around.

John winced at his fighting name. Tony had warned him not to fight until his head was straight. After these pints, it would be straight again. He was sure of it. Just one more pint.

---

THE KINSLEY BALL WAS SQUEEZED IN BETWEEN other established events, a last-minute party created —Lydia hoped—to announce the engagement of Lord Leighton, Jane's brother, and Miss Rose Dorchester. James would be a wreck, but he was the one who forewent the complete dissolution of the pact. He swore he wouldn't marry, wouldn't have children, hoping that the monster in his father, which lay dormant in himself, would never see the light of day in another Lord Andrepont.

Miss Dorchester was likely ignorant of all these machinations and likely didn't know that Lady Isabelle was competing for the honor of becoming Lady Leighton, who would then ascend to marchioness after the death of Leighton's father. Lydia had no doubt that Leighton was under enormous pressure to marry, given the scandal from last year, but she did feel sorry for Miss Dorchester. It was her debut Season and she was a quiet thing, unaccustomed to the gossip and rumor-mongering.

Tonight, Lydia wore her yellow gown with black muslin overlay, another unusual choice for an unmarried lady of the *ton*, but she was beyond caring. Her original plan was still in place: stay respectable for Agnes. Once her sister was squared away, Lydia would take her own money, hire a decrepit chaperone who was too tired to follow her on every ride, and go to the country—though she hadn't spent much time in the country, and things went awry every time she did. But, if left up to her own devices, and without the company of men, she was certain she would have a fine time.

Lord Elshire appeared with Margaret, followed by Miss Dorchester and James. Lydia frowned. James seemed to have escorted her even though they had agreed he was to leave her alone.

Lydia's stomach clenched. Was James so overwrought that he would poison Lord Denby? She waited for him to scan the room, and when he did, she motioned him over. He was dressed all in black, his green eyes feral.

"You're in quite a state," she greeted him.

"It's falling apart, it's all falling apart," he said, glancing back over his shoulder at Miss Dorchester.

"What's falling apart?" She asked gently.

"Someone bought the cargo debt for the *Europe*. I can't find out who," James's voice cracked.

"It will sort itself eventually. The *Europe* didn't have fire insurance, so claims against the marine insurance will be denied." She tried to soothe him. "Once that gets through the courts, the creditors will be knocking on Hackett's door."

"But if his friends have bought the cargo debt, they can use that as collateral." His hands snaked into his hair.

"You ought to go home, James," she said, sliding her arm through his.

"I can't. This—she—" Another glance back at Miss Dorchester, who was speaking with some young women.

"She has to marry Leighton," Lydia said softly.

Pain flared in his expression, but he nodded all the same. "She won't be happy, not forever."

"Are you certain that's how she feels? It's a good match for her," Lydia said, trying to find a way to soothe him. "An orphaned daughter of a viscount becomes a marchioness? She'll have enough money and power to do as she pleases."

"But she doesn't care about those things," James said. "I can't just let this happen. There has to be someone else."

"James. Miss Dorchester is her own woman."

James swore. "She has to know." He left her, pushing through the crowd as more people entered the ballroom.

"James!" she called after him, but he didn't respond. What did she have to know? Lydia stilled, watching as James pulled Miss Dorchester to the dance floor. The couple argued as they danced.

Jane freed herself from her previous conversation and came to join Lydia. She, too, watched James and

Miss Dorchester dance and argue. The whole world seemed to.

"The ballroom looks lovely," Lydia said.

"That's because you've already begun drinking the champagne," Jane said with a sigh. "I had my heart set on a few more flowers."

The room was already stuffed with vases holding wads of roses. Hothouses from around London must have been emptied out for the occasion.

"It appears we are low on dance partners this evening," Lydia said.

Again, Jane sighed. "I know—it was such short notice. But Mother wanted it to have a low ratio so that Henry could dance with Lady Isabelle more than once."

"Lady Isabelle?" Lydia kept her tone even. "Is she the new favorite?" The money of the estate was more than enough to bail out the Hackett name. Years of hard work would go down the drain. The burning of the *Europe* would still be quite a loss, but it wouldn't be the ruination they'd hoped.

"Mother thinks so," Jane said. "Though Henry is not keen on it."

"I daresay," Lydia said, sipping at her glass. She was not keen on it either. To ally those two houses was a severe mismatch in finances, not to mention politics. Lord Kinsley had been a more progressive sort, cheering on the American experiment, while Hackett had always been stuck in the past, focused on fortifying the family name, and ultimately digging himself deeper into a financial hole because of it.

Speaking of the devil, Lord Leighton came striding over in his signature blue. He was a handsome sight, golden hair and blue eyes that mirrored his sister's good looks. When he smiled, every woman, including Lydia, did her best to suppress a sigh. He greeted her, complimented her, took her by the hand to twirl her as if they were dancing. It was silly and girlish, but it felt nice to be petted in that way, even if it was by Leighton, whom she'd known for years.

Truthfully, she had never heard such words of praise from John. He wasn't the sort to lay on flattery. And while they had a physical attraction, he kept his professional distance when he could. It was she who pressed their closeness, she who sought him in the glade, she who asked for him to wrap her hands, and then the Orangery. Would he have kissed any woman who sought him out in such a way? Perhaps it wasn't her that he even had a physical connection with; perhaps she just happened to be there, happened to be interested, and he took advantage of an opportunity when he saw it.

James was no longer dancing and was nowhere to be seen in the ballroom, leading Lydia to suspect they were on the unchaperoned terrace. Inwardly she cringed. James was not thinking. "Where is Miss Dorchester? She must be here," she said, hoping to cover for them by pretending she hadn't seen them.

They pretended to look more, and Lydia saw Lady Isabelle and her mother hunting Leighton as a pair of vultures circled carrion.

"Don't bother," Leighton said. "She's on the terrace with Andrepont, keeping warm."

The women glanced over, able to make out the dark figure of the James embracing Miss Dorchester. Jane gasped, but Lydia winced. "No," Lydia said. "She does not want him, she told me."

Leighton shrugged, revealing for a fraction of a second a look of disappointment. It nearly broke Lydia's heart. She hadn't thought Leighton might truly like the girl, but it appeared she was wrong.

Lady Isabelle and her mother began to descend upon their group, but Leighton asked Lydia to dance before they could arrive. Lydia glanced over to the terrace doors where Rose and James still lingered behind.

"Of course," Lydia said. "I would be honored."

He smiled the dazzling smile that kept three-quarters of the *ton* reeling and put his hand out to her. She took it, and they made their way through the crowd of people. But before they could arrive, a servant appeared, whispering something in an urgent tone of voice. Lydia couldn't make out the words as she stood politely trying to ignore them.

Leighton dropped her gloved hand, bowing low as a signal of respect. "I apologize, Lady Lydia. A household matter has come to my attention. I will return to you as soon as I am able."

Lydia curtsied in response to show her acceptance. "At your convenience, my lord." He left in a hurry, though his control over his body language was practiced, and for anyone who didn't see he was following his servant out of the ballroom, he looked as relaxed and at ease as he had been when he asked her to dance.

She didn't mind being left. Instead of returning to Lady Isabelle, she parked herself near the terrace doors to catch whichever errant lover reentered first. Neither had shown good judgment. She didn't understand why, when everyone knew the role they had to play, there were so many problems with comprehending the parts.

James's reputation would never be bothered by an evening on an unchaperoned terrace, but Miss Dorchester's would suffer when she walked through those same glass doors. Lydia inched closer, her fan open and buzzing, as if she needed some air.

Miss Dorchester slipped through the small open space between the French doors. Lydia pounced on her, threading her arm through the other girl's as if they were the best of friends. The once active fan dropped, dangling from Lydia's wrist.

"Miss Dorchester, lovely to see you," Lydia said, steering the girl to the back of the ballroom. Here Miss Dorchester could do less damage if she intended to have a breakdown. Lydia suddenly wished for John. How his steady demeanor made it easier to keep herself calm.

"Did he see?" Miss Dorchester asked.

"Of course he saw. That's why James probably did it," she said, forcing them to stroll around the perimeter of the ballroom at an unnaturally slow pace.

"I bit him to make him stop," Miss Dorchester said.

Lydia barked out a laugh. She doubted James had ever been bitten by one of his conquests. It cemented Lydia's good opinion. The girl had more gumption than Lydia gave her credit for; she was glad Miss Dorchester fought back.

"Then I slapped him," Miss Dorchester admitted, pointing to a small wisp of discoloration on her handsome dove-gray glove. "That's his blood."

In a strange way, Lydia was proud of Miss Dorchester. She pushed back her attacker, even though he was known to her, even though he could have easily hurt her. This girl wasn't having any of James's nonsense, and when she said no, she meant it. Surely that was deserving of admiration. "If only Leighton had stuck around a little longer," Lydia said.

They strolled nearer to the door as Miss Dorchester looked towards the exit. Lydia plucked a champagne flute from a tray, handing it to Miss Dorchester. She steered them towards a group of women.

The Scottish lasses with whom they had become

acquainted during the Season lit up when Lydia and Miss Dorchester joined their circle.

Lady Isabelle approached, this time without her mother. Was she trying to follow Lydia everywhere? She didn't want to talk to the girl.

Lydia darted her eyes back over the far side of the ballroom, where James had slipped back in. There were enough dancers to keep the attention of most partygoers at the front of the room, allowing his movements to go mostly unnoticed. His lip was beginning to swell, but he didn't appear angry. No, he seemed resigned. Good, she thought. Perhaps he would finally go home.

Miss Dorchester, however, blanched the color of the Grecian gowns. Even the lasses picked up on her distress.

"I've heard Andrepont is the very image of his father," said Miss Moore, one of these hearty girls from the North.

The statement felt like cold water in Lydia's veins.

"In that he is very handsome," added Miss Brown.

Lady Isabelle had just enough time to overhear the remark. The satisfied smirk on her face spoke of a marriage contract. Lady Kinsley must have made an agreement with Hackett already. Lydia's heart tripped faster, just as it had on the dueling field.

"You look a tad pale, Miss Dorchester. Bad luck in love?" Lady Isabelle said with a thin-lipped smirk.

Lydia bit her tongue. If Miss Dorchester could stand up to James, she should have the bravery to deal with Lady Isabelle. There was power in facing one's demons.

"Would you excuse me?" Miss Dorchester said, setting down her glass on the nearest table. She curtsied low, the courtesy more for Lydia.

"I suppose I scared her off," Lady Isabelle said as they all watched Miss Dorchester leave the ballroom.

"I doubt that very much," Lydia said, watching a servant sweep Miss Dorchester's glass off the table.

"I'm told that I can be intimidating," Lady Isabelle said, attempting to preen.

"Only to those easily intimidated, and I assure you, Miss Dorchester is not," Lydia said, turning on her heel before her tongue let loose. She gave a curt nod to the group.

Lady Isabelle narrowed her eyes. "Then why did she leave so quickly?" Lady Isabelle challenged.

"A woman can have her own reasons," Miss Moore said.

Lydia was glad the girl defended Miss Dorchester. It was good to see that Miss Dorchester had the potential to make friends.

From behind her, a familiar voice boomed, "There you are."

Lydia turned to see Lord Hackett limping over with a cane. She hadn't seen him enter. She did her best to mask her horror, but she was afraid it was no use. He'd seen her expression.

"I may be a bit slower now, but I assure you, Lady Lydia, there is no worry of gangrene."

Clenching her teeth was all she could do. He was even more grotesque with his limp and his cane, his pallor a rough, splotchy purple. Cold tripped through her, and she willed herself not to start shaking. She would not tremble because of him. Hackett truly was the last one left. "Perhaps gangrene won't be your downfall, but life is full of traps."

"Isn't it just?" Lord Hackett said, his fat face mirroring the smugness of his daughter.

❧

PARSONS BROUGHT HIM SOME GIN, BUT JOHN DIDN'T know where to even sit in his own home. First he was in his bedroom, and then downstairs in the study. He wandered into the formal drawing room next. If he'd gotten things up to snuff, gotten Pearl a suitable chaperone, this would have been where she received callers. Proper ladies and perhaps a respectable fellow once in a while too.

He ought to stay with the middle-class folk. That was setting his sights high enough. Miss Franklin was a nice girl, and he liked her brother. She got along well with Pearl. But Miss Franklin seemed the type of woman who wouldn't respond to his charms, so to speak. So perhaps Miss Perry would be a woman to court instead. She was Pearl's friend, so that was good, knowing they already got along well. Her silly attempts to get his attention at the gallery bothered him, though. Why couldn't she just be straightforward? Why did she have to flutter her eyelashes and act so...so...*girlish*?

Because men like him were supposed to like girls who fluttered their eyelashes. But he liked women with strength. Women whose biceps had striations, whose focus could narrow to the width of a necklace chain. Women who followed their own code of ethics.

But it wasn't his fault that Lydia wouldn't let him in. He tried, good Lord, he tried. How many times could he knock on that door or outright ask to be let in? She wouldn't do it. And he had to accept that, for whatever her reasons, she didn't want him.

He wandered out of the dimly lit drawing room. To be fair, Parsons had attempted to anticipate his behavior by lighting candles ahead of his movements, but John was being so unpredictable the butler couldn't keep up. John returned to his study.

When Parsons burst into the room, John assumed it was to berate him for his movements. "I apologize,

Parsons," John said, his hands up in surrender. "I promise to stay in one place."

Parsons inclined his head to acknowledge the apology. "Thank you, sir. But I came to inform you of a visitor."

John set his glass down. "Now?"

"Shall I show her in to your study, or will you meet her in the drawing room?" Parsons asked.

The gin slid down his throat before he could think to swallow it. His thoughts immediately turned to Lydia, her dark hair undone, a hooded cape for disguise. She might tell him all of her secrets, the reason her cousin had shot Hackett, the reason for her weeping in the carriage, why she cared about that ship, all of it. Then he could kiss her senseless, strip off every stitch, and drink in every inch of flesh. He shook himself from his brief reverie.

"Here, please, Parsons," he said, getting to his feet. He burped, lessening the bloat; he shouldn't have drunk so much ale with Caulie. He bounced a little, hoping to sober up.

The butler gave a curt nod and turned on his heel, leaving John to sniff at his clothes. He lifted an arm. The stale smell of beer sweat permeated his shirt.

The desk drawers squeaked in protest as John opened each one, searching for some kind of scent to mask his own. They were empty but for a small pot of ink and an unsharpened quill. He had leased the place furnished, but apparently one needed to supply one's own stationery.

When he heard the footsteps down the hall, he stood. They didn't sound light enough to be Lady Lydia's. No, they were slow and heavy. He glanced at the clock on the mantel. It was late. Despite his poor manners in visiting her home near the midnight hour, he didn't think Lydia would repay in kind.

The door opened and Bess filled the entrance.

Her pallor was waxy and pale from exhaustion, the dark circles beneath her eyes even more pronounced. John left his post behind the desk and ushered her to a chair. "Are you well? What's happened? Denby?"

She held up her hand to stop his flow of questions.

"Would you like anything?" John asked instead. "Gin? It tastes awful, but it's a proper glass o' daffy."

Bess nodded as she dropped into a chair. John leapt up and poured a finger into a tumbler. She sipped at it without haste, shuddering as it went down. John seated himself in the chair next to her and waited, his own glass within reach.

"It's done," she said, her voice raspy and dry.

"Denby?" he asked.

She nodded, her limp hair oily and shifting with her gesture. There must have been no time to care for herself, or perhaps no one to help her care for an ailing man.

John took her hand, watching as his friend fought back tears. Despite all of her hardships, he had never seen her cry: not from a punch, not even the day he watched as she was evicted from a boarding house for being unnatural. "I'm sorry." He hadn't known she would be so attached to a client who had only contracted her for a few months. "You must have really cared for him."

Energy appeared as her anger reared. She wrenched her hand out of his. "I didn't care for that twat."

She tossed back the gin. Tears filled her eyes, and John hoped it was the burning of the alcohol.

"I watched a man die tonight, John." She stood, her sudden energy causing her to pace in front of the unlit fireplace. "He had money and influence, and he died alone in a house where even his loyal servants abandoned him. If he died alone, what will happen to me?"

"You still have fights and other income?" John asked. He wished Parsons had lit more candles in the room, for he could barely make out her expressions.

"I'm not talking about money," Bess said. "I'm talking about my deathbed. 'S a cold and lonely place."

Though his mind constantly worked on the future, setting up plans and strategies of money and work, training and security for Pearl, he hadn't once thought of his deathbed. "Why on earth do you think you'll die alone?" John asked, bewildered.

"Because look at me!" Her voice shook the room, an unexpected thunder.

John waited as she, in turn, waited for him. The painful tenor of her voice was unmistakable, but what she expected from him, he didn't know. "I don't understand," he said, drawing out his words. This felt like he was walking into an ambush.

"I have committed the worst sin a woman can," she said.

There were plenty of sins out there. What could be the worst? Did she murder Denby? No, she wouldn't have told him he was dying if she did. It was something else. Something more philosophical. "Plenty of men would forgive a lady boxer—it isn't that scandalous," John said. He almost went on to mention the other few notorious female fighters who were either married when they fought or married after their fame had waned.

"Not boxing, John. You can't even see it, can you?" Her voice thinned. She looked up at the ceiling, no doubt trying to stop what her exhaustion had loosed. "I am ugly. The worst sin of a woman is to be ugly, and I am she."

John stood. There was no way to argue, but there

was a way to soothe. She sagged against him as he wrapped his arms around one of the best fighters he'd ever known. Her body was more powerful than any other woman's, her spirit fiercer than any man's, and she was broken by the idea of spending her life as a solitary creature. It made him ache for her. More than he'd ever hurt for himself.

"You'll never be alone, Bess. No matter what, you'll have me," he said.

"Yes, but you'll never love me like that," she said, her voice weary. "No one will love me the way you love Lydia."

The truth of her words stung. He hadn't thought of that word at all. Love was a strange thing, weird and mystical. People used it all the time to describe all sorts of bits that couldn't be held up to the real feeling of love. People loved oysters. Sailors loved the sea. Debutantes loved the color sage. Rich people loved turtle soup.

But to love Lydia? He supposed that was true. When he went to tell her of Denby's illness, she had seemed stricken that he might think her capable of poisoning the man. And in turn, it had hurt him to cause her hurt. And he really didn't think she was responsible, but he'd given her the opportunity to deny it, to tell him everything, to let him in on the little club she'd formed but wouldn't give him access to. She'd let him rub his hands all over her, push his hand higher up her skirts—but tell him why she pursued those two men with the fervor of a starving dog? He wasn't good enough for that.

Holding Bess now was a comfort to him just as much as it was to her. Of all the people he knew, he was most like Bess. In some ways, they would be the perfect match. He had all the money in the world to keep her safe, and they had been training partners since they were knee high.

"It doesn't matter," John said, shushing her the way he would soothe an infant. His fingers combed through her short hair. "Because I love you anyway. You've not let anyone care for you, so let me."

He called for Parsons, who seemed to be close by. John didn't appreciate the man's eavesdropping, but no matter.

"A bath and the guest room?" Parsons whispered.

"And a tray," John said. "Food fixes everything. She likes the yellow cheese the best, the kind with the red rind."

"Very good sir," Parsons said, leaving the room without a sound.

"It'll be yer head if I stay the night," Bess said, sniffing. "They'll think we're basket-making."

"Let 'em think it." John pressed her hands between his. If his life was that he would live with Bess and Pearl, and not a wife, so be it. There were worse lives to be lived. He'd just ignore the gaping hole in his chest, the kind no amount of mills or friendly cups of gin could fill. He'd ignored an empty belly for years. This would be an old trick dressed up in new clothes. "You'll never be alone. I promise."

# 15

Sitting in her private drawing room upstairs, the room with the good light in the morning, she received a note from John, his handwriting now obviating the need for a signature, with no more words than

*D— has succumbed.*

She abandoned the drawing room with good light to go on a morning ride instead. It felt good to be alone, trees whipping by her in the dawn light. This was the hour when she would have met John for training, but instead she rode.

The horse, a three-year-old Arabian new to their stable, urged her faster. Lydia complied, giving the horse its head, the soft cushion of the grass beneath his feet in Hyde Park rebounding as the canter turned into a gallop. The wind threatened to take the pins out of her hair, a sensation in which Lydia reveled. She narrowed her eyes against the breeze and pushed the horse to a full run.

Four of the men from the horrid game were dead. The fifth limped with a gunshot wound. If he was successful in marrying his daughter to Leighton—and after James's antics last night with Miss Dorchester, he might be—then he wasn't as ruined as she would have liked. She turned the matter over in her mind as the miles spread out behind her. They were so close; it wasn't time to sit back.

James had been a mess last night. That was what love looked like, she mused. That's how a person felt when love slipped through her fingers. She was glad she didn't feel like that after her argument with John.

Because all of her feelings were crammed into the smallest jewelry box a person could imagine. Stuffed in, compacted, then closed up and lacquered over. Her heart could not be opened. It was impossible. She was, quite simply, incapable. Her arrogance was impenetrable.

Then, to test, just to experiment, as Margaret had taught her, she pictured the tall, ruddy-haired boxer. Especially as he'd looked in the Orangery, with the overcast day highlighting him as he moved toward her. When he told her the only good thing about being in the country was her.

But then, all the words he said came tumbling over one another. The prickles of hurt came from all directions, so she shoved them into that lacquered box for safekeeping.

She emerged from the wooded area, slowing the Arabian to a statelier pace as the paths of Rotten Row became more apparent. There were few other visitors, but enough to make her behave. She took the nearest exit. The sound of the horse's hooves clattering against cobblestone was not as pleasing as the swift pounding of them against the grass.

She found herself at Margaret's door, a small but well-appointed walk-up in a building shared with a few other young women. An older matron ran the house, with rules rivaling Newgate's.

Margaret was still styling her hair when she let Lydia into her small flat.

"How is Miss Dorchester?" Lydia asked, finding a place to sit on Margaret's bed.

Her cousin shook her head. "She cried all the way home." Margaret shoved more pins in her hair, not always successful at tucking away the thick strands.

"Expected," Lydia said. She went to the small window that looked out over the street. The Arabian stood tethered to the post, bored but content to wait for his mistress. "Lord Denby is dead," she mentioned, as if it were yet another ball.

Margaret gasped. "What happened? Did you—?"

Another casual accusation of murder. Was she such a believable murderess? A simple scowl eased Margaret's conscience.

"Of course not. Did James?" Margaret asked.

"I doubt it. Poison, from what I understand," Lydia said.

"Ah," Margaret said, a vague look coming over her face.

At this point, Lydia knew Margaret was cataloging possible poisons in her mind, cross-referencing them with availability and efficacy. No doubt there would soon be a list.

"That's four out of five," Lydia reminded her. "And Hackett is worse for wear, with the exception of one possible eventuality."

"If we eliminate the possibility, could you and James rest?" Margaret asked, her eyes owlish behind her spectacles.

Her cousin could calculate as ruthlessly as any of them, but she hated to do it. Perhaps her uncertain childhood, being pushed back and forth from abject poverty to opulent wealth, had made her desire for constancy seem soft-hearted. But no, Margaret was more compassionate than Lydia or James. Probably because she and Agnes had been so young they couldn't remember that night.

Margaret and Agnes had never woken in terror, a nightmare triggered by a sour scent or the sensation of someone standing too close.

"If we can ensure his insolvency, I think we can consider Lord Hackett taken care of," Lydia said, even though it meant breaking James's heart. Well, if she could handle not having emotions, so could he. But the thought worked at her—could she consider Hackett truly taken care of? They had dissolved the pact formally, but James had insisted on continuing. Perhaps it couldn't be done.

"Poor Lady Isabelle. And Lady Hackett, for that matter," Margaret said.

"What do you mean, poor Lady Isabelle?" She narrowed her eyes.

"Well, it isn't her fault her father is a monster. And she'll get stuck in some terrible marriage as a consequence. And Lady Hackett is equally blameless. I doubt theirs was a love match." Margaret turned back to her mirror.

But to pity those women would be muddying the waters. No. This was the way it had to be. No emotions, just action. "It doesn't really matter. Guilt by association."

Margaret eyed her in the mirror. "How do we finish this?"

"Lord Leighton must marry Miss Dorchester. If he marries Lady Isabelle, then Lord Hackett has access to the Kinsley fortune."

Margaret nodded, the facts clear. "It seems clear he wants to marry Rose."

"He has to," Lydia said. "But Hackett will fight and threaten. You must apply every bit of pressure you can."

Her eyes went wide. "I have no influence," she protested.

Lydia smiled. "Elshire loves you. He's wanted to

marry you for years. You have more power than you could possibly realize."

The apprehension in her expression was easy to read. Margaret loved Elshire too much to jeopardize their eventual marriage. It was the fairy tale she'd dreamed of her entire life.

"Just tell Elshire that if Miss Dorchester is shamed, he will need to care for her. If he marries you, his estate will pass to your future children, and Rose will be out in the streets. A penniless, scandalized, ruined light-skirt."

The last words hit home with the desired effect. Margaret gasped at the language. "But surely she could just retire to the country."

"Scandal sheets are delivered everywhere. It's only a matter of time."

Margaret's face softened. "I'll tell him."

Lydia left, giving Margaret ample time to break her fast before her work at Montagu House. She would visit James later in the day. After he had stormed out last night, Lydia could only assume that he'd stayed up all night drinking. It seemed like the kind of thing he would do.

Thinking that she was giving the horse its head to do what he pleased, she wandered the streets until she found herself in Marylebone. She was arrogant and self-centered. But he had no idea why she had to present herself so. And when he'd yelled at her, red-faced and clearly hurt, she hadn't defended her position. Hadn't told him that her single-mindedness was in service of the pact, to allow Margaret and Agnes and James a way out of their promises.

The horse slowed as she came to John Arthur's townhouse. Perhaps it was time he understood. She stared at the building. Her teeth tried to chatter, but she clamped her jaw.

There was no reason to be here. He didn't know

about their search for the person who'd bought the cargo debt, or about the pact. For all he knew, she'd poisoned Denby. Because he didn't really know anything about her.

She could tell him about William's illness, James's father, the faro game, the pact. The knowledge would make him eat his words. She would show him that lacquered box and dare him to open it.

In terms of scandal, it was a terrible idea to see him. She tied the horse to the post. Truly terrible—she hoped she wasn't seen this early in the morning. Any hopes of staying respectable for Agnes's sake would be dashed. But her feet shuffled forward, never wavering from the path to his front door. Would he talk her out of ruining Hackett for the sake of his wife and daughter? Would he think she was worthless?

When the butler opened the door, she asked to see Mr. Arthur.

"Mr. Arthur is currently disposed with another guest," the butler said, his voice somehow smoother than what Lydia cared for.

The hour was still early. What other guest could he have? A business colleague? A client?

"Will he be long?" Lydia pressed.

The butler's gaze left hers as he searched for words. "The guest in question has been here for some time. She will likely continue to occupy him."

The slow burn of a blush crept up Lydia's face.

"May I give him your card?" the man asked.

Lydia's feet already began their retreat. "No," she stammered. "I'd thank you to not mention my visit."

She untied the horse, her fingers flying through the knot. *The guest had been there for some time* could only mean through the night. Why should she be surprised? He had been frank about having past lovers.

Another piece of ephemera to push down into that box. That's fine. She leaned forward to brush the dark mane straight as they set off on an easy trot. No need to look as if she was in a hurry. Tamp it all down. Her head hurt. And something else hurt, but she could ignore that.

She knew she was difficult to love—her family had made that clear. There were so many reasons she held herself apart from the world, and she was working to solve that problem. Could he not see that to be soft was to break apart?

Women were expected to be soft, but it was their hardness that kept them going. Lack of choices, lack of opportunities, so many circumstances out of their control. And Lydia was a creature who was unable to absorb all of that. So, she was hard all the way around, and John clearly didn't want to have anything to do with that. Which was fine. She was broken, he was not.

The sun was beginning to warm her through her pelisse. The wrought iron fences gave way to sidewalks lined with manicured shrubs. Everything was fine. Better than fine. Her revenge was near complete. What else could she ever possibly need?

❧

"YOU SHOULD APOLOGIZE," BESS SAID, RUNNING her finger along the inside of her chocolate cup. When she came up with the thick sludge, she stuck her finger in her mouth.

"Your manners are atrocious," John said to her.

She grinned, the chocolate blacking out some of her teeth.

"What do I have to apologize for?" John asked. He stood and went to the sitting room window behind Bess. He'd never even looked out to see what view he had. Just the street. It was the second time he'd been in this room, the first being last night. A flicker of a dark-colored horse's tail caught his eye as it ambled south, out of view.

Bess snorted. "I may not know a thing about love, but what I do know is that no one wants to be accused of murder."

John sighed. "Oh, that." He'd told Bess about carrying her message to Lydia. But while she'd focused on that, all he could think about was that Lydia wouldn't let him in. It was another time where he'd tried to gain acceptance and couldn't.

"*Oh, that* is what you have to say? Jesus, John. You're the worst," she said.

"The worst what? You were the one who said Denby was poisoned. You were the one who told me she would want to know." He wanted to pull the curtains down.

"And I told you that I had a deal with Lydia. She wanted to know what happened to the man. Everything from his invitations to...other things." Bess clanked her cup back onto the tray and folded her arms.

He cracked his neck from side to side. "How do you think he died?"

She sighed, looking tired again. "It's only a guess."

"Tell me," he said.

"Remember Bennie Booth?" she asked.

"Yeah. Skinny kid. Died a few years back," John said, turning towards Bess, away from the window.

"Same kind of signs. Fatigue, then the puking and the runs—"

John held up his hand to stop her. "That's vivid enough," he said.

"You squeamish now? Is that what happens when you're swimming in lard?" Bess teased. "Bennie Booth took them pills to make him stronger. He got them from a Clyster Pipe on a street corner. I fed one to a rat after he died. Rat died too. Just like it was poison."

"So, you think Denby was taking some kind of quack pill? But he was a lord—he would have gotten medicine from reputable sources," he said.

Bess winced. "He would have, unless he was ashamed to be taking them."

John shook his head. "Like what?"

Her eyebrows went up, expecting him to supply the answer.

Except he didn't know the answer. "Haven't the foggiest."

"What sort of thing would you be ashamed of everyone knowing?" Bess prompted.

"I don't know," he insisted.

"What men are ashamed of?" she suggested, waiting as he huffed and sighed.

"Just tell me, Bess," John begged.

She rolled her eyes. "He took pills for prick problems."

"Oh," John said, understanding dawning. "Oh."

Bess watched John pace the room, not bothering to fill the silence with an explanation.

"And how do you know he was taking...such a drug?" John asked, finally looking up from his aimless meander around the room.

"Don't ask questions you don't want answers to," Bess said.

"I've prepared myself," John said.

"He attempted to initiate an inappropriate addendum to one of our sessions, which was then cut short by that particular problem." Bess shrugged, leaning against the window jamb.

"Addendum?" John asked.

"Fancy words make everything classier," Bess said.

"Tried to blow the grounsils, if you know what I mean."

John sat in one of the chairs. Bess returned to her seat on the settee. They were silent for a moment. He didn't want to ask if Bess had agreed to be the man's mistress or if the lord had assumed his rights and attempted to force it.

"Don't ask questions," she reminded him.

John stared out the window. How different their lives had turned out, despite how similar their childhoods had been. He'd tried to help her more when he'd started to make money, but she wouldn't take it. Instead, she gave him bits of blunt to invest as she earned it, clawing her own way up, just as he had. Was it a matter of his ambition, or was it a matter of their sexes that made this disparity so abominable?

"Thanks for the hospitality," Bess said. "I needed a friend."

John smiled. "Of course," he said. "Anytime you need. I told you, I'm here for you."

"I appreciate it. Maybe after you and Lydia marry, you could keep a room for me."

Color flushed John's face. "Let's not get ahead of ourselves."

"True, she might not accept you," Bess said, leaning back. "But if you both can get over yerselves, there's a shot there."

"What do you mean by that?" he asked, panic dousing the blush.

Bess shrugged. "Or maybe ye'll be too much of a coward to ask. She'll marry a toff, you'll marry some prissy girl who wants to spend yer money. And life will continue on."

"Are you trying to goad me into apologizing?" John said.

"I think this fuss is something that can be solved by

the two of you, a boxing ring, and maybe a pint of gin," Bess said, standing. She looked about, as if she were surveying the room for judgment. "I'd even say you could use those silly gloves they've started sporting at Gentleman Jackson's so you don't hurt each other. Silliest bit of prancy shite I've ever seen. But I'll be on my way now. I've left my flat unoccupied for too long. Mrs. Martin will be renting it out to someone else by now."

"It's been good to have you, Bess," John said.

She ducked her head, and John could tell she actually felt pleasure at the comment. "See you at Tony's?"

"As soon as he lets me fight."

She smiled. "He will. You haven't had a blackened peeper in too long."

❧

BESS WAS BUSY. JAMES WAS A DRUNKEN MESS. AND John? Well, that was out of the question. She crossed the ballroom practicing her one-two combinations, advancing carefully, maintaining form. Her shoulders crept up, but she noticed and forced them back down.

The wraps surrounding her fists were coming loose. She couldn't remember how to tuck the tail properly. Reaching the end of the ballroom, she caught her breath and stared at her hands. It had seemed so easy until she needed to do it without help.

"Do you have to use them?"

Lydia's head snapped up. She'd thought she was alone, but her mother had sneaked in somehow. "You never watch me exercise."

"I came to tell you that Margaret is here. She and Agnes are taking tea." Her mother approached, crossing the empty ballroom. It seemed so much more a proper ballroom with her in here.

"Oh? How is Margaret?" Lydia unwrapped her hand, trying to keep the long line of fabric untwisted.

"She's well. There is news," her mother picked up the bottom end of the wrap and began rolling it, straightening out the fabric as she did so.

"Wedding date?" Lydia asked.

"A marriage contract has been signed by Leighton and Elshire." Her mother gave her a soft smile. "I knew you'd be relieved."

Lydia did her best to return the smile. She was relieved. The only missing piece was the cargo debt, and it didn't trouble her as much as it troubled James. But it was the last thing on the list. The completion.

"You know," her mother said, taking up the rolled wrap, allowing Lydia to work on the other hand, "some women cry."

"I don't know what you're talking about," she said.

"When there is a broken heart, tears would be expected."

"I still don't know what you're talking about," Lydia said, unspooling the fabric of her other hand. It was much easier now that one hand was completely free.

"I couldn't help but notice that Mr. Arthur hasn't called. Properly, I mean."

"Haven't noticed." Lydia bit out. She moved past her mother to the chairs where she kept her equipment. "Do you mind?" she asked, plucking the rolled hand wrap from her mother's palm.

"Lydia." Her mother didn't move.

But Lydia kept on her path to the side of the room. Had to take good care of her things. It was hard for her to obtain boxing equipment. She needed James or Vasily to go to Covent Garden, and she was tired of relying on other people. She just wanted to be by herself.

"I know you're hurting."

The statement made her want to hurl the wraps across the room. "Of course I'm hurting," she ground out through gritted teeth.

"You've been hurting a long time," her mother said softly. "If I knew how to make it stop, I would."

She heard her mother approach her from behind, soft slippered steps.

Lydia shook her head. Her blood pounded in her ears. There was nothing anyone could do about anything. The best thing to do was just survive. They'd done their bit to punish those who deserved it.

"But you don't cry, do you?" She put her hand on Lydia's bare shoulder, which was slick with sweat.

"I did cry. I cried a lot. And it did nothing." She didn't have to bring up the event; her mother knew what she was talking about. "It made it worse, and everyone said I was hysterical."

"Nobody wanted to believe such a despicable thing," her mother said, leveling her gaze to her daughter. "Even me. And I was wrong." Her voice choked up.

Her mother's emotion made her throat close up, panic starting to claw at her. Lydia wanted to comfort her but also wanted to punish her at the same time.

"When you are connected to someone like that, married to him like my sister was, or invited him into your home, as I did, you don't want to believe it. Because if he's a monster, he makes you a monster, too." Tears glassed over her mother's eyes. "Sullied by association."

Lydia could feel it now—the hot tears in her eyes, the childish hysteria that had plagued her until she could grind it under her heel.

Her mother's nose began to redden, but the tears didn't fall.

"I knew something had happened, but I didn't want to believe it was James's father," she assured her daughter. "I wanted it to be a groom, or a man from the village. Something that awful couldn't be from our own house. But it was."

"But it was," Lydia repeated. "And I was broken."

"Broken?" her mother started. "You are not broken."

"I am. I remember the physician saying quite specifically that I was broken during one of those horrid annual visits. It was so humiliating, even though you gave me that awful bit of brandy to drink so I wouldn't remember."

She tried to pull Lydia in for an embrace but Lydia wrested out of her grasp. "Andrepont was clear about why he did it." Her mother's voice pitched higher. "Those men had all visited the same—a certain—" Her mother stumbled.

"Brothel," Lydia supplied.

"Yes. And they were under the impression they all had contracted a disease. A disease that could be cured by a—engaging in—" her mother's voice trembled. "I wasn't certain if you were about to start your cycles, and the idea that you could be with child was unbearable. You were still a little girl." Then her tears did fall.

It took all the self-control Lydia had not to match those tears.

"But the doctor never said you were broken. Not once. No one did. And I wouldn't have allowed anyone to tell you that."

It took all the self-control Lydia had to not match those tears."But I heard it. I heard him say it to you."

Her mother swiped at her tears and sniffed in a way very unbecoming to a countess. She thought for a moment, then cleared her throat. "The doctor told me your honor—the barrier—was gone."

"I don't know what you're talking about," Lydia snapped.

Her mother blushed. "It's the part inside of you that is supposed to prove that you are a virgin, but even that isn't always true."

Suddenly Lydia felt nauseated. "I need to sit down." The world whitened to where she could barely see. By the time she reached the chairs, a dark shadow encircled her vision.

Her mother followed her, a steadying arm across her shoulders. "That's one of the reasons why we encouraged you to ride horses. Sometimes that can break it. It would give you an excuse to tell a future husband." They sat on the chairs that lined the perimeter of the ballroom. "But you yourself were never broken."

"I think I'm going to—" Lydia's stomach heaved. Instead of scooting away, her mother put her arm around her.

"You aren't broken," she repeated over and over, rocking with her, fanning the back of her neck.

Instead of actually disgorging, Lydia did something far worse. She began to cry. And once it started, it didn't stop. Her mother kept her arm around her as Lydia laid her head in her lap. She wetted through her mother's skirts. The light waned. Her mother waved off Agnes when she came to check on her, and Robling left candles for when they were needed. Still Lydia cried.

"But what if I'm broken now?" she asked after a time. Her face was leaking in all ways, as if nothing inside her was solid anymore. The lacquered box had disintegrated.

"What would make you broken now?" Her mother asked gently.

"Everything I've done, hurting other people," she sniffed, but it was no use. There was no breathing happening through her nose.

"It wasn't the best idea," her mother admitted. "But what have you really done? You've sniped and been nasty in ballrooms, that's it."

"I paid a man to commit arson," she said.

"Oh," her mother said. "I thought you were just watching a particular ship."

Lydia shook her head. "James and I went to Wapping and paid a midshipman to set a fire after the cargo was loaded."

Her mother looked stunned. "Well," she said slowly. "We can't change the past."

Lydia shook her head. She didn't feel bad about it, exactly, especially since no one had lost their lives.

"But we can change how you move forward. It isn't like the man didn't have it coming."

A giggle escaped her. It was dark, save the candles Robling had brought in for them. She heaved a sigh. Control was hard to regain, but it was returning.

"As your mother, the only thing I want for you is happiness."

Lydia pulled up her sleeves and used them to wipe her face. The room had grown cold and she shivered in response. "I know."

"For other people, happiness is found in making their own lives. Finding someone to love."

She pulled on the dirtied sleeves. "That's really not a problem. The issue is finding someone who could love me."

Her mother reached up and took out the pins in her hair. Not that they were doing much anyway. "I don't think that's the issue."

"Are you talking about someone in particular?"

"Aren't you?" her mother countered, combing her fingers through Lydia's hair.

Lydia grunted, a noise that normally would elicit a snapping correction from her mother.

"What I think, and I know it carries very little weight, as I am your mother," she said, pulling out a knot. "Is that while we would have never revealed anything to a potential husband, you have an opportunity to trust a lover."

"Mother!" Lydia wrenched her head away. Her mother had actually said the word *lover* to her.

"Your husband can still be your lover, but not necessarily," her mother said coolly. "Don't look so surprised. Those are the best kinds of husbands."

"You'd think I was getting married tomorrow," she grumbled.

"But part of that," her mother continued as if she hadn't been interrupted, "is trust. If you don't give Mr. Arthur the ability to trust you, he can't. If you open your heart to him, I doubt you'll be disappointed."

---

JOHN THOUGHT HE HEARD A PIANO. HE STOOD IN Andrepont's library, a well-appointed room, but devoid of any character. Any room belonging to the brooding, clearly unstable viscount should have been over-the-top packed with eccentricities. Disappointing.

Finally, he heard steps and Andrepont burst into the room. He was not a man of subtle movements, which was why he didn't win in the boxing ring. Every thought was transmitted before he made his move.

"Mr. Arthur, I'm not accustomed to callers. I'm sorry to keep you waiting." His gait appeared concentrated, like he would wobble if he weren't careful. Man had already tied one on and it was ten in the morning. Or maybe it was just left over from last night. Andrepont slid behind his desk.

"No trouble. I came by to give you this." John slapped the papers on his desk.

"What is it?" Andrepont asked, pulling it across the expanse, squinting.

"It's the cargo debt from the *Europe*. I bought it when word came of the fire." John shrugged; it made him uncomfortable to go into details of what he'd actually done. It was such a murky territory of what was ethical versus what was legal. What he did was legal. But it didn't sit right with him, somehow. "And I did some maneuvering with the market. Some of the riskier investments have not panned out for, er, certain men. But I've paid myself back with the profits, so this is yours. I'm not giving it to you for nothing."

Andrepont nodded. "But it isn't for me, is it?"

John cracked his neck from side to side. "It's for your family."

"Lydia?" he asked with eyebrows raised.

"Whoever needs it," he said, turning to go.

"I could tell you, if you'd like." Andrepont leaned back in his chair, the pages of cargo listings, the values, the entirety of a man's debt forgotten on the desk. "I could tell you everything."

John turned, seeing Andrepont's calculated glare, his hands steepled. The ache inside John's chest throbbed. "I don't want to know anymore."

❧

"YOU'VE LOST WEIGHT," JAMES SAID, INTERRUPTING Lydia's reverie.

She didn't bother to look away from the gray splatters of rain on the window. "Thank you," she said.

"It wasn't a compliment. You look terrible. Or maybe your tailor went blind," he said.

"Women don't use tailors," she said, eyes still on the window. The only thing she enjoyed these days was training by herself. She attended all of her social engagements, dressing in finery, picking at plates, dancing when necessary. It was as if she weren't even there, counting down the minutes until she could strip off her sleeves and hide in the ballroom, trying to remember the last correction she'd been given. She hadn't the courage to send for Bess, because it wasn't Bess that she wanted.

"There's your problem," he said, flopping onto the furniture. "Tailors. Glad I could help. I'll tell your mother on the way out."

Lydia's head snapped over to look at him, lounged in one of the chairs, his leg kicked over the arm. "My mother sent for you?"

"Yes," he said, bobbing his foot up and down in midair.

"Did she tell you what Vasily found?"

"That was not the subject we discussed," he said, giving his head a lazy bob.

"He found the poison. Or at least, probably the poison from Denby's."

"How clever of him to have found it at another man's residence," James said. "His reach is further than I thought."

She glared at him. Her head hurt and she just wanted to get to the point. "According to some of Denby's staff, a disreputable sort of street apothecary was giving him pills for some problems."

"What kind of problems?" he asked.

"You know what kind of problems," she snapped. "Man problems."

"Chest hair, beard growth? Balding? We have a lot of problems." He grinned.

"I won't give you the benefit of my embarrassment. Anyway, one of the main ingredients in those pills is arsenic. Too much, and, well..."

"So, you no longer suspect me," James said.

"I never suspected you," she insisted.

"I'm not sure I believe that. I'm suspected of all sorts of horrid behavior."

"Well, sometimes you do engage in it, but I didn't ever really think you would have poisoned Denby. Not really your style."

"Not a signature move, I agree." James swung his legs around so his feet were flat on the floor for once. "Since we are being so candid, let me say this: Your mother is worried about you."

"Why?" Lydia asked, her temper sparking for the first time in weeks. "I've gone to all of the parties, danced when asked."

"But you've lost your glow," James pointed out.

"Is that what she said?" Lydia asked.

"Almost verbatim." James smiled at her, and she noticed for the first time that he had yellowing around his right eye and a cut on the bridge of his nose. "Quite certain it was your *glow* she mentioned."

"Have you been at the mills?" she asked.

"Why? Does it matter?" his eyes gave a cold glint. "Are you concerned for my well-being?"

Her stomach clutched. "Have you seen him?"

He stopped swinging his foot. "Yes. He stopped by for a visit, even."

An ache lodged in her chest. It wasn't the anxious panic she had felt before, nor was it the cold tremors —it was something else entirely. And she didn't like it. "What did he say?"

James pulled a thick collection of papers from his jacket's interior pocket. They were tri-folded, held together with twine. He held it out to her.

"What is this?" She stepped forward and took

them. She slid the twine off and flipped through them. "Is this a copy?"

James shook his head. "And to be clear, he didn't just give this to us. He did some sort of money magic and has been compensated. So, don't think he did it out of the goodness of his heart."

"But he did," she whispered. A tiny light of hope lit inside her. "I know what we have to do with it."

"Wait until the creditors come for Hackett and then go pick out his best furniture when they open the house to repay the loans?" James suggested.

Lydia shook her head. "It's a much better revenge than that."

## 16

It had been a long time since he'd had fight night jitters. The air was somehow electrified, and every hair on John's body stood on end, ready for a bolt of lightning to surge through him. He shifted his weight from foot to foot, light on his feet, trying to be ready for anything. His body felt light as air, empty.

"What's wrong with you?" Tony asked him, chewing on a long, thin piece of hay.

"Nothing," John said, pulling at his shoulders, willing the muscles to loosen up even more.

Tony shook his head. Caulie stood next to him, looking worried. The small jobber had agreed to be his cornerman, like old times. Small comfort, at least. The basement of the butcher was filling up with people of all types. Mostly working men in shirtsleeves, holding their beers, some already red-faced from their efforts. The Fancy hadn't shown yet, but they preferred to be fashionably late. By the time the last fight started, there'd be a few dandies tripping about. A few women trickled in, some there to work the crowd of men, some to find their husbands and sons, and others to watch the mills.

Bess was in the far corner talking to the man who

owned the butcher shop above. They looked to be arguing, with Bess pointing to the small ring marked out in the middle of the floor by large squares of butcher paper. The dimensions did look small, and he could understand if she were asking for a remeasure. Bess had agreed to fight tonight if a competitor could be found, and with her height advantage, she hated to be shorted her space.

Basil came up, all scrawny limbs and elbows every which way. "Millin' tonight, I see," he said to John with an appraising eye. "Who's the lucky cove?"

John shrugged. "Whoever comes up."

Basil eyeballed Caulie. "What about you? Coming out of retirement for a little extra blunt?"

Caulie gave him a dirty look and spit.

"Who's he fightin', Tony?" Basil asked, holding Caulie's gaze. The pissing contest had been going on for years, the disdain mutual and long lasting.

"Coupla coves have volunteered for duty," Tony said.

"That cove with the broken nose from up north," John said.

"He's down again?" Basil sniffed and looked around. "Thought last year's beating was enough, but sometimes losing comes in handy, too."

John cracked his knuckles, letting his head fall from side to side, the joints making noise as he moved.

"And the other Corinthian?" Basil asked.

Tony looked sideways at John.

"We don't know yet," John said.

Basil gave him a strange look. "Whaddaya mean, you don't know?"

"He don't. I do," Tony said.

"You do?" John said, finally turning to look at Tony, who was dressed like a back-alley king in a moth-eaten, claret-red waistcoat. "Who?"

"It's a rematch," Tony said, shifting his mass from foot to foot, his belly rolling under his tight clothes like waves on the ocean.

John cocked his head.

Basil clapped his hands. "Lurve it. I can whip the crowd into a right frenzy with a grudge match."

"That toff sort, from a few months ago," Tony said it, throwing the piece of hay he'd been chewing onto the dirt-packed floor. He wouldn't meet John's eye.

"The toff sort who was the Beastly Baron?" Basil asked.

"The night the crowd got all unruly?" John asked.

"Which toff?" Caulie asked.

"Yeah," Tony said. "The Beastly Baron. He came in this morning, asking to mill tonight for a rematch."

"Why? He seemed like a sane enough cove," Basil said.

Maybe it was fear, but it smelled an awful lot like hope, and a new emotion drifted over John. His palms began to sweat. He cracked his neck again, but no sounds came out.

Caulie raised an eyebrow. "Ye nervous?"

John shook his head no, but everyone standing there could tell it was a lie.

"Yer white as the Virgin Mary's ass," Basil said.

"Don't say that," Caulie said.

"I'm Catholic, I can say what I please about her. You, on the other hand, can't," Basil said, jabbing a skeletal finger at Caulie's chest.

After these weeks of Lydia's complete silence, he would see her. She would show for her cousin's mill. He could only hope she missed him as much as he had missed her.

"What's taking so long?" John asked.

The other men exchanged glances. "What *is* what taking so long?" Caulie asked.

"The preliminary fights should be starting," John complained.

Basil took out a pocket watch and checked the time, shaking his head. "Almost, lad."

Tony shook his head.

"It's a woman problem," Caulie said to Tony.

"Shut it," John said.

"Of course it's a woman problem," Tony said. "At his age, if it weren't, I'd be worried for him."

Basil slunk off, kicking one of the butcher sheets, expanding the ring dimensions without the butcher being any the wiser.

"It isn't a problem," John said.

Caulie scoffed. "Never seen you this bad, mate. And never known you to deny it when it were true."

John scuffed his foot along the hard-packed dirt. This building didn't have any back rooms he could hide in. He had to stand in full view of everyone, nowhere to hide from Tony and Caulie and Basil while they had their fun.

Basil finished talking with Bess across the room, pulled her away from the argument with the butcher, checked his pocket watch, and went to the middle of the ring. He was quiet for a moment, watching the crowd churn about. As his gangly body coiled its energy, he would transform into the loud showman who would whip the spectators into a betting frenzy.

The crowd ignored him as he straightened his smudged cravat, his elbows nothing but hard angles and lean bones. He seemed to grow taller, straightening out his bony body, as if he were a bit of rubber being pulled at both ends. He took a breath big enough that John could see the man's lungs expanding in his chest.

"Ladies and gents! Corinthians and coves!" Basil bellowed, and the crowd's attention, which had been so randomly dispersed, scattered wide and then focused in on him in the middle of the ring. "We are gathered here tonight to witness some excellent fighting. The best London has to offer. Nay, the best England has to offer, and as we all know, England is the best. In. The. World!" He used his skeletal finger to jab into the air for emphasis. Basil took off his hat and swept himself into a low bow. Most of the gentlemen also doffed their hats at the sentiment.

"God save the King, and God save our illustrious fighters," he said, topping his hat back on his head. "Now, first up in this fine evening. Originally, we had planned to give you a right good show. But sadly, our fighter is so fierce we couldn't find an opponent. Please give your regard for your favorite lady boxer, Bess Abbott!"

Basil pounded his hands together, causing the rest of the crowd to follow suit. Bess pushed her way through the crowd to stand next Basil. She was wearing the fighting clothes that Lord Denby had created for her, with the wide-legged pants making it appear as if she were wearing a dress.

"We want to see her fight!" someone from the crowd screamed.

"We would as well, my good man," Basil said, pointing towards the door from where the voice came from. "But if we have no challenger, then our Bess remains undefeated."

Many of the men looked about the crowd for another woman, any woman, who they could shove into the ring. John couldn't blame them. Watching Bess work was a pleasure every time.

"I'll fight her," a man yelled from the crowd.

Basil helped point out the man to Bess, so she could see. She whispered something to Basil, who laughed and called out, "She said she would be happy to fight you, but only with a longstaff so she doesn't have to touch you."

The crowd guffawed, including the heckler. More people filtered into the basement, pushing the spectators closer together. They were densely packed in the low-ceilinged basement, the heat of the people and their breath making the air thick and humid.

"Get on wiv it!" someone yelled.

"The best lady pugilist ye will ever have a chance to meet, Bess Abbott," Basil yelled, and the crowd hooted for her as she curtsied and pushed her way out of the makeshift ring. "Next up, we've got some young coves you haven't seen before. They're hungry for claret, and by God, they'll have it."

John tried to concentrate on the ring, but he found himself peering around the audience, trying to spot Andrepont. Halfheartedly, he watched the opening fight, two scrawny boys who had not yet grown into their tempers. He caught himself scanning not just for the lord, but for pelisses with large hoods.

But no, he knew that wasn't the way. She'd been clear, and he would be an idiot for thinking she would magically change her mind. He'd spent the last week training for real again, nothing but beef broth and long runs through Regent's Park. There was nothing left inside him, nothing for her, nothing for anyone.

❧

LADY ISABELLE RECEIVED HER WITH NARROWED eyes. "Your visit is such a delightful surprise."

Lydia sank into a settee in the Hackett drawing room. "Thank you for receiving me in private."

The other young woman blinked in response, a tight smile pasted on her face.

"I've come to deliver this," Lydia said, pulling out the bundle of documents that made up Hackett's cargo debt.

"And what is it?" Lady Isabelle asked.

"Your freedom," Lydia said.

"How delightful. I'll let my father know," she said, reaching out to take the bundle.

"If you show your father, you've lost every advantage you have. Keep these under lock and key."

Lady Isabelle froze. "But he's my father."

"You have some serious decisions to make," Lydia said. "If you give this to him, his debt will effectively be erased, and your financial life will be as it has always been. He will still need you to marry a wealthy man. But if you keep this to yourself, then you may marry even the poorest man, and as the holder of your father's debt, you may demand this money in full from your father at any time, down to the last silver candlestick."

Lady Isabelle took the bundle and sat back in her chair. The tight politeness had evaporated from her face. She looked at the fire, her features softened in thought.

"This is your freedom." Lydia stood.

The other woman stood reflexively, still clearly puzzling over her new predicament. As Lydia moved toward the door, Lady Isabelle stopped her.

"Why are you just giving this to me?" she asked. "Surely you want something in return."

Lydia shook her head. "I had meant to ruin your father," she confessed. "But in doing so, it would have ruined your life and your mother's life as well. There are so few options for us. Rather than fighting each other for them, I'd rather give you the opportunity to make new ones."

❧

THE MILL ENDED WITH ONE BOY ON THE GROUND bleeding and the other boy bleeding from his nose, his arms lifted over his head in triumph. Basil stepped back into the ring to shuffle the event along. John slipped back behind Caulie and Tony to shadowbox. There would be another few matches before his, but he didn't want to stiffen up.

John stayed focused as more mills came and went. He slowed his jab, feeling how his shoulder moved when the punch was true. After finding the feeling, he sped the movement back up, throwing combinations as quickly as he could without compromising the integrity of the blow. The muscles in his back warmed. He danced a little on his feet, keeping his body light and in control. Control was what he needed most. His body could fight on autopilot if it had to, but that wasn't what he wanted. To be the best fighter, he had to maintain a resilient focus, a mental control that had been escaping him since Lydia had come into his life.

A hand touched his shoulder and John swung around, arm cocked. Caulie held both his hands up, an instinctive response on his part.

"Whoa now, John. I only wanted to tell you that she's here," he said.

"Where?" he said. He should have said, *who?* But only one woman mattered, and Caulie knew it.

"Should I go get her?" Caulie asked, his face frowning.

John made a face, too. What would be the etiquette for this event? Could Caulie retrieve the lady? Was that done? "If she'll go with you," he said.

Caulie pushed off into the crowd. John meant to go back to shadowboxing, but he found himself looking after Caulie, trying to see the flash of color in the crowd that would signal the lady. A feather on her bonnet, a brightly colored hood on a pelisse. He couldn't pick her out.

"Forget her for now, friend," Tony said, clapping

him on the shoulder and turning back around to face the wall. "Keep warming up."

John nodded, obeying. The star-shaped beauty mark that dotted Lydia's face dogged his thoughts, so he practiced his uppercuts. Behind him, he could feel the crowd surge and push. He redoubled his efforts at concentration, delivering body shots to the air in front of him.

"Let him work," Tony said behind him.

And then there was her voice. Her elevated accent cut through the chatter of the basement. He winced. He should be able to continue to work even if she was standing in front of him.

He turned and met her gaze. "Hello," he said.

She wore a cheap, ill-fitting dress, a man's coat over it. A straw bonnet covered her dark hair. Her deep-blue eyes locked into his as if she could see into every depth he had. There was nothing he could hide from her. Just seeing her here made him feel stripped bare.

"I thought I should wish you luck," she said. He watched as her fingers twisted around the fabric of her dress.

"I don't need it," he said. Her face fell and he wished he could take it back. That wasn't what he'd meant at all.

❧

ALREADY THE BASEMENT OF THE BUTCHER'S MARKET smelled of men's sweat mixed with drying pig carcass. She was glad she'd worn her boots, though the heels still sank into the soft dirt floor.

John was beautiful to watch, shadowboxing with his back to her. She clutched at her dress, another one of Agnes's old dresses that they'd converted, putting buttons down the front, Vasily's overcoat hanging off her shoulders as if she were child-sized. She wanted to tell John why she was the way she was. He needed to know the source of her arrogance, the drive inside of her. And if he thought she was broken, that was fine. But he needed to know why she took the risks, why she had to box, why she was who she was.

John turned back again, his shirt undone and open, his face creased with concentration. His voice was low, almost as if he hadn't spoken for days at a time. His bright-blue eyes focused in on her, making her feel like the world fell away from them. "I meant that I make my own luck," he said. "I've trained hard."

According to James, John had been at every match, growing leaner and stronger every day.

"I look forward to watching," she said, backing away. The short man who had retrieved her out of the crowd stood behind her. She bumped into him, but instead of him apologizing or even moving, he just stood there with his arms crossed.

"You could help me warm up, if you wanted," John said.

Lydia glanced to the far corner of the room where James leaned against a wall, drinking whiskey out of a flask with the butcher. He seemed to be enjoying himself just fine.

"He isn't in it for the fight," she said.

John raised his eyebrows, the red-gold of his hair rich in the low, smoky light of the paraffin lamps.

"He wants the punishment," Lydia finished.

John looked past her, over at James. "I can understand that," he said. "Come over here."

She followed him to his small corner, sliding off the bulky coat and throwing it over her arm.

"Mikey," the large man who had initially blocked her bellowed.

A small boy darted out of the crowd.

"Take the lady's coat," he said, chucking his thumb over his shoulder.

The boy, serious in expression and missing a tooth, gathered up the dark garment from Lydia's arms. "Ma'am," he said. "I'll watch it for you."

Lydia cautioned a glance in the large man's direction. He acknowledged her out of the corner of his eye but went back to watching the fight, never turning in her direction. She unpinned her straw hat and handed it over to the boy as well. He gave it a serious look and scampered away.

"Can you throw combinations at me? Nothing hard, and don't get too close," John instructed.

Lydia nodded, glad for the first time that she was wearing her boxing attire. She took a big step backwards, assuring that none of her blows would connect, and neither would any of his. Not that she believed he would ever purposely hit her outside of a sparring round.

She started slow, throwing jab-cross-uppercut combinations as he dodged and blocked each round.

"Faster," he said, his voice flat and methodical.

Obeying, she sped up her combinations. Still, he blocked and dodged with ease, dancing around her in a circle. She pushed back with her own footwork as she threw, forcing him counterclockwise. "The crowd won't like it if you shift too much."

"Faster," he said, ignoring her advice.

Her feet went faster, her fists went faster, and she felt as if they were in a dance, moving as if already choreographed. Her hair loosened in the careful pins. It felt good to throw jabs again, to move in this way, left foot forward, eyes quick, and stomach muscles tight. Her body sprang back to life as they worked, the speed as necessary for her as it helped to ready John.

"'Ay, 'ay, Bess Abbott!" A large-mouthed man who stood nearby brayed. "We got you a contender right 'ere!"

Lydia heard Bess's name but focused back on John. Their world was small, the two of them, the feel of a shoulder loosening with use, stretching and lengthening in its strength. She continued to circle John, changing up her combinations, making her assault last longer.

He dodged and blocked, threw his own assault back, fists never connecting to her flesh, always a handbreadth away. Still, she dodged and blocked in return, the sweat beginning to bead at her temples. It felt good; it felt right.

More eyes watched her, but she narrowed her vision even further. She refused to look over John's shoulder. The world was not there. Only she and John, locked in their dance, his form the most elegant sculpture she'd ever seen.

"How much?" she heard the big man say. Then there were more calls to Bess Abbott, many voices, louder and louder.

"Good," John said, straightening. He wasn't out of breath, but at least there was some dampening at his temples. "You haven't lost your form," he said.

She straightened as well, yanking up the sleeves of her dress as far as they would go. "Thank you," she said.

"Done," the fat man announced.

John looked up in alarm. "What's done?"

Lydia looked over to see the fat man shaking hands with a number of men. Bess elbowed her way over.

"Let's see her, brave little soul," Bess crowed, but stopped short when she made her way to John's side. She turned to the large man. "No, Tony."

Tony, the big man, shrugged his shoulders. "What's done is done."

"You agreed to this?" Bess hissed at Lydia.

"I didn't agree to anything," Lydia protested, looking over at John. "Did I?" Her pulse quickened. Was this a match? Was she being pulled into an underground bare-knuckled boxing ring? Now there was a scandal.

"She was never asked," John said.

"I spoke as her manager," Tony said.

"You are not my manager," Lydia said, pointing her finger. She pulled herself up to her most regal height.

"That's true, but watching you move wif John, I can tell what you are. And this here is an opportunity. A chance to fight the best in the land. That's more than most fighters can ever claim," the fat man said. "Plus, you get thirty percent of the take for just showing up."

Lydia narrowed her eyes. "Thirty-five."

"Done! Miss, um...Miss, uh," the fat man stammered.

Her mouth was dry and her insides felt like they'd been turned upside down. She was suddenly grateful that she hadn't been able to eat much at dinner. She'd never fought Bess without Bess pulling her punches.

"Miss, er...?" They all looked at her.

She certainly wasn't going to advertise who she was, but she'd never needed another name. "Mrs. Arthur," she said. It came out before she could think.

Both Bess and John looked at her sharply. The shorter man with the strange ears sighed and cursed.

"One round, we don't go to knock-out, just to the ground, understood?" Bess said to Tony, Lydia's apparent manager, and the men crowded around him.

"Done," Tony repeated. One of the other men leered at Lydia from the side.

Bess finished her negotiations and came over to speak with Lydia. "I have another chest bandage," she said.

The thought hadn't even occurred to Lydia, but she was grateful for Bess's foresight.

"I always bring two," she said.

"Thank you," Lydia said.

"I'll not throw this fight," Bess said, her tone grave. "I don't want to hurt you, my lady, but I fight fair or I don't fight."

"I understand," Lydia said. "I'll do the same."

"Good," Bess said, reaching out to clap Lydia's shoulder. "I'll get you the band." Bess elbowed her way back out of the crowd.

"Don't do this," John said, taking her arm. His fingers felt like they could melt through her skin. "You don't have to."

"I've never fought," Lydia said. "Not for real stakes."

"I beg to differ. I've seen you plant a facer on an earl."

Lydia scoffed. "That was just a brawl. This is a match. A real match."

His blue eyes went wide. "A real match with an opponent who has fought for her life. She won't pull her punches, Lydia. She could hurt you for good."

"I can block and shift," she said. The more she thought about it, the more excited she became. She knew Bess's style from the years of instruction. The pulse that had beat so slowly for weeks began to quicken. A smile crossed her lips. "I want to do this. I want to fight."

"If ye'll be fightin', you best learn the terms. 'S called a mill. Ye'll be millin'," the fat man said.

John put his hands on his narrow hips and looked over at the man with strange ears. "This is Caulie."

"Yes, Caulie, lovely to meet you."

He tipped his hat. "M'lady. I mean, ma'am." He cleared his throat. "Ma'am," he repeated for good measure.

"He'll be your bottleman. I'll be your kneeman if you need one."

She stopped and frowned. A kneeman? Then she remembered. John would sit in the corner of the ring with one knee up, providing her a place to sit and rest. Could she be focused in a moment like that? Panting, sweating, pressed up against him, flesh to flesh? Their stolen time in the Orangery came to her mind. She could feel the blush creeping up her face.

His expression changed, and she knew he must know what she had been thinking. "I'll be in your corner," he said. "Listen for my advice if you can, and I'll be there with you every step of the way."

She looked up at him, and someone jostled her from behind, pushing her closer. Maybe there was a tendril of emotion he still had for her. Some small way she could patch things. "I'm sorry, John."

He shook his head. "Don't be sorry about this fight. I understand the need."

"Not that," she shook her head. "I'm sorry I didn't tell you everything. I'm sorry I didn't trust you. There's so much history that I didn't want to tell you because..." she cleared her throat. He looked at her expectantly, but she could swear there was some hope in his expression. "Because I was afraid you would think of me poorly."

He took her hands and squeezed them. "Think of the fight now. Concentrate."

The fight. Yes. It wasn't about her history. Tonight was about her fists. Blood pounded in Lydia's ears. Bess made John and Caulie and the fat man, Tony, turn their backs to form a wall. Lydia glanced over her shoulder at the people-turned-dressing-room, looking beyond them to the crowd that ignored them. She pulled down the loose gown, slid her arms out of the tapered sleeves, removed her loose leather stays, and then pushed down the thinner straps of her chemise. She used Bess's binding cloth to cover her breasts, tightening the bandage with shaking fingers.

She still wasn't certain how she had agreed to fight, but somehow a bargain had been struck. Did she want to fight? The small voice in her head said *Yes* without hesitation. The fighter in her, the newly named Mrs. Arthur, longed for a chance in the ring. Bess warned that she would give no quarter, but wasn't that what she wanted? A chance to prove herself, test her skills. She was a little slow after a few weeks of training alone. But that just meant she was rested.

She pulled her chemise and her dress back up over her shoulders. "You can turn around now," she said.

Caulie whispered something to John, and John elbowed Caulie in the ribs. Behind them, the crowd surged as the next fight ended.

"Just in time," Tony remarked, giving Lydia a cool look.

The gangly Basil elbowed his way through the crowd to the center of the ring. He lifted the fallen man's arm to test his level of consciousness. The arm dropped on the man's face, causing a sucking sort of sound as the blood streaming from the man's nose splattered across the fallen hand.

The audience reacted with disgust.

"Clear 'im out," Basil called.

The kneeman came out of the corner, and between him and the bottleman, they picked up the unconscious fighter by his arms and feet.

"Don't worry," John said, leaning in close to her. She could smell him, the way his sweat smelled cleaner than anyone else's she knew. It was a peculiar scent, but it was his.

"No further damage gets inflicted," he said with a grin.

Their eyes met, and suddenly that tripping pulse felt like it might not be nerves about a fight, but rather the possibilities that could lie ahead.

The gangly man in the ring began chattering. She wanted to block him out, keep in this time where she and John were the only people in the world. Could they have that? In the humid, dusty basement of the butcher shop, it seemed possible.

"The lovely ladies of the ring 'ave come to show off their skills. You all know her, you all love her, the fiercest woman in London, Bess Abbott!" The spidery man screamed, then the crowd screamed, and Bess strode into the makeshift ring.

Lydia's stomach clenched.

"Keep your mind on your basics," John said, gripping her upper arm.

In the ring, Bess took down her sleeves, much to the hooting and hollering of the crowd. Lydia could barely see her through the sweaty bodies of unwashed men.

"Her brave opponent, new to the ring but fierce of heart, meet the sweetheart of your favorite, Mrs. Corinthian John!"

The crowd whooped. Lydia looked to John, her heart in her throat. The spectators turned towards her, giving her a path to the ring. He was supposed to say "Mrs. Arthur."

"I don't think—" she started to say, but John pulled her into a searing kiss. Her hands went to his shoulders, kneading the muscles, as if her body could tell him how much she had missed him. How much she wanted him. How she probably—not to get too carried away here—might actually be fond of him in a way that could be construed, by some, those who felt that sort of way, anyway—

The crowd whooped. John pulled away. "You're the bravest person I've ever known. Go fight."

Lydia licked her lips as if she could still taste him. She turned to her path, cleared of strangers, which led her to the small ring, marked out by rolls of paper, where Bess waited. Lydia unbuttoned her dress at the neck and pulled her sleeves down, tucking them and then tying them to keep them out of the way. Just like Bess had taught her so many years ago.

Her blood was throbbing in her ears, and she could hear nothing but her own breath coming fast and shallow. She needed to calm down. Bess was across from her, looking both proud and terrifying. There was no way to count how many times Lydia had fought Bess, but it had always been as a student sparring with her teacher.

John had said to stick to her basics. Bess had almost a foot of height on Lydia, so her wingspan was that much longer. For success, or even to minimize her own damage, she needed to stay in close. Bess was stronger than her, no question. One hit from Bess would equal at least ten from her. This was a game of aggregate aggression.

They matched their toes on the line. The umpire bade them to begin.

Bess began to circle, so Lydia circled back. It was hard to ignore the sea of faces, open-mouthed and red, that formed the background. Bess darted in closer and took a swing, but it was a long enough swipe that Lydia ducked and rolled out of the way.

Lydia thought she could hear booing, but she ignored it. The crowd didn't like too much footwork —it was seen as cheating to get out of the way of a fist, but Lydia wasn't about to sit down and have a discussion about it when Bess was attempting to give her a black eye.

Lydia stepped in closer, managing a quick jab to the stomach before darting away. Some of the crowd hollered in appreciation for her daring. She heard Bess snort, a noise that she could only interpret as amusement.

Instead of going after her, Bess stayed away. The taller woman waited on the other side of the ring for Lydia to come to her. She would have to breach the bigger woman's defenses again.

Glancing over to her corner, where both John and Caulie stood, clapping and shouting, she took what she needed: John's look of serious confidence. Lydia turned back to the problem at hand. There was no other option than to take a run at her opponent.

Curious how despite the years of training, Lydia couldn't see Bess as herself anymore. She just saw the other fighter, the opposite of herself. She ran in quick, managing to sidestep a jab, and delivered a few hits to Bess's body. But this time she stayed too long and Bess shot a heavy blow to her side. Lydia staggered back.

Over the years, there had been countless bruises. She'd suffered hits from fists and sticks and elbows, but nothing prepared her for the jarring shock of a hit from a real fight.

John's voice rose over the din of the crowd. "Yer fine."

Lydia staggered back. This time Bess advanced on her, and Lydia retreated further.

"Get away from the edges," John called.

There were things in that moment that she knew, and things she thought she knew. For instance, she knew she would be hurt. She knew she should get away from the edge of the ring, but she couldn't make her feet move. All she could see was the towering presence of her opponent.

The twitch of Bess's shoulder told Lydia to duck, so she did, rolling underneath the long arm and moving to the center of the ring. But Bess was faster, and she spun, clocking Lydia full in the face with a right cross.

The floor was softer than Lydia had thought it would be. Her face felt puffy, as if it were expanding, like egg whites being fluffed by a Parisian chef. She blinked. Her head hurt on the inside, like her brain had hit against her skull. Interesting; she had always thought she would cry in this moment, but she didn't. Her brain couldn't comprehend what had happened.

"I'm sorry, my lady," Bess said, standing over her, hands on her hips. The wide legs of her fighting uniform swayed in Lydia's field of vision. "But please stay down."

The spidery rat-man came to her other side and examined her, then yelled something to the crowd. More noises, and then there was John, kneeling next to her with a warm cloth.

"Now we go to the recovery room," he said gently. "Do you want me to carry you?"

Carry her? She had been hit in the face, not the feet. Pressure was building in her head, making it feel like it would swell larger and larger until it popped right off her neck. She shook her gargantuan head, her brain swishing along inside. "No, I'd prefer to walk." Her voice was haughty once again—her stage voice, the one she used at balls and on the sidewalk when rude stockbrokers approached and asked to walk with her.

She felt shaky, but she made it to her feet. The crowd hooted at her, eyes still on her. Blood dripped out of her nose onto her upper lip. Any other room and she would be mortified. She touched it, checking the pads of her fingers smeared with red liquid. She'd fought. She had fought in a real underground match. The coddled aristocrat had finally made good on her training.

Lifting her hands over her head, she felt like she'd had a victory. The crowd roared in approval. She laughed, tasting the blood in her teeth. Even Bess applauded. The ring was surrounded by men shouting, and she felt safe—better than safe. She somehow felt invincible, despite Bess proving otherwise.

"Come on, Champ," John said, his hand on the bare small of her back, steering her up the narrow stairs.

She glanced back at the crowd as she ascended the stairs, money changing hands, a few arguments being had. A man in the corner was picking his nose with abandon, and his friend swilled the last of his flask. They weren't a clean lot, or a savory one, but she felt a sudden kinship with the people in the room, as if she were a part of them.

❧

JAMES LENT THEM HIS CARRIAGE. IT WAS unbecoming of an unmarried woman to be in an enclosed carriage with a gentleman without a chaperone present. But she'd had a full night of unbecoming behavior.

Lydia's face was absolutely hurting. But John was there, a little worse for wear, too. James had done his best on a rematch, and while John had won again, it was not without some damage.

"I can't breathe through my nose," Lydia said.

"It's the blood clots," John said, his tone just as nasally.

"How romantic," she said, holding her handkerchief, already well-ruined, to her nose.

"Did James tell you about the cargo debt?" he asked.

She nodded, even though it made her whole face hurt to do so. "I gave it to Lady Isabelle. It's not her fault who her father is."

John smiled. "You can't help what you're born into." He reached over and squeezed her hand.

She squirmed. "I didn't want her to be sullied by something she had no choice in." Staring down at their intertwined hands, she knew it was time to tell him. But she didn't want to. She wanted to skip right past it all, just as if it didn't matter. "There's a lot to tell you."

"You don't need to all at once," he said, grabbing her hand. "Just as long as you let me in."

She looked at his hand with its scraped knuckles. "That's precisely what I'm afraid of, you know. That once you hear it, the very idea of touching me will be disgusting."

"That seems impossible."

So, she told him. Starting with William's death and the family's escape to the country. She mentioned James's father, the whispers of the staff. Margaret's parentage. But that was when she began to falter.

"That sounds like a difficult situation," John said, his hands still clasping hers.

She took a steadying breath. "That's not the bad part."

He raised his eyebrows in expectation.

"You know faro?"

"Of course," he said. "I've won a lot of money at faro."

"Then you know that betting is a key aspect. Escalation is expected. So what better bet than the cure for the pox they all have?" She removed her hands from his, gesturing for effect.

John shook his head. "What cure?"

"To bed a virgin." Lydia looked down, her hands now in her lap, dormant.

John sat back and cocked his head cocked to one side, as he did when he was thinking. She liked that about him. His eyes slid to hers, and she waited.

"And the one female in the house that could be guaranteed a virgin was—" His voice broke.

She nodded. He nodded in return, his jaw taking on a hard set. "How old?"

"I was ten. James was twelve."

"He was there?" John all but roared.

"He was asleep. We all were."

"All?" John asked.

"We were in the nursery. Me, James, Agnes, Margaret."

"Where was your nursemaid? Surely you didn't go unchaperoned."

"She was there too, also asleep. When I woke up, he told me he would hurt her if I made a sound."

"Did it happen again?" John winced.

She shook her head. "But every year a physician would come, look me over and make sure I hadn't the pox. It was humiliating."

John reached over and grabbed her hands. "You are not disgusting to me."

A lump formed in her throat. "Even if I do have the pox?"

"I don't care."

"But—"

"Lydia." His ice-blue eyes bored into hers. "It makes no difference to me."

She couldn't hold his gaze. It might not make a difference to him, but it made a difference to her.

He slid to the seat next to her. "I'm deeply sorry

for you. I'm hurt for you. I'm angry for you. But I don't hold you to blame. And it would kill me to see you carry that shame another day."

Gently, he traced the curve of her face with his fingers. "You know, if my face didn't hurt, I would ravish you in this carriage," he said.

She laughed. "If my face didn't hurt, I would let you."

"You've got a good bruise on your side, I bet."

Her hand reflexively went where Bess had hit her. "I do. It hurts to breathe, a little."

He cradled the side of her face with his hand and kissed her temple. The streets clattered beneath the wheels of the carriage. They would be to her house soon. She laid her head against his shoulder.

"I love you," he whispered.

In the darkness of the carriage, all the colors seemed to glow. Her chest felt about to burst. "I know."

# 17

"And that is that," Lorian said, dropping his pen back in its holder.

John stared at the wet ink. This definitely felt odd. He was all but a married man, and he was standing in the room with his bride's father, not his bride. "Are you certain?"

Lorian frowned at him. "If you had second thoughts, we should have negotiated before we signed."

"I don't mean that," John said. This is the toff stuff he couldn't ever get used to. "Isn't there something Lydia needs to sign as well?"

Lorian laughed. "Verbal agreements in front of a bishop are binding." He stuck his hand out to John. "Welcome to the family."

John shook his hand. He ought to be grateful. He ought to be jumping out of his skin with happiness. And he would be, if he was standing with Lydia. Lorian pushed him upstairs to the drawing room, where Lydia and Lady Agnes sat with their mother.

"Deed is done," Lorian announced.

"You look a little green," Lady Agnes said, looking up from her embroidery.

"It's the bruising still," Lydia said, her face bearing the marks of her fight.

"Two weeks," John said.

Lydia smiled so big her lip split again. He felt better.

❧

BESS ADVANCED ON HER AGAIN, BUT THIS TIME, instead of getting in a thwack at her thigh, Lydia blocked the move. Agnes sat at the sidelines with her embroidery.

Lydia countered, driving Bess back. Their sticks clacked faster and faster.

"No bruises!" Agnes called.

"Not even one for John to find?" Bess cackled.

Lydia landed a blow on Bess's thigh and almost crowed about the accomplishment. Bess redoubled her efforts, and back they went the other way. The door opened and closed, but she didn't want to look up. She couldn't look up. The state of her face on her wedding day depended on it.

"I'll take next round," called a masculine voice.

Lydia pushed Bess back with all the strength she had, giving her room to glance over. John watched them, taking off his jacket.

Agnes stood. "Bess? Would you like to take tea with me in the drawing room? It would be delightful. Do you have a favorite treat? I'm certain we could whip up whatever you'd like. It would only be a matter of time."

Lydia could kiss her sister.

Bess exhaled loudly, swinging her arms to cool down. "Tea." She glanced over at John, then back at Lydia. "I'm in need of something extra special fancy. Oughtta take at least an hour just to find the ingredients."

Bess joined Agnes, Lydia following at a slower pace. John unbuttoned his waistcoat. They hadn't found any time together since the papers had been signed. Or since the boxing match. Really, since the Orangery.

"Positively indecent," Agnes muttered.

Bess pulled up her sleeves and followed Agnes to the door. "You know," the boxer said, giving Lydia a wink, "I think one of the ingredients is this here key."

They shut the door behind them, and there was a click as the door locked. "Ah, no, my mistake," Bess said, her voice muffled by the barrier. The key came sailing in underneath the crack in the door. "Don't need it."

"Oh dear," Lydia said. "I believe we're in a locked room."

"How very unsettling," John said, whipping off his shirt. "My reputation will be in tatters."

"I won't compromise you," she promised. His bruises had healed. She liked looking at him. She was proud of him, proud of his power, of his past.

"How very disappointing. I was looking forward to having a tattered reputation," he said, advancing on her.

"Then you'll have to do something about it." She raised her fists to prepare to fight. Her pulse ticked faster as she waited.

He charged her, only to slide to his knees at the last minute. "I forfeit."

"You can't forfeit!"

"Watch me. Because when I forfeit, I'm really, really good at it." He leaned forward and kissed her stomach through her chemise.

SECOND CHANCES WERE, IN MOST CASES, RARE. He had dreamed of this moment so often that to get a second chance, with a locked door and a lenient eye, he had to take it.

The last time they had been here, in a ballroom, ready to box, he'd been stunned by her, bewildered, unsure of himself. Now, though—now she was to be his wife. His match. The woman in his corner. He'd meant to be gentlemanly and gallant, to wait until their wedding day and be all manner of soft and generous. But the heated spark in her eye made him think differently.

He gripped her hips and kissed the triangle bit of flesh under her ribcage. The one that had haunted him the last time he was here, forfeiting. This would be a much better forfeit.

Her sharp intake of breath was not quite a moan, but he'd get there. His brain was fogging over with all the things he wanted to show her, but he was doing his best to maintain focus. "May I rise?"

She nodded her assent but didn't speak. That was a good sign; kissing her senseless was another goal, and he was an ambitious man. He kissed her, cradling her perfect jaw in his hands. He was going to go slow, keep it easy and steady, let her inexperience be his guide.

But she broke away from his kiss to run her mouth along his neck. Heat and need radiated off of her, ablaze in his arms. It was damned hard to keep it slow when she was going so fast. Not that he minded fast. He thought she minded fast.

"We don't have to hurry," he said. He pushed the straps of the chemise off her shoulders. He'd wanted to bite those shoulders last time he was here. Perfect, strong, real in front of him, not just the illusion of his dreams.

"Don't we?" she asked. "We aren't married yet."

"A matter of days."

"Still days."

A bit of worry nagged at him, and he pulled away from her kiss. "What do you think is going to happen in a few days?"

She shook her head, like it was an obvious answer. "I don't know." She kissed him again, her hands running down his chest to his stomach, to the waistline of his trousers. He was already hard, but this made him harder.

She was making it really difficult to speak. Her hands roamed across his body. She landed a kiss on the hollow of his neck, and his brain stopped working. All his plans, all of the words he'd hoped to say, all the ways to calm her, seduce her, make her feel loved, they all disintegrated when her lips touched his skin.

Instead of sweet words, he ripped the ragged banding off of her. "I hate this thing," he said.

She laughed, and it was the most delicious thing she could have done. Her breasts shifted, and he leaned her back to catch her nipple in his mouth. She gasped and gripped his shoulders.

Encouraged, he slid one arm underneath her bottom and the other behind her head, then lowered her to the ground. She sighed, and he looked up at her face to find her glowing. Her face was absolutely incandescent.

"May I?" he asked. Whatever she wanted, he would find a way.

"Please continue," she said, as if he were holding forth on a lecture and not doing his damnedest to avoid stripping her bare and having his way with her like the beast he felt he was.

He ran his hands up underneath her skirts while he nudged her other breast, waiting until she squirmed in frustration before taking it into his mouth.

"You did that on purpose," she accused.

He hummed his assent and his hand crawled above her knee, finding new territory on her thigh. Her hands worked through his hair. Finally, he reached her juncture. He cupped his hand there, letting her grow accustomed to the feeling.

She moved against his hand, arching her back into him. It killed him. It would be so easy to slip a finger in, to begin down the path that had to—had to—finally happen.

"Before we go any further," he said, lifting his head.

She swore.

He chuckled. "It's a simple request." Her frustration was palpable. And it was funny. She let her head fall against the floor with a *thunk*.

"What is it?" she groaned.

"I want to see all of you. No skirts around your waist, no bindings, no nothing. Just. You."

She raised her eyebrow. "The same goes for you."

"Done."

She sat up to unbutton her boots, and he did the same. He couldn't help but grin at her. This was his wife, his partner, the person in his corner. For life. He planned to be a very old man.

She lifted her hips and slid off the dress, the petticoat, the chemise. He unbuttoned his pants, happy he had finally started wearing trousers instead of breeches. Trousers had fewer buttons. Fashion had finally come in handy. He wasn't sure how she would react to him, but he was so hard, there was no way he could change that now.

He kicked off the trousers entirely. She reclined on her elbows, watching him. There was not a stitch on her. Finally. He took his time taking her in. The strong shoulders, the soft slope of her breasts, the small belly, and what he'd always suspected: long legs. Long, well-muscled legs.

"You're looking at me like a starving man looks at a ham," she said.

"Yer the best kind of ham," he said. She laughed and he lay down beside her, rolling up onto his hip, letting his hand graze all over her. He tried to keep his straining erection at a respectful distance, which was impossible. He didn't want to scare her. "The kind of ham with long legs." He kissed her neck. She lifted her head to accommodate him. "The kind of ham who gets what she wants." He kissed her shoulder. "I love ham."

She laughed again and squirmed as he stole his hand across her belly, encircling her, pulling her close. His cock pressed against her thigh.

"I love you too."

He knew it was silly, unmanly really, for a prizefighter, a bare-knuckled boxer, a man who could down another man in a single round, to grin so wide.

"I wouldn't marry you otherwise," she said, her hand tracing the yoke of his shoulders. "I'm looking forward to being Mrs. Arthur instead of Lady Lydia."

"It doesn't matter to me what you call yourself, as long as you're happy." The lazy tracing of his fingers along her torso began to meander. He cupped her breast.

She looked him in the eye, letting her hand trace down his chest and find his cock. "Do you know what would make me happy?"

"I have some very good ideas," he said.

He meant to take his time. He meant a lot of things that got lost in the taste of her skin. Her gasps gave him more satisfaction than he could have imagined. But he waited, wanting her to be ready, wanting her to enjoy what he hoped would become a regular occurrence.

Stroking the nub between her legs, letting her wetness consume his hand, he couldn't remember a time in his life when he was as hard as this. She squirmed against him. Bending his head to suck on her nipple, he thought he should get a medal for his restraint. Her body arched and he could feel her muscles shudder against his hand.

He moved between her legs and slowly pushed in, letting her relax as he went. She watched him, midnight-blue eyes pulling him further, her hands gripping his arms. Not wanting to hurt her, he stopped. It took all his concentration not to spend himself immediately. He had some dignity, after all.

"John," she gasped.

"I—"

"I need you," she commanded.

There was no choice for him. Slowly he started again, lowering himself all the way. They were joined completely. Together. Consummated. But he didn't feel like two into one. He felt like he was suddenly whole. He searched her expression to see if she felt the same, and her face was like a mirror.

Controlled, he began moving again, thrusting against her as she moved against him. He couldn't think anymore, and his pace increased. Her grip on his biceps tightened. She angled her body, and the shift increased their friction.

"For the love of—" She shuddered again, pushing him over the edge.

He cried out, spending himself. He shuddered, falling onto his elbows, protecting her from his full weight.

Their heavy breaths were the only sound in the ballroom. He held his temple next to hers.

"I should have pulled out, I'm sorry," he said. "I didn't think to ask."

She wrapped her arms around him, enveloping him further. He moved off his elbows, putting his weight on her.

"I wouldn't have asked you to. It doesn't matter," she said. "What matters is that you're mine."

"Isn't it the other way around? You're mine?" John asked.

Her midnight-blue peepers sparkled. "I'll fight you for it."

# EPILOGUE

Marriage agreed with her.

Until it didn't.

After the wedding, which was a small affair in a small church, followed by a quick wedding brunch, Lydia was packed up to Marylebone. They still received social invitations, though John grumbled about the turtle soup. They even expanded Lydia's circle to include the more radical thinkers of the Marylebone set, people she'd never thought to know if they hadn't been her neighbors.

John hadn't been talking out of turn when he had said he could afford anything. They stayed in the same townhome, and within minutes of requesting any item or luxury, he or Parsons procured it. One of her requests was his time, and thus he had begun going into the Exchange less and working from his private study more. He hired on a host of runners and messengers to keep his trades going. Caulie came and went without ceremony, still doffing his cap in terror if he spotted Lydia in the hallway.

They opened up the ballroom, another room he'd never explored, and it became a training room. Bess was a regular visitor. Agnes and Margaret still refused to learn, though James was interested in an occasional sparring session with John.

But it wasn't long until Lydia realized she hadn't needed her monthly rags. And by the time she started paying attention to the calendar, certain smells—including turtle soup—became overwhelming. But being that she'd thought she was broken in every way, her thoughts took a more dire turn.

When the nausea set in, every day at eleven in the morning, she knew Death was imminent.

Despite her vow not to interrupt his work, Lydia finally could no longer keep it to herself. She had just a few minutes before the nausea would set in and she would have to position herself close to a chamber pot.

John was in his study, papers stacked high, a young boy waiting at his elbow for the piece of paper he was signing. She cleared her throat to catch his attention. He looked up, surprised. He slid the paper to the boy and told him to sand it himself. John crossed the large room with its half-empty bookcases and cavernous ceiling.

"You look pale," he'd said, taking her elbows. "You aren't ill, are you?"

"I'm always pale," she said, scared now of this moment. But she couldn't keep the tremor out of her voice.

They stared at the boy until he slunk out and John closed the door behind him. "What's wrong?"

She swallowed hard. "I think...that is, I believe..."

John searched her face, which only made her more nervous. To say this out loud would be like wishing it true. "I think I'm dying."

He became very still, the way he did before he started to fight. His concentration was focused entirely on her. "What makes you think that?"

She ticked off her reasons, the fatigue, the smells.

Then, she told him of the impending clockwork nausea, just moments away.

And then the horrible man broke into a grin.

"Why are you smiling?" she demanded. "I've just told you you'll be a widower!"

He stifled a laugh. "I'll call a physician. But I'm pretty sure you just told me that you're with child."

"Don't be absurd." But then she thought about it. And for any other woman, that would make sense. But for her? She had been so convinced that she was broken in every way. A nursery full of redheaded boys and serious, violet-eyed girls seemed as probable as going to the moon.

She stared at the half-empty bookcases. Suddenly she was like everyone else. She was no longer different. She was a person doing exactly what people did: getting married and having a baby. Quite ordinary, in fact. "Do you really think?"

"I wondered. You haven't used rags in three months," he said.

"You've been counting?" she asked.

"Not exactly, but you've performed your wifely duties every day for several months straight. Not that I'm complaining." The look on his face made her wonder if he was going to want her to perform them right then.

Her hands went to her middle. "We're going to have a family," she whispered.

His face split with a smile wider than the Channel. He kissed her then, her lips, her forehead, her nose. He buried his face in her neck. She wasn't certain, but for a moment, she thought he might be weeping. When he pulled away, his eyes were clear, but his ruddy skin flushed. "Are you happy?"

The door opened, and Lydia jumped away. Old habits still clung. Pearl entered the room. "There you are. I wanted to discuss—oh. Am I interrupting? Has something happened?"

Lydia shook her head, pulling herself together, shoulders back, chin tucked.

"It's good news," John said, his eyes shining.

And then Lydia realized that she didn't have to be pulled together. Pearl didn't need her to be strong or firm or self-contained. Pearl was living her own life, with them, under their roof.

Pearl took a breath in and clasped her hands together. "Is it what I'm thinking?"

John nodded.

"What are you thinking?" Lydia asked, envious of the shorthand that was happening between the siblings.

Pearl began dancing a little jig as she approached. "I'm so happy for you!" she squealed, throwing her arms around Lydia. "I knew it! I just knew it!"

Lydia wrapped her arms around Pearl in return but looked over at John in bewilderment. "How did you know?"

Pearl pulled back. "Oh, Lydia, when you are around babies as much as we were, you can just smell it on a person." She scooted over to her brother and embraced him.

John stepped to Lydia and wrapped her in his arms as well. He buried his nose in Lydia's neck. "I'm so happy," he said.

Pearl extracted herself. "We'll catch up later, Lydia. I'll let you two have some time together. Oh, I'm so excited. A baby!" Pearl left the room with her hands clapping to an invisible song.

"Are you happy, wife?" John asked, gripping Lydia's hips, as if he would carry her from room to room for the next months of her confinement.

"I'm surprised," she said. "I never thought." And then the tears got the better of her. They weren't from sadness but from surprise. He wanted a child, wanted a family, and wanted her. She hadn't known what she wanted, hadn't been able to see that far. But now that she was here, with him and Pearl, and they were safe and loved, she realized this was more than she had ever hoped for. When does a person stop thinking they don't deserve to be happy?

John thought they deserved to be happy, and for once, she didn't want to argue.

# HISTORICAL NOTE

Boxing was *the* sport of the Regency era. Pugilism was considered the noblest and manliest pursuit, and thus, the most English pastime. Prizefighters were celebrities, and as they gained fame, some escaped pugilism, others wallowed in it. The inspiration for John Arthur's lifestyle came from a boxer named John Gully (1783-1863), who managed to use pugilism to get out of debt. He then gambled well, married, and eventually became an MP. Pierce Egan, the sportswriter of the day whom I relied heavily on for my information, wrote of Gully, "...proving, in himself, a lively instance, that ALL pugilists are not deprived from entering into polished society."

Regency is also a time period of great upheaval in pugilism itself. Handwraps and boxing gloves appeared at Gentleman Jackson's. Serious training included going for runs and a modified diet. They used bags filled with sand, hung from the ceiling to train with. Dodging punches, while often despised as something only foreigners would do (because it wasn't noble to get out of the way of a fist), was starting to gain popularity amongst all fighters. Modern rules would not appear until in 1865, known as Queensbury Rules, which outlawed biting and wrestling (all well within bounds for boxing matches during Georgian and Regency eras), and also instituted boxing gloves for every participant.

But much of my book is about women boxing. That too, has historical basis. The most famous boxer of the Georgian era (the century before the Regency) was Elizabeth Wilkinson Stokes. She fought for money, taught boxing, got married, and continued to fight. There is very little record of her private life, though one can look up her advertisements in the newspaper where she trash-talks her rivals. She was very entertaining.

Sometimes women fought in chemises, as depicted in my book, and other times, stripped to the waist, as men fought. It's currently thought that female fighters who stripped to the waist were likely also advertising their wares for later.

As for women of the aristocracy, there is record of titled women behaving badly and coming to blows in private brawls. There is also record of titled young women learning fencing, another sport considered exclusive to men at that time.

In non-pugilism matters, I would like to note that the *Europe* did, in fact, meet its fiery end in Antigua's bay. However, there was a casualty, a Mr. Fletcher. I did not look into Mr. Fletcher, nor his demise. For the sake of fiction, I overlooked his death in this book.

What John Arthur did to obtain Hackett's cargo debt was not, at the time, illegal. It is now. Don't do it.

A note on Lydia's trauma: I based her response off of another real woman, but from a different time period: Lee Miller. Elizabeth Miller was born in 1907, in the US, and was raped by a neighbor at age seven. She contracted gonorrhea. Her childhood was filled with medical treatments, but the life she led afterwards was extraordinary. She was a model for *Vogue* and also an art student. In 1925, she moved to Paris to study with Man Ray. After World War II broke out, she became a photojournalist, and was the first to Hitler's apartments after his fall. She photographed the Buchenwald and Dachau concentration camps as they were liberated.

All this to say, she was victimized, but not a damn thing stopped her. She was a pretty face, but she also had courage and bravery and wit. She was more than a model. She was more than Man Ray's lover. She was more than the sum of her trauma. Lee Miller lived at a time when her virginity was her value, just as in Regency years. Instead of shrinking in and holding the pain, she used it as a rock beneath her feet.

## ACKNOWLEDGMENTS

"Thank you" can seem insincere if you say it enough, just like an airline attendant walking down the aisle at the end of the flight with an open bag, saying, "Trash? Trash?"

But I do mean it. I mean Thank You so earnestly that it is embarrassing for everyone.

Thank you to the critique group in Savannah, Gail Byrd and Victoria Steele-Logue, for reading and critiquing a week at a time. And also for letting me cry when I was eleven weeks pregnant and nauseated and tired and strung as tight as piano wire.

Thank you to everyone at the University of Anchorage MFA program approximately one million years ago. Thank you to my fellow students who became professionals, from Signe Jorgenson who has done editing for this book and other work, and to Brian Hendrickson for having coffee with me one day over a decade ago in Albuquerque, and telling me not to be so hard on myself. Thank you to Leslie Ward for sparkling in every circumstance. Thank you to Haden Polseno-Hensley for introducing me to my husband.

Thank you to Anya Kagan at Touchstone Editing for the developmental edit that was so desperately needed. Thank you to Signe Jorgenson for the copy edits and all news from Wisconsin. And thank you to Fiona Jayde at Fiona Jayde Media for the incredibly spot-on cover. She's perfect.

Thank you to the Beau Monde group of RWA for the random tidbits, pointed answers, and to several members volunteering their time to read for historical accuracy.

Thank you to Mike Tyson for his original quote: "*Everyone has a plan 'till they get punched in the mouth.*"

Meghan Tierney, you've done some damage. Thank you. At her wedding, I met her best friend who is a romance author, and I liked that romance author so much as a person that I read her books. And it changed the way I thought about romance as a genre. It wasn't the same formula as the Victoria Holt and VC Andrews that I'd read as a teenager, and it wasn't always where the women were abused or abandoned. I learned then that Romancelandia is large, sprawling, and inclusive. It was a breath of fresh air to find out that somewhere the woman doesn't have to die at the end. I wanted to write something where my audience wouldn't think a happy ending was cheap, but rather, that it was *supposed* to be that way. And thank you, to that author, for being passionate about what you do. Thank you Meghan, for being a great slab neighbor. Those were the days.

Thank you to Jill Trumble and Julie Bench for being my early beta readers. I'm wondering if you even recognize these characters after all this time!

Many, many thanks to Coach Steven "Big Fish" Bass at Savannah Combat Club for letting a middle-aged lady come fight with you. And thank you to the athletes I met there, who showed up to work. In particular, thank you to the women boxers, who require just as much dedication for far fewer opportunities.

Thank you to Rick Stine, who put his money where my mouth is.

Thank you to my family, but especially my husband, Andy, who has been trying to get me to push my work out the door for well over a decade. I love you.

# *the* BOXER *and the* BLACKSMITH

Edie Cay

# THE BOXER AND THE BLACKSMITH

## LONDON, 1818

Bess swung her arms as she walked, an empty bottle in one hand, stretching out tight shoulders as she sidestepped piles of frozen horse dung. Her muscles were still warm, the sweat of her back causing her dress and cloak to cling, and she enjoyed the feeling of looseness in her body in the not-quite-icy spring air.

The narrow roads snuck between buildings, cramped and crowded, with occasional midden piles dotting the maze. The smell of humanity wasn't masked by perfumes in this neighborhood. Strange maybe, that these odors made Bess feel at home, just like the uneven street and occasional squawk of a chicken.

The promise of a meal quickened her step. Her landlady, Mrs. Martin, put some kind of herb in that big pot that required a bit of ale to enhance the flavor. When Bess had arrived home after sparring with John Arthur, Mrs. Martin had sent Bess out to fetch some more.

The streets fell dark fast in this part of London, the lamplighters coming late to the streets of Paddington, not near so important as those in Mayfair or Marylebone. Mrs. Martin preferred Tuck's ale to Tony's, though Tuck's was a bit further of a walk in the twilight. Perhaps she'd grab a small beer while she waited for him to fill the bottle, and hopefully the gas lamps would be lit soon, so she could better watch her step.

"'Ello, lovie, yer a two-handed cat," a man crooned from a drunken perch in front of a now-closed market. He sat on empty apple boxes piled up awaiting the next days' fare, shrouded. Three other men lounged with him, the glass bottle glinting as they passed it amongst themselves.

Bess ignored them, continuing on her way.

"Awful big, ain't ya? A right whapper," another called. Their dockyard speech wasn't slurred, but rather thick with gin. If they were from Paddington, they would have recognized her and known to leave her be.

"Off it, lads," she warned them, never breaking stride. Their jeers didn't bother her, but something in their tone made her prickle like she did just before a bout. She was glad she was still wearing her boxing costume, a gift from her late sponsor, Lord Denby. He had designed it for her alone: wide-legged trousers that looked like a skirt, with extra fabric in the shoulders to allow better range of motion. It was a terrible bother when relieving herself, but far better to fight in, especially in a moment like this. When outnumbered, hands could still scrabble up underneath skirts.

The empty apple boxes clattered as the men shifted their weight and stood, their boots heavy as they hit the ground.

The lamplighters were still far off, and Bess sighed and turned hoping they'd see her better as the meager gaslight spilled down. This usually put off any would-be brawlers. "I said, go home, lads." Bess planted her feet and put down the bottle.

"Cor, not a beaut by any measure," one of them said as he stalked closer.

"What's with yer nose, pretty?" The men chuckled.

Bess took the insults without blinking. These jabs didn't hurt, but she steadied her breathing, readying for the moment to come.

"Jeezus, Harry, look at her ears!" another said.

Bess had tried to take pride in the uneven scarring of her cauliflower ears. Male pugilists were proud of the physical sign of their profession, but somehow, Bess didn't care for them, despite her status as a fighter being apparent in so many other ways.

"Eh," the one who was probably Harry said. "Put a bag over 'er head."

"You should be grateful some blokes want to have a bit fun with you," one insisted.

"Such a compliment," another said, daring to pluck at her sleeve.

It was the sleeve that pushed her over the edge. She kicked the man closest to her and went after the one who had touched her. A quick right cross followed by a left uppercut and right kidney shot put him on the ground.

She pivoted to survey the other three. The man she'd kicked had stumbled, but was on his feet. "Go home, lads," she said, her hands still ready. She wasn't above running, but with a group like this, it would be easy for them to overcome her if her back was turned.

They didn't speak for a moment, still unable to understand how their chum ended up on the ground.

"Let's go, Mickey," the one who had been kicked urged.

The man on the ground slowly got to his feet, clutching his side. It was Harry who stood his ground before capitulating to the others.

"But I'm taking yer bottle," Harry cried, darting forward to snatch it up.

Bess took two quick strides forward. "You won't," she said.

"Come get it," Harry sneered.

She took another step forward and Harry dropped the bottle, hurrying off behind his friends.

The silhouettes faded into the darkness of the streets. Bess sighed and scooped up the bottle, inspecting it for damage. There was a chip on the lip now, which no doubt Mrs. Martin would ask about. She was careful about her things and didn't care for scuff marks.

Suddenly, she heard clapping from behind her. She spun towards the noise, her heart ticking faster just as it had begun to slow down.

"Well done," a low voice boomed.

Searching the dark shadows of the storefronts, Bess felt the voice almost in her bones. "Show yourself," she said.

A large dark-skinned man stepped out of the shadows and into the light. He was at least two hands taller than Bess, and twice as wide. In his hand, he carried a blacksmith's hammer.

"I'd prefer if you put down the weapon," Bess said. Again her nerves prickled, but this time in a way she could not identify. The man was powerfully built, but likely slow on his feet. If nothing else, she could slide in a few hits and then run. The hammer swing would be slow enough to dodge, but a mistake would be fatal.

He chuckled, another low noise that sounded more like the shifting starts of an iron locomotive. She felt it in her ribs, and it made an ache bloom almost as if she had been knocked by a belly-go-firster.

He put up one of his massive paws as a show of

peace. “I’d not raise a weapon to the great Bess Abbott,” he said, lowering the hammer to rest on the ground.

“You have me at a disadvantage,” she said, still not abandoning her defensive stance, but no longer thinking about running. The ache in her chest eased, and she was distracted by the roping power in his bare forearms, the low light etching him in silver and gold.

The man shook his head. He had no hair, and the dark skin of his bare pate gleamed. “I don’t believe you could have a disadvantage. You’re too quick.”

She watched him a minute more, waiting for something else to happen: an insult, a shout, or even for him to slide back into the shadows. Instead he smiled at her, which made her suspicious.

“I’ve watched your fights,” he said.

Bess harrumphed, relaxing. “Hard to get a set-to going.”

“So fight men. I’ve wondered why you didn’t. I’m glad I got the opportunity to ask.” His accent was strange, the lilting sounds of the West Indies came through, tempered by what sounded Northern, maybe a Manchester accent. The odd mix was pleasing to hear.

Bess put her hands on her hips. “That a compliment?”

“You’re my favorite fighter,” he said, leaning back against the building. “I suppose that’s a compliment.”

It sounded so wrong to hear, it almost struck her as a joke. She shook her head and walked over to where he stood, his great bulk leaned against the bakery. The hammer leaned against the wall next to him, the handle coming near to her waist. It was no ordinary tool. Suddenly, she forgot how to breathe, being this close to a man that wasn’t trying to train with her. "Then I thank you," she said, gasping for no reason. "You a smug?"

"My foundry is up there," he said, gesturing with his chin back toward Edgeware.

Bess frowned. "Isn't that Barnsworth's?"

"Took it over when he died," the blacksmith said, shifting his weight to better look at her.

"I didn't hear." So many people from her childhood were passing, she could barely keep track of the old neighborhood anymore. The foundry was a landmark in everyone's mind, a place of perpetual fire, the sound of metal on metal at all hours.

He lifted his massive shoulder and let it fall. The motion only showed how much power was poised inside of him. If he'd an inclination, there'd be plenty of money to be found in the ring.

The lamplighters approached, giving them both more to see. Bess was glad to get a better glimpse of him, but embarrassed that he might see her in such disarray. The cuffs of her boxing costume were frayed, and he'd undoubtedly figured out that her skirt was in fact trousers. She liked the costume, but knew how the rest of the world saw her. She tired abruptly, wishing for sleep.

"So why don't you fight men if you want to have more matches?" he asked.

Bess looked up at him. It was so strange to lift her chin to speak. "What man would agree to fight me? What if he lost?"

He chuckled again, the rumbling deep. It made her breath catch and finally start to regulate on its own. In this bit of shadow, on this bit of street, she felt as if she knew this stranger, as if they got to skip past all of the formal speech, all of the dances people did, and went straight to speaking truth.

"It's a risk." Could be he felt that she wasn't a stranger in this bit of light, either.

She felt him weighing her, taking in all these odd pieces. It was only a matter of time before he ran away, having identified her for what she was. Unnatural. Strange. She braced for the impact of his judgment.

"I've always wanted to tell you that I like your ears," he said. "I thought if I met you someday, on the street, I would tell you that."

Heat flushed Bess's face. Without thinking, her hand went to cover the tell-tale scarring. "It makes me ugly." She pulled her cap down lower, covering the dirty-dishwater color of her unwomanly short hair.

He lifted his dark eyebrows, the whites of his eyes near glowing. "It makes you powerful," he said, picking up the heavy blacksmith's hammer with ease.

"I never got your name," Bess said, reaching out with her hand before she thought better of it.

"Come by the shop and I'll tell you," he said before he slung the hammer over his shoulder and sauntered away.

Bess stared at his receding figure before remembering the empty bottle in her hand. The glass was warm from where she clutched it. Talking to the blacksmith had been so distracting she had almost forgotten if she was coming or going.

Turning to finally head down to Tuck's, Bess kept looking back at him, this blacksmith who liked her ears.

## ABOUT THE AUTHOR

Edie Cay writes Feminist Regency Romance. Her debut, A Lady's Revenge, won the 2020 Golden Leaf Best First Book. The next in her series, The Boxer and the Blacksmith won the 2019 Hearts Through History Legend Award, a Man for All Reasons as an unpublished manuscript. She obtained dual BAs in Creative Writing and in Music from Cal State East Bay, and her MFA in Creative Writing from University of Alaska Anchorage. She is currently at work on the third in the series, A Lady's Finder. She is a member of RWA, the Beau Monde, the Historical Novel Society, and a founding member of Paper Lantern Writers. You can keep track of new releases by signing up for her newsletter, or following her on Instagram or Facebook, @authorediecay.

CPSIA information can be obtained
at www.ICGtesting.com
Printed in the USA
LVHW032107200323
742055LV00001B/52